EXTREME PLANETS

Fiction Across Time and Space from Chaosium:

These, and more, can be found on our catalog at
www.chaosium.com

EXTREME PLANETS

EDITED BY DAVID CONYERS,
DAVID KERNOT AND JEFF HARRIS

CONTENTS

INTRODUCTION

DAVID BRIN

Planets. Self-contained worlds that need little other than the gentle tug and consistent light of a reliable nearby star, in order to nurture biology and—possibly—minds to contemplate the universe. Planets appear to be the "cells" of interstellar life. Each one solitary and self-supporting.

And each *unique*—we knew this would turn out to be so, long before the 1990s, when humans started learning just how strange and diverse planets might really be, out there.

Until the Space Age, we were free to imagine, so other-earths were everywhere. And nearby! The dangers on our threat horizon be invading Martians. The princesses on our exogamy horizon might be found amid the jungles and islands underneath the shrouding clouds of Venus. I was a teenager when the Mariner probes crushed those dreams, and forced us to set them farther away.

But the space missions gave back, even as they took away. Some of you out there remember 1968, the most exhausting year anyone could imagine living through, with wild gyrations of emotion packed into every week—(along with incredible music). After a seeming-endless chain of assassinations, invasions, calamities and declarations of despair, what was the very last news item, before we collapsed into 1969? Like a diadem, glittering at the bottom of Pandora's Box, that final item was the greatest gift of NASA. It came from the astronauts of the Apollo VIII mission. An image no one had ever seen before—the blue marble. A floating, fragile oasis in the great vacuum desert. The oasis that is our shared, nurturing home, our **Earth**. And, for the time being at least, the only known abode of life. That image changed us! Perhaps, it is even the reason that we turned around, starting to take our role more seriously. Perhaps even in time. Such may be the power of art.

But art also looks outward! And no art form does that so earnestly as science fiction—the literary genre that not only accepts the possibility of change, but embraces it! Peering obsessively toward the *next* horizon. Then the next and so on. If *fantasy* dwells on the nostalgically conceivable (though impossible), and regular sci-fi cavorts amid the possible-though-barely-plausible...then *hard SF* is the variety that tries to probe the most interesting frontier of all. One that Einstein himself explored when he coined the term *gedankenexperiment*, or thought experiment.

The territory of the perhaps-plausible. Informed by real science. Constrained by its known laws and phenomena...yet somehow liberated by all that!

And now that territory includes a new panoply of planets. Planets galore! Far beyond Sol's mundane and placid nine, we now know of—since just over a decade—several hundred worlds beyond this little system. A bestiary of strange objects that were barely imagined before land based telescopes refined the art of tracking stellar wobbles and inferring the orbits of dark objects near glowing stars. Or before the marvelous Kepler spacecraft detected score after score of tiny eclipses, taking place light years away, teaching us about astonishing worlds beyond.

Now we know of *hot Jupiters* boiling away closer to their suns than Mercury orbits ours! We know of *super-earths*. We've begun to suspect that carbon rich solar systems may host planets made of diamond or feature oceans of soupy proto-life (both of these notions appearing in stories that are featured in this volume.)

To an extent, this weirdness is a selection effect—our detection methods naturally favor objects that are large and close to their stars. There are already signs of some though that orbit in their Continuously Habitable Zones (CUZ) or "goldilocks" realm where temperatures might allow water to be liquid on a planet's surface. And now it is no longer thought strange that Jupiter's moon, Europa, might host a sea under its icy-protective surface. It may be that a vast majority of those worlds out there that host life may do so under frozen roofs.

And then there are comets. Ah, I did my doctoral research on comets. Love-em. Amazing creatures, bizarrely strange, and possibly the very font of life itself.

These are the topic-grist for **EXTREME PLANETS**, an anthology that makes no extreme promises other than to be both daring and fun, taking you to exceptional places, the way the great SF author Hal Clement did, in his fantastic series of novels about strange life on strange worlds. Tales like *Mission of Gravity* and *Close to Critical*, that did what hard sci-fi does best, conveying the reader to places he or she has never been, and where even the human imagination is like Robinson Crusoe, stepping across a virgin beach, apparently unoccupied.

Until—there in front of us—we spy footsteps in the sand.

Banner of the Angels

By David Brin and Gregory Benford

October 2061

*He that leaveth nothing to chance
will do few things ill,
but he will do very few things.*
—George Savile, Lord Halifax

Kato died first.

He had been tending the construction mechs—robots that were deploying girders on the thick black dust that overlay the comet ice.

From Carl's viewpoint, on a rise a kilometer away, Kato's suit was a blob of orange amid the hulking gray worker drones. There was no sound, in spite of the clouds of dust and gas that puffed outward near man and machines. Only a little static interfered with a Vivaldi that helped Carl concentrate on his work.

Carl happened to be looking up, just before it happened. Not far from Kato, anchored near the north pole of the comet's solid core, eight spindly spires came together to form a pyramidal tower. At its peak nestled the microwave borer antenna, an upside-down cup. Kato worked a hundred meters away, oblivious to the furious power lancing into the ice nearby.

Carl had often thought the borer looked like a grotesque, squatting spider. From the hole beneath it came regular gushes of superheated steam.

As if patiently digging after prey, the spider spat invisible microwaves down the shaft in five-second bursts. Moments after each blast, an answering yellow-blue jet of heated gas shot up from the hole below, rushing out of the newly carved tunnel. The billowing steam jet struck deflector plates and parted into six plumes, fanning outward, safely missing the microwave pod.

The borer had been doing that for days, patiently hammering tunnels into the comet core, using bolts of centimeter-wavelength electromagnetic waves, tuned to a frequency that would strip apart carbon dioxide molecules.

Carl felt a faint tremor in his feet each time a bolt blazed forth. The horizon of ancient dark ice curved away in all directions. Outcroppings of pure clathrate snow here and there jutted out through thick layers of spongy dust. It was a scene of faded white against mottled browns and deep, light-absorbing black.

Kato and his mechs worked near the microwave borer, drifting on tethers just above the surface. The core's feeble gravity was not enough to hold them down when they moved. Overhead, thin streamers of ionized, fluorescing gas swayed against hard black night, seeming to caress the Japanese spacer.

Kato supervised as his steel-and-ceramic robot mechanicals did the dangerous work. He had his back to the spider.

Carl was about to turn back to his own task. The borer chugged away methodically, turning ice to steam. Then one of the giant spider legs popped free in a silent puff of snow.

Carl blinked. The microwave generator kept blasting away as the leg flew loose of its anchor, angling up, tilting the body. He did not have time to be horrified.

The beam swept across Kato for only a second. That was enough. Carl saw Kato make a jerky turn as if to flee. Later, he realized that the movement must have been a final, agonized seizure.

The beam blasted the ice below the man, sending luminous sheets of orange and yellow gas pouring into the blackness above, driving billows of dust. Vivaldi vanished under a roar of static.

The invisible beam traced a lashing, searing path. It jittered, waved, then tilted further. Away from the horizon. Toward Carl.

He fumbled for his control console, popped the safety cover, and repeatedly stabbed the countermand switch. His ears popped as the static storm cut off. Every mech and high-power device on this side of Halley Core shut down. The microwave finger ceased to write on the ice only a few score meters short of Carl.

The spider began to collapse. Halley's ten-thousandth of a g was too weak to hold down a firing microwave generator, but without the upward kick of expanding gas and radiation pressure, the iceworld's own weak attraction asserted itself. The frame lurched and began its achingly slow fall.

—What the hell you doin'? My power's out.—

That would be Jeffers. Other voices babbled over the commline. "Mayday! Kato's hurt." Carl shot across dirty-gray ice. His impulse jets fired with a quick, deft certainty as he flew, unconsciously moving with the least wasted energy, the result of years of training. Crossing the rumpled face of Halley was like sailing adroitly over a frozen, dusty sea beneath a black sky.

Against all hope, he tried calling to the figure in the orange spacesuit, splayed, face downward, on the gouged snowfield. "Kato...?"

When he approached, Carl found something that did not resemble a man nearly so much as a blackened, distorted, badly roasted chicken.

Umolanda was next.

The timetable didn't leave much room to mourn Kato. A med team came down from the flagship, the *Edmund Halley*, to retrieve Kato's body, but then it was back to work.

Carl had learned years before to work through unsettling news, accidents, foul-ups. Shrugging off a crewmate's death wasn't easy. He had liked Kato's energy, his quick humor and brassy confidence. Carl promised his friend's memory at least one good, thoroughly drunken memorial party.

He and Jeffers fixed the spider, re-anchoring the foot and reflexing the leg. Carl cut away the damaged portion. Jeffers held the oxygen feed while he slapped a spindly girder segment into the opening. At Carl's signal, the other spacer played the gas jet over the seams and the metal leaped to life, self-welding in a brilliant orange arc. They had the repair done before Kato's body was back on the *Edmund*.

Umolanda came over the rim of Halley Core, pale blue jets driving her along the pole-to-pole cable. The easiest way to move around the irregular iceball was to clip onto the cable and fire suit jets, skimming a few meters above the surface. Magnetic anchors released automatically as you shot by, to minimize friction.

Umolanda was in charge of interior work, shaping irregular gouges into orderly tunnels and rooms. She met Carl near the entrance to Shaft 3, a kilometer from the accident site. The pile-driving spider labored away again on the horizon.

—Pretty bad about Kato,— she sent.

"Yeah." Carl grimaced at the grisly memory. "Nice guy, even if he did play those old junk movies on the 3D all the time."

—At least it was quick.—

He didn't have anything to say to that, didn't like talking a whole lot out here anyway. It just interfered with the job.

Umolanda's liquid eyes studied him through a bubble helmet spattered with grime. The neck ring hid her cleft chin. He was surprised to see that this omission revealed her as an otherwise striking woman, her ebony skin stretched by high cheekbones into an artful, ironic cast. Funny, how he'd never noticed that.

—Did you investigate the cause?—

"I checked the area where the spider leg got loose," Carl answered. "Looked like a fault under it gave way."

She nodded. —Not surprising. I've been finding hollows below, formed when radioactive decay warmed the ice long ago, as Halley formed. If some hot gas from the spider's digging worked its way back to the surface through one of those hollows, it could undermine the spider's anchor.—

Carl squinted at the horizon, imagining the whole cometary head riddled with snaking tunnels. "Sounds about right."

—Shouldn't the spider have cut off as soon as it lost focus?—

"Right."

—The switch?—

"Damn safety cutoff was defective. Just didn't kick in," Carl said sourly.

Her eyebrows knitted angrily. —More defective equipment!—

"Yeah. Some bastard Earthside made a little extra on the overhead."

—You've reported it?—

"Sure. It's a long walk back for replacement parts, though." He smiled sardonically. There was a brief silence before Umolanda spoke again.

—There will always be accidents. We lost people at Encke, too.—

"That doesn't make it any easier."

—No... I guess not.—

"Anyway, Encke was a pussycat of a comet. Old. Sucked dry. Lots of nice safe rock." He scuffed the surface softly with a boot tip. Snow and black dust puffed at the slightest touch.

She forced a grin. —Maybe all this ice is supposed to keep us alive over the long haul, but it's killing us in the short run.—

Carl gestured toward three mechs which stood nearby, waiting for orders. Already the machines were pitted and grimy from Halley's primordial slush. "That's your team. Kato was shaping them up. But you might want to give 'em a once-over, anyway."

—They look okay.— Umolanda whistled up the color-coded readout on the back of the nearest one and nodded. —Some luck here. The microwave beam didn't hit them. I'll take them down, put them to hollowing out Shaft Three.—

She tethered the boxy, multiarmed robots and gracefully towed them to the tunnel entrance. Carl watched her get them safely aligned and disappear down the shaft, leading the mechs like a shepherd, though in fact the mechs were as smart as a ten-year-old at some things, and a lot more coordinated.

He went on to check out more of the equipment that other crewmen were ferrying down from the *Edmund*. It was dull labor, but he had been working in the shafts for days and needed a break from the endless walls of rubble-seamed ice.

Overhead, gauzy streamers wove a slow, stately dance. Halley's twin shimmering tails were like blue-green silks. They were fading now, months past the brief summer crisping that came for the comet every seventy-six years. But still the banners of dust and ions unfurled, gossamer traceries waving as if before a lazy breeze, the flags of vast angels.

The expedition had elected to rendezvous with Halley's Comet after its 2061 perihelion passage, when the streaking planetoid was well on its way outward again. Here, beyond the orbit of Mars, the sun's violent heating no longer boiled off the huge jets of water molecules, dust, and carbon dioxide that made Halley so spectacular during its short summer.

But heat lingers. For months, as Halley swooped by the fierce, eroding sun, temperature waves had been diffusing down through the ice and rock, concentrating in volatile vaults and scattered clumps of rock. Now, even as the comet lofted back into the cool darkness of the outer solar system, there were still reservoirs of warmth inside.

The gritty, dark potato shape was a frozen milkshake of water, carbon dioxide, hydrocarbons, and hydrogen cyanide, each snow subliming into vapor at a different temperature. Inevitably, in some spots, the seeping warmth melted or vaporized ices. These pockets lay waiting.

Carl was partway through assembling a chemical filter system when he heard a sharp high cry on suitcomm.

Then sudden, ominous silence.

His wrist display winked yellow-blue, yellow-blue; Umolanda's code.

Damn. Twice in one shift?

"Umolanda!"

No answer. He caught the polar cable and went hand over hand toward the mouth of Shaft 3.

Mechs milled at a cave-in, digging at the slowly settling ice amid swirls of sparkling fog. No signal from Umolanda. He let the mechs work but popped pellet memories out of their backpacks to scan while he waited. It was soon apparent what had happened.

Deep in the ice, the mechs had dutifully chipped away at the walls of the first vault. Umolanda controlled them with a remote, staying in the main tunnel for safety. The TV relay told her when to sequence the robots over to a new routine, when to touch up details, when to bore and blast. She hung tethered, and monitored the portable readout board, occasionally switching over to full servoed control of a mech, to do a particularly adroit bit of polishing.

She had been working at the far end of what would soon be a storage bay when a mech struck a full-fledged boulder of dark native iron two meters across. Captain Cruz had asked them to watch out for usable resources. Umolanda put all three mechs to retrieving it. Under her guidance they slipped levers around the boulder and tried to pry it free. The sullen black chunk refused to budge.

Umolanda had to come in close to inspect. Carl could envision the trouble: mechs were good, but often it was hard to see whether they were getting the best angle.

Carl had a dark premonition. The boulder had been absorbing heat for weeks, letting it spread into a slush that lay immediately behind it, a pocket of confined carbon dioxide and methane. This frothy soup would be perched at its critical point, needing only a bit more temperature or a fraction less pressure to burst forth into the vapor phase.

Oh for chrissakes, Umolanda don't...

A mech slipped its levering rod around the boulder, penetrating into the reservoir of slush. Umolanda saw the robot lurch, recover. She told it to try again, and moved a little closer to observe.

The mech was slow, gingerly. Its aluminum jacket was spattered and discolored from several days in the ice, but its readouts showed it was in perfect running order. Using as its pivot its own tether in the wall, it levered around the boulder, lunged—and the iron gobbet popped free.

No!

Release of pressure liberated the vaporization energy. The explosion drove the pry bar out of the mech's grip like a ramrod fired through the barrel of a cannon.

Umolanda was two meters away. The lever buried itself in her belly.

The pellet-memory readout terminated. Carl blinked away tears.

He waited while the mechs cleared the way. There was really no need to hurry.

Mission Commander Miguel Cruz called off operations for two full shifts. The setup crew had been working to the hilt for a week. Two deaths in one day implied that they were making errors from plain fatigue.

Umolanda's accident had spewed forth a pearly fog for an hour as the inner lake of slush boiled out. Had anyone Earthside been watching through a strong telescope, they could have detected a slight brightening at the cometary head. It was a fleeting memorial. The blinding storm had driven her mechs out into the shaft, dislodged enough ice to bury her. Carl and the others were kept outside until it was too late to recover her and freeze her down slowly for possible medical work. Umolanda was lost.

Carl came up on the last ferry. The mottled surface seemed to darken with distance: the cometary nucleus dwindled to a blackish dot swimming in a luminous orange-yellow cloud. Though the fuzzy haze of the coma was still visible with a small telescope from Earth, from near the head itself the shimmering curtains of ions were lacy, scarcely noticeable. Gas and grains of dust still steadily popped free of Halley's surface, making cargo piloting tricky. Most of the outgassing now came not from the sun's ebbing sting, but from the waste heat of humans.

As the ferry pulled outward the twin tails—one of dust and the other of fluorescing ions—stretched away, foreshortened pale remnants of the glories that had enthralled Earth only two months ago. Ragged streamers forked out toward Jupiter's glowing pinpoint. Oblivious, Carl stretched back and dozed while the ferry rose to meet the *Edmund*.

When they clanged into the lock, he peeled off his suit and coasted toward the murmuring gravity wheel at the bow. He climbed down one of the spoke ladders and stumbled out into the unfamiliar tug of one-eighth g, feeling bone-deep weariness descend with the coming of weight.

Sleep, yes, he thought. Let it knit up whatever raveled sleeve he had left.

Virginia came first, though. He hadn't seen her in ages.

She was in her working module, of course, halfway around the wheel. She seldom left the thing nowadays. The door hissed aside. When he slipped into the spherical world of encasing memory shells there was an almost cathedral-like hush, a sense of presence and humming activity just beyond hearing. He sat down quietly next to her cantilevered chair, waiting until she could extract from interactive mode. Tapped into channels through a direct neural link and wrist servos, she scarcely moved. She had to know he was there, but she gave no sign.

Her slim body occasionally fidgeted and jerked. Like a dog dreaming, he thought, and trying to run after imaginary rabbits.

Her long, half-Polynesian features were pointed toward the banks of holographic displays suspended above her, and her eyes never even flicked to the side to see him. She gazed raptly at multiple scenes of movement, sliding masses of ever-flickering data, geometric diagrams that shifted and evolved, telling new tales.

He waited as she worked through some indecipherable problem. Her long face momentarily tightened, then released as she leaped some hurdle. She had delicate, high cheekbones, too, like Umolanda. Like a third of the expedition's crew, the Percells, products of Simon Percell's program in genetic correcting of inherited diseases. Carl wondered idly if fine boned, aristocratic features were traits the DNA wizard had slipped in. It was possible; the man had been a genius. Carl's own face was broad and ordinary, though, and he had been 'developed,' as the antiseptic jargon had it, within a year of Virginia. So maybe Simon

Percell had taken such care only with the women. Given the gaudy stories told about the man, he couldn't rule out the possibility.

By anyone's definition, Virginia Kaninamanu Herbert was clearly a successful experiment. A Hawaiian mixture of Pacific breeds, she had a swift, quirky intelligence, deliciously unpredictable. There was restless energy to her eyes as they moved in quick, darting glances at the myriad welter before her. Below, her mouth was a study in quiet immersion, slightly pursed, thoughtful and pensive. She was not, he supposed, particularly attractive in the usual sense of the term; her long face gave her a rangy look. The serene almond smoothness of her skin offset this, but her forehead was broad, the mouth too ample, her chin was stubbed and not fulsomely rounded as fashion these days demanded.

Carl didn't give a damn. There was a compressed verve in her, a hidden woman he longed to reach. Yet all the time he'd known her she had stayed inside her polite cocoon. She was friendly but little more. He was determined to change that.

On the main screen, obliquely turned girders filled together in precise sockets. The frame froze. Done.

Abruptly Virginia came alive, as though some fluid intelligence had returned from the labyrinths other machine counterpart. She stripped the wrist inputs. The white socket for her neural connector flashed briefly as the tap came off and she fluffed her hair into shape.

"Carl! I hoped you'd wait for me to finish."

"Looks important."

"Oh, this? She waved away the frames of data. Just some cleanup work. Checking the simulations of docking and transfer, when we take everybody down. There'll be irregularities from random outgassing jets, and the slot boats will have to compensate. I was programming the smarter mechs for the job. We're ready now."

"It'll be a while."

"Well, a few more days… Oh, yes." She suddenly became subdued. "I heard."

"Damn bad luck." His mouth twisted sourly.

"Fatigue, I heard."

"That too."

She reached out and touched his arm tentatively. "There was nothing you could do."

"Probably. Maybe I shouldn't have let her go down that hole right after Kato bought it. Thing like that, shakes you up, screws up your judgment. Makes accidents more likely."

"You weren't senior to her."

"Yeah. But—"

"It's not your fault. If anything, it's the constraints we work under. This timetable—"

"Yeah, I know."

"Come on. I'll buy you some coffee."

"Sleep's what I need."

"No, you need talk. Some people contact."

"Trading arcane jokes with that computer crowd of yours?" He grimaced. "I always come out sounding like a nerd."

She flexed smoothly out of her console couch, taking advantage of the low gravity to curl and unwind in midair. "Not at all!" Something in her sudden, bouncy gaiety lifted his heart. "Blithe spirit, nerd thou never wert."

"Mutilated Shelley! God, that's awful."

"True, though. Come on. First round is on me."

BROOD

BY STEPHEN GASKELL

ena had to hand it to her brother. He didn't shy away from the system's most inhospitable places. She'd used to think he was testing her, testing to see how far she would go to forge a bond with him, but now, twenty-seven years after she'd become his little sister, she wasn't so sure. Maybe he did want to be alone, and she should just stop trying. She could certainly do without his so-called *charm*.

They'd lost contact with his research team hours ago. They'd swept past the same pitted plains, the same mountainous ridge of volcanoes, the same abandoned derricks, four times in their low-slung orbit. He'd known something was up, but all she'd got out of him was a dismissive "You can't land yet" before the link had turned to white noise.

"I say we set down." Nik Magyar, the Miura-Sagan Prize-winning journalist, spun head-over-heels, bored out of his mind.

Lena sighed.

She wasn't cut out for chaperoning. She didn't know how much longer she could hold him off. Corporate-sponsored gigs like this weren't his usual bag. This was a man who was used to working alone, getting his own way—much like her brother, Artem.

"I said 'I say we set down.'"

"I heard you. And *you* heard my brother. We're not—"

"They might be in trouble."

Possible, but unlikely. More likely a fried RF relay or EM interference had crippled the comms. She had to be careful. Obtaining the license for the experimental trial had taken the better part of a year of legal wrangling with the Astronautical Control Agency, the United Interplanetary Space Authority, the Biotech Ethics Committee, and the rest. It might never be granted again. Artem—not to mention the Genotech board—would be mighty pissed if rockstar writer Nik Magyar saw something he shouldn't. They wanted a PR coup, not a PR disaster. "We wait."

"Do you do *everything* he tells you?"

His question needled her. "I trust him."

Nik shrugged. *If you say so.*

Lena liked that even less. "I'll tell you what. We're not landing, but maybe we can take a closer look."

Nik smiled. "Now we're getting somewhere."

Ancient lava flows coated the crust in a glittering mineral of deep red hue. Sea-green gashes laced the ochre fields where shallow impacts had exposed the olivine mantle. In places, meadows of purple grass clung to the stone. It was a form of needlegrass geneered from archea microorganisms, and one of Artem's greatest triumphs. It survived solely on solar energy and silicates, a marvel of resilience—and a steady source of food for the harvesters.

"There," Lena whispered, spying one of the giant insects.

Nik studied the lone forager, rapt. "Surreal."

"On Mars their size would cripple them."

Nik shook his head, disbelieving. "How do they survive?"

"Mucus."

"Mucus?"

"Their bodies are coated in the stuff. Traps enough air and warmth for them to survive outside for a time."

Lena explained how after Vesta's precious ores had been excavated, cleaned, and brought to the surface, a specialized flinger caste would toss it into space. Through reference to the star field—and this was another stroke of genius on her brother's part—the flingers could be trained to send the ore through solar windows like the Kirkwood Gap, ensuring their capture at the Lagrange points or in Earth's or Mars' gravitational wells. From there, orbital mining scoops would collect the ores. "This is going to be revolutionary."

Twenty years ago they'd lost their father in a drilling accident on Ceres. Extraction tech hadn't fundamentally changed since the pre-space era, and Artem dreamed of dragging the industry into the Twenty-Second Century, breaking the corps' monopoly of medieval practices.

"Now we definitely have to land," Nik said.

Lena rattled the small aerosol can of pheromone. "You know, this stuff hasn't been tested yet."

The chemical had been manufactured in the Genotech labs from data transmitted back by the Vesta team. A fine spray over their suits would identify Lena and Nik as members of the insect colony, and allow them to wander unchallenged—that was the theory, anyhow.

"Nik," Lena gasped. "Look."

On the holo an entourage of smaller insects swarmed around one of the colossal flingers. Lena's mouth went dry. The smaller insects weren't cleaning the flinger as they should've been. They were *attacking* it. She watched on, couldn't help herself as they slashed and tore at the behemoth, gouging its eyes, puncturing its carapace. It fought back, but its immense size hindered its attacks on its small, nimble foes. Straw-yellow ichor spilled from its wounds, marking the rocks.

"You okay?" Nik asked.

She shook her head. "I'm afraid for Artem, for the others."

"Shit, you don't think—"

"I don't know!" Lena imagined the insects clashing in the dark, musty tunnels of the nest. It'd be no place for a person, pheromoned or not. Stupidly, she felt guilty too. She'd been angry when they'd last spoken, lived up to the childish image he had of her.

"Lena—"

"What?"

"Easy there. I was—"

"*Easy there?* My brother's down there, not a fucking story!" She raked her hands into her hair, pulled hard. "I'm sorry."

They stared at one another, the silence festering. Landing would be suicidal. Backup was weeks away. They were both about to speak, when the navigation holo blinked to life. A compact object tore into the heavens not twenty klicks away. Lena neuralled the holo, began instructing it for an object composition analysis.

"Don't bother," Nik said. "I'd recognize that trail signature anywhere." He spun towards the vacsuit lockers. "That was a rescue flare."

The survivor trekked across a crystal plain, gunmetal vacsuit contrasting with the prismatic red stone. He—Lena assumed it was a he from the survivor's languid bearing—waved. His lack of urgency unnerved Lena. She tried hailing him on the close-range frequency, but only got static.

"Funny," she said, speaking into her helmet's mic, "radio's off."

Like Lena, Nik had put on his vacsuit. He stood by the entry hatch, impatient, eyes glued to a small holo that relayed a grainy feed of the survivor. "Maybe he can sign?"

Lena didn't appreciate the joke. "I just want to know who it is."

"So do I. And before they're made into very modern art."

They set down on a small plateau, not two hundred meters from the survivor. "Hold tight," Lena said.

The hatch groaned opened. Lena felt a chill enveloping her, the buzz of her thermal sleeve responding. She didn't like the sensation, didn't like the situation, either. "Off and on, Nik. No dallying." She listened to herself inhale, exhale, the noises amplified by the helmet. "Nik? You get that?"

Nik hunkered down, staring out the hatch. "I got it," he said, distractedly.

"And watch your step, you'll be practically weightless."

She wondered who it would be—maybe Carlson, or Petronis, or perhaps it was Miera, the short, tough Brazilian. She didn't dare imagine that it was Artem—

"Get us out of here!" Nik's footsteps thrummed through the starsloop's metalloceramic skeleton. He jammed himself into the co-pilot's seat. "Now!"

Lena blinked, confused. Survivors need rescuing.

Nik didn't wait a second time, leaning across Lena and wrenching her command field into his lap. His fingers rippled through the light. The starsloop lurched upwards pressing Lena down hard.

"What is it?" she stuttered.

Nik ignored her, slammed his right hand forward. The starsloop responded likewise, plowing forward, engines screeching. Lena's head cracked against the headrest with a dull thump. Pain bloomed. The external cam was still slaved on the survivor, and in a dozy slo-mo she watched the man begin to raise his arm.

Poor soul, she thought.

Except what she'd thought was a last desperate plea *wasn't*. A pulse of earth-sky blue flashed across the vacuum followed by a tremendous crash. They went into a terrifying spin, the whole craft churning and whining and shaking, while everything blurred. Nik shouted something, but his words were lost as his teeth chattered and the warning sirens blared. She tasted blood on her tongue.

The low gravity prolonged their descent into a long drawn-out affair putting klicks between themselves and their attacker. Lena's life didn't so much flash as amble before her eyes.

Then, with a thunderous rumble, the ground reared up and swallowed them.

She woke dazed and bruised in darkness.

Down was sideways and up was somewhere else. Her arm felt sore, trapped. With a determined effort she cracked it free. She waved the other arm, carved out some space in front of her, and neuralled on her shoulder-mounted torch. Shockfoam, white and crispy like meringue, had saved her life. She kicked her legs, amazed they were still willing and able, broke the foam. Suit vitals on the inner arm indicated that its integrity had held, but comms, meds, and data were all shot. A red light on the sleeve blinked every few seconds; air supplies were low but not critical. She must've been out for the better part of an hour. No sign of fear. Perhaps she was still in shock. Whatever, at least she could think straight.

She breathed calmly, excavated Nik from his foam crypt. His body was doubled up, hanging. She pressed her helmet against his, her busted comms meaning he wouldn't hear a peep without direct contact. "Nik! Wake up!"

He groaned, slowly came round.

"Check your vitals."

He gazed at his arm then gave her a groggy thumbs up.

The starsloop had corkscrewed in the crash. Getting out was no picnic. After swinging and grappling and climbing, they stood on the starsloop hull surveying the carnage. Thank Sol we hadn't closed the hatch before we were hit, Lena thought. The starsloop was deader than Mercury now, even the emergency hydraulics were busted good. Nik pointed to the rough track where it had skidded to rest.

S-'s that way he mouthed.

"What?"

He loomed close, cracked their helmets together harder than he intended. "I said, the slicer's that way." His voice sounded hollow, distant.

The slicer? She'd get the story later. Right now they had to get inside, avoid asphyxiation. "Let's head away from him."

"Where's the nest entrance?"

Good question. The vacsuits couldn't help them, their data cores corrupt or broken. Lena scanned the dead horizon. Nothing. Nothing except the odd flutter of motion. Insects. And insects meant access—

The pheromone! "Do you have the aerosol?"

Nik cursed, then peered down into the dim interior of the starsloop. He clambered inside, moments later hoisting up a couple of compact harpoon guns and a couple pairs of Hi-Gain IR goggles. As Lena clutched the second gun her eyes wandered back in the direction of their arrival.

Something glinted in the sunlight, far off.

The slicer? She went horizontal, pressed herself against the starsloop shell, and motioned the danger to Nik. He hauled himself out, touched helmets. "If you can see him, he can see you. We go. Now."

"Where's the aerosol?"

"Lost." He grabbed one of the guns, stuffed the goggles into a pouch on his vacsuit. "Come on."

Lena picked up the other gun, clasped the barrel of the harpoon gun tight, glad to feel its heft. Then, crouching, they scampered down the curved belly of the starsloop and onto the asteroid. The stone was cold and hard. Dread assailed her. This was supposed to be a cakewalk—babysit a journo, collect some hard samples, go home.

She slapped her helmet as she ran. *Stop it.*

Nik was a few paces ahead, his steps controlled but fast, as if he was running on the spot. The microgravity was a nightmare, and she tried to emulate his action, all the while keeping her eyes peeled for outcroppings or loose rocks. And then they needed to find an insect—

The whole ground shook. She nearly tumbled.

Nik turned, pointed into the sky. She twisted, watched a piece of debris pirouette between the stars and crash mere meters away. Burnt and mangled as it was, she still recognized it as the remains of the landing ramp. Beyond it the starsloop was a blackened smoldering thing.

Nik gestured with his head. *Come on.*

She nodded, tried to ignore her hammering heart. She pointed at a dead insect ahead and to the right, not two hundred paces away. They moved fast, and not long after, wheezing hard, Lena pulled a hunting knife from her shin pocket. Hand shaking, she crouched down and began examining the underside of the insect's head with the tip of the blade. A thin film coated its exoskeleton.

There.

The gland was easily visible beneath the insect's leathery skin, a thick rope of a vessel. She beckoned Nik over, motioned for him to cup his hands. He did, and she sliced through the gland. Hot spurts of fluid pooled in his makeshift bowl, dripped between his fingers. He threw the liquid over himself and rubbed it into the folds of his vacsuit. Lena did likewise with the ebbing flow.

It felt like a pathetic shield against the insects.

She shook away the thought, found herself listening to the quickened beep of her sleeve. Oxygen supply was getting low.

Not waiting to speak, they hiked up a gentle rise. A vast expanse of the magenta needlegrass stretched across the shallow valley beyond. Foraging insects toiled in the field, coming and going from a fissure in the cliff on the far side. Hundreds of kilometers of nest tunnels, not to mention the team research station, lay within.

Lena nodded. *Onwards.*

An insect approached as they slid down loose rock. Lena tried not to hesitate, tried not to quicken her breathing, but she couldn't help it. She wanted to run, but she held firm as the insect loomed close. Feelers roved over her, analyzed her chemical signature. A bulbous head, less than a foot away, rocked from side to side, while its sharp jaws flexed in slow pulses. She hadn't felt so uncomfortable since she'd been subjected to Artem's withering gaze after she'd flunked her Highers all those years back.

Eventually, satisfied, the insect moved on.

They headed for the fissure. At the thick spongy membrane—five paces wide and twice as tall—that sealed the entrance to the nest, Nik turned and shrugged. *Open sesame?* he mouthed.

Lena placed her hand, palm flat, against the membrane. The organic material was semi-translucent, but the multitude of layers made the whole thing opaque, like staring into deep water. She pulled her hand away, gelatinous tendrils caught between her fingers. As she studied the strands, marveling at the ingenuity of the system, motion within the membrane drew her eye.

Dark forms shifted, grew.

Lena bundled into Nik, moving both of them out of the way.

Two legs came first, then the antennae, then the head. Remarkably little of the material adhered to the insect as it passed. The membrane wobbled, then stilled.

"Amazing," Lena whispered. As she said the word, splinters of rock exploded from the cliff, rained over them. She glanced back, watched the figure descending on the far slope. It fired off a few more pulses, killing any approaching insects in a cloud of gore and dust.

Nik untangled himself from Lena's grasp. He took a few steps back, rocked on his heels, and sprinted forward, harpoon at his hip like an infantry charge. Lena neuralled her torch on, swept it up and down where he'd entered.

No evidence of his passage remained.

She took a few paces backwards and charged. The membrane was deeper than she'd imagined and she found herself trapped as if a fly in amber. Her breaths came in shallow gasps as she struggled. The vacsuit beeped faster than her heart. The pain in her chest worsened. Ahead, in the attenuated light of her torch, his outline fractured and morphed by the membrane, she thought she could see Nik moving freely.

His form got bigger, before his harpoon gun speared into the area to her right. She flexed her fingers, slowly moving her arm until she could clasp the end of the barrel. She tugged as best she could to indicate she had purchase, then gripped tighter.

Three heaves later, chest burning, arm feeling like it'd been wrenched from its socket, she was inside.

Save for the lances of light emanating from their shoulder-mounted torches, the interior of the nest was pitch black. Lena swept her beam down the passage, fighting a growing sense of claustrophobia. The pockmarked walls looked ancient and alien. Occasional motion blurred the edge of her vision. Part of her wanted to take her chances with the slicer. *What would Artem do?*

She drew the light back to Nik, who blocked the beam with his hand. She dipped the light. He gestured with his hands. *Remove the helmets?*

She nodded. As Nik lifted off his helmet, Lena unclasped her own. A faint hiss accompanied the outrushing high-pressurized mix, before she caught her first breath of the nest. The air was warm and thick, rich with an unpleasant yeasty scent. Strange clicks and tapping noises could be heard from distant tunnels. Nik spluttered.

"It's the fungi." Back on Mars, Lena had helped geneer the carbon-dioxide fixer. She'd been proud. "You'll get used to it."

She slipped on her goggles. The darkness transformed into a web of ochre filaments, the contours of the passage walls clear. Dead insects littered the tunnel. They ran. Despite the low gravity, lifeless carapaces and spindly limbs cracked under their feet. As they made their way deeper, their weight would only lessen from this point. Their passage would be a mixture of scrabbling on all-fours as much as hiking. "That thing outside," Lena shouted, "you've seen it before?"

"Maybe not one and the same." Ahead, beyond the splayed forms, the passage opened up into a bigger chamber. Bright flashes of cadmium orange and sodium yellow slashed across Lena's vision. More insects. "But I've seen others like it—other slicers. It's a remnant of the Fringe Wars."

Fringe Wars. Lunatic factions fighting bitter wars for Europa, Titan, and the rest. What the hell was it doing here?

Nik seemed to read her mind. "That war made a lot of crazies, a lot of killers," he said, breathing hard. "Deadly, augmented crazies more machine than man. We called them *slicers*. Some of the more sane ones do a steady line as guns for hire."

She recalled the name now. On Mars, children were told that slicers roamed the red plains outside the domes looking for easy kills. It helped keep kids away from the 'locks. First she'd feared them. Later she'd thought them no more real than ghosts. Now she knew different. "You think the mining corps sent it?"

"Makes sense. They've got the funds—and the reasons."

They stumbled into the cavernous chamber, came to a halt. The smell of butchery was almost overwhelming. The place thronged with insects. Some were clearing the fallen—hoisting severed limbs, cutting gasters into more manageable pieces, scampering off with their bloody pillage—while others raced from one side to the other. They paid little heed to the two newest members of their colony.

Nik gagged, his vomit a sickly yellow color in the infra-red. A small worker ate it up. "What *happened* here?" he asked, wiping the back of his hand over his mouth.

"Looks like the colony went to war with itself."

"Why?"

"Starvation? Disease? I don't know." A heavy rumble from the passage they'd left broke Lena's train-of-thought. The slicer.

"Which way?" Nik asked, beads of perspiration hot on his brow. A dozen passages led off in a myriad directions.

Lena glanced around the chamber, watched a couple of workers carry off their booty through a tunnel high and to the left. They'd be taking the bodies to the garbage pits, close to the fungal gardens—and the source of food for the team. The research station would be nearby. "Up there," she said, pointing.

She didn't wait for a reply.

"Now I feel safe," Nik said, sneering.

They'd torn through the dark riddle of tunnels, descending and climbing when they'd had to, sweating hard, not speaking much. They'd pretended that was to conserve their energy, but the reality was something else: they didn't want to be heard.

The maze-like place was their best ally and worst enemy. The tunnels forked and multiplied so much that there was no chance the slicer could've followed them, but equally, the sense of being lost, of being at the whim of the deranged geometry of the nest, was a nasty, itchy feeling that only got worse with each step.

They'd made it to the research station, though. Lena blinked, dazzled, as she ran into its artificial white light. The yeasty smell was still strong, but here it battled with more familiar aromas: coffee, disinfectant, plastics. Somebody or something had trashed the room, the wall of computing cores smashed, glass crunching underfoot. Lena sifted through the electronic rubble left on the large table that dominated the middle of the room, but anything that wasn't in pieces had been wiped.

"Nothing," she said. No clue as to Artem's or the others' whereabouts. No clue as to how they might escape.

"What now?" Nik's suit, like hers, was in tatters, ripped and useless. He fumbled a packet of flashfeed, scattering the freeze-dried contents over the floor. "Dammit!"

She needed his smarts, not his anxieties. "Why'd you think it came now? Why not two years ago?"

"What?" Nik crouched, ferrying morsels of food into his mouth with his fingers.

"Genotech's been here two years. Why did the corps wait two years before they sent this thing?"

Nik looked up, stopped chewing. "Maybe they never thought this crazy idea would come to anything." He got up, ferreted about. If he got out of this, he'd have one hell of a story to tell. "Or maybe sending the slicer was a last resort after the usual channels failed." He proceeded into an adjoining room—the researcher's dorm by the look of things—and his voice grew quieter. "You know, the bribes, the—"

There was a loud crash from the other room.

"Nik?" She felt her stomach pit.

"Don't come in."

What had he seen? She had to know. If it was Artem—

Nik came out of the dorm, stood in the threshold. He raised his hands in a stopping motion, using his frame to block her view. "They're dead," he said. He grabbed her wrists. "And messed up."

His words only made her more frantic, and she tried to writhe past him. The room smelt rancid. "Let go of me, for dust's sake!"

He didn't.

Lena stopped struggling. "I need to know if it's him." She held his gaze, and finally he relented, flinging her arms down before letting her past. She should've taken a moment to compose herself, but her eyes were drawn to the spectacle like vultures to a carcass.

No surface or fixture had escaped the blood. Misty, ferrous-colored arcs daubed the walls. Congealed slicks caked the bunks. Thick plum-shaded puddles pooled around the bodies. The scene had a surreal, artistic quality—at least until Lena caught a glimpse of a man's face. Despite some decomposition, she recognized him.

It was Carlson, the myrmecology expert.

They were only acquaintances, but she remembered a snatch of conversation they'd shared in the Genotech cafeteria. She retched, tasted bile. She took a deep breath, then moved closer to one of the other bodies that slumped upside-down off a lower bunk. Please don't let it be Artem, she thought, hating herself for it. She twisted her head—

Petronis. Climatology.

Last one. The body was splayed on the floor, face down. She pivoted, careful not to step in the surrounding viscous fluid, and crouched. She steeled herself, then rolled the body. She gasped. The face was bruised and bloody. She tugged free the corpse's arm, spat on the sleeve and scrubbed away the gore.

It was Miera. The team petrologist. Lena and the man used to play shuttle ball together. She stumbled backwards, fighting another wave of nausea.

She turned round, fell into Nik's arms, numb. She squeezed her eyes shut as if she could undo all of this in that simple act. They stood holding one another for a long while, gently swaying. When she opened her eyes, she cried out in shock.

Somebody was standing in the doorway.

It was her brother, Artem.

He placed a finger over his lips, then led them in silence through the wrecked research station and out into the musty passage. They hadn't gone five paces when he pointed to an area high on the tunnel side. He clambered up and disappeared into the wall. Next moment an arm shot out with an open hand. Lena went first, Nik second, and shortly the trio sat in a tiny cubby hole, legs tangled.

Lena pressed the palm of her hand against her brother's face, grateful to feel his warmth, but he swatted it away, angry. She was going to say something, but his glare made her hold her tongue. He nodded at the small hole through which they'd scrambled. Over their breaths, Lena could hear the sounds of the nest—unsettling clicks and burrs—and something else…a whirring sound…regular…*artificial*. It grew louder, and she realized what it was: mechanized servos.

The slicer.

It grew louder still, and Artem indicated for them to hunker down as best they could. Lena's heart was beating so hard, she was sure the slicer must've been able to hear it.

The noise of the servos stopped.

She pictured it mere paces away, gaze combing the walls. After a long moment it moved off. She could still hear it, though. It must've gone into the research station. Her body ached, and she felt a pain where a sharp tuft of rock dug into her side. Her legs went numb. Eventually the slicer came out of the station, strode past them, rock quaking at its every step. When all they'd been able to hear was the sounds of the nest for several minutes, Artem spoke in a low whisper. "You shouldn't have come here."

"We had no choice!" Lena snapped back, immediately regretting her tone.

Nik nodded. "That thing shot us out the sky."

Artem dropped his head between his knees.

Lena gripped his hand. "The corps sent it, didn't they?"

"Only after I told them where to shove their money." He pulled his head up, met her eyes. "I was stupid, Lena. I thought I could handle them alone."

They sat in silence for a while. "Why are the insects fighting?" Nik asked.

Artem narrowed his eyes, glanced between the pair of them, calculating. "My guess is that that thing brought some kind of phage that sent them into a frenzy."

He pulled a holostick from his coveralls. A complex web of light filled the space between them. "This is a map of the nest." He delved a hand into the holo, and a green path appeared. "And this is your route to safety. The phage hasn't spread to this area yet. There are emergency space-rafts here."

"You're not coming with us?" Lena could hardly believe Artem wanted them to split up already.

Artem clicked off the holostick. "The others might still be alive—"

"Then we'll look for them together."

"No, we won't."

Lena had heard that tone many times over the years. Conversation closed. "Fine."

They grabbed essentials from the research station—water, food, meds, power modules—then trekked off in silence, twenty yards apart. Nik took point. It was slow going checking the map all the time. Shallow veins of color—the residue of excavated minerals—marked the sides, drawing the eye away from the dangers underfoot. Every passing insect unnerved Lena. Her knees, elbows, and shoulders became grazed from where they had to get down on all fours and squeeze through choked channels.

Often, Nik disappeared from view as the passages turned hard or pinched tight. At these moments, Lena would up her pace, terrified that he'd be gone by the time she turned the corner, but he was always there, a ghost of hot light in the darkness. Sometimes her mind played tricks on her and she thought she could hear a mechanized whirr. The fact they'd left Artem to fend alone gnawed at her constantly.

Ahead, she noticed Nik had stopped. "I need some chow," he said when she caught up with him. He slung off his pack, and flopped down. Even in the thick yeasty air, she could smell his sweat. He needed a distraction.

A worker approached. Before she lost the nerve she leapt in front of the insect and tapped out a complicated pattern on the side of its head. The bristled carapace felt like coarse sandpaper against her knuckles. She'd learnt the simple stimulus-response action from some researcher's notes she'd read on the journey out, thinking it would've made a nice party trick. The insect twitched, disgorged a clotted clump of regurgitate, and scuttled off. A layer of mucus clung to the food, but underneath it felt doughy in her hands. She tore off a piece, offered it.

"You're shitting me," he said, but he took the food, curious. He sniffed it. "Eughh. After you."

Lena broke off another piece and wolfed it down. It tasted like rich, chewy bread; weird, but not unpleasant. "Beats the slop blocks."

Nik nibbled a corner, devoured the rest. "Not bad."

They ate the remainder in silence, listening to the weird clicks and taps of the nest. A faint and odorous breeze, rich with a yeasty scent, blew past.

Lena said, "I shouldn't have left him."

"He didn't give you any choice."

"It wasn't his choice to make. It was mine. And I left him."

Nik got to his feet. "Stop beating yourself up. He didn't want us with him." He slipped on his pack.

Lena hauled herself up, wondering if she'd ever see her brother again.

Ahead, the passage opened up into a low-ceilinged chamber. An explosive profusion of fungi sprouted wildly from its sides and roof. Delicate swollen saucers, tangled spaghetti-like tubules, and massed bifurcating thickets crowded every surface. A dim mist of exhaled spores charged the air, the moldy smell overwhelming. A couple of workers scurried past, jaws loaded with long shoots of needlegrass.

A fungal garden.

Nik cupped his hand over his mouth and nose, coughing. "Let's stock up and get out."

Lena nodded, slipping off her pack. At the sides of the chamber, where the workers had dumped the needlegrass, other smaller castes worked the organic matter. One type chewed down the grass, then added it to a growing mound of vegetative pap, while another distributed the mulch to the roots of the fungi. She watched one wind its way down a hanging tendril—

Hell.

Near the base of the tendril slumped a human. Her head was shaved, her hands and face filthy, and her body so emaciated her jumpsuit looked like a deflated balloon, but there was no doubting it was a woman.

"Ana?"

The technician lay on one side, barely alive, the rise and fall of her chest slight, her eyes closed in peace. Laser scorch marks streaked her midriff, her flesh blistered and seeping.

Nik joined Lena. "What—"

Ana's eyes opened. She screamed, began trying to scramble away, her body flexing in ugly spasms. The insects in the chamber responded to the shrieks, spiraling around in tight circles. Workers streamed in, alert and ready.

"Ana," Lena said, but it was to no avail, the woman's mind reeling.

Nik crouched down, the aim of his harpoon gun shifting between the chamber's three exits. "Calm her down!"

"Ana!" Lena grabbed the woman's shoulders. Up close, she stank of burnt flesh and decay. "It's me, Lena—from Pavonis Majoris, from Genotech!"

The woman still floundered, but less aggressively.

"You're safe now," Lena said. "No one's going to harm you."

"Lena?" Ana asked in an awestruck tone, as if the name were a foreign word. One side of her face was red raw where it had scraped the ground. Spittle flecked her chin.

"Yes. Lena." She stroked the woman's cheek with the back of her fingers, wiped off the saliva as best she could. She cradled the woman in her lap for a long while, waiting until her breathing calmed before giving her a few mouthfuls of water. "We're going to help you get out of here," Lena said, pulling a med kit from her pack.

She pressed a sterilizing pad against the first wound, making the woman gasp in pain. After the lacerations were cleaned and dressed,

Nik tapped Lena on the arm. "Give her this," he said, pushing a slop block into Lena's hand. "She must be sick to death of this fungal crap."

It was a smart move. The block would help distance her from the place. Lena offered the food. "Here. Eat."

Ana snatched the slop block, tore open the wrapper, devoured the bar in three bites. Afterwards, she almost retched it straight back up.

Nik helped the woman to her feet, arm around her shoulder, while Lena swathed her in a creased flash blanket. "For a second there, I thought we'd run across some infected insects."

"Infected?" Ana looked confused.

"Yeah. Infected with the phage-virus from the slicer."

Ana tottered as she glanced around the chamber. "Who told you that?"

"Artem. We were with—"

"Where is he?"

Lena glanced at Nik, her stomach pitting. "He's looking for the others."

Ana wrapped the blanket around herself tighter. "The others are all dead."

Artem had lied. There was no phage virus.

The insects were fighting, Ana explained, because Vesta contained not one, but two, insect colonies. The second had never been planned, but when the researchers had discovered that the original queen was suffering a terminal, degenerative disease—a disease that would one day stop the flow of precious ores dead in its tracks—Artem had argued in favor of a second colony with a tweaked geneline.

The team had been divided.

The second colony would have to be kept secret, since Genotech had only been given license to establish one insect colony, not two. "Semantics," Artem had argued. "We owe it to the drilling crews who risk their lives every day."

Eventually, the dissenters had backed down.

"Everything was working out okay," Ana whispered, "until that thing arrived."

Nik shifted his weight, Ana still leaning on him. "Are you saying the slicer caused the fighting between the colonies?"

"Yes." Ana coughed, brushed away a handful of spores that floated by her head. "The slicer hacked the commsat, eavesdropped on us.

It must've realized there were two colonies—and that making them meet would cause chaos."

"And how did it do that?"

Ana laughed bitterly. "It used one of the abandoned drilling rigs to connect the nests."

Lena was sure Artem would've appreciated the irony.

Ana went on, eyes on the ground. "It was only me and Artem who weren't torn to pieces during the first wave of attacks. We holed up while the insects fought. Afterwards, as we fled, it found us." She stroked the laser wound on her side. "I couldn't go on. I told Artem to carry on without me." She glanced up, must've seen the unspoken question in Lena's eyes. "My life was saved by my brood."

Brood. The bond between Ana and the insects was strong, familiar. The notion unsettled Lena. "My brother isn't looking for Nikerson or Singh—or anyone else, is he?"

Ana shook her head sadly.

Lena bit her lip. "What then?"

Ana met Lena's eyes. "He's hunting the hunter."

They went their separate ways from the fungal garden. Ana and Nik, arms draped over one another, headed for the space-rafts, while Lena headed deeper into the nest.

Before they parted Ana had explained that Artem would've made for the second colony's queen to ambush the slicer. "He knew that thing wouldn't be content until this place is a lifeless rock again," she'd said. "Killing the healthy queen is the only way to be sure that no more ore leaves Vesta."

"I didn't think there were any weapons here."

"There aren't."

She'd decided there and then that she would go back—try and find him before the slicer did, before he threw his life away. Nik had tried to argue her out of it, but a stubborn streak she was all too familiar with made her hold her ground. She'd glanced at the passages out of the gardens. "Which way—?"

"You can't waltz in like the slicer." Ana had leaned close, reeking of sweat and piss. "With the scent of this nest you'd be swarmed."

"I have to—"

"There's another way," Ana had said. "But you must hurry. Listen."

She moved as fast as she dare, harpoon gun in hand, keeping light on her feet. Sometimes she tripped, grazed a knee. Sometimes she stumbled, slammed a shoulder. Scrapes and bruises littered her body.

Nest activity increased as she made for the heart of the original colony, the insects dug in, guarding their dying queen. Workers carried the scars of fighting—broken antennae, missing legs, fluids seeping from cracked carapaces. The air was thick with the smell of acrid blood. Terrifying, alien shrieks echoed from afar. A party of soldiers hightailed past. Lena followed, fighting the urge to flee, the noises growing louder. Fallen insects, reeking fluids seeping from their wounds, clogged the route. Their splayed limbs crunched and cracked underfoot. Some were probably soldiers from the invading colony, but she had to be sure so she carried on.

Rounding a corner, she was nearly pitched into the front line of the fighting. Legs and jaws blurred as the two sides clashed. Gouts of blood sprayed the air, accompanied by awful, spine-chilling wails. The enemy ranks stretched away as far as the eye could see, only the narrow passage preventing the defenders from being overrun.

The original colony wouldn't hold out much longer.

Lena ducked backwards, tripping as she avoided the lunge of an enemy soldier. Instinctively, she raised her harpoon gun to shield herself. The insect's head surged forward. Its jaws clamped around the barrel with a terrible gnash. It drew back for a second attack. And a third.

Saliva dripped onto her cheek, hot and putrid. As she warded off more blows, she imagined Artem laughing at her. *You, little sister? Save me?*

She fired. The bolt ripped through the insect's head, and the monster went limp. She scrambled back and let out a deep breath, then gasped in pain. When she brought her fingers back from her cheek they were dappled in blood, her face sliced wide.

At least she had her enemy insect. With shaking hands, she collected its glandular fluid in a small canister. One spilt drop on herself would see her ripped apart. A few paces away the two colony's insects crashed together like the armies of old, a tremendous din reverberating around the choked tunnel. A scrambling leg knocked her arm, but she held firm. She screwed on the cap, allowed herself a small sigh of relief.

She didn't have much time, though. At the head of the tunnel that led to the queen, a phalanx of an elite caste bristled, barring her way. They didn't attack, but they made it clear she wasn't to pass, raising their forelegs while they nipped at her arms. She wasn't the enemy, but she had no place there.

Ana's words came back to her. *If the entrance to the queen's nest is blocked look for a tunneller.*

It didn't take long to find one, the tunneller ambling across an intersection, uncertain. It was a strange paddle-limbed beast, its head a mass of sharp grinding jaws and blunt armored acid spouts. Before she could change her mind, Lena grabbed onto one of its chitinous plates and heaved herself up onto its segmented body. *If you could see me now, Artem.*

The tunneler barely acknowledged her presence, carrying on its way. Bobbing up and down, legs rubbing against its prickly exterior, Lena shifted her pack about, pulled out the holostick, and flicked on the map. There was only one path into or out of the queen's chambers—and the nurseries beyond—but some of the surrounding tunnels skirted close. Hanging tight, she waited to where she thought the walls came closest, then tapped out the quick fire pattern that Ana had shown her on the tunneler's head, careful to avoid its vicious jaws. The monster responded, pitching right and going to work on the rock.

Splinters of mica and basalt ricocheted from the wall accompanied by a heavy grinding sound. Now and then, the tunneler edged backwards to shoot geysers of acid or paw away the growing mound of debris underfoot. Steam fizzed from the rock face, shone white hot through Lena's goggles.

After it had broken through, Lena rapped out a retreat command, and the tunneler padded away. She stepped through the breach to an overpowering smell of mucus and decay. The chamber was enormous, cathedral-sized, matched by the colossal girth of the colony queen. Its spiracled abdomen bulged, while rounded billows of soft flesh undulated with machine-like churning and gurgling. A slow stream of eggs coated in a thick hormonal paste emerged from an orifice near the rear. Even from this distance Lena could tell the spawn was rotten. Workers inspected the latent, diseased offspring, before carting them off to a nearby graveyard pit. From the entry passage where her way had been barred, she heard shrieks and the clash of battle. The colony was in its death throes, a last stand being made against a new wave of invaders.

Lena hurried onto a nursery chamber off to one side. A few workers tended a depleted collection of larvae, bedding them down on discarded cocoons. Soon the larvae would be plundered by the invading army and taken to *their* nurseries. There they would be chemically instilled with new allegiances. There they would forget their true lineage. Nature's means could be profoundly frightening at times.

Lena stepped to the nearest larva—a rubbery oval, half a man tall—and roughly cut a slit along its top, releasing a putrid stench. She delved her hand inside, coating herself in the nutrient goop, and sought out the rudimentary form. Finding it, she pulled it out with a puckered slurp and cast it away. She tipped the larva over and let the goop sluice out.

A mighty squeal came from the adjoining chamber. Nursery workers rushed past to defend their imperiled queen. Enemy soldiers swarmed over the matriarch's bloated abdomen, stabbing and tearing and biting. Spouts of clotted fluid sprayed from her wounds. She made a half-hearted effort to shrug them off, tossing a few off with a flaccid crunch, but their numbers were too great.

The larva was a hollowed out shell now. Lena stared at it, heart pounding. *Artem, you sure as hell better show me some gratitude.* She clambered inside, wiping the lubricant over herself as she hunched down into a fetal position. She nearly gagged from the stench, but forced herself to pull the slit closed, leaving only a small gap for air. The last thing she heard before the enemy surged into the nursery was a lurching crash and an awful, otherworldly screech.

In the darkness and decay, she waited.

Soon enough, Lena was hoisted up by an enemy worker. She dared not move, but by tilting her head she was able to catch glimpses of the world outside. Most of the view was obscured by the underside of the worker's head—a thick bristled hide, tapering to its claw-like mandibles—but she also saw the enormous gasters of others ahead. With the constant patter of the insect's legs against the rock it felt like she was in the middle of a stampede.

Tensed up, it didn't take long before her muscles began to ache. Then burn. Her right arm went dead. She gritted her teeth against the pain, tried to transport her mind somewhere—anywhere—else. She wondered what she'd say to Artem to make him listen. He wasn't easily swayed once he'd made up his mind.

Her bearer slowed up.

Was she there already? The insects moved fast, but it didn't feel like she'd traveled far enough. *Maybe some kind of bottleneck?*

And then she glimpsed it.

Head shaved down to fine stubble. Two whirring, mechanized eyes—hot coals in a cold inhuman face. A muscular arm with a metallic exoskeleton. The slicer. Oh yes, slicer was the right word, no simple mercenary here. This *thing* was an efficient blend of sinew and purpose and engineering. It was heading in the same direction, gaze roving over the passing insects. She prayed it hadn't found Artem yet.

She ducked a little deeper into the cocoon, held her breath. The sound of the slicer's motorized rhythms receded. The stampede settled down into a more ordered march. She was in enemy territory.

She risked a small stretch, releasing the pressure on her arm. She lost track of her bearings, their path a hodgepodge of sharp turns and inclines. Without a decent map—the second colony's nest still largely uncharted—she was terrified that she might never find her way back. She sought landmarks wherever she could: a skein of minerals in a chamber ceiling; the shape of an arch; an unusual rock formation.

If the nest was anything like the first—a chaotic riddle of thousands of passages and hundreds of chambers—it was probably an exercise in futility. She might walk dozens of kilometers and never find her way out. She repeated a mantra to herself, mouthing the words in the darkness. *Artem will know the way. Artem will know the way.*

She tried not to think of the unspoken conditional: *If he's still alive.*

They left her with the rest of the stolen larvae and pupae in a cavernous storage chamber. When she could only hear the background hum of the nest, she heaved herself out of her cocoon. She stripped off her sodden undergarments, lodged the clothes in the pod, and swiftly applied the new colony's pheromone.

A worker at the chamber entrance rushed over. It seemed confused to find her there, but after probing her it turned its attention to a pupa that was nearing maturity. Lena rapped out a pattern on its head. Ana had taught her the action—a command to retrieve fungal pap for the queen. The worker set off. Lena grabbed her pack and jogged after it, grateful that it paused at the chamber entrance to pick up the right trail. She kept her harpoon gun in hand, ready to fire.

Unlike the original colony, the tunnels teemed with activity. She encountered several castes she hadn't seen before: a small, frenetic beast that ferried debris away from tunneling sites; a type with a proboscis-like extrusion sensitive to mineral deposits; and a lumbering insect with a long balloon-like sac on its underbelly. The last was one of the fabled kamikaze caste. An insect loaded up with more toxic acids than Genotech's entire biochemical division. The other nestmates gave it a wide berth. Lena did likewise.

After the worker collected some pap in a nearby garden, it led her off to an almighty chamber. The chatter of several hundred insects and a thousand myriad rumblings filled the cavern, while the smell of moist organics prickled Lena's nose. In contrast to the dying queen, this gargantuan matriarch positively glowed with vitality. The great curving bulk of its abdomen shone, while its flesh beat with powerful pulses. Lena wondered if it had any inkling its colony had won the battle for Vesta.

"Lena!"

Artem. Thank God.

Lena tracked the sound of his voice to one of the side vestibules, where she found him gesturing her over. She went to embrace him, but he grabbed her hard and pulled her down amongst the giant fungi. "What the hell are you doing here?" he spat, keeping his voice low.

Only trying to save your ungrateful ass.

"How did you find me?" His face lit up. "It's Ana, right? She's alive."

His mind worked fast. Too fast, sometimes. Lena nodded, glad to be the bearer of good news.

Artem's smile was short lived, though. "If you've come to talk me out of this, forget it. And if you've come to give me help, I don't need it."

"Like you didn't need help when the corps came knocking?" It felt good to stand up to him for once. "Look where that got you."

He blinked, shocked.

"I'm not blaming you." She took a deep breath. "You don't have to fix everything on your own, Art."

He bobbed his head up, looked across the chamber towards the entrance. "Were you followed?"

"Shit, Artem, are you listening to me?" Lena punched a saucer shaped fungi head. "No, I wasn't followed."

"Good, we've still got time then."

"Artem, stop! You got a death wish? For what? Revenge?"

"Revenge? You think this is about revenge?" He gritted his teeth, stared hard at Lena. "Okay, I admit it. I won't be sorry to put this animal down, but that's not it. I'm doing this for all those miners who live short, shitty lives, for those guys who if they don't cop it out in the belt, die of the raddies when they get back home. If she dies,"—he nodded at the monstrous queen—"belt mining stays in the dark ages."

"No, stupid. If she dies, we lose six months work. If *you* die,"—and here, suddenly, a knot of emotion choked her—"we lose everything."

He examined her face, which she held up, proud. Then he picked up a loose rock, rolled it in his hands, while he stared across the chamber. "She's beautiful, isn't she?"

Lena didn't say anything, just listened to the rhythms of the nest, inhaled the pungent smells of life and death. There was a harsh beauty to this world.

After a while, Artem got to his feet.

They left together.

She thought he was leading her to safety.

She thought their fleetness of foot, their silence, their persistence in keeping to minor passages, were tactics to *avoid* the slicer. Any moment she thought they'd emerge from the riddled, evolutionary-honed chaos of the nest and come across the clean engineered lines of the space-rafts.

She thought wrong.

Artem wasn't *avoiding* the slicer, he was *tracking* it. The realization came too late to argue the toss—came when they almost ploughed straight into the back of the monster. It was trudging away from them, crossing a large pit-shaped chamber, the space churning with insects. She imagined they would've met a swift death if it hadn't been for the noise and motion of their nestmates.

Artem ducked down, pulling Lena with him so they were hidden by the monstrous bodies. A din of clicks and burrs and taps echoed off the hard igneous walls, but Lena could still hear the whirring, metronomic stride of the slicer. *Zzzt-klank. Zzzt-klank. Zzzt–*

It stopped.

She would've been furious if she wasn't so shit scared. She slowed her breathing, held herself still. Her legs trembled, muscles exhausted. Artem motioned for the harpoon gun. *Wait*, she wanted to say, but his face was hard and unyielding. She leaned over to pass him the gun, the reflex to obey as natural as blinking. Still the compliant sister, a small part of her whispered, taunting. *Only as a last resort*, she tried to tell him with her own face set stern. It was almost in his hands, when she had an idea. She drew it back from him, delicately twisted the pack off her back, and retrieved the aerosol from inside.

Artem's eyes lit up, understanding. The aerosol held the original colony's scent. If he were forced to fire, dousing the slicer in the scent would give them a fighting chance of escape. She passed him both the gun and the aerosol.

The slicer began moving again—began moving away from them. Lena let her head slump, felt her tension draining. Then she turned to Artem, and watched in horror as he stood up, jammed the aerosol can into the harpoon tip, and took aim—

Stupid, stupid, stupid.

The slicer turned full about, unleashing some type of explosive pulse.

Artem fired.

A tunneler took the full brunt of the pulse—its heavy abdomen flying apart with a terrific crack—but they were still thrown like rag dolls by the blast. The spiked harpoon must've hit the slicer because around it a storm of fighting broke out. The shot didn't have the consequences Artem had intended though. The slicer was like the calm eye of a hurricane, impervious to the carnage that whipped about it, blade fields cutting its opponents to pieces in a carnival of false color. This thing—this cold-hearted killer, this inhuman machine of flesh and blood and metal, this monster of rhymes and nightmares—would kill them.

She couldn't move, could barely breathe for the thought. "Artem," she screamed.

No reply.

Artem wasn't going to save the day. Artem was still down, keeping a low profile, licking his wounds—or worse.

Dazed, she watched the strange caste of insect with the pendulous, bulbous sac amble past. Before she lost her nerve, she clambered onto the bloated insect, gripped its antennae like reins. She wheeled it about to face the slicer, struck a simple pattern on the side of its head. As the insect charged, its enormous sac inflated. Ten yards from the target, she leapt off, landed painfully on a rocky outcrop. She got up just in time to see the immense gland burst, throwing searing, toxic fluids all over the slicer and the pit floor and a few of the fleeing insects and, to her horror, her brother.

"Artem, oh Jesus, Artem."

He hadn't been cowering. He'd been crawling closer, still fighting whatever the odds.

She stumbled to his side, glanced at the wound that slashed across his torso, neck, and around the side of his face. He was alive, but in so much agony that it was a curse as much as a blessing. Nearby, an acidic whorl rose off the seared tissue and corroded metal of what remained of the slicer. The gurgled scream that had greeted the monster's demise still echoed in her mind.

"You did good," Artem croaked, spittle flecking his lips. "You make sure that newsman knows you're a hero."

"Shh, shh."

She used all the elements of her limited med-kit: painkillers, salve strips, gauze pads. Still he cried in pain. She lifted him to lean on her shoulder, felt a sticky warmth against her arm. His pain hurt her deep.

What hurt her more though was his betrayal of her trust.

Their space-raft looped in a high eccentricity—five hundred klicks at furthest, two at closest—orbit around Vesta. Nik had switched on the emergency distress beacon as soon as his and Ana's space-raft had launched, and help was on its way from Pallas. He'd also had the smarts to inform the United Interplanetary Space Authority that he'd sighted outer system pirates—another remnant of the Fringe Wars—in the vicinity. Military vessels, bound by standard protocol, would be vectoring in to secure the local volume. There'd be no more slicers.

The colony was safe.

They were safe.

Lena set Artem up in a loose mesh-cradle, pumped him full of meds. The weightlessness helped him deal with his blistered skin and corroded flesh, but he still moaned in pain. He'd make it though.

"What will you write?" she asked Nik when their space-rafts had line-of-sight comm as they shot close over Vesta's plains.

"What I always do."

Below, Lena spied movement. A flinger stood on its hind legs, antennae twitching at the stars. It circled about, drew back its muscular tail. A whiplike blur later, a glittering speck raced into the heavens. "What's that?"

"The truth."

The truth meant revealing the unlicensed second colony. The truth meant Genotech prosecuted, Artem incarcerated. Even though ore was leaving Vesta again, even though the experiment was a success, with the truth, the corps would sink the technology in a legal mire as dangerous as quicksand. Nobody would touch it. Belt mining would remain trapped in the dark ages.

"What about the bigger picture?"

"The bigger picture? Not my concern. I just write what happened."

"What happened? What happened?" she stuttered. Everything was slipping away. Was it all going to be for nothing? She had to try. "What happened is that my brother saved your fucking life. If he hadn't tracked that monster, if he hadn't killed it, where'd you think you'd be now? I'll tell you where: blasted to slag. All of us would be."

Artem moaned softly.

"He killed it?" Nik asked.

Lena gripped her brother's hand. "Rode one of those suicide bugs straight into its ugly cybernetic side," she lied. "Nearly killed himself for his efforts." Artem's eyes opened wide. Lena pressed her index finger over his lips. "My brother's a hero and you want to write a story that'll see him locked up, see his work abandoned, and see the corps carry on, business as usual, all because you have some misplaced allegiance to a code. Tell me, how many miners' deaths could you live with? Ten? A hundred? A thousand?"

"Not my concern," Nik said again, although this time there was less conviction in his words.

"Ten thousand?"

"Not my concern." Barely a whisper.

"A hundred thousand?"

Vesta receded, plains and prominences merging into a grainy wash. "I'll think about it," he said eventually, but the subtext was clear.

Lena severed the connection. He'd write the story they wanted. There'd be no mention of the second colony. Only his pride stopped him saying as much now. She should've felt happy, but where the feeling should've been there was only hollowness.

"You lied for me," Artem whispered.

"Not for you." Lena peeled off a dressing-salve from her brother's shoulder, inspected the salmon-pink tissue.

The space-raft carried on into the darkness, silent as the vacuum.

Haumea

By David Nordley

Captain Karl Krull glared at his second in command—not me, thank goodness. Krull made the Lieutenant, John Ellison, sit because the two-meter first officer would otherwise tower over him. Ellison ignored the glare, smiled and presented his case as smoothly as any lawyer or Martian real estate agent would.

"Karl, we've traveled beyond Pluto and it's only one more astronomical unit to Haumea. We are getting some well-earned relief at Samios."

Relief was an understatement, as I well knew. The memory of Thera's legs wrapped around me was still fresh. I'd said goodbye, but not wanted to.

"We have a mission," Captain Krull said, tonelessly. "We will get to Haumea before the Cislunar Republic."

"We will," Lieutenant Ellison said. "Captain Duluth is months behind us, if coming at all. It's just a rumor. The documentary crew would like to stay here a few more days as well."

Captain Krull drummed his fingers on his faux-wood desk. "We serve the International Space Authority. We are not the employees of the supercargo…"

That was a fine point, I thought. They *were* paying for the mission, after all.

Ellison smiled. "The ISA is a long way from here."

Captain Krull scowled even more. "We *are* the ISA. We break seals at ten-hundred tomorrow."

"Karl, the days of that kind of autocracy are past. Leadership…"

"Don't lecture me about leadership, Lieutenant." Krull's voice had a shrill, nasal quality that was especially irritating when he raised it. "Ten hundred hours. Any crew not aboard can apply for Samiosan residency. Understand?"

"Karl…"

"Captain Krull!"

He pronounced it "kruhl," not "kroo-el." Born in Garmisch, his astronautical English still held a hint of German in it. That was perhaps unfortunate.

Ellison shrugged. "I will let them know, then. May I tell them that we will stop at Samios on the return trip?"

"Are you all that horny? Have your brains migrated to some southern part of your anatomy? We will return on the planned trajectory on the planned schedule. That is all."

"Karl… Captain…"

"THAT. IS. ALL."

Ellison shrugged again and left the wardroom.

Captain Krull then noticed my existence. Departure prep was in my department.

"And Tony…"

"Yes?"

"Delegate. Lieutenant deWalt can watch the AI. I'll assist, if needed. I see no reason why you can't attend to personal business, do you?"

"No, Captain." Lieutenant Kari deWalt was my second; a very disciplined and competent woman who got along better with machines than people, with Captian Krull as the odd exception.

"That is all."

I messaged Thera before the wardroom doors hissed closed.

She didn't have the evening free when I called. Ten minutes later, she called back and said she'd arranged for someone to take her shift at the Samios Protective Services watch desk.

A warm tropical sea circled Samios inside its belly. Thera and I basked on its shore, our bare bodies soaking up the last rays from the interior reflector as it retreated toward its evening nest in the north polar hills.

"We can still tan out here!" I remarked.

"Aluminized graphene reflectors can do wonders."

I smiled. Samios had 30,000 square kilometers of them: a huge silvery flower. "A lot of work to be so far away…"

She laughed. "Why do you think we are so far out?"

I gave a safe answer. "Nitrogen?"

Ice Chip was a hundred-kilometerish Kuiper Belt object tumbling near Samios, full of water and ammonia. A space colony is an almost closed system, but nothing is perfect.

"Hmm, interesting, but easier to ship the nitrogen in, I think. No, we don't want to be overwhelmed by bluenosed missionaries and sexual tourists."

I ran my finger along her firm, tan, breast. "Overwhelmed?"

She repaid the favor. "Even me, I think." She went on for several minutes about the problems of sexual tourism, ending with, "So, it is your job to bring our culture inward."

I smiled. "Let's see. Partnership is not ownership. Let the robots do the work; that's what they are for. If the lower needs are satisfied, the higher needs rise to the fore. Very idealistic. Do people here actually spend that much time on engineering and science?"

"And writing and music and all the arts. We make more patents per capita than Germany."

I touched the local net. Okay, they did, by maybe about a tenth of a percent.

"We have more fun, too." She flowed around me and assumed a position that precluded further conversation.

The problem with exporting their culture, I thought, was that most people would just rather stay here than fight another culture war on Earth.

The *Dag Hammarskjold* looked like a 200-meter-wide spinning dragonfly with pods at the end of its radiator wings. It flew 'backward'; the reactors and engines were in the dragonfly's head, and the segmented, despun 'tail' was a train of reaction mass modules surrounding the long access tunnel that kept the rotating part clear of any obstructions when we docked.

Surprisingly, the entire crew made the ten-hundred departure deadline. Two documentary techs stayed in lotus land, but the supercargo were overstaffed, anyway.

I told *Dag* to undock as soon as the access tube was clear.

"Mind the exhaust clears the solar collector," I said, unnecessarily. It did get a nod of approval from Captain Krull, however, who could go on at length regarding how human beings should still be able to fly spacecraft.

The *Dag* reported readiness, Krull got clearance, and I gave the ship the execute order. We backed out to ten kilometers on the steam jets, while the reactors came back up to flight power. Our wings began to glow cherry red and the floors of our life support spheres adjusted to the gentle thrust of our plasma exhaust.

As we pulled away, Ice Chip caught the Sun just right, a wink that reminded us of what we'd left behind.

Two weeks before Haumea orbit, documentary team leader Tehn Wan Do addressed his audience in English with a carefully cultivated British accent. The audience was pretty much everyone in the solar system.

Behind him, an image of our destination tumbled ponderously end over end. Time lapse of course; Haumea's four hour rotation rate held the record for planets, but that's still less motion than people can perceive as such, four times slower than the minute hand of an old analog clock.

"It is extreme: extremely small, barely enough mass to achieve hydrostatic equilibrium and planethood; dwarf planethood to be precise. It's extremely elongated; like a rugby ball. It's covered by an ocean of ice, but only a few hundred meters deep; above solid rock. Robots can only see what they are built to see. We shall now find out what the human eye and mind can accomplish on the scene."

As someone who has built and maintained robots, including the spacecraft we were on, I shook my head. The robotic exploration of Haumea had been far deeper than anything people could accomplish. But Earth had been playing second fiddle to the Cislunar Republic in space exploration lately. So we were on an ISA flag and footprints publicity mission: it was almost the year 2100 and no person had yet bothered to place a boot on Haumea. It was an opportunity to point out that in the modern era of orbital towers, a gravity well was not the handicap it used to be.

"Who will be the first human to set foot on Haumea?" Tehn asked. "If that has been decided, we have not been told. There are only sixteen planets around the Sun and only three that have not felt the presence of the human foot. This will be an historic moment. The entire solar system wants to know."

My earchip buzzed. "Wardroom oh-eight-twenty sharp. Disciplinary board."

Chaos! Who was Captain Krull going to alienate now?

Dr. Tehn addressed the Captain formally and only when necessary. Lieutenant Ellison was the only person who made any pretense of camaraderie with the Captain, and everyone knew it was a pretense.

I chafed under his paternalism myself, but kept calm so as not to add to the general malaise. Kari deWalt, on the other hand, seemed to be of a similar mind to the Captain when it came to shipboard things. Formalities could be a defense against dealing with the messiness of relationships and neither had ever gotten anywhere near marriage to anyone, to the best of my knowledge.

I had half an hour to freshen up and slip into a formal uniform and do some research.

Captain Krull's victim this time was Biotech Linda Rodrigues. She'd made a still. As chief engineer, I got to sit on one side of the wardroom with Captain Krull and Lieutenant Ellison. Second Officer Lieutenant Leena Diel read the charges.

"Biological Technician Rodrigues constructed a still in her quarters and with said still did produce at least ten ccs of alcoholic beverage in violation of ISA Regulation 2035-143857-B.3.c banning the unauthorized production of alcoholic beverages on ISA spacecraft."

"For the record, how do we know this?"

"You discovered the still on an unannounced inspection on the third of February, 1400 UT."

"Has the output of the still been analyzed and the results recorded?"

"Yes."

"Enter it into the record. Is there any disputation with respect to the facts of the case?"

Rodrigues shook her head.

"Ms. Rodrigues?" Captain Krull asked.

"My lawyer has a statement."

"Lawyer?"

"He's on Samios."

Krull sighed. "Let's hear it."

The image on the wall introduced himself and explained that the regulation was intended to keep astronauts safe from amateur distillation efforts which could be poisonous and endanger their health. Since Rodrigues was a Biotech and had made wine and beer before and knew what she was doing, the regulation should not be applied to her.

"Do you have anything more to say on your own behalf?" Captain Krull asked when the lawyer was done.

"I'm from Hawai'i. It would be very good public relations if I continue to be part of the Haumea expedition." She pronounced it Ha-oo-MAY-eh, not HOW me ah.

"Noted. Wait outside while we discuss this. That will be all."

Once the others left, Captain Krull looked at each of us, then asked, "Does anyone have anything to say before I start recording?"

Lieutenant Ellison responded quickly. "Clearly, the harm to the expedition's reputation and morale of carrying this on greatly exceeds any benefit of terminating Tech Rodrigues' experiments, let alone punishing her for them. This is an embarrassment. Since the board has been convened, I suppose we have to do something. Maybe we can create a local licensing board?"

"Noted," Captain Krull said. He then looked at me.

I liked Linda. I'd spent a couple of very sweet nights with her, as had many of the ship's company, men and women. She had a wild streak to her; nobody would ever own her. If she obeyed rules, it was because she thought they were good rules, not because of authority. She'd had lots of cautions from Captain Krull, but she'd never hurt anyone. Now we had to decide whether we could allow her judgment to replace the codified 'wisdom' of decades of spaceflight. No, I realized, that actually wasn't the question, yet; at this point, we simply verified the facts.

"Sir, the facts show that Tech Rodrigues violated the ISAR."

"Yes. I agree. Lieutenant Ellison, do you dispute that she made the still? She doesn't."

Ellison shot him an angry look. "Okay. She made a still. But I don't think the spirit of the regulation was violated."

Captain Krull nodded, expressionless. "Very well, for the record the vote is two to one on the facts."

"Lieutenant Diel, given the finding what is the range of corrective action?"

Diel sighed. "It's a class three violation, with a maximum punishment of dismissal from duties and transportation to the nearest appropriate ISA facility by most expedient means. The minimum is forfeiture of one week's pay, which may be suspended by convening authority."

"Thank you, Lieutenant Diel." Captain Krull was silent for a few moments, then pronounced, "I'm inclined to forfeiture of one month's pay, confinement to quarters for one week, *with no visitation*, and confiscation of all elements of the still. I think that covers us should there be an investigation. I'm not going to put her aground at Samios. She'd take that as a reward. Any comments?"

He stared at each of us in turn. It was clear he didn't want any comments.

Lieutenant Ellison stared back. "On the record, I think that is unnecessarily harsh and detrimental to morale. I recommend the minimum, suspension of the sentence, and ignoring such activities hereafter."

"Noted," Capt. Krull said. He looked at me.

"I might drop confinement, suggest a counseling course on the philosophy of regulation and discipline aboard ISA spacecraft, and suspend the fine retroactively if there is no subsequent violation."

"Probation, in other words. For a first time violation, I might be inclined to agree. But this one has a history and needs to be brought up short."

He looked at both of us. "I need to take your views into account, and so will suspend the forfeiture of pay at the end of the mission given no further violations. I will also take your suggestion," he nodded to me, "concerning the course. It will give her something to do in quarters. We are done, gentlemen."

And that was that.

Linda's jaw dropped as Captain Krull pronounced the sentence, and she walked to her quarters alone, with tears in her eyes.

We took station over Haumea's prime meridian one hundred and ten kilometers above the furthest point on Haumea's surface from its center. The landers would go down to the north pole, now in continuous sunlight, a convenience for the documentary team; over much of the dwarf planet, the Sun set every two hours.

You could cut the tension aboard with a knife. The rumor mill about who would be first to set foot on the Solar System's tenth, twelfth, or fourteenth planet, depending on who counts, ground away and Tammy Kling of the documentary crew started a pool. The lead of the documentary team had the best odds, followed by our staff planetologist, then the lander pilot (someone has to check things out first), and even Linda Rodrigues, because she was from Hawai'i and female; the only woman to be first on a planet so far was Ingrid Karinsdottir of Mars. But Linda's recent misadventure lowered her odds.

So we all gathered in the maintenance shop next to the small craft hanger. At precisely 1400, Captain Krull walked in, dressed in EVA gear.

"Quiet please, quiet please," he said and waited for the hubbub to die down. "As you know, this is an ISA mission. It has been decided that, as the senior ISA official present, it is my duty to be first off the lander platform and plant the UN flag." There were several groans and he looked around at everyone as if he expected some kind of challenge. There was none, unless one considered the cynical smirk on Lieutenant Ellison's face a challenge.

Krull nodded. "Landing party, we leave at 1420. Tony, you have the con."

"Yes sir," I said, surprised.

Lieutenant Ellison's mouth became a tight, grim line. We had the same rank and I was senior to him by a year in ISA service, but he was in a line slot while I was technically in a support billet. We both shared watch duty with the Captain; nine-hour shifts with an hour overlap. The Captain was leaving in the middle of his shift; Lieutenant Ellison would have the next one. Perhaps he was simply trying to manage the workload. But as the first officer, Lieutenant Ellison could take it as an affront, and blame it on me.

The first landing party entered the elevator up to the hanger in the zero-g core of the ship in near silence. At the last moment, someone started clapping, and a couple of others joined in, including myself, for form. It was a feeble sendoff, all recorded for posterity by the documentary group's robocam—the last thing to scurry into the elevator.

I headed for the control room to finish off the remaining three hours of the Captain's shift. Leena Diel sat folded in a lotus position on the Captain's chair, watching the documentary feed on a main screen window and made no move to leave it. I shrugged and took my usual position at the engineering board.

"So Old Rude-and-Rule is going to get himself a planet," she said.

I shrugged. "Orders are orders."

She laughed. "What orders?"

She had a point. If there were any instructions nominating Captain Krull to be the first person on Haumea, we hadn't seen them. Then again, "We don't necessarily see everything. The UN should have made some public statement," I said, "to take him off the hook."

"Off the hook? He has Vesta, Amalthea, Chiron, and Nereid. But nothing big. So I think he wants this. Our captain has a compensatory ego inversely proportional to his stature." She sighed.

"He didn't look all that happy. Maybe he was taking *them* off the hook."

"Fat chance."

Kari deWalt joined us then. The women shared unsmiling glances. Kari thought Diel's area of greatest competence was Lieutenant Ellison's bed, but I'd not noticed either the technical shortcomings nor the sleeping arrangements.

"Best view of the main event," Kari said.

Lieutenant Diel got up. "I'll be taking the second lander down. Time to check it out." She sauntered out.

Not being Captain Krull, I simply said, "That will be all, Lieutenant" softly to her swaying derriere.

Kari stared at me with steel-blue eyes boring into me from beneath a dome of short steel-gray hair. Her body said she was about thirty, her head said she was about fifty. But her language was of another era.

"You don't have to take that BS, Captain."

I shrugged.

"I'd just love to see Diel bust up an effing lander."

I wasn't sure Diel was out of earshot, so I didn't laugh.

We watched lander one depart. It was basically a cylinder with a bunch of boxes attached here and there, some of which sprouted thruster cones. They'd been designed all-video; in the command seat, you'd think you were sitting out in open space, except for the windows Captain Krull had put in the lower front. We got the view from the documentary crew's camera bot.

Three hours later, Krull brought the first lander down. From a couple of momentary hesitations, I surmised that he was piloting manually.

The attention tone sounded. "Lieutenant Delgado, Captain Ellison needs to speak to you," *Dag* said. I looked at Kari and she looked back. I was 'Captain', and however 'acting' my status might be, there was only one Captain on a spacecraft at a time. This wasn't good.

Before panicking, though, I tried the simplest thing first. "*Dag*, I have the con."

"That status has just changed. Captain Ellison needs to see you immediately. He will explain the change in status."

"It's an effing mutiny," Kari said.

I held a finger to my lips, too late as it turned out.

We were escorted to the wardroom by Linda Rodrigues. She was holding a dart gun.

"Linda, this isn't right. You can't just take over a spaceship in this day and age."

"You can if it's being run by people like you and Captain Krull," she said.

"Me?"

"You're part of it. You voted to convict me for nothing. And I thought we were friends."

"I didn't have much choice. You built the still."

"You had a choice. You voted with *him*."

The way she said 'him' made me realize that Captain Krull's morale problem was much worse than I'd thought. But Lieutenant Ellison should have been trying to help hold things together instead of looking at it as an opportunity.

When we got to the wardroom, Lieutenant Ellison sat at the center of the wardroom. Linda took the seat to the left.

"What in the hell do you think you're doing?" I asked him.

"Sit down, Tony." He smiled. "By the way, you're officially relieved of watch."

"Under whose authority?"

"Mine. I have succeeded to the Captaincy under ISA regulation 1.0094-72."

"You can't do that. The Captain has to be found incompetent by a board of officers..." I looked at them. "Rodrigues isn't an officer."

"She is now. Lt. Diel participated as well."

I spread my arms. "He gets to defend himself, doesn't he?"

Linda smiled, very much enjoying this. "He didn't answer summons."

"If you have any questions," Ellison said, "ask *Dag*."

I thought furiously. The mutineers must have somehow compromised the ship's computer. But I shouldn't just assume this. I touched the net. But the *Dag* affirmed the change of command and its legality.

"Sit," Ellison said again, a bit more peremptorily. "You too, Kari."

Once we were seated, he began. "The situation is this. I have replaced Captain Krull under ISA 1.0094-72. Captain Krull was informed of this ten minutes ago by the crew of the lander. As he, unfortunately, did not accede to the regulations' implementation, he has been detained on the surface."

"Lieutenant deWalt, you referred to this entirely legal and necessary action as a 'mutiny', did you not?"

Kari sat tense as a cat. If there were anything physical she could do about it, she would, but she knew, as we all did, that at the Captain's order, the *Dag* could quickly anesthetize anyone—and it thought Ellison was in charge.

"Lieutenant?"

"I was not fully aware of the circumstances at the time."

Ellison laughed. "And now that you are, you plan to lie low and try the same thing on me." He shook his head. "Give it up. I want your formal concurrence to the change of command."

"There's an 'or else'? What is the 'or else'?"

He smiled at her. "There's no coercion here. You know the former Captain's behavior as well as anyone. Do you, freely and of your own will, agree that his replacement was necessary? While you are thinking about that, I'll need Tony's answer to the same question. Perhaps he will set an example."

Choosing my words carefully, I said. "I know Captain Krull has his faults, but I don't know enough about this proceeding to validate it. There are a number of irregularities…"

Ellison cut me off. "Both of you fall far short of the standard of the complete support I need to run this ship. Wait outside."

"*Dag*," I asked aloud, "are Asimov's laws still in force?"

"Yes."

Ellison laughed. "No, I can't execute you. Now go to your quarters."

Ellison gave us and two other 'recalcitrant' crew, a choice. We could be confined to quarters until the *Dag* reached Samios and turned over to the authorities as, technically, mutineers, for failing to accede to Ellison's takeover. Or we could be put aground on Haumea, with supplies, to be picked up later. One of the crew, Commtech Jensen, chose confinement to quarters.

Besides myself and Kari, only Biotech Samuel Levi chose to stay with Captain Krull.

They left us with Captain Krull at the derelict robot base on the north pole in the middle of a crater-pocked field of dusty ice as hard as rock. They took the lander, of course, and our personal comps, leaving us with no outgoing communications.

We had a standard emergency kit with a hemispherical six-person vacuum tent, a field printer-refiner, and a thirty-square-meter roll-up solar array rated at ten kilowatts—which out here would generate about five watts. At least, given Haumea's 287 year orbit, the arctic summer would last longer than any of us would live.

I looked up toward the departing lander, now a blue-violet pin-prick with a ghostly tail against a jet-black sky. Distant as it was, the Sun reflecting off the surrounding ice field gave more light than would allow our eyes to see stars.

Sam started rummaging through our rations. "The schlemiel didn't leave us with enough to survive," he said. "Not in this place of no return, this land of darkness and the shadow of death."

I stared at him. The Sun wouldn't set at this latitude for years.

"It's a quote. Job. That guy came out of it okay."

"Well, we aren't effing intended to survive," Kari said. "Too inconvenient. There'll be some kind of exculpatory narrative, with doctored video."

"Kari, Tony, Sam," Captain Krull said, "we are going to do much more than survive. But we have much work to do."

We all turned to him. All kinds of questions went through my head. Was he still in charge? The spaceship was gone. He was Captain of nothing.

"There's 200-watt radiothermal generator at the east pole data node. That was thirty years ago, of course, but it should still be good for 100 watts or so."

We stared.

"Yah, yah, I studied lots of stuff about Haumea before we came here."

"The east pole is about 1200km away," I said. Haumea may be a 'dwarf' planet, but as someone said about Pluto, a Chihuahua is still a dog. "And the east pole is 500km higher than the north pole. We'd have to lift everything up five hundred kilometers!"

"Yah, yah. We have a big mountain to climb. Where I come from we have lots of mountains to climb. But Haumea gravity is only a few percent and it is smooth, yah? Two Charon-sized objects merged and the heat of that melted everything, drove off most of the water but not all. For a while there is an atmosphere and an ocean, which had time to freeze. So it is sea level all over, because of isostatic equilibrium."

Captain Krull continued. "So we build a sled. We build a platform for the vacuum tent, a mast and struts for the array. That," he pointed at the small robot base, "is our mine for stuff to build with. Then we move, while our bellies are still full from the ship. The gravity will get lower as we go."

On Earth, I weigh about a kilonewton. Here, I weighed a bit less than fifty Newtons, maybe sixty in my vacuum gear. The emergency gear was likely another twenty or thirty.

Sam perked up. "We do have to move. Except for the base, there's nothing but ice around here to feed the printer and not much power. We'd starve after the rations are gone."

That would be the big problem. Our skin-tight suits powered themselves from our motions moving fluid through their capillaries, as well as the temperature differential between our bodies and the 30 Kelvin or so radiative temperature of the surface. But our bodies had to be fed to power our suits.

"Yah. There's some bare rock at the east pole. So you'll be able to feed the printer some real regolith."

"If that field printer eats regolith," Kari said. "Okay, I'll check it out."

In spite of myself, I started thinking about the engineering problems, too.

We explored. There was a generator; its hydrogen fuel supply was long gone, but maybe we could crank it by hand. Some of the batteries worked. There were some hollows and cracks in which some dust had collected, and the ice itself was slightly dusty.

That night, we slept in the vacuum tent, a hemispherical thing with a frame on the bottom to make it flat. One inflates the sides, goes in, seals the opening and pressurizes the rest; a quarter bar, mostly oxygen, some nitrogen. To get out, you need to pump it down, but complete vacuum is hard to achieve with the field pump; we lost some air on every cycle. Modesty consisted of sleeping bags, or looking at the wall. We had a glorified chamber pot.

The next day, Kari got the printer to eat dust. Its refining operation was partly exothermic, so it didn't use as much of our scarce power as it might have otherwise. But that power had to be split in a delicate balance of printing toilet paper and printing anything else. Speaking of the TP, I can tell you from personal experience that the difference between 5% and zero gravity does matter.

We built the *Ernest Shackleton* in six days. Its mast, yardarm and runners were salvaged from pallet supports. Haumea has one of the highest albedos in the solar system, and we doubled our effective collecting area by tilting the array down slightly. We salvaged some batteries. Every Earth day, we recycled oxygen, printed some sugar, protein, and some TP; supplies went down, but not too rapidly, Sam thought.

Captain Krull drove us hard, but there was a certain exhilaration to it. We made sixty or so kilometers every day.

Navigation was simple. The east and west pole stations had launched data tethers—strong fiber-optic lines—to the poles, which were out of view to the satellites. The data had flowed overland to the dishes on either end of Haumea. We followed the data tethers.

Grunt, pull. One's mind drifts while man-hauling a sledge. A few hundred kilometers below me might be a lake. I thought of fish and swimming East.

After six hundred kilometers south, we got short nights every four hours.

We came up against an exception to flatness. Pressure, apparently, tipped a huge hunk of the ice crust up about four meters, creating a wall that ran east and west to Haumea's horizon.

Captain Krull nodded. "That big impact near the east pole broke off the moons. That all happened, what, a billion years ago? Haumea continues to lose angular momentum to its moons, and the ice slips toward its center faster than the rock. So we get pressure ridges, like this."

The *Ernest Shackleton* massed maybe twenty tons—only a couple of kilonewtons.

It was my bright idea to lever up the front end to the top of the ridge and just push it on up and over. That would save time, and we were all tired. Captain Krull frowned and looked at Kari. Kari frowned and looked at me.

"If it doesn't go, we can always unload and lift it that way."

"Yah, yah, okay."

We stood two on a side, a bit forward. If we got the center up and dipped the back, the front runners ought to just clear the wall.

It worked just like that, and we were congratulating ourselves when Kari simply went limp and slid slowly to the ice, under the runner. The sled started to slip back. Captain Krull and I were on the other side of the sled and Sam was looking in the other direction at the lip of ice beginning to give way.

"Sam," Captain Krull said, calmly but urgently, "Kari has fallen. Get her out from under the runner."

Sam turned, and it was a race. I moved as fast as I could to the back of the sled and tried to halt its slide, while Captain Krull ducked under the runners and tried to lift from below. Sam got Kari out while, in slow motion, the sled made a mockery of the Captain's effort to clear two kilonewtons overhead.

The runners had some clearance, but I could not remember how much.

"I am okay, Tony," the Captain said. "It's tight and you will probably have to dig me out. But see to Kari first."

She was non-responsive. By virtue of his biological training, Sam was our doctor, but this was way out of his comfort zone. He stood frozen.

As a ship's officer, I had some EMT training, but in this era of robots, hand comps, and so on, I hadn't taken any of it too seriously.

"Where's the med kit?" I asked, thinking that a place to start.

"Is she breathing?" Captain Krull asked, in gasps, from under the sled.

I couldn't see any evidence that she was. Maybe…some slight fogging on her faceplate. Not enough, I thought.

CPR? I could do the 'C' part from outside the space suit. Then my eye caught her suit air controls. Maybe that could take care of the 'P' part; I turned the oxygen up to max. I spread her out and pushed down hard on her chest, I hoped not too hard, where I thought her heart was. A bit faster than once a second, I remembered. I did this for about twenty seconds and was rewarded by more fogging of the face plate. Her eyes opened, but she didn't look good.

"My gut, I want to puke. My back is killing me."

In 5% gravity? Sam showed up with the med kit. It wasn't sealed and its comp had been removed. Among other things, it was a long range communications device, of course. But it was also the brains of the kit. I looked at its contents; right near the top were smart caps of aspirin and cardiol.

Heart attack? She didn't complain about chest pain, but when all you have is a hammer, everything looks like a nail. The space suits have a passive oral lock built into them. I put the cardiol and aspirin in, closed the cover, and continued compressing as the tube found its way into her mouth.

That was everything I could think of or remember to treat a heart attack.

For whatever reason, after a few anxious minutes, she began to breathe easier.

"Hang in there, kid," I said. "I'll be right back. Sam?"

Sam came alive and followed me to the back end of the sled.

"Captain, if we lift up the back, can you wriggle out?"

"You'll need to hold it up about five seconds, Lieutenant," he said.

I looked at Sam. He seemed puzzled for a moment, then nodded.

"Okay. One…two…three." Up the back end went. Easily at first and then my muscles started to burn.

Captain Krull shot out from under the rear in much less than five seconds.

We all got back to Kari, now sitting up.

"Geeze, what hit me?"

"We don't know," Sam said, "but we treated you for a heart attack, and you're still with us."

"Heart attack?"

"We're guessing. They vanished the kit's med comp. What did they think they were doing?"

Captain Krull interrupted. "To the problem at hand. Women having different symptoms for heart attacks, yes?"

"Oh, of course. How old are you, Kari?"

"I'm sixty-three. I know… I guess I can't fool Mother Nature forever."

Sixty-three, and she'd been through three weeks of backbreaking labor on short rations with inadequate sleep in not enough gravity for circulatory health.

"My sincere apologies, Lieutenant," Captain Krull said. But, in contrast to the formal words, he knelt down by her and took her hand and held his helmet next to hers. What he said, off radio, I will never know.

The Captain stood and gestured to the *Ernest Shackleton* with its nose against the four-meter ice wall. "The three of us will have to take care of this the hard way. In an hour, it will be night. We should have all the cargo above the wall by then. Then we rest, then heave the frame over when again it is light."

We managed, just barely. The pinprick sun vanished from the near airless sky as if cut off by a shutter. Then, more slowly, our eyes let us see the stars.

The ice wall was but the first hint of the much rougher terrain leading to the meridional pole. But the gravity was much lower. After another day of sledging, we discarded all the ballast, rails, mast and solar yardarm. That left about a ton of mass—two-hundred newtons of weight. We simply lifted the remaining framework, with Kari on it, and carried it the remaining hundred and twenty kilometers to the pole.

The last fifty kilometers were more rock than ice, and jagged, fractured rock at that, showing little of the expected space weathering.

"It's been uncovered in the last million years, maybe," Captain Krull said. "Maybe our time scale is wrong. Or the moons have found new games to play. Chaos is like that."

"Life is like that," Sam said. "Long periods of steady, sane, stability, and then it all goes to hell."

Later, when by chance, we were alone in the tent, making a minor repair, Captain Krull touched my arm. "I do not pry into crew files. I know their qualifications and assignments. The rest I left to others whose job that is. I now regret that I had not looked deeply into Lieutenant Ellison's file; there may be nothing there, but I did not look. And I did not look into Lieutenant deWalt's file."

"You had visions of a relationship?"

"Yah, yah, something like that. I am forty-eight years old. She is sixty-three. God laughs at our visions."

I did not share my own visions of Kari, and I was thirty-two.

The next day we reached the east pole station and found it had been vandalized. That wasn't totally unexpected; the lack of communications meant that some thought had gone toward our demise, and there was a bright new crater next to where the big telemetry dish had been. There was another impact near the site of the radio thermal generator, which was also missing.

Two storage sheds at the South end of the facility seemed intact, however.

Captain Krull pointed to them. "Let us see what we find. Since this base had no people to maintain it, and robots were primitive, they relied much on simple redundancy."

The result brought the first grin I ever remember seeing on Captain Krull's face. "My enemies do not research well. We have an intact backup radiothermal generator—150 watts. We can stay here a while."

Sam enlisted my help in collecting regolith and organic salvage for the printer. It drew about a kilowatt. With a lash-up of batteries and power conditioning, he could run an hour for every ten that the RTG was on, with an allowance for other power needs. Keeping us warm was not one of them. There was only a trace of nitrogen and argon around us.

"Think of living in the world's biggest thermos bottle. As long as we keep our floor above the rock or ice, our problem is not getting warm, it is in losing warmth by radiation at the same rate we generate it," Sam said. "But, we're still in trouble. 150 watts still isn't enough and I can't print all the food we need."

"How much power do we need?"

"We burn about 100 watts each from food and air. Even with the most efficient technology, we'd have to gather about twice that from the Sun or nuclear sources. We need better than a kilowatt, probably two. And that doesn't even address the nutrition problems. I can do sugars, simple proteins, some vitamins…but in a year we'll start falling apart. We're toast"

"So we just give up? We're toast so why bother?"

Sam shrugged. "Eh? Not yet. I just need to kvetch a bit."

Tiredness and fatigue kicked in for me. "Sam, I am getting a little tired of being everybody's kvetching board! Do I have a sign on my head that says 'tell me all your troubles?' Do I look like a shrink?"

"Actually, you and my uncle Benjamin could..." He must have seen my face. "Sorry."

"It's okay, Sam. Just not now."

A week later, we all met in the pressure tent. It stank, but it was good to be out of our airtight space underwear.

"We can't survive on 160 watts," Captain Krull said.

Kari nodded. "But how about 310 watts? I'll bet there's another one of these on the west pole."

Kari was returning to her old spunky self, as long as she didn't push herself. Back in civilization, she'd be fixed up good as new in a fortnight. Here, she might drop dead tomorrow.

Sam shrugged his shoulders. "It wouldn't do it."

Captain Krull nodded. "We need to call for help. There's enough metal around that we can build a big dish, and we can use the batteries to provide the power for a brief burst."

That sounded good to me, but Kari spoke up. "Sir, Ellison thinks he's finished us off. As soon as he finds out otherwise, he'll come back to finish the job. He has to. Either that or try to leave the solar system."

"His hatred is that much?" Captain Krull asked, softly, with what seemed a sense of wonder in his voice.

"It's beyond hatred now, Captain," Kari said. "He's burned the bridges, he's staked himself out, he's painted himself into a corner, crossed the Republican."

"Rubicon," Sam said.

"Rubicon, okay, whatever. If he's found out now, he'll go to prison forever. They all will. So they will come back first and make sure we aren't talking."

"Yah, yah. So, we need to be elsewhere. For that we need more power."

"Can we convert the RTG's to actual reactors?" Sam asked.

I shook my head. "They use the wrong kind of fuel, plutonium 238. It won't sustain a chain reaction."

There was a long silence. "Maybe we have enough for one or two of us to make it," Kari said. "I've had a long life..."

"Quiet, Lieutenant!" Captain Krull snapped.

"Captain, we have to face…"

"I SAID QUIET!"

We sat in shocked silence. Kari's heart! I thought.

Captain Krull was oblivious; he had gotten his silence. "Now, we *all* make it through this or we all die. So, unless you propose a mutiny within a mutiny, that is the way it will be. My will is that we make it. Is that understood?"

There were tears in Kari's eyes, the one person in all my experience who had actually liked Captain Krull, or perhaps more than that. He had struck at her like a snake with perhaps as much forethought.

"Very good. Now, I know where there's a two-megawatt reactor," Captain Krull said.

"Huh?" we all said.

"Where?" I asked.

"Namaka."

Namaka was the inner satellite of Haumea.

"That is where the mother ship for everything on Haumea ended. It disassembled itself, of course, but its propulsion reactor should still be there."

"It may as well be on Earth's moon," Sam said

Captain Krull frowned coldly. "Not your field, is it, Sam?"

"No, uh, sir, but I know we'd need a rocket to get there."

"Oh?" Captain Krull stared at him in a way that made me very glad he was not staring at me. That would only be a matter of a minute or so, I realized, and I was thinking furiously.

"Oy vey. Captain, it would take months to make enough rocket fuel from the power we have, and by then we would be all dead. So unless you have some kind of Indian rope trick up your sleeve…"

"In a way," Captain Krull said with a glimmer of a smile. "That is very much what I have in mind."

Of course! The rope trick! Our position was ideal for an orbital elevator. Haumea rotated so rapidly that its synchronous orbit was only a little ways above the elongated poles. But how would we get something even a couple hundred kilometers up?

"The mission is very redundant. For almost everything, there is an unused backup. Look for spare data tether launchers."

A days search found two unexpended launchers. I pointed them straight up, and got one of them to work, giving us a twelve-hundred-kilometer orbital tower under tension. We printed out a tether climber—well, actually, a clothes wringer, from the emergency printer-refiner's eclectic library; the same machine might have ended up in an emergency somewhere in Earth's tropics.

"Remember always," Captain Krull said at being shown the device. "Once it is built, what a piece of equipment was *designed* to do matters not. What matters is what it can do."

We modified the *Ernest Shackleton* by adding pressure tanks to the frame, for crude cold gas maneuvering rockets.

All of an orbital tower, of course, rotates at the same rate as the planet to which it is attached. Beyond synchronous orbit, everything on the tower moves faster than orbital velocity for that altitude. It took three excruciating days in shifts to crank ourselves by hand up out to where our velocity would get us to Namaka. That was at 394,661.42 meters above Haumea's east pole. I think I will remember that number the rest of my life. I had to work it out five times on my suit calculator before Captain Krull was satisfied.

We spent several days hanging at 1.3% of an Earth gravity, with Haumea overhead, getting our position on the tether exactly right and waiting for Namaka to be in just the right place to let go.

This leap of faith resulted, five days later, in a half-meter-per-second crash landing with dry gas tanks—but the harpoon on our underside stuck into Namaka's ice and caught us up before we bounced away.

We found the main reactor, pretty well exhausted.

We found its backup, essentially untapped.

Our last ration bars were consumed as a feast when we got it on line. The robot base station had a printer-refiner as well, much more capable than our emergency version. With Sam's help, it could print vitamins.

Kari, bless her, found a way to 'talk' to the base computer through our suit helmet displays. It was dumb in the ways of humans, but she could teach it some tricks.

I found the discarded base ship's engines. They were useless junk.

Sam found some plasma ice boring tools still attached to defunct construction robots. He thought they'd greatly reduce our ice-chopping labor.

"Those shoot out hot hydrogen plasma, with magnetic fields focusing it into a tight stream, right?" Captain Krull asked when shown the borers.

"Yes, sir, that's how they work."

"How fast is this plasma they shoot out?"

Nobody even thought to suggest to Captain Krull that they weren't designed to be rockets. At this point, we were following him on faith and the force of his bullying personality.

After a couple of days of clever testing, we found their plasma exited at six to sixteen kilometers per second, depending on how fast we fed them water. They didn't make really great electric rockets; their efficiency was low. But they were much better than cold gas, and could get us to Samios in about six months, if we took enough ice.

So the *Ernest Shackleton* was reborn as an interplanetary spacecraft. Imagine a ladder spinning about its middle with its rungs parallel to its intended direction of motion. I lashed the reactor and generator from Namaka to one end of the ladder and our vacuum tent at the other and stuck a ball of ice, ice mining machine, and the torches in the middle. Radiator panels covered the ladder from the center to the reactor, and the solar array, all ten watts of it, filled in the rungs on the other side.

We could conceivably make Samios on short rations, but our plan was to fabricate a communications system and call for help once we were well away from Haumea.

None of us had ever made a radio, but we all knew in principle and had several low-power systems to cannibalize. We mainly needed an amplifier.

"There's probably a robot comm unit in the printing file, if I could find it," Kari said. "But the printer memory isn't designed to be searched..."

Captain Krull's head spun instantly.

"Maybe something else will work," Kari finished softly.

We could print Sam's organic molecules, because he knew where every atom in one of those things belonged. A radio amplifier was different.

I told them what I remembered of the subject, which wasn't much. The earliest such things used something called vacuum tubes.

"Okay, that sounds good," Captain Krull said. "We can print the parts. We'll have weeks in which to experiment. At least the vacuum part of a vacuum tube wouldn't be a problem."

Captain Krull laughed at his joke.

Sam and I laughed nervously too. Kari kind of smiled, but there was a tear in her eye.

Then something quite unlikely happened. Captain Krull apparently noticed the tear, and said very softly, "Yah, yah. Sometimes things, they get so tense one must laugh or cry. For me, I had better laugh." He looked around at all of us. "You must not see me cry, yah?"

We didn't quite have enough thrust to lift off of Namaka. With Kari handling the cold gas thruster valves, the three of us men got upside down below the ship and with our feet securely gecro'd to the girders, we pushed the little moon away from the *Ernest Shackleton* as hard as we could. That, we figured, should give us about ten meters per second up to start with.

Without radar or anything like it, it was hard to tell how successful our maneuver was and Kari kept her hand on the gas thruster controls. But once we were about four kilometers up, we seemed to draw away. At about three and a half hours, Captain Krull figured that we'd reached escape velocity, judging by the change in size of a crater below.

Navigation was simple. We found Ice Chip, blinking brightly every three hours, with a salvaged robots' camera. This far out from the Sun, any interplanetary trajectory is close to a straight line, so we just pointed at it.

Which was almost our undoing.

"Up! Everyone! Keep the lights off!"

I groaned and opened my eyes. A few red equipment diodes provided enough light for my dark-adapted eyes to see Kari rapidly shove herself into her dirty spacesuit.

"What is this?" Captain Krull asked.

"They are coming to kill us, I think," Kari said, as if reporting the unchanging outside temperature.

Captain Krull abandoned the modesty of his sleepsack for the tent window.

"Toward Samios," Kari said, handing him the camera, "it's very, very faint, but it's blinking every forty-five seconds."

I sat up. The *Dag* normally rotated every ninety seconds, but it had two outboard hulls.

"Suits, everyone," Captain Krull said. He said it unhurriedly, but there was tension in his voice. "Tony, you will have to take down the reactor. Kari, kill the plasma thrusters, god help us they will start again. Then kill our spin and keep us pointed at that blinking thing, wings edge on. Sam, start pumping the tent down, then get your suit on. Oy vey, first things first," he complained but moved quickly to the tent controls.

Pumps soon started whirring. It would take about ten minutes to get the tent down to a millibar; we'd dump the rest of the air. I concentrated on getting into my suit; I can't breathe a millibar.

I didn't have to ask why to take down the reactor. The radiator was an infrared beacon. But it would take an hour or more to get everything down to merely room temperature. It would still be noticeable at 300 kelvins, but not a beacon. Our only real hope was that they wouldn't look in our direction, or at least wouldn't be expecting to see anything.

"You all know what you have to do," Captain Krull said. "Radio silence from now on." His voice was starting to get a bit tinny. He put his helmet on.

The reactor take-down required turning valves on the center end of the radiator. We hadn't taken time to automate that; except for Kari, we hadn't expected to have to go non-critical. One would not normally go outside alone, but this was decidedly un-normal. Despite the rush, I took extra care to keep my carabiners on the frame as I moved up to the center.

The ice-mining bots had done a pretty good job of hollowing out our fuel iceberg; we were very near the turn around, with only a third of the ice left.

The engines and the radiator controls and the power supplies all sat bolted to a metal grid salvaged from the floor of the utility shed on the east pole. The spin gravity was almost negligible this near the spin center. I brachiated over to the reactor controls and hit the scram button. At the end of the other wing, drums rotated, neutrons were absorbed, and the reaction went subcritical.

Now I had to cut the radiator flow off at just the right speed. Too fast and the reactor core would melt. Too slow and the working fluid would freeze up in the radiator pipes. There was no manual on this, but I knew it would take one point five rotations to close each valve. I settled for a quarter rotation every five minutes, and hoped.

Kari kept our 'nose' pointed at the *Dag*, minimizing the radiator exposure. This put me on the other side, unable to see our adversary for all the ice in between us. Turn the wheel.

Not moving, I started to get a bit chilly. I touched my toes about twenty times to build up some heat.

Turn the wheel.

The plasma torch…it would run for a few minutes on batteries. Long enough to cut the old *Dag* to shreds. It would take just a few minutes to unbolt them.

Turn the wheel.

The men and women aboard her had been coworkers, friends, and in a couple of cases lovers. All their lives, for mine? Could I do that?

I looked at the beast. It microwaved water into atomic ions and directed the exhaust with magnetic fields.

I nearly broke radio silence then and there.

Instead, I turned the wheel. Nuclear gods must be served.

In reality, I did not have to wait long. I was joined by Captain Krull and the others; we would wait out the closest approach in the ice shell. We would not be able to see them, but they would not be able to see us. The deflated tent might make them think the best (for them) had happened.

I put my helmet against Captain Krull's. "The plasma is heated by microwaves…"

The *Dag Hammarskjold* missed us by no more than two hundred kilometers on its return to Haumea. For all we could tell, its crew remained blissfully unaware of our existence.

We cobbled together a radio, modulating one of the torch microwave heaters and, about a hundred days out from Namaka, I called Thera.

"You get to call your girlfriend," Sam said. "I should be so lucky, I should be so lucky."

Captain Krull laughed for the first time that I remembered since his 'trial.'

"Sam," I said, "she's a cop."

Then Captain Krull reached over to touch Kari. "We will make it now, I think," he said.

After a long time, without smiling, but relaxing ever so slightly, Kari put her hand over his.

"Yah, yah, we will make it."

The relatively huge, beam-boosted Cislunar Republic Spaceship, CLRSS *Elizabeth Reynolds* came up behind our ramshackle vehicle. It was a sleek, tri–hulled, ring-winged construction, obviously able to use an atmosphere, if available. My mouth watered to see it.

"So, we are rescued by our enemies," Kari said. "We could have made it to Samios."

"Yah, yah. But this situation has its own definition of friends and enemies," Captain Krull said. "Politics aside, we are all spacefarers. We live by doing things right. Stow everything properly, as if we are to come back."

"I should live so long," Sam said. "I should live so long."

But he tidied up, tethered down, shut lids and closed valves just like the rest of us. Someone, Captain Krull must have thought, would come back to the *Ernest Shackleton* and judge him by what they saw. Whatever his faults, they would see Captain Karl Krull's determination in this ramshackle ship. They would see the discipline that held us together and alive for two months. I had no problem with that, but I hoped that a few years in vacuum would ensure that in some distant future, they would not judge us by what they smelled.

I powered the reactor down again, but our rescuers were still very careful. They came in from the front along our spin axis, matched our one-sixth-g spin rate and grabbed our 'ladders' with a couple of robot arms. Thus secured, they sent a pinnace, which dropped lines down to our tent. We deflated, emerged, and allowed ourselves to be drawn up and aboard the small tubular craft.

Once aboard the '*Lisa*', we made use of the facilities in the locker room immediately next to the airlock. The joy on Kari's face lit up the whole room. There we found that Captain Krull had somehow managed to keep a clean, lightweight ISA coverall with him throughout the entire ordeal. The rest of us made do with ill-fitting CLR utility coveralls. Only then did we accede to meeting our rescuers.

Captain Duluth, a short, muscular woman of about seventy years, received us with full honors. Then she had a private meeting with Captain Krull while the rest of us enjoyed recounting our tale to the crew of the *Lisa* and getting caught up on the fate of the mutineers.

Which, to this day, is unknown. Their stay at *Samios* was brief; Thera hadn't been fooled by Krull's trial and scheduled their big interferometer to check out the site of the 'crash,' that had supposedly killed us. Before she could, Ellison had dumped the documentary crew and headed out again on a 'rescue' mission. The *Dag* is still out there, somewhere.

And needs to stay there for the rest of their lives. Tech Jensen was not on the ship when it arrived at Samios.

Captain Krull asked Captain Duluth if he and Kari could take the *Ernest Shackleton* on into Samios, after suitable repairs. Saner heads prevailed, however; fix it up as one might, the *Ernie* was not to be considered spaceworthy by any reasonable standard. Kari actually seemed more disappointed than Captain Krull.

We had our final meeting on Samios, after all the interviews, the trial—some of the documentary crew had participated in the mutiny, and the wedding. I kissed the bride, for the first and only time in our two year long and occasionally all too intimate relationship. We had shared a chamber pot in a vacuum tent, a circumstance that did not encourage any other kind of nether sharing.

Unless, of course, one is hopelessly smitten. In a rare example of diplomatic ice-thawing, Captain Duluth married Kari deWalt and Karl Krull. They headed inward; him to take charge of a prison in the Earth-Sun L1 orbit, she to be its chief engineer. Media hero or not, Karl Krull had lost a very expensive spaceship, and the ISA did not want any unlucky Captains. He would never command an ISA spaceship again. But no terrestrial before the merger of the CLRSS and the ISA into the Interplanetary Administration would ever come close to his legendary career.

I stayed on Samios, recording this, and waiting for an opportunity, perchance, to salvage the *Ernest Shackleton* when it bullets by the big space colony.

Sam decided to stay with me a while. He dreams about building an even more remote space colony around Proxima Centauri, a new promised land too far from terrorists and tourists to worry anybody. At a tavern on a river leading to the equatorial sea of Samios, he hoisted a glass to Thera and me.

"To Captain Krull, who saved our lives and our honor. Nobody else could have got us off that planet, made us make that spaceship, and gotten us back to civilization alive. And I should live so long as to ever be within an astronomical unit of him again!"

We laughed and raised our glasses.

A Perfect Day off the Farm

By Patty Jansen

The giant shadow slides towards the horizon and the air comes alive with sparkles, rising off the ground like negative snow. Jewels of pale blue, yellow and pink. Sprinkles of diamond. The eclipse is over, and Io's whisper-thin atmosphere of sulfur-dioxide sublimates back into the air.

Ed stands by the cubicle door, listening to his breaths hissing through his mask—in, out, in, out. With one hand on the lift's doorframe, the other feels the lumpy presence of the tools within his gear bag. The floor vibrates with the lift's ascent up the cliff face.

His fellow inmates, in thick pressure suits, stand behind him. No one speaks over the helmet comm. When that bastard Hickey supervises the day's shift, every word can, no, *will*, be used against you.

The plain recedes below, soft rolling dunes of yellow dust, sharp and crumbling sulfuric cliffs and a lava lake which belches lazy plumes of smoke. The sky is grey except for the massive sliver-crescent that is Jupiter, orange-red and growing visibly, trailing massive clouds of vapor into the sky.

On the other side of the valley, the wan sunlight hits the metallic domes of Calico Base. The spaceport's landing lights blur into four-pointed stars in the scratched visor of Ed's helmet, and with the tears of yawning after two hours of deep sleep.

Maybe more than sleep.

Freedom is over there, under those domes. Sabine is there. In a locket around his neck, positioned over his heart, he carries a scrap of plasti-paper on which is scribbled in clumsy, uneven letters *I love you, Daddy*. The letter had been much longer, but he cut the rest of the paper with a fork—no inmates are allowed sharp implements. Words describing how much she enjoyed the crèche and her friends. Words written while a warden looked over her shoulder. A message smuggled to him by a sympathetic guard, because he's not allowed any outside news. *I love you, Daddy*, four words. That's all he needs for now.

The lift jerks to a halt at the top of the six-kilometer-high track. The stick farm.

Ed hesitates in the opening. The younger guys push past him and jump out of the cab. The dust is so fine that it puffs up even though there is hardly any atmosphere.

"Hasegawa, don't hold up the traffic, old bag o' bones!" Hickey pokes Ed in the back. "Out, out, out. Assemble at the shed."

Ed wishes the man would stop shouting. Many of the men might be mentally dulled from treatment, but they're not deaf. He wishes for a few quiet moments so that he can speak to Song Chee, a new inmate, and ask him about life outside. Song Chee is big and beefy with tattoos on his arms. He looks like he's worked in the warehouses, places where gossip travels fast. Sometimes the drug's effectiveness has not been complete and new inmates remember shards of happenings from prior to their sentencing. Mostly unimportant things, like gossip or personal memories, but anything helps. The rumor goes that these days *tourists* come to Io, although Ed finds it hard to believe that the rigid, secretive regime would have changed that much. Still, if it's true maybe Jezra could sneak in and help to get him out of here, if he can contact her.

He braces himself and jumps out of the lift, knee-deep into the yellow dust. He holds his gear bag aloft so the crap doesn't get into it. But it always does, and after each shift outside, he'll spend hours cleaning his instruments. Because if he doesn't, he may well be the next victim of an arc. He's seen too many men leave horizontally in a bag.

The stick farm. Nine square frames with impossibly tall rods that reach into the sky further than he can see. About a kilometer in fact.

Here at the subjovian point, Jupiter's magnetic field runs parallel to the surface. It's strongest when Io slides into the giant planet's shadow, when it's dark and so cold that the atmosphere freezes out in a thin layer of sulfur dioxide snow. Especially during that time, the magnetic field induces a current in the wire, aided by the electron pumps underneath the platform. Giant transformers and batteries sit in a chamber under the shed, and feed Calico Base and its manufacturing plants which churn out products made from locally mined materials.

It's the inmates' task to maintain the installation and keep it free of dust, to prevent arcing.

Today there seems to be a different kind of job to be done.

In the dust stand a bunch of man-high cylinders wrapped in the ubiquitous blue plastic used for space transport. Print on the plastic says *Juno Station*, a vacuum manufacturing plant for electronics.

"Right, the job," Hickey says, and he taps one of the rolls. It's kind-of strange how the sound comes through the loudspeaker in Ed's helmet. "As some of you may know—" He glares pointedly in Ed's direction. "—the farm is about ten years old. The conducting wires are old, so we're going to replace them." Hickey has funny metaphors. The word *we* means the *inmates* and has nothing to do with him. "We divide our usual groups in two teams. One will strip the sticks from below. The second will string the replacement wire from above. You, Jules, and Song Chee, you disconnect the electron pumps. Then you will loosen the clamps and pull each wire down, make sure the insulation comes off as well, and as the trolley comes down with the replacement, clip that in place—What?" He gives both men a sharp look. He must have seen Song Chee stiffen. Yes, the new guys usually get those jobs because Hickey thinks it's funny to watch their fear of arcs.

The period after the electron pump is disconnected is the most dangerous part of the job. The array may only run at about twenty-five percent capacity during daylight, the voltage induced in the wires as a result of the magnetic field is enormous. Disable the electron pumps and the wires *will* arc, that's a given.

"Hasegawa, Pearson, you will winch the new wire up and start threading it down."

Ed grits his teeth. Stringing the wire requires climbing up the stick frame, on a narrow ladder wearing a pressure suit. Climbing the ladder means heights, about a kilometer worth of *heights*. Hickey loves giving the old hands jobs they hate, too.

Song Chee whispers to Ed, "Want to swap?" His eyes still carry that dumb expression that comes with having one's memories recently wiped.

Ed waves his hand to make him shut up. Yes, he'd swap in an instant, and no, that's not allowed and if Hickey hears this, if Hickey realizes Ed remembers far more of his previous life than he should—

Behind their backs, Hickey yells, "Did I say you two could chatter? Get on with it. Up you go, up, Hasegawa!"

Ed is tired, so tired. Everyone is tired. The human body isn't made for working days forty hours long, not even with medicated deep sleep for the remaining two hours a day.

Ed climbs up the platform's walkway and clips his tether onto the ladder's safety belay, and starts climbing. Up, up, up, hand over hand, rung over rung. He doesn't look down, but his heart is pounding. His breath hisses heavy in his mask.

Think about different things.

A lunch meeting, a long time ago, which would change his life. He'd become friendly with Emily, a fellow scientist, through his work. They got talking about humanity, and she invited him to meet her friend, the dissident journalist Jezra Amami. Because he didn't adhere to the doctrine of Earth-centric life, because he dared to suggest that humanity would evolve, *should* evolve, and adapt to life in space. Because he saw no problems with doing some of that evolving artificially. *Tampering with genes!* the naysayers yelled, *Playing God.*

There was scientific evidence that permanent inhabitants of space colonies had already changed. But it contradicted policies, and suggested there were valid grounds for discrimination, and provided distinctions between groups of people that could be enshrined in law. But the differences were there. They were statistically significant. All he had done was report his data, and when his superiors dismissed it, gone to the independent press. Evolution was happening under their noses, but of course under the fairness laws, evolution had been branded a theory a number of years ago, and given the same importance as a lot of crackpot ideas. That is fairness for you. No scientific evidence needed.

Jezra is still free. The rumor goes that she's a politician these days. If only he can contact her, she will kick up a stink against the authorities, such as that baby-faced creep Michael Rankin from the New Pure party who Ed strongly suspected of having a hand in his arrest. Ed never planned attacks on government. Talked about it, yes, in a theoretical sense, but he doesn't possess a violent bone in his body. He's a scientist.

In his memories, he hears harsh voices, Sabine's screams at the door of the apartment, the men who ripped Emily from the warmth of his arms. He's never seen either of them again, but he's found out that Emily is dead. Exposure, the authorities called it, an accident, another euphemism for suicide. Emily would rather kill herself than be forced to take drugs to make her forget her science.

Sabine is six now, and he needs to get her out of that horrible crèche. Ed is afraid he won't recognize her, and that she won't know who he is.

Have hope, Eduard Hasegawa, one day you'll get out of here.

On the top of the kilometer-high frame, there is another platform that surrounds the array of sticks. Here, the bundles of wires end in bare metal tips. The metal looks corroded and tired. He knows some wires are irreparably damaged, the insulation eaten away.

He unlashes the safety of the lift, and sends the trolley careening down the rails, makes the mistake and looks down—

A sheer vertical drop to the mountain top. A further drop to the lava lake, almost eight kilometers in total. There is no safety railing around the platform. The abyss calls to him, *just a look or maybe you could jump off, flap your arms and fly.* He freezes. Gravity on Io isn't much, but with nothing to stop his fall, it would kill him.

"Hasegawa, what are you doing up there?" That's Hickey, in his helmet comm.

Ed gulps a breath he'd forgotten to take. "I'm getting to it." His heart is thudding.

The lift cable is moving. The roll of wire is coming up.

Jack Pearson has climbed up below him, and he's using his gas gun to blast clouds of sulfur dust off the installation, their eternal job of cleaning crud off this installation. Like Song Chee, he's much bigger than Ed and has deep scars on his right cheek. He doesn't speak. He seldom does. Having their memories wiped makes some of the inmates go funny like that.

Ed gets out his own gun, clamps in a canister of liquid helium and helps with the cleaning. He can feel the bursts of hissing gas through his gloves.

Then a light flashes and the trolley is up with the roll. Ed drags it off, cuts away the casing and unrolls the wire. It feels light, insubstantial. He knows there have been some advances with superconductors, revolutionary alloys produced in vacuum, but this wire seems strange, too light to be as strong as it should be. He tries to thread it through the clamp on the trolley, but he ends up missing the clamp and poking his glove instead. It takes him a few tries to realize what is wrong.

The wire vibrates. Jupiter's magnetic wind moves around the wire, it generates a force that pushes the wire perpendicular to the direction of the current running through it. Up in this case. He's never felt it this strong. He uses his other hand to push the recalcitrant wire in, screws down the clamp, and sends the trolley back down at a slower speed, unrolling wire as it goes, and still feeling the tug. This is a strange new material indeed. The world has moved on while he's been stuck in this hellhole.

He wonders… He gazes over the lava plain to the glimmering dome of the base, a few kilometers and a world away. Something glints in the feeble sunlight, the roof of a truck, he guesses, since the dome authority has been working on a paved road to the shore of the lava lake. A new inmate told him a few months ago that tourists love the place, and that locals go for relaxing strolls along the lake's shore and even lie on the hot ground as some sort of remedial treatment.

If that is true, much has changed indeed. Ed remembers only a claustrophobic research base where every breath was monitored and every move recorded.

If those rumors are right, then the smoking expanse of lava is the only thing standing between him and freedom. He looks at the unrolling wire. He wonders… As he has just experienced, the magnetic field exerts a force on the wire, the same force that, before he was locked up, some engineers were experimenting with for space ship propulsion by using huge loops of superconducting wire. Jupiter's magnetic field is strong, but would it generate enough force to make the wire fly, if he used a very *long* piece? Below him, Pearson is blasting clouds of dust from the array. Soon, Ed will have to join him on the ladder and start stringing the wire in the frame.

Pearson puts away his gas gun and yanks at something.

The trolley trundles down. Sparks crackle along the wire.

Pearson gets out his laser—

Ed guesses what's going to happen a microsecond before it does. He yells, "No, don't, Pearson!"

Pearson squeezes the trigger.

Flash. Arc. A blinding sizzle of blue. A sharp crackle in his helmet comm. When the black spots clear from Ed's eyes, the ladder is empty.

"Pearson!" he yells, and looks down, but it is too dark to see anything. There are shouts in his helmet comm, and the platform shakes with something heavy hitting the frame.

Ed writes on the pad, his radiation-wrinkled hand sliding over the smooth surface.

My dearest Sabine,

I love you. Not a day goes by that I don't think of you. You know that I can see the dome when I go out to work. Whenever I see it, I think of you, playing, and learning…

What a load of rubbish. She's in an *education center*, education being a euphemism for indoctrination. Maybe she's been told he is crazy and needs to be fixed. Maybe they've told her he's a bad man who plays God and turns creatures evil.

His hand shakes when he writes the next words.

Today we lost another man to this madness and may lose a second. Jack Pearson fell off the ladder and hit Song Chee on the way down, ripped his suit. The work is dangerous, and the operators of the stick farm know that, but most of the inmates are damaged by the memory-wipe and no longer care. The authorities don't care either. This is a place no one is meant to survive. His writing is angry, all long loops and poorly-controlled scribbles. Not that he will ever be allowed send it. His courage has withered to careful whisperings in the dark where no one can hear what you are saying. Speaking out loses its gloss when people hurt you and your family for it.

A faint rustle behind him and Ed wipes that last paragraph. It's only Jules, though. Poor Jules who cries at night for having forgotten why he's here.

"Song Chee needs you, Doc." The young guys all call him Doc, but he has a degree in biology, not in medicine. He's explained, but none of them knows what biology is.

Ed puts down the pad, making sure with a quick glance that it contains no incriminating text. Jules leads Ed across the dorm.

Song Chee is on his bunk, his face covered in sweat.

Ed sits down on the edge of the bed, sliding into the dark hollow under the bunk above. There is an empty drum next to the bed, with a small puddle of brownish liquid in the bottom. Ed doesn't need to smell the rank scent of vomit to know what it's been used for.

"It's bad, Doc, isn't it?" Song Chee whispers. His voice is hoarse.

Ed nods. He doesn't know anyone who has survived a ripped suit.

"How long?" His voice is thick with emotion.

Ed shrugs. "A few days, maybe."

"Can you…" Song Chee grabs his hand. He's hot with fever. His eyes drift and the thought vanishes.

Ed tries to prompt his memory-wiped brain. "You want me to tell your family?"

"Nina," Song Chee whispers, and his eyes widen as a measure of clarity returns to them. "Nina!" He pushes Ed aside and sits up. He hits his head on the bottom of the top bunk, but doesn't seem to notice. "Nina. Don't let the bastards get you!" His eyes are wide and crazy.

Jules and a few others jump on top of him. "Quiet, man, or do you want Hickey—"

But it's already too late.

"What's going on here? Why are all of you out of bed?" Hickey marches into the dorm in precise, angry strides that match his sharp face and the regulation stubble on his head.

A spot of hatred ignites in Ed's chest. Hatred that he knows is a bad idea.

"We've got a man sick," Jules says, still holding a hand over Song Chee's mouth.

"And whose fault was that?" Hickey says. There is another guard with him, one of the younger ones who rarely gets a word in when Hickey is around. "This is not a charity institution. We're running a business here and if you stuff up, I will be getting complaints from Calico about intermittent power supply. I do *not* like getting complaints." He glances at Song Chee. "Sedate him."

One of his lackeys unbuckles his tranquillizing gun, puts it against Song Chee's beefy arm and presses the trigger. Song Chee ceases to struggle almost immediately. Ed shivers with the memory of the stifling numb hollowness that stuff inflicts.

Before Song Chee fades completely, he whispers to Ed, "Tell Nina I love her."

"She knows," Ed says, but the words hurt to speak. He's afraid to go there. Like Emily, Nina might no longer be alive. Like Sabine, she might have been imprisoned and brainwashed and might believe what the soldiers told her about her missing husband. She might have married someone else. What will Sabine think of him when he gets out, if he gets out? His hand strays unbidden to the locket under his clothes. His eyes burn with unshed tears.

Not knowing is punishment. For someone who's grown up talking to humanity in the entire solar system, isolation is hell. The world moves on without you. He's heard of people asking to go back into isolation after their release.

"Are we done with the love scenes?" Hickey asks.

Ed glowers at him, and Hickey meets his eyes. Ed tries to do his best *stupid* expression, but he never knows if it's good enough. Sometimes he feels that Hickey knows his memories are still intact.

"What are you doing here anyway?" Hickey asks. "Why aren't you in bed?"

Ed begins, "Song Chee is—"

"I asked about you, not about him. I want all of you to take your medication and go to sleep. Now. Or we'll have more of these types of accidents."

He grabs a handful of Ed's shirt and pulls him off the bed.

Ed is angry, angrier than he has been for a long time. He meets Jules' eyes across the dormitory, pools of resignation. Even though these men are much diminished, they all liked Song Chee. They all respected Pearson. Tomorrow, they will have two new team members to whom they're not allowed to speak and who will likely remember little of their life.

"Can you do anything for Song Chee?" Jules asks when they clamber into their bunks.

Ed shakes his head. "Besides making him comfortable, I'm afraid not."

Radiation damage cannot be reversed. For all of humanity's wonders, no one has found a miracle medicine that will do that. The young boys will know it, too. And still they hope, and still he feels like he's failed them. As he will fail them time after time, until it is his turn to be involved in a fatal accident.

Ed takes out the infuser band, but the ampoule he clips in is an empty one he's forgotten to put in the recycler.

He closes his eyes and lies very still until Hickey's footsteps and his yelling at other inmates have faded. His mind is churning with numbers, and currents and magnetic fields. He has to get out of here, for Sabine, for Song Chee and all the others.

The inmates are asleep when Ed switches on the light above his bunk. He clicks open the locket and takes out the scrap of plasti-paper. Somehow it's fitting that he uses his most precious possession. He kisses the paper with Sabine's handwriting.

"I love you, too, Sabine."

He turns the paper over and scribbles in tiny letters on the blank side: *Eduard Hasegawa, Jack Pearson, Jules Santorio and others are political prisoners at the stick farm outside Calico Base. Contact Jezra Amami.*

He slips out of the bed and sneaks through the dorm. Into the change room, where he puts on two layers of insulation and climbs into his suit. It's tight with the extra clothing. As best as he can, he sneaks into the lift and hopes Hickey won't hear the mechanism as it trundles up the cliff face.

He drags a roll of wire out the store, outside, into the lift. At the stick farm, he loads it onto a trolley and sends it up the frame. Then he disconnects one of the electron pumps. He climbs after the trolley, not looking down, not thinking about arcs. It's the eclipse and it's pitch dark. The array is working at maximum capacity. He can feel the air hum with power, although surely that must be his imagination. His helmet light casts a small pool of light on the ladder. He climbs and climbs and climbs.

At the platform, the roll of wire waits for him. He cuts away the plastic, opens the casing and unrolls the wire, unrolls and unrolls, letting the loop drape off the platform. It vibrates and jiggles in his hands. Small arcs jump from one end to the loop to the other. He freezes, waiting for the arc, but it doesn't come. Keeps unrolling. He reaches the end of the wire, which means he holds both ends of a full kilometer of it in his hands. He grabs a connector from his gear bag, clips it onto both ends of the wire to form a giant circle. Then. Deep breaths.

Ed jams the connector onto the naked tips of that part of the frame he's just disconnected from the electron pump. Electricity crackles. The wire stiffens with the massive current running through it. The sides move away from each other as if an invisible hand pulls them apart. The wire forms a big oval.

So far, so good. He'd been afraid the wire would tangle and arc, but the insulation must be wonder material. Or he's just plain lucky.

He cuts a strip of the blue plastic and wraps it around the wire, securing his note inside.

He lets go, and watches the wire as it falls away from the tower, first straight down, but then it gains sideways momentum and starts floating towards the opposite side of the lava lake, where the trucks are. The occasional crackle of electricity licks the wire like flames on a giant circus hoop. But it's dark and soon his magnetic sail disappears from sight. He can only hope the current will take it all the way to the other side, and that the construction workers will find it.

Hopefully.

He clenches his fists.

Sabine, I'll save you from that dreadful place.

Ed climbs up the ladder, holding his gas gun. He's sore all over after Hickey caught him sneaking back into the dormitory last night. Ed denied having sabotaged anything, and failing to find evidence for such, Hickey gave him a beating anyway. Hickey is clever. He never hits in places where inspectors from Calico Base can easily see it. He never hits so hard that the inmates remember it for long…except Ed.

Ed can see the building activity on the other side of the valley, and hopes his message has arrived safely. His hand goes automatically to the locket around his neck, before realizing Sabine's message is no longer in there.

I love you, Daddy.

He blows a kiss on the imaginary wind.

Not much later, Jules calls out, "Hey, Ed look at that!" He points.

A truck trundles up the zigzag path that leads from Calico the stick farm. Sunlight flashes in the windscreen every time the truck turns a hairpin bend. It is not the white vehicle that usually brings the inspectors. This truck is much bigger, and a glance through the binoculars reveals an unfamiliar logo and the word *News* on the roof.

A moment later, Hickey yells in his helmet comm, "Hasegawa, come down here immediately."

There are a lot of people in Hickey's office. They shuffle aside when Ed comes in, and it is then that he becomes aware of the cameras and the woman in uniform. A familiar woman.

"Jezra," he says. "I'm so glad to see you…"

His old friend is no longer young. Five years have taken their toll on her dark hair and figure. Next to her is another familiar face: Michael Rankin. Grey-haired, but still baby-faced.

Ed stares. "Why are…." *Why are you sitting next to that creep?*

She smiles. "Meet my husband, Governor Rankin."

What? Whatever happened to their ideals, and freedom of opinion?

She chuckles, uncomfortably. "A lot has changed, Ed."

"I see that." He glances at the cameras. So the news is now under her control?

"If you want to change something, it is better to work within the system than outside it. I saw that, when working as a journalist. When people like you, they will agree with your ideas. I guess I was always a better politician than activist. I was elected into the government."

Ed's mind is still reeling. "So—all this time, you've had the power to let me out, but you never did."

"You had been treated. I didn't think you would remember."

"I was treated, but it didn't work. You…you never even thought to check on me?"

"I did check. I was assured that you were happy and oblivious."

"You never checked me in person."

Her brown eyes hold a sad look, one that says, *I couldn't check you, because it would destroy my career.* He had become an inconvenience to her.

"I'm sorry, Ed."

But he saw, *You were an old man, Ed, never willing to give in to anyone who didn't agree with you.*

Michael Rankin says, "It seems there has been a mistake in your case and we're here to deliver an apology. We will organize for you to be rehabilitated."

So that's it? They're turning this into a publicity stunt? Ed wants to shout, *I will never accept anything from you,* but he has Sabine to think of. He says nothing while Jezra rises and makes for the door.

When she passes him, he says in a low voice, "We had ideals and principles. We swore by them."

"Most people grow out of those childish ideals."

"You betrayed me."

"The world has changed. The old arguments are no longer relevant. It turns out the International Space Force has been using our science all along, even while the politicians were pretending to know nothing about it."

With every word she speaks, Ed feels more like a naïve idiot. No, he's not a terrorist, but he was never a politician either. He hates dishonesty.

Is this truly Jezra the dissident activist he hears speaking?

"And what about the others, then? You believe all the dissidents should remain locked up here?"

"There are no more dissidents. All the people sent here recently are criminals. Thieves and murderers. Of course they work. We cannot afford to let people sit idle and do nothing."

Ed's world unravels further. So *that* is why the newer inmates are more beefy and less talkative. He rages with the sense of betrayal. They let him rot in here, while the ground shifted.

Then he lets his shoulders slump. There is no point arguing. He is alone, old guard. No one cares about his ideals of pure science anymore. "Can you at least let me go? The penalty for dissenting has never been five years in labor camp, has it?"

He meets her eyes, and sees some of the fire still there. Her eyes say, *careful what you say and you'll be free.* They tell him, *Don't fight us, and we'll talk.*

How the power has corrupted her.

He hates her for the hypocrisy, but he nods.

Ed is nervous when he walks into the childcare room. The children are sitting on the floor facing the caregiver who is reading them a story. The room is light and airy, the furniture clean and bright-colored. The children wear pretty clothes. It doesn't look like a prison. It doesn't feel like a horrible place at all. Nothing is as it is supposed to be. While he was locked away, someone has changed the rules of the game.

If these people are not bad, does that mean he is a criminal?

As he comes in, young faces turn to the door.

He expected to recognize Sabine immediately but he stands there staring at these unfamiliar children, tears pricking in his eyes.

Finally, a girl with dark hair gets up.

"They say you're my daddy." Her voice is clear.

She doesn't look like him. She doesn't look like Emily. Although she does have black hair and she has big hazel eyes. And the shape of her face…

She bursts into tears.

He drops to his knees so his eyes are level with hers. He doesn't know what to do. Touching may not be appropriate, so he takes her hand. It is small and soft, and her skin has tiny freckles. Emily's freckles.

"Don't cry," he says. "I won't harm you."

She meets his eyes. "They're saying that you are going to take me away from Jackie and Stella."

The two sit against the back wall, identical twins accompanied by a uniformed mother, watching Sabine intently.

Warden's children. He wants to say, *but they are bad* but can't bring himself to do so. What do these children know? What does he know?

"Don't you want to live with me?"

She hesitates. His heart is thudding in his chest.

"You'll have everything you want, your own room, toys…" And when she still says nothing, he adds, "You know how you wrote in your letter you loved me?"

"Oh. Sandra told me to put that in. She said it would look better." And then she adds, "But I do love you."

The damage is done. Ed understands. Of all the words she wrote to him, *I love you, Daddy* were the only words she didn't mean. They are words a six-year-old girl can't possibly mean to say to a father she doesn't remember. The love of a child has to be earned, and so far, he's done a poor job at being a father.

"You can stay here, then." For now, until he gets his life organized, until he gets a place where she wants to stay.

She smiles through her tears. It cuts him inside.

He desperately doesn't want her to stay here, but he has to try harder, for Emily's sake.

"If you'll let me, I can come after class and teach you fun things, like how to make a kite that flies itself."

Her eyes widen. "Really?" She's interested now. Ed sees it in her eyes. Like him, like Emily, she wants to understand the science of the world around her. Maybe there is hope yet.

"Yes. We can make flaming hoops out of kites, and play games with them. And I can tell you how you make the lights work, and how to make rocks burn, and…" *Let's not forget about human evolution.*

While he speaks, the other children come closer, wide-eyed, and then a little girl says, "Wow, Sabine, it looks like your dad knows a lot of fun tricks. Can I borrow him?"

Sabine gives the girl a sharp look, and takes Ed's hand. "No, he's mine."

DAYBREAK

BY JEFF HECHT

We've heard from a spacecraft called the Interstellar Comet Explorer," Maria said. "It spotted a giant incoming iceball."

"Are you sure? That probe is older than I am." Aaron sounded more surprised than Maria had expected. "ICE has been drifting in the scattered disc for decades. It has to be at least a light day out."

"It was new to me, but that's what the deep space system said." After twenty months of working with Aaron, Maria was still learning about the fringes of the solar system. She expected to be calling him long after he finally retired. "The system said it had dispatched a drilling probe and set up relay circuits."

"How did it find an iceball?" Aaron wondered, leaning back in his chair and running a hand through his sparse white hair. "Its radioisotope thermal generator is too weak to keep it awake very long, so it spends most of its time sleeping."

Maria punched keys, gestured at the screen, and muttered commands. Words appeared, and an orbit animation. "The Infrared All-Sky Survey spotted the object, and the system requested observations from the closest spacecraft. The data shows it's an iceball coming from deep space on a hyperbolic orbit. It won't come close enough to the sun to be a bright comet, though, just a little closer than Saturn."

"How large is it?"

Maria punched more keys and voiced more commands. "Big enough to have internal heat and emit in the deep infrared." She pointed to a spectrum displayed on the screen.

"That's not just a stray comet," Aaron said, slowly. "At that temperature, it must be a wandering planet with a hot core and an ice-covered ocean. Who knows what could be in that ocean! On an interstellar scale, it's coming close enough that we can almost touch it. I never thought that would happen."

The instruments reported a warm spot high above the watch station, where the world-ocean met the endless ice. The temperature in that area had never changed before, so junior watch officer Seventh Upwelling checked again and again, but the anomaly would not go away. Finally he said, "Sir, the temperature gradient above us is changing."

Senior officer Twelfth Cycling floated slowly closer, lethargic from the coming Change. "How?" he asked.

"It is warming, sir," Seventh answered. Cycles of cycles of generations ago, the swimmers had built the watch stations to see if other world-oceans might lay beyond the endless ice. After generations of finding nothing, the elder thinkers decided to look down instead, and monitor the mineral-rich water seeping from the hot core that fed the drifters that the swimmers ate.

"The ice is warming?" Twelfth was incredulous. The elder thinkers had always said the ice would only cool until the final freeze came to the world-ocean.

Seventh swam to the command post and spread out a screen embossed with readings. Twelfth's face-fingers ran across the textured surface, picking out the results. If the instruments had made a mistake, he would find it.

"It is odd," Twelfth said after a long silence. "The instruments show a point-source thermal anomaly. I concur with you that it is in the ice itself. Something must be out there."

"That is why I showed you, sir," said Seventh.

"That is supposed to be impossible," Twelfth said, his words taking the Tone of Authority of a commanding officer. "The elder thinkers say that no energy can come from the ice. Energy comes only from the radioactivity that melts the core. It cannot originate in the endless ice."

"Indeed, sir," Seventh said, with the uncertainty of a junior officer. He knew that rising molten rock touched the liquid ocean a few times in a life cycle. For an instant, the horrible heat of the molten rock would turn the water into searing steam trying to explode away from the core. Then the tremendous pressure near the core would crush the steam back to liquid in an implosion that would send shock waves bouncing around the world-ocean, tossing the swimmers about.

"The instruments may be deceived." Twelfth's fin-fingers pulled away from the embossed screen. "Molten rock that shatters at the edge of the core contains potassium and the lesser energy sources uranium and thorium. Strong currents can carry those pieces of rock high above the core, even above the watch station. A rock laden with radioactive isotopes would look warm if it is above us." Twelfth turned back to the screen, and dropped the Authority from his voice, telling Seventh that he was no longer speaking as commander. "Yet I do not see any evidence of such a rock above us. How smooth is the ice surface in that region?" Twelfth asked.

"Sonar shows the surface is even, but we are too far away to observe details. We must take the probe near the ice to observe the warm spot." Seventh had gone up toward the ice twice before, because junior watch officers must learn how. He did not like the feeling, and would assign the task to the junior who came when he became senior watch officer.

"It should be my task to verify your measurements," Twelfth said. "Yet I feel too close to the Change to go up safely. Do you concur?" He turned his head, conveying the Authority of decision to Seventh.

The test of Authority was to know the truth. Bits of female shading showed on the senior's tail fins. The color would spread from tail to head, then the swimmer's body would thicken as organs changed from male to female. Within a few feeding cycles, the nesting instinct would take hold, and the female Twelfth would swim down toward the core, where she would breed, bear neuters, raise them to become males, then spend the last part of her life cycle as an elder thinker. "I concur," said Seventh.

Twelfth's face-fingers sagged with sadness. Then he swam away from the touch-screen and led Seventh to the top of the station to prepare.

The swimmers had evolved in the deep ocean; they needed pressure balls to survive close to the ice. Like the probe, the station's pressure ball was old and precious, and kept in a sealed case.

Seventh clacked his tongue to make a sonar pulse, listening for an echo as Twelfth lifted the probe from its case. It was a metal sphere with a window made of a rare transparent crystal that could survive in the world-ocean. The probe contained a mechanical sonar to examine the edge of the endless ice from a safe distance. It also contained the brightest mechanical source of light that Seventh had ever seen, and instruments to detect the light returned from the ice and the ocean. A tether cable would carry the instrument readings back to the station.

Twelfth ran his fin-fingers over the controls. "This is buoyancy. Turn it up, and the probe will rise. These buttons tell the instruments to measure water composition, temperature, pressure, and flow." He showed Seventh the steering controls on the tether cable, then pointed to another control. "This opens the capture net, but I do not think you will not find anything to capture above us." Then they stowed food for Seventh's journey, because no edible drift floated above them.

After sealing Seventh in the pressure ball and attaching the probe to it, Twelfth swam beside it, tapping with his fin-fingers. "Go now, before the Change comes any closer and I must go down to the vents. They will send a new junior for you to train, but that will take time, and I do not want to leave the watch station empty."

The controls beeped to verify their links to the probe and to the station. Seventh began to rise, clicking his tongue, and listened as the sonar echoes of Twelfth and the station faded. Alone, he wondered if the ice went on forever, and why its pressure was not great enough to crush the world-ocean.

Rising, Seventh scanned the water. Almost nothing lived so high above the life-sustaining vents. His sonar sensed a small floater below him, grazing on the few single-cell drifters that escaped from the nutrient farms down near the vents. Once large floaters had been common, but few remained. After it drifted out of view, Seventh read the gauges, checking temperature and pressure as he rose slowly, and rested.

A door opened behind Maria. "The drill has 1300 meters left to go through the ice," she said, knowing Aaron had come to ask about the probe's progress.

"After drilling 160 kilometers, it's detected liquid?"

"It's 163 kilometers down now. Temperature and pressure rise with depth. I expect the interface will be slushy."

"It's strange. None of us had expected an iceball the size of the Earth." Aaron sounded tired.

"The ice shell makes its diameter larger." Maria insisted on accuracy, as Aaron himself had told her was essential.

"What has the drill found?"

"Layers," Maria said. "The top is polymerized hydrocarbons with a large excess of carbon. The interstellar ultraviolet blasts hydrogen atoms from light ices, but the process is very slow. The object is very dark, so it must have been in deep space for a very long time."

Aaron sat beside her. "The modelers say it's too big to form in deep space. It must have been in a planetary system, maybe a satellite of a gas giant."

"How could it escape from such a deep gravity well?"

"A close encounter with another gas giant might have ejected it from the star system. The modelers say it's big enough to retain a liquid ocean for more than four billion years." He looked at Maria.

"So it may have been wandering since the Earth was born?" she asked.

Aaron nodded.

Waking from his rest, Seventh saw a warning flashing on the instruments in the pressure ball. He was approaching the hot spot; it was above him, in the mushy layer between ice and water. His fin-fingers coded a message to Twelfth.

Looking up, Seventh wondered what the hot spot was. Was he chasing a warm rock containing gas that expanded as the pressure dropped, so the rock floated upward? Or had the hot spot come from somewhere above the ice? Legends told of hot spots inside the endless ice when the swimmers first learned to think, but the instruments built to find them had recorded nothing. Were hot spots a myth?

The instruments showed the pressure was much lower than at the watch station. Did that mean the ice did not go on forever? Long ago, an elder thinker had told Seventh that the ice was not infinite, but instead closed upon itself in four dimensions, like the surface of a sphere closed upon itself in three. But then she said nothing lay beyond the ice, and that made no sense.

Frustrated, Seventh shook his body and focused on the informa-tion from the probe. Sonar mapped the uneven surface of the ice. Flow meters monitored water movement; thermometers sensed tem-perature. Running his face-fingers across the touch-screen, Seventh saw that the heat source now was at the very surface of the ice. He wondered if he could catch it with the probe.

The pressure ball shook. The probe reported that water was rush-ing upward, and Seventh felt it pull on him.

The controls shrieked. A flash of green light hit the probe and the pressure ball; its color meant that it must have passed far through the water. The instruments showed his face-fingers a beam sweeping through the water, moving past the probe. The light faded and shrank almost to a point, then grew brighter and longer.

The probe traced the light to an object floating below the ice, near where water rushed up into the ice. Seventh realized the object was turning, pointing a beam of light that scanned through the water that surrounded it as it turned. A burst of green light illuminated the probe, then swept onward and faded. The cycle of fading away then scanning back repeated five times, with the object steadily coming closer to Seventh and the probe. Then the beam swept back and forth across the pressure ball and the probe, examining them. The beam was so bright it was almost painful.

Seventh ran his fin-fingers across the pressure ball's controls, and felt the levers that controlled the capture net. Twelfth had taught him how to use it near the station; they had caught a floater, let it go, and carefully packed the net back into place.

Now Seventh used the controls to move the pressure ball toward the lighted thing, his fin-fingers ready. When it came in range, he sprung the net, which sprang open in front of the object, then closed over it. Seventh's sonar showed a cable rising up from the object into the hole where water flowed upward. The flow pulled the pressure ball and probe upward as well.

When he felt himself moving up, Seventh hit the controls to dive, pumping more water into the pressure ball, and switched it to diving. As he struggled against the flow, he fired water jets to push away from it. The net pulled the lighted object with it, tightening over it, but the cable held on. Seventh remembered the emergency blade, and his fin-fingers pushed it into the water and upward. Turbulence blocked Seventh's sonar view, but he yanked mightily on the controls, slashing the blade. As he moved back from the flow, he felt something snap and a severed end of the cable drifted into view.

Momentum kept Seventh going, but fear made him turn and click his tongue to fire a sonar pulse. The light had stopped, and he thought that he must have lost the object. Yet the return showed that the net still held the thing, which had stopped moving and shining light into the water, as if stunned. He turned and continued down toward the high station.

At the comfortable pressure of the station, he opened the pressure ball and examined the thing he had caught inside the net. It was still, as if dead or drained of power. The texture of its surface was unlike anything he had ever felt before; its sonar response was unlike anything he knew. He fastened the net, the probe, and the pressure ball to the station, and went to get Twelfth.

When Seventh reached the station, he found the Change was coming quickly to the senior; his body had thickened further. He swam in restless circles around Seventh and the object, examining it with a light he had brought from a cabinet. "I have never seen such a thing," he said, waving his fin-fingers in excitement.

Seventh told Twelfth how the thing had seemed alive when it shone lights into the water just below the ice, and how water had flowed up into the hole. He pointed to a limp stub of broken cable. "That must have gone to a power source, like the probe draws power from the pressure ball. That power fed the warmth we saw."

"What else came from the hole?" Twelfth asked.

"Nothing came from it, sir. Water rose into it. The water pulled me upward, and I had to swim fast to escape, and pull hard to rescue the probe and the thing. Did you receive the data from the probe?"

"It was logged." Twelfth swam loops again. "The Change is on me, and it muddles my mind and makes it hard to think. This thing muddles my mind further. It was made, but it was not made by us. And water should not be going up into the ice." He paused and stopped cold in the water. "Where is the water going?"

"Up through the ice," Seventh answered. "What is beyond the ice?"

"Someplace where the water can go," Twelfth said, moving his fin-fingers very slowly to hold him in place against the slow currents. "So the endless ice is not endless. We must go and tell the elder thinkers."

"We cannot abandon the high station," Seventh said, programmed by his training and sense of duty.

Twelfth stopped circling, and brushed his face-fingers against Seventh. "This is more important than the high station. As Senior Watch Officer, I command you to come with me. I need you to bring the thing and the probe, and to tell the elder thinkers what you saw and how you captured it. With the Change, I cannot do this alone."

The camera panned slowly in circles, keeping phase with the illuminating beam scanning the ocean beneath the ice. "This is typical of what it's seeing," Maria said. "The data rate is much too low to show realtime, even with full compression, so I had the probe send one-minute low-res samples every two hours. I also told it to watch for changes, and send us a minute after every change."

Aaron watched intently. The screen displayed a series of one-minute clips, each virtually the same as the other. "Not a very busy place, is it?"

"It's an ocean on an alien planet. Isn't that enough?"

"Drilling the hole should have stirred something up. The pressure down there should be high enough to squeeze liquid up the tunnel, so if anything is floating in the water, the flow should bring it close to the probe."

"If the ocean gets its energy from the core, maybe nothing lives high up in the water, away from all the energy?" Maria groped for an explanation. They both wanted to see something.

"Maybe," Aaron said, and leaned toward the screen. "I just saw something. Run that back."

Maria spoke a command. The screen flashed back 60 seconds. This time she saw a greenish glint where Aaron pointed.

"That's it," he said, pointing to where the green spot had been. They waited and the spot appeared a second time. "Dark object. I wonder what it's doing."

They watched the spot grow brighter and larger as the probe and the object approached each other. Maria keyed in commands and numbers appeared at the bottom of the screen. "It's changing its course to follow the probe," she said. Lacking references, they couldn't estimate its size as it grew larger on screen.

They were trying to trace the object's shape when it ejected something that swept over the probe like a net.

"What is that!" Maria shouted.

"Call headquarters and get them in on this," Aaron commanded. "Now!"

Seventh and Twelfth swam downward swiftly, to the high ridge where the elder thinkers pondered the world-ocean. Seventh had only seen the ridge from afar. Neuters and young males were too unruly to visit the refuge where the elder thinkers lived. The youngest of the elder thinkers taught the neuters about the world-ocean and the ways of the swimmers, but the oldest never left the ridge.

Twelfth led the way to a worn level space on one side of the ridge. As Seventh settled alongside, he realized that the Change had passed as they swam downward. Twelfth now looked fully female, and she seemed calm for the first time since they had spotted the anomaly. "What do we do?" he asked her.

"Wait. This is the waiting spot. They will come for us when they are ready."

The waiting seemed long but was not. A single elder thinker swam toward them, long, thin, and pale, and settled beside the probe, feeling it with her fin-fingers. Twelfth pointed to the net and the thing inside, without saying a word. Instinctively, Seventh kept his own silence as the elder thinker felt the thing.

"It does not feel like ours. You were a watch officer, and he still is one. Where did you find this?"

Twelfth turned to Seventh, "He found it."

Seventh looked at the elder. "It was moving near the ice, shining a light into the ocean as it turned around. A cable led upward from it, through a hole in the ice where water flowed up. I caught it in the net and as I swam down the cable broke."

"Wait," the elder said, and swam away.

As they waited alone, Seventh felt hungry, and began eating the food left from his trip to the ice. He gave some to Twelfth, and she ate hungrily until the elders began arriving.

Many came, and one at a time they swam to the net and examined the thing with their fin-fingers and face-fingers, their sonars, and with lights some carried. Then they swam away and joined a circle that swam in a slow, growing circle above the level spot. Seventh could feel the noise of them talking among themselves, but could not understand the words.

Then seven of them broke from the circle and swam toward them. By their number, Seventh knew they came for him.

The palest of them spoke for the group. "What do you think this is, Seventh Upwelling?"

"It is like nothing I have seen before. It came from a warm spot within the endless ice," he said. After so long at the watch station, he felt uneasy with so many swimmers around him. "But you would know better than I."

The elder thinkers held their places in the water, looking at Seventh. "We, too, have seen nothing like it. It could have been made by others, within the ice or beyond it," the palest one said. "Or it could be something that the first swimmers made, which drifted into the ice long ago and was forgotten. What is it?"

Their uncertainty confused Seventh. The elder thinkers were supposed to know the answers, not to ask him for them. He said nothing.

"We want you to find out, Seventh Upwelling. You must form a special watch to study this hole in the ice and see where it goes. It may tell us where this object came from. You started the quest, and you must finish it."

Floating uneasily, Seventh looked at the seven elder thinkers. Twelfth's Change had not been easy, but they had known it was coming. This was different. None of them knew what was out there. But Seventh would be the first to know what came from the endless ice. "Yes," he said, "Yes, I will."

A dozen people crowded the control room, standing behind Maria and Aaron and looking at their screen. Maria had patched the signal into headquarters, so the dour director of trans-Neptunian exploration stared at the same screen in her office hundreds of miles away.

"How hard is that thing pulling on the probe?" the director asked.

"No data yet," Maria replied. "The surface transmitter at the drill head is storing the monitor data until time is available to transmit."

"How strong is the tether cable?" the director added.

"Searching," Maria said, as she waited for results. A minute passed. Data scrolled across her console, but nothing matched "The only specifications I can find for the probe cable are its length and transmission capacity."

The director cleared her throat.

The screen blanked. For a moment, it was black as deep space without a sparkle of starlight. Then bright yellow letters appeared in overlay: CABLE CONTINUITY FAILURE.

"It's gone," a man in back said.

"Something's out there," said Aaron. "They can't be like us, but they must be curious. They're yours, Maria. Tell me what they are when you find them."

Maria turned and stared at Aaron. She had known her turn would come, but she had not expected it to come so suddenly. His words echoed. Eyes turned toward her. "Yes," she said, "Yes, I will."

GIANTS

BY PETER WATTS

So many eons, slept away while the universe wound down around him. He's dead to human eyes. Even the machines barely see the chemistry ticking over in those cells: an ancient molecule of hydrogen sulfide, frozen in a hemoglobin embrace; an electron shuttled sluggishly down some metabolic pathway two weeks ago. Back on Earth there used to be life deep in the rocks, halfway to the mantle; empires rose and fell in the time it took those microbes to draw breath. Next to Hakim's, their lives blurred past in an eyeblink. (Next to all of ours. I was every bit as dead, just a week ago.)

I'm still not sure it's a good idea, bringing him back.

Flat lines shiver in their endless march along the x-axis: molecules starting to bump against each other, core temp edging up a fraction of a fraction. A lonely spark flickers in the hypothalamus; another wriggles across the prefrontal cortex (a passing thought, millennia past its best-before, released from amber). Millivolts trickle down some random path and an eyelid twitches.

The body shudders, tries to breathe but it's too soon: it's still anoxic in there, pure H2S gumming up the works and shutting the machinery of life down to a whisper. The Chimp starts a nitrox flush; swarms of fireflies bloom across *Pulmonary* and *Vascular*. Hakim's cold empty husk fills with light from the inside out: red and yellow isotherms, pulsing arteries, a trillion reawakening neurons stippling across the translucent avatar in my head. A real breath this time. Another. His fingers twitch and stutter, tap a random tattoo against the floor of his sarcophagus.

The lid slides open. His eyes, too, a moment later: they roll unfocused in their sockets, suffused in a haze of resurrection dementia. He can't see me. He sees soft lights and vague shadows, hears the faint underwater echo of nearby machinery, but his mind is still stuck to the past and the present hasn't sunk in yet.

A tongue dry as leather flicks into view against his upper lip. A drinking tube emerges from its burrow and nudges Hakim's cheek. He takes it in his mouth and nurses, reflexive as a newborn.

I lean into what passes for his field of view: "Lazarus, come forth." It anchors him. I see sudden focus resolving in those eyes, see the past welling up behind them. I see memories and hearsay loading in the wake of my voice. Confusion evaporates; something sharper takes its place. Hakim stares up at me from the grave, his eyes hard as obsidian.

"You asshole," he says. "I can't believe we haven't killed you yet."

I give him space. I retreat to the forest, wander endless twilit caverns while he learns to live again. Down here I can barely see my own hand in front of my face: grey fingers, faint sapphire accents. Photophores glimmer around me like dim constellations, each tiny star lit by the glow of a trillion microbes: photosynthesis instead of fusion. You can't get truly lost in *Eriophora*—the Chimp always knows where you are—but here in the dark, there's comfort to be had in the illusion.

Eventually, though, I have to stop stalling. I sample myriad feeds as I rise though the depths of the asteroid, find Hakim in the starboard bridge. I watch as he enters painstaking questions, processes answers, piles each new piece on top of the last in a rickety climb to insight. Lots of debris in this system, yes: more than enough material for a build. Call up the transponders and—what's this? No in-system scaffolding, no half-constructed jump gate, no asteroid mining or factory fleet. So why—?

System dynamics, now. Lagrange points. Nothing on this side, anyway, even though there are at least three planetary bodies in— whoa, those *orbits*—

Our orbit…

By the time I join him in the flesh he's motionless, staring into the tac tank. A bright dimensionless point floats in the center of that display: *Eriophora*. The ice giant looms dark and massive to port, the red one—orders of magnitude larger—seethes in the distance behind. (If I stepped outside I'd see an incandescent barrier stretching across half the universe, with the barest hint of a curve on the horizon; Tac reduces it to a cherry globe floating in an aquarium.) A million bits of detritus, from planets to pebbles, career through the neighborhood.

We're not even relativistic and still the Chimp hasn't had time to tag them all.

None of those tags make sense anyway. We're aeons from the nearest earthly constellation; every alphabet, every astronomical convention has been exhausted by the stars we've passed in the meantime. Maybe the Chimp invented his own taxonomy while we were sleeping, some arcane gibberish of hex and ascii that makes sense to him and him alone. A hobby, perhaps, although he's supposed to be too stupid for anything like that.

I slept through most of that scenery. I've been awake for barely a hundred builds; my mythological reservoir is nowhere near exhausted. I have my own names for these monsters.

The cold giant is Thule. The hot one is Surtr.

Hakim ignores my arrival. He moves sliders back and forth: trajectories extrude from bodies in motion, predict the future according to Newton. Eventually all those threads converge and he rewinds time, reverses entropy, reassembles the shattered teacup and sets it running again. He does it three times as I watch. The result never changes.

He turns, his face bloodless. "We're going to hit. We're going to ram straight into the fucking thing."

I swallow and nod.

"That's how it starts," I tell him.

We're going to hit. We're *aiming* to hit, we're going to let the lesser monster devour us before the greater one devours it. We'll lower *Eriophora* by her own bootstraps, sink through roiling bands of hydrogen and helium and a thousand exotic hydrocarbons, down to whatever residual deep-space chill Thule's been hoarding since—who knows? Maybe almost as long as *we've* been in flight.

It won't last, of course. The planet's been warming ever since it started its long fall from the long dark. Its bones will survive the passage through the stellar envelope easily enough: five hours in and out, give or take. Its atmosphere won't be so lucky, though; every step of the way Surtr's going to be stripping it down like a child licking an ice cream cone.

We'll make it through by balancing in the ever-shrinking sweet spot between a red-hot sky and the pressure cooker at Thule's core. The numbers say it'll work.

Hakim should know this already. He would have *awakened* knowing if not for that idiotic uprising of theirs. But they chose to blind themselves instead, burn out their links, cut themselves off from the very heart of the mission. So now I have to *explain* things. I have to *show* things. All that instantaneous insight we once shared, gone: one ancient fit of pique and I have to use *words*, scribble out *diagrams*, etch out painstaking codes and tokens while the clock runs down. I'd hoped that maybe, after all these red-shifted millennia, they might have reconsidered; but the look in Hakim's eyes leaves no doubt. As far as he's concerned it all happened yesterday.

I do my best. I keep the conversation strictly professional, focus on the story so far: a build, aborted. Chaos and inertia, imminent annihilation, the insane counter-intuitive necessity of passing *through* a star instead of going *around* it. "What are we doing here?" Hakim asks once I've finished.

"It looked like a perfect spot." I gesture at the tank. "From a distance. Chimp even sent out the recon vons, but—" I shrug. "The closer we got, the worse it turned out to be."

He stares at me without speaking, so I add context: "Far as we can tell something big came through a few hundred thousand years back, knocked everything haywire. None of the planetary masses are even on the ecliptic any more. We can't find anything orbiting with an eccentricity of less than point six, there's a shitload of rogues zipping around in the halo—but by the time those numbers came back, we were already committed. So now we just buckle down through the heavy traffic, steal a gravity-assist, get back on the road."

He shakes his head. "What are we doing here?"

Oh, *that's* what he means. I tap an innerface, timelapse the red giant. It jerks in the tank like a fibrillating heart. "Turns out it's an irregular variable. One complication too many, right?" Not that we'll be able thread the needle any better than the Chimp can (although of course Hakim's going to try, in these few hours left to him). But the mission has parameters. The Chimp has his algorithms. Too many unexpected variables and he wakes up the meat. That's what we're here for, after all.

That's *all* we're here for.

One more time, Hakim asks: "What are *we* doing here?"

Oh.

"You're the numbers guy," I say after a moment. "One of 'em, anyway." Out of how many thousand, stored down in the crypt?

Doesn't matter. They probably all know about me by now.

"Guess it was just your rotation," I add.

He nods. "And you? You a *numbers guy* too, now?"

"We come back in pairs," I say softly. "You know that."

"So it just happened to be *your rotation* as well."

"Look—"

"Nothing to do with your *Chimp* wanting its own personal sock-puppet on hand to keep an eye on things."

"Fuck, Hakim, what do you want me to say?" I spread my hands. "That he might want someone on deck who won't try to pull the plug the first chance they get? You think that's *unreasonable*, given what happened?" But he doesn't even know what happened, not first-hand. Hakim wasn't up when the mutiny went down; someone obviously told him, down through the epochs. Christ knows how much of what he heard is truth, lies, legend.

A few million years go by and suddenly I'm the bogeyman.

We fall towards ice. Ice falls towards fire. Both spill through the link and spread across the back of my skull in glorious terrifying first-person. Orders of magnitude aren't empty abstractions in here: they're life-size, you feel them in your gut. Surtr may be small to a textbook—at seven million kilometers across, it's barely big enough to get into the giant's club—but that doesn't mean shit when you meet it face to face. That's not a star out there: that's the scorching edge of all creation, that's heat-death incarnate. Its breath stinks of left-over lithium from the worlds it's *already* devoured. And the dark blemish marching across its face isn't just a *planet*. It's a melting hellscape twice the size of Uranus, it's frozen methane and liquid hydrogen and a core hot and heavy enough to bake diamonds. Already it's coming apart before my eyes, any moons long since lost, the tattered remnants of a ring system shredding around it like a rotting halo. Storms boil across its face; aurorae flicker madly at both poles. A super-cyclone pinwheels at the center of the dark side, fed by turbulent streamers fleeing from light into shadow. Its stares back at me like the eye of a blind god.

Meanwhile, Hakim pushes balls around inside an aquarium.

He's been at it for hours: a bright blue marble here, a sullen red basketball over there, threads of tinsel looping through time and trajectory like the webbing of some crazed spacefaring spider. Maybe pull our center of mass to starboard, start gentle then ramp up to max? Break some rocks on the way, suffer some structural damage but nothing the drones won't be able to patch up in time for the next build.

No?

Maybe cut smooth and fast into full reverse. *Eri's* not built for it but if we keep the vectors dead along the centerline, no turn no torque just a straight linear one-eighty back out the way we came—

But no.

If only we hadn't already fallen so far down the well. If only we hadn't slowed down to open the trunk, all these N-bodies wouldn't have been able to get such a grip on us. But now we're only fast, not fast enough; we're big but still too small.

Now, the only way out is through.

Hakim's not an idiot. He knows the rules as well as I do. He keeps trying, though. He'd rather rewrite the laws of physics than trust himself to the enemy. We'll be deaf and blind in there, after all; the convulsions of Thule's disintegrating atmosphere will fog our sight at short range, the roar of Surtr's magnetic field will deafen us in the long. There'll be no way of telling where we are, nothing but the Chimp's math to tell us where we should be.

Hakim doesn't see the world like I do. He doesn't like having to take things on faith.

Now he's getting desperate, blasting chunks off his toy asteroid in an attempt to reduce its momentum. He hasn't yet considered how that might impact our radiation shielding once we get back up to speed. He's still stuck on whether we can scavenge enough in-system debris to patch the holes on our way out.

"It won't work," I tell him, though I'm wandering deep in the catacombs half a kilometer from his location. (I'm not spying because he knows I'm watching. Of course he knows.)

"Won't it now."

"Not enough mass along the escape trajectory, even if the vons *could* grab it all and get it back in time."

"We don't know how much mass is out there. Haven't plotted it all yet."

He's being deliberately obtuse, but I go along with it; at least we're talking. "Come on. You don't need to plot every piece of gravel to get a mass distribution. It won't work. Check with the Chimp if you don't believe me. He'll tell you."

"It just *has* told me," he says.

I stop walking. I force myself to take a slow breath.

"I'm *linked*, Hakim. Not possessed. It's just an innerface."

"It's a corpus callosum."

"I'm just as autonomous as you are."

"Define *I*."

"I don't—"

"Minds are holograms. Split one in half, you get two. Stitch two together, you get one. Maybe you were human back before your *upgrade*. Right now you've got about as much standalone soul as my parietal lobe."

I look back along the vaulted corridor (I suppose the cathedral architecture might just be coincidence), where the dead sleep stacked on all sides.

They're much better company like this.

"If that's true," I ask them all, "then how did you ever get free?"

Hakim doesn't speak for a moment.

"The day you figure that out," he says, "is the day we lose the war."

It's not a war. It's a fucking tantrum. They tried to derail the mission and the Chimp stopped them. Simple as that, and perfectly predictable. That's why the engineers made the Chimp so minimalist in the first place, why the mission isn't run by some transcendent AI with an eight-dimensional IQ: so that things will stay predictable. If my fellow meat sacks couldn't see it coming, they're more stupid than the thing they're fighting.

Hakim knows that on some level, of course. He just refuses to believe it: that he and his buddies got outsmarted by something with half his synapse count. *The Chimp.* The idiot savant, the artificial stupidity. The number-cruncher explicitly designed to be so dim that even with half the lifespan of a universe to play around in, it could never develop its own agenda.

They just can't believe it beat them in a fair fight.

That's why they need me. I let them tell each other that it *cheated*. No way that glorified finger-counter would've won if I hadn't betrayed my own kind.

This is the nature of my betrayal; I stepped in to save their lives. Not that their lives were really in danger, of course, no matter what they say. It was just a strategy. That was predictable too.

I'm sure the Chimp would have turned the air back on before things went too far.

Thule's graduated from world to wall while I wasn't looking: a dark churning expanse of thunderheads and planet-shredding tornadoes. There's no sign of Surtr lurking behind, not so much as a faint glow on the horizon. We huddle in the shadow of the lesser giant and it's almost as though the greater one has simply gone away.

We're technically in the atmosphere now, a mountain wallowing high above the clouds with its nose to the stars. You could draw a line from the hot hydrogen slush of Thule's core through the cold small singularity of our own, straight out through the gaping conical maw at our bow. Hakim does just that, in the tac tank. Maybe it makes him feel a little more in control.

Eriophora sticks out her tongue.

You can only see it in X-ray or Hawking, maybe the slightest nimbus of gamma radiation if you tune the sensors just right. A tiny bridge opens at the back of *Eri's* mouth: a hole in spacetime reaching back to the hole in our heart. Our center of mass *smears* a little off-center, seeks some elastic equilibrium between those points. The Chimp nudges the far point farther and our center follows in its wake. The asteroid tugs upward, falling after itself; Thule pulls us back. We hang balanced in the sky while the wormhole's tip edges past the crust, past that abraded mouth of blue-sanded basalt, out past the forward sensor hoop.

We've never stretched ourselves so thin before. Usually there's no need; with light-years and epochs to play in, even the slowest fall brings us up to speed in plenty of time. We can't go past twenty percent lightspeed anyway, not without getting cooked by the blueshift. Usually *Eri* keeps her tongue in her mouth.

Not this time. This time we're just another one of Hakim's holiday ornaments, dangling from a thread in a hurricane. According to the Chimp, that thread should hold. There are error bars, though, and not a lot of empirical observation to hang them on. The database on singularities nested inside asteroids nested inside incinerating ice giants is pretty heavy on the handwaving.

And that's just the problem *within* the problem. Atmospheric docking with a world falling at two hundred kilometers a second is downright trivial next to predicting Thule's course inside the star: the drag inflicted by a millionth of a red-hot gram per cubic centimeter, stellar winds and thermohaline mixing, the deep magnetic torque of fossil helium. It's tough enough figuring out what "inside" even *means* when the gradient from vacuum to degenerate matter blurs across three million kilometers. Depending on your definition we might already be in the damn thing.

Hakim turns to me as the Chimp lowers us toward the storm. "Maybe we should wake them up."

"Who?"

"Sunday. Ishmael. All of them."

"You know how many thousands of us are stacked up down there?"

I know. Hakim might guess but this traitor knows right down to the last soul, without checking.

Not that any of them would pat me on the back for that.

"What for?" I ask.

He shrugs. "It's all theory. You know that. We could all be dead in a day."

"You want to bring them back so they can be awake when they die?"

"So they can—I don't know. Write a poem. Grow a sculpture. Shit, one or two of them might even be willing to make their peace with *you* before the end."

"Say we wake them up and we're *not* all dead in day. You've just pushed our life support three orders of mag past spec."

He rolls his eyes. "Then we put everyone back down again. So it spikes the CO2. Nothing the forest won't be able to clear in a few centuries."

I can barely hear the tremor in his voice.

He's scared. That's what this is. He's scared, and he doesn't want to die alone. And I don't count.

I suppose it's a start.

"Come on. At the very least it'll be a hell of a solstice party."

"Ask the Chimp," I suggest.

His face goes hard. I keep mine blank.

I'm pretty sure he wasn't serious anyway.

The depths of the troposphere. The heart of the storm. Cliffs of water and ammonia billow across our path: airborne oceans shattered down to droplets, to crystals. They crash into our mountain at the speed of sound, freeze solid or cascade into space depending on the mood. Lightning flashes everywhere, stamps my brain stem with half-glimpsed afterimages: demon faces, and great clawed hands with too many fingers.

Somehow the deck stays solid beneath my feet, unmoved even by the death throes of a world. I can't entirely suppress my own incredulity; even anchored by two million tonnes of basalt and a black hole, it seems impossible that we're not being tossed around like a mote in a wind tunnel.

I squash the feed and the carnage vanishes, leaving nothing behind but bots and bulkheads and a ribbon of transparent quartz looking down onto the factory floor. I kill some time watching the assembly lines boot up in there, watching maintenance drones gestate in the vacuum past the viewport. Even best-case there's going to be damage. Cameras blinded by needles of supersonic ice or sheets of boiling acid. The whiskers of long-range antennae, drooping in the heat. Depending on the breaks it could take an army to repair the damage after we complete our passage. I take some comfort from the sight of the Chimp's troops assembling themselves.

For an instant I think I hear a faint shriek down some far-off corridor: a breach, a decompression? No alarms, though. Probably just one of the roaches skidding around a bend in the corridor, looking for a recharge.

I'm not imagining the beeping in my head, though: Hakim, calling down from the bridge. "You need to be up here," he says when I open the channel.

"I'm on the other side of the—"

"*Please*," he says, and forks me a live feed: one of the bow clusters, pointing at the sky.

A feature has emerged from the featureless overcast: a bright dimple on the dark sky, like a finger poking down through the roof of the world. It's invisible in visible light, hidden by torrents of ammonia and hydrocarbon hurricanes: but it shimmers in infrared like a rippling ember.

I have no idea what it is.

I draw an imaginary line through the ends of the wormhole. "It's in line with our displacement vector."

"No *shit* it's in line. I think the wormhole's—provoking it, somehow."

It's radiating at over two thousand Kelvin.

"So we're inside the star," I say, and hope Hakim takes it as good news.

If nothing else, it means we're on schedule.

We've got so little to go on. We don't know how far we are from the ceiling: it keeps ablating away above us. We don't know how close we are to the core: it keeps swelling beneath the easing weight of all this shedding atmosphere. All we know is that temperature rises overhead and we descend; pressure rises from beneath and we climb. We're specks in the belly of some fish in empty mid-ocean, surface and seabed equally hypothetical. None of our reference points are any more fixed than we are. The Chimp presents estimates based on gravity and inertia, but even those are little more than guesses thanks to wormhole corruption of the local spacetime. We're stretched across the probability wave, waiting for the box to open so the universe can observe whether we're dead or alive.

Hakim eyes me from across the tank, his face flickering in the light of a hundred cam feeds. "Something's wrong. We should be through by now."

He's been saying that for the past hour.

"There's bound to be variability," I remind him. "The model—"

"The *model*." He manages a short, bitter laugh. "Based on all those zettabytes we collected the *other* times we hitched a ride through a red giant. The model's *shit*. One hiccup in the magnetic field and we could be going *down* instead of *out*."

"We're still here."

"That's exactly the problem."

"It's still dark." The atmosphere's still thick enough to keep Surtr's blinding interior at bay.

"Always darkest before the dawn," Hakim says grimly, and points to that brightening smudge of infrared overhead.

The Chimp can't explain it, for all the fresh realtime data he stuffs into our equations. All we know is that whatever it is, it hasn't budged from our displacement vector and it's getting hotter. Or maybe closer. It's hard to tell; our senses are hazy that far out, and we're not about to stick our heads above the clouds for a better view.

Whatever it is, the Chimp doesn't think it's worth worrying about. He says we're almost through.

The storm no longer freezes on impact. It spits and hisses, turns instantly to steam. Incessant lightning strobes the sky, stop-animates towering jigsaw monsters of methane and acetylene.

God's mind might look like this, if He were an epileptic.

We get in the way sometimes, block some deific synapse in mid-discharge: a million volts spike the hull and a patch of basalt turns to slag, or *Eri* goes blind in another eye. I've lost count of the cameras and antennae and radar dishes we've already lost. I just add it to the tally when another facet flares and goes dark at the edge of the collage.

Hakim doesn't. "Play that again," he tells the Chimp. "That feed. Just before it fratzed."

The last moments of the latest casualty: *Eri's* cratered skin, out-croppings of half-buried machinery. Lightning flickers in from Stage Left, stabs a radiator fin halfway to our lumpy horizon. A flash. A banal and overfamiliar phrase:

NO SIGNAL.

"Again," Hakim says. "The strike in the middle distance. Freeze on that."

Three bolts, caught in the act—and Hakim's onto something, I see now. There's something different about them, something less—random—than the fractal bifurcations of more distant lightning. Different color, too—more of a bluish edge—and smaller. The bolts in the distance are massive. These things arcing across the crust don't look much thicker than my own arm.

They converge towards some bright mass just barely out of camera range.

"Static discharge of some kind," I suggest.

"Yeah? What *kind*, exactly?"

I can't see anything similar in the current mosaic, but the bridge bulkheads only hold so many windows and our surface cams still number in the thousands. Even my link can't handle that many feeds at once. "Chimp: any other phenomena like that on the surface?"

"Yes," says the Chimp, and high-grades the display:

Bright meshes swarming over stone and steel. Formations of ball lightning, walking on jagged stilts of electricity. Some kind of flat flickering plasma, sliding along *Eri's* crust like a stingray.

"*Shittttt...*" Hakim hisses. "Where did *they* come from?"

Our compound eye loses another facet.

"They're targeting the sensors." Hakim's face is ashen.

"They?" It's electrical. Could just be electricity arcing to alloy.

"They're blinding us. Oh Jesus fuck being trapped inside a star isn't bad enough there's gotta be *hostile aliens* in the bargain."

My eyes flicker to the ceiling pickup. "Chimp, what are those things?"

"I don't know. They could be something like Saint Elmo's Fire, or a buoyant plasma. I can't rule out some sort of maser effect either, but I'm not detecting any significant microwave emissions."

Another camera goes down. "Lightning bugs," Hakim says, and emits a hysterical giggle.

"Are they alive?" I wonder.

"Not organically," the Chimp tells me. "I don't know if they'd meet definitions based on entropy restriction."

No conventional morphology there. Those aren't legs exactly, they're—transient voltage arcs of some kind. And body shape—if *body* even applies—seems to be optional and fluid. Auroras bunch up into sparking balls; balls sprout loops or limbs or just blow away at Mach 2, vanishing into the storm.

I call up a tactical composite. Huh: clustered distribution. A flock gathered at the skeletal remains of a long-dead thruster nozzle; another flickering across an evagineering hutch halfway down the starboard lateral line. A whole party in *Eri's* crater-mouth, swarming around our invisible bootstrap like water circling a drain.

"Holes," Hakim says softly. "Depressions. Hatches."

But something's caught my eye that doesn't involve any of those things, something unfolding overhead while our other eyes are fixed on the ground—

"They're trying to get in. That's what they're doing."

A sudden bright smudge in the sky. Then a tear; a hole; the dilating pupil of some great demonic eye. Dim bloody light floods down across the battered landscape as a cyclone opens over our heads, wreathed in an inflammation of lightning.

Surtr's finger stretches down from Hades, visible at last to naked eyes.

"Holy *shit*..." Hakim whispers.

It's an incandescent tornado, a pillar of fire. It's outside reaching in, and if anything short of magic can explain its existence it's not known to me or the Chimp or the accumulated wisdom of all the astrophysicists nesting in our archives. It reaches down and touches our wormhole, just so. It bulges, as if inflamed by an embedded splinter; the swollen tip wobbles absurdly for a moment, then bursts—

—and fire gushes down from the heavens in a liquid cascade. The things beneath scatter fast as forked lightning can carry them; here in the bridge, the view sparks and dies. From a dozen other viewpoints I see tongues of soft red plasma splashing across *Eriophora* crust.

Some rough alarm whispers *fuck fuck fuck fuck* at my side while *Eri* feeds me intelligence: something happening back at that lateral hutch. All those cams are down but there's a pressure surge at the outer hatch and a rhythmic hissing sound crackles in along the intercom.

Hakim's vanished from the bridge. I hear the soft whine of his roach receding at full throttle. I duck out into the corridor, grab my own roach from its socket, follow. There's really no question where he's headed; I'd know that even if the Chimp hadn't already laid out the map in my head.

Way back along our starboard flank, something's knocking on the door.

He's in the prep compartment by the time I catch up. He's scrambling into an EVA suit like some panicky insect trying to climb back into its cocoon. "Outer hatch is breached," he tells me, forgetting.

Just meters away. Past racks and suit alcoves, just the other side of that massive biosteel drawbridge, something's looking for a way in. It could find one, too; I can see heat shimmering off the hatch. I can hear the pop and crackle of arcing electricity coming through from the other side, the faint howl of distant hurricanes.

"No weapons." Hakim fumbles with his gauntlets. "Mission to the end of time and *they don't even give us weapons.*" Which is not entirely true. They certainly gave us the means to *build* weapons. I don't know if Hakim ever availed himself of that option but I remember his buddies, not so far from this very spot. I remember them pointing their weapons at me.

"What are we doing here?" I gesture at the hatch; is it my imagination, or has it brightened a little in the center?

He shakes his head, his breathing fast and shallow. "I was gonna—you know, the welding torches. The lasers. Thought we could stand them off."

All stored on the other side.

He's suited up to the neck. His helmet hangs on its hook within easy reach: a grab and a twist and he'll be self-contained again. For a while.

Something pounds hard on the hatch. "Oh shit," Hakim says weakly.

I keep my voice level. "What's the plan?"

He takes a breath, steadies himself. "We, um—we retreat. Out past the nearest dropgate." The Chimp takes the hint and throws an overlay across my inner map; back into the corridor and fifteen meters forward. "Anything breaches, the gates come down." He nods at an alcove. "Grab a suit, just in—"

"And when they breach the dropgates?" I wonder. The biosteel's definitely glowing, there in the center.

"The *next* set goes down. Jesus, you know the drill."

"That's your plan? Give up *Eri* in stages?"

"*Small* stages." He nods and swallows. "Buy time. Figure out their weak spot." He grabs his helmet and turns towards the corridor.

I lay a restraining hand on his shoulder. "How do we do that, exactly?"

He shrugs it off. "Wing it for fucksake! Get Chimp to customize some drones to go in and, and *ground* them or something." He heads for the door.

This time the hand I lay on him is more than a suggestion. This time it clamps down, spins him around, pushes him against the bulkhead. His helmet bounces across the deck. His clumsy gloved hands come up to fend me off but there's no strength in them. His eyes do a mad little jig in his face.

"You're not thinking this through," I say, very calmly.

"*There's* no time *to think it through!* They might not even get past the gates, maybe they're not even *trying*, I mean—" His eyes brighten with faint and ridiculous hope. "Maybe it's not even an attack, I bet it's not, you know, they're just—they're *dying*. It's the end of the world and their home's on fire and they're just looking for a place to hide, they're not looking for a way in they're looking for a way *out*—"

"What makes you think that inside's any less lethal to them than outside is to us?"

"They don't have to be *smart!*" he cries out. "They just have to be *scared!*"

Fingers of faint electricity flicker and crackle around the edges of the hatch: heat lightning, maybe. Or maybe something more *prehensile*.

I keep Hakim pinned. "What if they *are* smart? What if they're not just burrowing on instinct? What if *they're* the ones with the plan, hmm?"

He spreads his hands. "What else can we do?"

"We don't give them the chance to breach. We get out of here *now*."

"Get—"

"Ditch the ice giant. Take our chances in the star."

He stops struggling and stares, waiting for the punchline. "You're insane," he whispers when I fail to deliver.

"Why? Chimp says we're almost through anyway."

"He said that *half an hour ago!* And we were an hour past predicted exit even *then!*"

"Chimp?" I say, not for the AI's benefit but for Hakim's.

"Right here."

"Say we max the wormhole. Throw out as much mass as we can, shortest path out of the envelope."

"Tidal stress tears *Eriophora* into two debris clouds of roughly equal mass, each one centered on—"

"Amend that. Say we optimize distance and displacement to maximize velocity *without* losing structural integrity."

I can tell by the wait that there are going to be serious confidence limits attached to the answer. "*Eriophora* is directly exposed to the stellar envelope for 1300 corsecs," he says at last. "Give or take 450."

At 2300 Kelvin. Basalt melts at 1724.

But the Chimp hasn't finished. "We would also risk significant structural damage due to the migration of secondary centers-of-mass beyond *Eriophora* hardlined displacement channels."

"Do we make it?"

"I don't know."

Hakim throws up his hands. "Why the hell not? It's what you *do!*"

"My models can't account for the plasma invagination overhead or the electrical events on the hull," the Chimp tells him. "Therefore they're missing at least one important variable. You can't trust my predictions."

Down at the end of the compartment, the hatch glows red as the sky. Electricity sizzles and pops and *grabs.*

"Do it," Hakim says suddenly.

"I need consensus," the Chimp replies.

Of course. The Chimp takes his lead from us meat sacks when he gets lost; but looking to us for wisdom, he wouldn't know whose to follow if we disagreed.

Hakim waits, manic, his eyes flicking between me and the hatch. "Well?" he says after a moment.

It all comes down to me. I could cancel him out.

"What are you waiting for? *It was your fucking idea!*"

I feel an urge to lean close and whisper in his ear. *Not just Chimp's sock puppet* now, *am I, motherfucker?* I resist it. "Sure," I say instead. "Give it a shot."

Wheels begin to turn. *Eriophora* trembles and groans, torqued by vectors she was never designed for. Unfamiliar sensations tickle my backbrain, move forward, root in my gut: the impossible, indescribable sense of *down* being in two places at once. One of those places is safe and familiar, beneath my feet, beneath decks and forests and bedrock at the very heart of the ship; but the other's getting stronger, and it's *moving...*

I hear the scream of distant metal. I hear the clatter of loose objects crashing into walls. *Eriophora* lurches, staggers to port, turns ponderously on some axis spread across too many sickening dimensions. There's something moving behind the wall, deep in the rocks; I can't see it but I feel its pull, hear the cracking of new fault lines splitting ancient stone. A dozen crimson icons bloom like tumors in my brain, *Subsystem Failure* and *Critical Coolant* and *Primary Channel Interrupt.* A half-empty squeezebulb, discarded decades or centuries or millennia ago, wobbles half-levitating into view around the corner. It falls sideways and slides along the bulkhead, caught up in the tide-monster's wake.

I'm standing on the deck at forty-five degrees. I think I'm going to be sick.

The *down* beneath my feet is less than a whisper. I give silent thanks for superconducting ceramics, piezoelectric trusses, all reinforcements brute and magical that keep this little worldlet from crumbling to dust while the Chimp plays havoc with the laws of physics. I offer a diffuse and desperate prayer that they're up to the task. Then I'm falling forward, upward, *out*: Hakim and I smack into the forward bulkhead as a rubber band, stretched to its limit, snaps free and hurls us forward.

Surtr roars in triumph as we emerge, snatches at this tiny unexpected prize shaken free of the larger one. Jagged spiders leap away and vanish into blinding fog. Wireframe swirls of magnetic force twist in the heat, spun off from the dynamo way down in the giant's helium heart—or maybe that's just the Chimp, feeding me models and imaginings. I'm pretty sure it's not real; our eyes and ears and fingertips have all been licked away, our windows all gone dark. Skin and bones will be next to go: warm basalt, softening down to plastic. Maybe it's happening already. No way to tell any more. Nothing to do but fall out as the air flattens and shimmers in the rising heat.

I'm saving your life, Hakim. You better fucking appreciate it.

Yeats was wrong. The center held after all.

Now we are only half-blind, and wholly ballistic. A few eyes remain smoldering on the hull, pitted with cataracts; most are gone entirely. Charred stumps spark fitfully where sensors used to be. *Eri's* center of mass has snapped back into itself and is sleeping off the hangover down in the basement. We coast on pure inertia, as passive as any other rock.

But we are through, and we are alive, and we have ten thousand years to lick our wounds.

It won't take anywhere near that long, of course. The Chimp has already deployed his army; they burned their way out through the slagged doorways of a dozen service tunnels, laden with newly-refined metals dug from the heart of the mountain. Now they clamber across the surface like great metal insects, swapping good parts for bad, cauterizing our wounds with bright light. Every now and then another dead window flickers back to life; the universe returns to us in bits and pieces. Surtr simmers in our wake, still vast but receding, barely hot enough to boil water this far out.

I prefer the view ahead: deep comforting darkness, swirls of stars, glittering constellations we'll never see again and can't be bothered to name. Just passing through.

Hakim should be down in the crypt by now, getting ready to turn in. Instead I find him back in the starboard bridge, watching fingers of blue-white lightning leap across the hull. It's a short clip and it always ends the same way, but he seems to find value in repeat viewings.

He turns at my approach. "Sanduloviciu plasma."

"What?"

"Electrons on the outside, positive ions on the inside. Self-organizing membranes. Live ball lightning. Although I don't know what they'd use as a rep code." He shrugs. "The guys who discovered these things didn't have much to say about heredity."

He's talking about primitive experiments with gas and electricity, back in some prehistoric lab from the days before we launched (I know: Chimp fed me the archive file the moment Hakim accessed it). "*We're* the guys who discovered them," I point out; the things that clawed at our doorstep were lightyears beyond anything those cavemen ever put together.

"No we didn't."

I wait.

"*They* discovered *us*," he tells me.

I feel a half-smile pulling at the corner of my mouth.

"I keep thinking about the odds," Hakim says. "A system that looks so right from a distance and turns out to be so wrong after we've committed to the flyby. All that mass and all those potential trajectories, and somehow the only way out is through the goddamn star. Oh, and there's one convenient ice giant that just *happens* to be going our way. Any idea what those odds are?"

"Astronomical." I keep a straight face.

He shakes his head. "Infinitesimal."

"I've been thinking the same thing," I admit.

Hakim gives me a sharp glance. "Have you now."

"The way the whole system seemed primed to draw us into the star. The way that thing reached down to grab us once we were inside. Your *lightning bugs*: I don't think they were native to the planet at all, not if they were plasma-based."

"You think they were from the star."

I shrug.

"Star aliens," Hakim says.

"Or drones of some kind. Either way, you're right; this system didn't just happen. It was a sampling transect. A trapline."

"Which makes us what, exactly? Specimens? Pets? Hunting trophies?"

"Almost. Maybe. Who knows?"

"Maybe *buddies*, hmm?"

I glance up at the sudden edge in his voice.

"Maybe just *allies*," he muses. "In adversity. Because it's all for one against the common enemy, right?"

"That's generally good strategy." It felt good, too, not being the bad guy for a change. Being the guy who actually pulled asses *out* of the fire.

I'll settle for *allies*.

"Because I can see a couple of other coincidences, if I squint." He's not squinting, though. He's staring straight through me. "Like the way the Chimp happened to pair me up with the one person on the whole roster I'd just as soon chuck out an airlock."

"That's hardly a coincidence," I snort. "It'd be next to impossible to find someone who *didn't*—"

Oh.

The accusation hangs in the air like static electricity. Hakim waits for my defense.

"You think the Chimp used this situation to—"

"Used," he says, "or *invented*."

"That's insane. You saw it with your own eyes, you can *still* see—"

"I saw models in a tank. I saw pixels on bulkheads. I never threw on a suit to go see for myself. You'd have to be suicidal, right?"

He's actually smiling.

"They tried to break in," I remind him.

"Oh, I know *something* was pounding on the door. I'm just not sold on the idea that it was built by aliens."

"You think this whole thing was some kind of trick?" I shake my head in disbelief. "We'll have surface access in a couple of weeks. Hell, just cut a hole into Fab right now, crawl out through one of the service tunnels. See for yourself."

"See what? A star off the stern?" He shrugs. "Red giants are common as dirt. Doesn't mean the specs on this system were anywhere near as restrictive as Chimp says. Doesn't mean we had to go *through*, doesn't even mean we did. For all I know the Chimp had its bots strafing the hull with lasers and blowtorches for the past hundred years, slagging things down to look nice and convincing just in case I *did* pop out for a look-see." Hakim shakes his head. "All I know is, it's only had one meat sack in its corner since the mutiny, and he's not much good if no one will talk to him. But how can you keep hating someone after he's saved your life?"

It astonishes me, the degree to which people torture reason. Just to protect their precious preconceptions.

"The weird thing," Hakim adds, almost to himself, "is that it worked."

It takes a moment for that to sink in.

"Because I don't think you were in on it," he explains. "I don't think you had a clue. How could you? You're not even a whole person, you're just a—a glorified subroutine. And subroutines don't question their inputs. A thought pops into your head, you just assume it's yours. You believe everything that miserable piece of hardware tells you, because you don't have a choice. Maybe you never did.

"How can I hate you for that?" he asks.

I don't answer, so he does: "I can't. Not any more. I can only—"

"Shut the fuck up," I say, and turn my back.

He leaves me then, leaves me surrounded by all these pixels and pictures he refuses to accept. He heads back to the crypt to join his friends. The sleeping dead. The weak links. Every last one of them would scuttle the mission, given half a chance.

If it was up to me none of them would ever wake up again. But Chimp reminds me of the obvious: a mission built for aeons, the impossibility of anticipating even a fraction of the obstacles we're bound to encounter. The need for *flexibility*, for the wet sloppy intelligence that long-dead engineers excluded from his architecture in the name of mission stability. Billions of years ahead of us, perhaps, and only a few thousand meat sacks to deal with the unexpected. There may not be enough of us as it is.

And yet, with all that vaunted human intellect, Hakim can't see the obvious. None of them can. I'm not even human to those humans. A subroutine, he says. A lobe in something else's brain. But I don't need his fucking pity. He'd realize that if he thought about it for more than a split-second, if he was willing to examine that mountain of unexamined assumptions he calls a worldview.

He won't, though. He refuses to look into the mirror long enough to see what's looking back. He can't even tell the difference between brain and brawn. The Chimp drives the ship; the Chimp builds the jump gates; the Chimp runs life support. We try to take the reins of our own destiny and it's the Chimp who hammers us down.

So the Chimp is in control. The Chimp is always in control; and when minds merge across this high-bandwidth link in my head, surely it will be the mech that absorbs the meat.

It astonishes me that he can't see the fallacy. He knows the Chimp's synapse count as well as I do, but he'd rather fall back on prejudice than run the numbers.

I'm not the Chimp's subroutine at all.

The Chimp is mine.

Maelstrom

By Kevin Ikenberry

Jaret Vralik loved to open media interviews with the story where he'd hugged a utility pole at three-hundred and fifty kilometers an hour and lived. Smiling, his blond hair combed away from his face, tanned and fit in his close-fitting Kevlar jumpsuit, Jaret spread his arms and said, "It was right there and I just grabbed onto it for a second. When you're riding a monster twister, you never know what you're going to see! You're just trying to stay alive!"

The pretty blond reporter did her part, smiling and leaning closer. "So what's it really like? Flying inside a tornado?"

Jaret winked and leaned closer. "Honey, there ain't nothing about it that's flying." He let it drawl out a little, sounding like every pilot since Chuck Yeager made it famous. "It's like riding an angry cobra. I'm just holding on with everything I've got."

"So it's dangerous then?"

"Deadly." Jaret grinned. "But you have to remember that I'm a professional with years of experience going for me. I'm the only big tornado rider on Earth right now, so I'm the perfect candidate to go to Epsilon Eridani b. I'm proud to be part of the mission."

The reporter smiled. "So, the Space Consortium is not bringing you along as a publicity stunt?"

Jaret forced a chuckle. *What was her name again? She's kind of cute.* "Not at all. There is a considerable amount of scientific data I can gather from a very unique perspective."

"Everyone knows about the nine-month storm cycle on Epsilon Eridani b. We've had only one successful colony expedition land safely in three attempts. If it's too risky to land, logic says it's more dangerous to have you jump into planet-wide storm system. This sounds like the perfect opportunity for an adrenaline-seeking thrill jockey to pad his resume at the expensive of Earth's tax paying citizens."

Jaret stopped smiling. "What are you—"

"The Charon Sentinel is reporting from sources close to the expedition that you're planning no less than three separate exojumps through megacyclones. How much will those jumps cost?"

Going to Charon had been a mistake, and having a fling with a holonews reporter disastrous. "I don't have those figures in front of me."

"I do," the reporter smiled brightly. "Ten trillion Euros, Mister Vralik. Is the data you're promising to gather worth such cost?"

Emily. That's her name. "My jumps will ultimately save lives. Epsilon Eridani b has the most volatile atmospheric conditions ever observed on a rocky planet. You said yourself that only one in four landing attempts has been successful. Unless we learn about these storms, our colonies risk crash landings. If they happen to survive the landing, we have to help them live on the planet! Nobody can go outside for half their year, and when the storms die down, it's too cold to farm, fish, or enjoy their planet. If we can give them data to help them cope with the conditions and make the most out of their expedition, we'll have done our job. That's the essence of the mission."

The blonde sat back and seemed to relax a bit. Jaret wondered if she was married. The married ones always flirted the most. "Now, I've learned a little about your instrument pack. Let me see what I can remember?"

She was good. "Absolutely."

"You'll be able to determine wind speed and direction, wind shear and divergent velocities, atmospheric composition, pressure, temperature, solar radiation intensity, water vapor analysis, cloud density and composition, and electrical activity. Is that everything?"

Jaret grinned. "That about sums it up."

"Not quite."

Jaret looked through her smile to eyes that were hard blue steel dots staring back at him. *What could she know?* Putting on a grin he knew would fail, Jaret replied, "What's that, Emily?"

"This is the fourth iteration of your data pack, is that right?"

"Yes, the first version flew successfully three years ago."

"And how long did you test the instrument pack? It's heavy, ungainly, and hard to fly. Didn't you say that?"

Jaret chuckled. "Four years ago. We've made significant improvements since then."

"Under what kinds of conditions?" Emily crossed her legs and Jaret had a hard time not gawking at them.

"We've flown the pack successfully in seventeen test flights including Afghan sandstorms, EF-5 tornados, and a Category Five hurricane two years ago. The system is as refined as we could make it."

"And what about your first tornado test? Into an EF-4 tornado near Wellington, Kansas in August of 2069? What can you tell me about that?"

Jaret reeled and heat rushed into his face. "What about that test?"

"It was the first time you attempted to attach the pack as a part of your jumpsuit, right? A very important test flight you deemed necessary for your partner, Kristen Smalls, to make in your place. Isn't that right?"

Panic crept up Jaret's spine in icy rivulets. "At that point, our testing showed the gear was ready."

"Five years ago, how many tornadoes had you jumped into?"

"Six," Jaret said.

"How many had Kristen Smalls jumped into?"

"None."

"So you sent an untrained tornado jumper into a powerful tornado with unproven gear? Can you explain that decision?"

Jaret took a deep breath, brushed at his right ear, and said, "Kristen had hundreds of hours in tunnel simulations. She flew more with the pack in the tunnel than I did while we tested the gear. To suggest she was untrained is blatantly false."

The reporter leaned in for the kill. "Then tell me why you decided to let her fly into that tornado, Mister Vralik. Was it fear? Uncertainty? Why Kristen Smalls?"

Jaret let out a long slow breath. "You had to know her."

The lone fish-eyed portal in Gossamer's airlock door lied. At one hundred kilometers above the surface, Epsilon Eridani b's atmosphere was calm and pleasant. Jaret saw the slender crescent of the planet's horizon clearly outlined in grays and blues against the black of space. Somewhere down there, the maelstrom waited. Jaret flexed his hands into the exojump stanchions that would hold him in place when the door slid open. Eyes on the distant horizon, Jaret ran the power up sequence with his eyes on the inside of his visor. Data began to populate almost immediately.

"Control, I have full start on all data systems."

"Roger, Birdman. Standby for decompression."

The pressure icon began to blink as the airlock door opened a fraction of a centimeter. His suit readings didn't budge. "All systems nominal."

"Thirty seconds to drop. Handing you over to Ground Control. Good luck, Birdman."

Jaret chuckled. There were worse nicknames. "Roger, switching comms to Ground Control." Using his lower lip, he cued the suits receiver and listened.

"Birdman *hzzzzzz* control *zzz* conditions are *hzzzzz* improving. Go for drop *hzzzzz*."

As expected, the tight-band communications were spotty. When the eye of one of Epsilon Eridani b's mini-cyclones passed over the ground station in three minutes, there would be uninterrupted communications until Jaret penetrated the deepest parts of the storm. *How could a simple storm have so much impact?* Jaret blinked the thoughts away. *Fly straight and true. Let everyone else worry about the data.*

The airlock door opened fully and Jaret looked down. Epsilon Eridani b bared her fury up to nearly twenty-seven thousand meters. Dark gray clouds swirled counter-clockwise around a twelve-hundred kilometer wide eye. The low pressure system would have stretched from Los Angeles to Adelaide. Around the perimeter of the storm, multiple smaller eddies swirled opposite the megastorm's rotation, each with winds at least as strong as the fiercest storms on Earth. The megastorm's eye was nearly over the ground station. They'd have twelve hours of peace and quiet, Jaret would have twelve minutes of hell. Selecting an eddy, Jaret locked the storm's position in his navigation set and tried to calm himself.

Knees buckling, Jaret tried to laugh. Exojumps were so much easier than the traditional method. He'd not been afraid like this since that first jump. *Take it easy. Just another jump.*

A sheet of purple lightning rippled across the breadth of the target storm. Fingers of electricity danced outward across the cloud tops. Grounded to more than two million kilojoules, a lightning strike wouldn't kill him.

It might just curl your hair.

Kristen's voice jumped up from memory, demanding attention. He'd not thought of her since his last mission interview.

Stop worrying, Jaret! I'll be fine.

More lightning danced below Jaret's feet as the jump light turned red. Fifteen seconds to drop. Closing his eyes, Jaret tried to pray, but the memory was too strong and his heart ached. *It should have been me, Kristen.*

The Vralik Aerospace vans roared off the Kansas Turnpike onto Highway One-Sixty to the west, heading toward Wellington. They stopped for gas on the edge of town and, with police escort, skirted downtown crossing a series of railroad tracks and passed a golf course before breaking out into the countryside again. Jaret was driving the lead van. The storm was now twenty-two kilometers to the west and just south of the town of Argonia. Moving northeast at ninety kilometers per hour, Kristen worked on the computers to find a suitable intercept point. The dark sky reached high enough to block the sun, starkly contrasting the eastern horizon of clear blue skies. Jaret tingled in anticipation. "This is gonna be a big one!"

Legs curled under her on the front seat, Kristen tapped on her tablet computer. "Norman is reporting a tornado on the ground southwest of Argonia." The National Severe Storms Tracking Laboratory in Norman, Oklahoma was both a familiar haunt of theirs, and a partner for this mission.

"Can you see it on Doppler?"

Doppler radar showed storm relative velocities among other things. Where there were divergent, or shearing, winds, tornadoes were likely. Most of the time, these conditions settled at the extreme southern end of storms like the one ahead in an area where the forward velocity of the storm created a vortex of swirling winds coming from the rear quarter of the storm. On a Doppler radar set, that would appear as a hook. Kristen whistled through her teeth. "Big nasty hook echo on it. Looks like it's gonna be a big one. I'm guessing a three or four."

The Enhanced Fujita scale measured winds above the traditional Beaufort scale. A minimal strength storm, with winds around one hundred and sixty kilometers per hour, registered as an EF-0. Devastating tornadoes, like the Greensburg and Tuscaloosa storms, were EF-5s with winds in excess of three hundred and fifty kilometers per hour. The kind of storm to literally wipe humanity off the face of the Earth. "Got an intercept point?"

"Yep." Kristen grinned. "Winds aloft are looking around three hundred already, so it's nearly a four now. Let's do it."

Jaret started to respond, but Kristen sat down her tablet and bounded through the space between the front seats to the rear of the van. "What are you doing?"

"This one is mine."

"I don't think so, Kristen." He looked up into the rear-view mirror. "It's too big."

Kristen was already tugging the jumpsuit on. "I'm taking this one, Jaret."

"Not for your first jump, babe."

She snorted and zipped up the Kevlar suit to her navel. "Your first was a five, Jaret."

"It's not the tornado, Kristen. It's the pack. We haven't flown it—"

"I've flown it more in the tunnel than you have."

"Yeah, but—"

"No buts." Kristen finished zipping up the suit and started tying back her long brown hair. Their eyes met in the mirror. Her girlish smile was there, but her eyes were different. Focused. Serious. "My jump."

Jaret knew the look. "First sign of trouble, you bail out and pop that chute."

"Anything else, coach?" She crept over the gear and hugged him from behind.

"Don't hesitate."

The airlock light clicked from red to green and Jaret pulled his hands from the stanchions. Falling face first, Jaret sucked in a quick gasp at the swirling storm beneath him before tumbling so that he could see Gossamer's tail rip overhead. Spreading arms and legs, Jaret settled into the descent. "Control, I'm stable in position one. Clock shows descent time is twelve minutes, thirty-two seconds. Altitude is a shade over ninety-six kilometers. All systems are functioning nominally."

"Roger, Birdman. Enjoy your flight." Like he was flying from Dallas to La Guardia. Not ninety kilometers straight down.

"Roger that." Jaret replied. He was committed now, and plotting his entry point became a high priority. Ideally, a buffer zone existed between the swirling eddies and the megastorm where winds would only be in the four to five hundred kilometer an hour range. As the storm rotated under him like a massive circular saw blade, Jaret used his targeting cursor to pinpoint a likely spot and adjust his course. Pulling his arms to his sides triggered glide panels to deploy between his thighs and under his arms. Accelerating now, and with his suit generating more than its fair share of lift, Jaret slid into a perfect descent angle of thirty-seven degrees to maintain maneuverability and speed when he would reach vortex interface.

So much easier than laying face down in a field. Or standing up. The flash of memory was enough to make Jaret shake his helmeted head.

Get down, Kristen!

From a kilometer and a half away, all Jaret could see was the flashing strobe light mounted to the top of Kristen's helmet. That was the problem. In a perfect intercept point, surrounded by six hectares of corn, Kristen should be lying down with her head about ninety degrees off the predicted path of the twister. Jaret shouldn't have seen her at all. She was standing up.

"Get down, Kristen!"

The radio crackled. "I can't see it coming. I need to be able to adjust."

"You're not gonna be able to adjust to anything! Get on your stomach, head away from the path!" Jaret roared. "You're a target for debris or a lightning strike!"

"A strike won't kill me," Kristen laughed. "Might curl my hair."

The distance from her to the twister now less than six hundred meters. The twister was fifteen or twenty seconds away. "You're green for intercept. Lay down and let it pick you up."

"I'm gonna stand. I'll turn my back."

"No!" Four hundred meters. "You're in the debris zone now. Lay down!"

"You wanted to test a standing deployment, Jaret."

"Not today." The distance display clicked to two hundred meters. "Not with you."

"Stop worrying. I'll be fine."

The giant black wedge tore through the tree line a kilometer from Kristen. Jaret didn't have time to say anything as the snarling darkness swept into the cornfield. Kristen's strobe lifted suddenly, blinking twice before disappearing around the curve of the vortex.

Passing seventy-five thousand meters, everything looked as promising as Jaret could have hoped except for the dark gray clouds billowing and swirling below. Tweaking his position with subtle rolls of his shoulders and hips, Jaret flew an imaginary track displayed on his visor to the heart of his target.

"Birdman, Ground Control. We're in the eye now, and reading your telemetry perfectly. How copy?"

Jaret replied. "Right on time, Ground. I'm ready to start recorded observation when you are."

"Roger, Birdman. You're live in five seconds."

Jaret counted slowly before switching his transmitter on. "Hello, this is Jaret Vralik. I'm currently passing sixty-seven thousand meters above Epsilon Eridani b. I've got about five minutes of flight until I reach the cloud tops. Do the math and you'll see I'm traveling more than a football field every second. Not too bad for a guy in a Kevlar suit."

Jaret licked his lips. Science time. "All instruments are sending data to both flight and ground control as we speak. There's too much of it for me to follow, but let me give you the low down. Up here the temperature is cold enough to freeze me solid without my suit. The air pressure is negligible and the flight is as smooth as you can imagine. I won't be able to say that in a few minutes. Once I reach the cloud tops I won't have time enough for anything other than trying to fly. Let me turn on the cameras and show you what I'm talking about."

Focusing on a swirling eddy off the main storm, Jaret said. "That's my target. It might not look like much, but the eye you see in the middle of the storm is about ten kilometers across. Winds at my target are about five hundred kilometers per hour. That's calm for one of Epsilon Eridani b's monsters. Let me pan north and you'll see what I mean."

The swirling edge of the megastorm dominated the horizon. "The eye of the megastorm to the north is more than one hundred and thirty kilometers wide. The winds in the eye wall are upwards of eleven hundred kilometers per hour. Along the cloud tops, the megastorm is rotating faster than the speed of sound. On the Enhance Fujita scale, that would be an EF-10. Thankfully, we don't get anything like that on Earth.

"Here on Epsilon Eridani b, the result is massive destruction. The only flora that can survive these conditions are mosses and fungi that can get in the crevices and rocks of the surface below. If we can figure out what makes these storms get so powerful, the hope is that we can actually reduce their intensity and allow this planet to be successfully colonized. Without the storms, the planet is very much like Earth. On Earth we only occasionally see Class Five hurricanes and EF-5 rated tornadoes."

Kristen's strobe disappearing into the tornado swam back to his mind. "Usually."

The sudden whooping over the radio let him know that Kristen was alive. A full twenty seconds passed from the disappearance of the strobe to her joyful screaming. "Speed is three sixty one, and altitude is one thousand two hundred AGL. Pack is nominal at position two." In a maximal lift position, Kristen would be ascending quickly, gaining as much as one hundred and fifty meters per minute above ground level.

Jaret grinned. "What can you see?"

"Not much right now. There was some big stuff down low. Ducked around a couple of trees. It's clearer up here."

Jaret's control console beeped. "What's your speed reading up there?"

"Four hundred and twenty. We're at EF-5 now! First woman!"

"Save it for landing, Kristen. Give me thirty seconds of data and then bail out."

She didn't respond for a few seconds. Jaret nearly keyed the radio again. "Speed is four sixty! Four seventy!"

Jaret keyed the radio. "Kristen, bail, bail, bail!"

"Not yet!" Static burst into the conversation coinciding with a flash of lightning. "You're getting the data right?"

"All of it." Sweat stung Jaret's eyes. "Now get out of there!" The control console showed the impossible dream, a tornado swirling at over four hundred and fifty kilometers per hour. Driving parallel to the storm on the deserted highway, Jaret fingered the radio button. "Kristen?"

"Holy shit! Five hundred! My speed is Five hundred! It's an EF-6! Do you read me?"

Jaret's heart raced like a jackhammer. "Bail, Kristen. Get out of there. The storm is eight kilometers from Conway Springs. When it gets there at that strength there's no telling how high the debris will get. You've done enough! Bail out!"

"Roger. Crossing inner boundary heading *hzzzzzzz*."

"Kristen? Say again?"

"*Hzzzzzzz…* bailing now."

Jaret stopped the van hard enough to smoke the tires and brakes. Scanning the sky, Jaret dismounted the van and stepped out towards the storm with his eyes skyward. The strobe came out of the wall cloud north of the storm and about one thousand meters off the ground. Shooting from the vortex like a cannonball the light streaked away from the storm on a long arc, hesitated for a moment, and then began to tumble.

Jaret spared a last look up at *Gossamer* orbiting above his entry point. "Thirty seconds to interface. Cloud base is at four thousand meters. We'll pick up voice then. Good luck. Ground control out."

At Ground Control, colony settlement known as Keystone, the weather was calm for the first time in weeks. Storm season was nearly over, a four-month long respite from the storms as the planet rotated to give Keystone a brief, cold winter. The storms would move to the southern hemisphere, where no colonies had been successful in landing. Jaret couldn't imagine a place where the storms could be worse than this. *And these people want to live here.* Jaret shook his head in admiration. Maybe they'd generate enough data to find a way to negate the formation of megastorms, continent-wide lightning, and frightening wind speeds. Maybe it would make a difference.

The first shear slammed Jaret out of his stable descent posture like a feather. Tumbling, Jaret snapped to the familiar stable one position like a terrestrial skydiver and righted himself. *Here we go*, he thought as the gray clouds reached up to grab him and hell swallowed him whole.

Winds are six-seventy-three, twenty-six thousand seven hundred meters. Is this an EF-7? EF-8? His shoulders rolled as air currents shook him in all directions at once. *Visibility nil, all telemetry nominal. Approach posture is good. Ground speed is six twenty.* The air cleared for a moment, a layer within a layer of clouds at twenty-three thousand seven hundred meters. Jaret relaxed a little and took a deep breath.

The microburst slammed into his back with no warning. Alarms sounded from the pack. His descent rate almost twelve kilometers per minute and the hammerblow of air wouldn't let up. The glide panels between his legs tore away, as did the panel under his left arm. Back to a stable free fall position, there would be no more gliding.

The altimeter bleeped its first warning at fifteen thousand meters. Jaret finally righted himself by tearing away the glide panel under his right arm. Under control, chest raised, he began to slow.

"Microburst," Jaret spoke into the mission recorder. "Pressure differential was huge. Lost two of three glide panels, had to tear away the other. Pack is okay, all instruments functioning."

There was nothing more he could do. Turning his shoulders toward the center of the swirling eddy and calmer winds, Jaret abandoned the experiment. Another burst at a lower altitude and he would be eating rocks. *Not today*, he thought with a grin. *Always know when and how to get out of Dodge.*

Kristen's readings didn't make sense. The pack showed a constant speed of nearly five hundred and twenty kilometers an hour, but the gimbals swung wildly, as if the pack was tumbling. The strobe on Kristen's helmet was clearly accelerating under gravity away from the vortex. Friction or drag or a combination of both should be slowing her down some, even if she were tumbling. *Unless...*

Jaret began to run in the direction of the falling strobe. The three kilometer wide tornado churned to the northeast and tore through farmland. The strobe arced downward without a shred of control. Impact came a few seconds later, far enough away that Jaret could not see or hear it. Realization that she was dead crashed onto his shoulders and drove Jaret Vralik to his knees.

It was his fault. The pack rated more than five hundred kilometers an hour in testing. Those conditions were benign compared to an actual twister. The pack must have failed. The loss of radio communication meant that the leads tore away from Kristen's helmet when the pack failed. Along with the instruments and the radio was the parachute. Without the pack, Kristen had no chance.

The first recorded EF-6 became the most famous tornado in history. Jaret and Kristen were heroes for the data the jump recorded, and Kristen became an overnight media sensation, posthumously. A picture of Jaret kneeling, crying, by her casket won the Pulitzer Prize.

Kristen was nominated for the Nobel Prize, and received the Presidential Medal of Freedom. A blockbuster motion picture was made with the title taken from Kristen's chosen epitaph: "IT WAS WORTH IT!"

The dark grey maelstrom cleared and Jaret gathered his wits. Survival would take every ounce of his skill and considerable luck. Out of the clouds at three thousand three hundred meters, Jaret tried to get as much glide as possible without his panels. The weight of the pack meant he wasn't getting anywhere near the amount of lift, and that meant he'd land short of the center of the eddy. Had the suit held up he'd not be gliding into dangerous terrain short of the drop zone. He would have flared three hundred meters off the ground, activated his chute and landed as close to the armored recover vehicles as possible. That wasn't going to happen now.

Two and a half thousand meters and just over twenty seconds to impact. Jaret knew that in fifteen seconds, he'd have one chance to fire the carbon filament parachute. In five hundred kilometer per hour winds and a rain-wrapped twister the size of Rhode Island somewhere behind him. *God help me.*

Fourteen.

Thirteen. I hope you're right, Kristen.

Eleven.

Ten.

Nine.

Eight.

I'm so sorry, love.

Five. Fire chutes!

Three. All open. Brace for-

Zero.

Jaret slammed into the granite escarpment with a wet thud. His right leg snapped in multiple places, his right lung collapsed under broken ribs, and his helmet cracked down the center in the milliseconds between impact and when he came to rest. Adrenaline coursed through his body, enough that he was able to crawl three meters to the relative shelter of a rock outcropping. His parachute tore away under the force of the wind. Off to his left, the monster storm barrelled across the horizon. Thankful for small miracles, Jaret activated his recovery beacon. Rescue would be delayed by his position and the strength of the storm.

Under the eave of rocks, Jaret panted and scrolled through some of the pack's data. Even smiling hurt. The data package was complete from upper atmosphere to impact. By quick analysis Jaret made two decisions: First, that no one would ever participate in extended activities on Epsilon Eridani b's surface during storm season. Second, that the amount and quality of data, combined with his injuries, made the need for subsequent jumps unnecessary.

The rain began to fall hard enough to obscure his vision more to no more than a few meters. Jaret scrolled through the pack's computer and pulled up his favorite picture of him and Kristen. In her running shorts and University of Oklahoma shirt, fresh-faced and ready for anything, Kristen was beautiful. Her arm was around Jaret's neck. They'd kissed a moment before the picture was taken at the gas station outside Wellington by a wild-eyed man who smelled of gasoline. The kiss had been clumsy, like first kisses tend to be. The second kiss as infinitely better, except it was their last. Six hours after the photo was taken, they'd stood in that blustery cornfield near Argonia.

In the crystal clear portal of Jaret's memory, Kristen lifted her arms around his neck, and he slipped his hands behind the small of her back, underneath the instrument package as the kiss began. Jaret forgot whether or not he'd tightened down the pack and Kristen's shoulder straps as they kissed. Their lips met, tongues danced for a few seconds, and all too quickly it was over. Kristen pulled away, her wheat blond hair blowing in the wind and the tornado that would take her life looming on the horizon.

"It's worth it, Jaret. Every second of it." Kristen smiled.

Five years and twenty-three-and-a-half light years distant, Jaret Vralik huddled in a frigid alien rain against impenetrable winds and wondered.

Murder on Centauri

By Robert J. Mendenhall

Captain Christopher Manning pulled the goggles from his face and steadied the sonic-rifle on the snow-berm, bringing the digital night scope to his eyes. The joints of his servo-frame whirred at each of his movements as the sophisticated exoskeleton surrounding his limbs and torso compensated for the crushing pull of gravity 3.17 times Earth normal.

The cold bite of alien snow cut through the layers of Manning's thermal utility uniform, chilling him despite the suit's military-grade insulated material. The high mineral content of the planet's thick atmosphere gave its precipitation a pale yellow tinge and the distinct odor of spoiled eggs. The urge to retch was constant when he was outside, even more so when he lay prone in the sand-colored snow, his face only inches from it.

The scope's cross hairs focused, then flashed a sharp green as they locked onto the figure's head, fifteen hundred meters away. Manning didn't need the weapon's enhancements to see the reddish glow of the cigarette, even from the icy bluff overlooking the compound. The ice crystals of the predawn mist acted as tiny lens, reflecting and intensifying the pinprick of light until it glittered like a holiday sparkler.

The figure below was clad in standard-issue fatigues and furry parka beneath a servo-frame like Manning's. Manning couldn't make out who it was, but guessed it was a man by the size and build, and the way the cigarette was held. That narrowed it down to about three hundred and fifteen, but he had a good idea who it was just from the arrogance of the security violation.

"Greco." Manning drew out the name in quiet disgust.

Greco, the chu'a—the snake.

Major Dominic Greco was the executive officer of Early Warning Station Centauri. Second-in-command. Yet there he was, violating a rule as basic as light discipline.

He watched as Greco trod awkwardly across the snow-covered quadrangle, his gait hampered by the driving wind and his bulky servo-frame. Greco's tracks led from the officer's billets, one of the dozen-and-a-half insulated Quonset huts that made up Centauri Station. As he thought of Greco coming out Alina's quarters, not Greco's own, the back of Manning's neck burned the way it always did when he became angry.

Manning's grandfather, a Navajo of the old ways, once told him his warrior spirit lived at the base of the brain, in the medulla. Most often the spirit slept. Sometimes it would speak to Manning in his dreams. But when angered…

He didn't like his warrior spirit. It reminded him of his ancestors' early history. Savage, brutal, nomadic, and predatory. So unlike the modern, benevolent Navajo of the late Twenty-First Century whose cultural evolution began its slow growth toward a pastoral lifestyle in the waning years of the 1800s.

Greco paused outside the alloy structure of the Headquarters Quonset and drew deep on the cigarette. The embers flared with the long drag, glistening and cascading off the mist crystals. Greco flicked the butt into the mist and watched it rocket to the ground.

That son-of-a-bitch.

Manning steadied the barrel on the berm, raised the scope again and locked onto the smoldering cigarette at Greco's feet. The weapon gave a soft, unremarkable puff when it fired, jumping just a bit in recoil. The round hit the snow with a dull report, and while the explosive force of the ultrasonic bullet expanded only a few centimeters, the concussion blew clumpy snow several meters in all directions.

Greco jerked back in surprise, nearly toppling over in the servo-frame. He flattened his body against the chilled metal of the hut and twitched his head back and forth, searching the distance for the source. He glanced up toward the bluff, stared a moment, then turned and darted into the hut.

Manning rolled onto his back and looked up into the dark, early-morning sky, letting the perpetual cloud cover work on his stress with its monotony. The servo-frame allowed him to move in the dense surface gravity, but it didn't nullify the unrelenting influence of the planet's massive core. His body weight was still more than three times normal when he was outside, and it exhausted him just to lay flat on his back, doing nothing more than sucking in the stinking air. He still felt the insane pull on his organs and blood.

The servo-frame whirred quietly as he reached into his thigh pocket and pulled out the fist-sized, turquoise talisman he always carried. He fingered the carving absently, not feeling its lines through his thick glove, but sensing its shape and creamy texture, nonetheless.

His father had passed the talisman down to him the day Manning left Earth, reminding him of its history and importance. It had been in his family for generations and held great traditional value, even to Christopher Ahiga Manning, who had never completely embraced the old ways.

He hated night watch. He hated the entire planet, for that matter. Spending most of his life in the scorching desert of the North American Southwest, cold and snow had been only vague, intangible ideas. But here on Centauri, the super-gravity and the constant cold and the reeking snow continually reminded him he was far from the Navajo Reservation and no longer a tribal policeman.

No, he was here. On Centauri. The fourth planet circling the primary star of the Alpha Centauri binary and an exacting, hostile place. A super-Earth with more than three times the gravity of home. The planet lay just within the binary's habitable zone, but only just. More months were spent in winter than the other three seasons combined. Centauri's strong magnetic field caused havoc with external electronics, reducing surface surveillance to low-tech labor.

To be sure, Centauri was not the vacation getaway of the galaxy. But they had to be here. Absolutely had to.

For Manning, the alien snow was the planet's worst attribute, more so than the high gravity. The color he could almost live with; it often resembled the dusty New Mexican wasteland he had grown up on. But he had never become accustomed to the constant odor. During the morning fogs and frequent snow-squalls, when the mineral-rich moisture condensed and plummeted fresh from the sky, the stench was so pungent it could turn a steel stomach. And often did.

And this damn cloud cover never broke. He hadn't seen a star in, Gods, how long was it? Nearly five years now. *Five years*. After the thirteen-month FTL trip to Alpha Centauri, he thought he'd had his fill of looking at stars. But now, weeks before his tour was up, he was eager to look at them again. COMM had made contact with the transport last week and it was right on schedule, carrying supplies, new personnel, and a return berth with his name on it. He closed his eyes…

The transport enters orbit, trumpets blaring. Confetti drifts down through the atmosphere. He stands on the hull of the surface-to-orbit shuttle as it rises to meet the transport, his hands firmly on his hips, oblivious to the icy cold and wind and gravitational grip. Above him, the mustard clouds part and scores of monstrous raco-dons descend and circle the shuttle as if in escort, their bulbous, hydrogen-filled belly's and long, leathery wings keeping them aloft. Below him, the six hundred plus personnel of Centauri Station wave frantically at him in good-wishing tribute. And then, Alina breaks free of the crowd and calls to him, her rich Russian voice cutting through the cheers. "Please take me with you, Christopher, I beg of you!" He smiles gratuitously and nods to her. She rises from the ground, the wind tossing her auburn hair, pasting her chiffon nightdress to her firm body—

A sudden gust of wind blew a loose clump of moist snow onto his face, stinging his exposed cheeks. His nostrils flared. He shook the fantasy away, and turned over.

The mist was dense and he could see the squall beginning. Soon the snowfall would be driving. Visibility would be near zero, and the air would stink even more.

He pulled his field glasses from the gear bag, set the mode to NIGHT and scanned the area. The image in the glasses was as clear as the night-scope of his rifle, but more panoramic and augmented with luminescent compass points and distance indicators.

He focused on Post One, the only structure on the entire north face of the quad. Through the blowing snow, he could still make out the sign next to the door.

HEADQUARTERS
359th COMMUNICATIONS DETACHMENT
15th SIGNAL DIVISION, FORWARD
UNITED NATIONS DEFENSE FORCE
EARLY WARNING STATION CENTAURI

The rest of the quadrangle was quiet and dark, although the dining facility on the narrow east end would be busy soon enough as the mess crew shuffled in to prepare breakfast. But, in the stink of the churning snow, the thought of eggs was repulsive.

He scanned the south side of the quadrangle, and the row of Quonsets. There was no activity at the NCO Quarters, and both double-story Enlisted Barracks were quiet as well. Likewise, the Rec Hall was dark. Manning focused on the far hut, the Officer's Billets, and on one blacked-out window in particular.

What are you doing now, Alina? Sleeping? Bathing? Oh, the thought of her wet…

Reluctantly, he shifted his focus to the west end and the Medical Center. It, too, was dark, but even money said Han was there. Doctor Hannah Lang maintained a room in the Med Center, often preferring to sleep there rather than in her own billet. She hated the servo-frames. And as long as the buried gird-work of the counter-gravity generators were able to siphon off two-thirds of the planet's gravitational field, essentially providing an Earth-normal gravity environment in the Med Center, she was content to remain there.

CG-Gens required a massive amount power, in fact 78% of the total energy output of the station's nuclear reactor was distributed to the CG-Gen grid-work. There wasn't an erg to spare for much else, so only the living quarters and the daily-use work facilities were equipped with them. But, they provided relief for the high-gravity and freedom from the servo-frames. Manning was ever-thankful for that.

He scanned past Post One to the large structure behind it. The COMM Center was why they were there, to scan deep space for any indication of the Threat. COMM was nothing more than a series of cargo containers strapped together to hold the sensitive early-warning sensor equipment and FTL hyper wave communication instruments. Two huge dish antennae and a large microwave tower to receive data from the orbiting Hubble-Sagan sensor array, were surrounded by a low-tech fence made of coils of barbed concertina wire.

Manning shifted his sights north of COMM and keyed in the tele-photo mode. But four kilometers from the base proper, the supply hut, machine shop, and hanger were too far to be seen in the rapidly degrading weather. Berthed inside the hanger, along with a couple of ground skimmers and a dozen or so tracked snow-sliders, was the surface-to-orbit shuttle which would bus him and about half of the assigned personnel to the transport vessel when it finally achieved far orbit. He would be inside the shuttle, of course, not riding it bareback.

Manning picked up the perimeter fence (chain-link and more concertina) and inspected it one meter at a time. He scanned section after section of the fence, as he did yesterday and the day before—twisted, heavily oxidized, rolling coils of barbed wire—each section the same as the one before.

The fence was necessary to keep the local wildlife out. Occasionally, one of the mountainous brontos would stray from their herd and wander toward the base. Mostly vegetarians, the brontos were not aggressive; the greatest danger was being trampled beneath one of the creature's massive legs. Occasionally, a bronto would get caught in the exterior concertina and Manning would have to send a squad out to cut it loose. The creature had the most gut-wrenching moan, like a rabbit in pain only a few octaves lower and a few hundred decibels higher.

The fence was also meant to keep out the local humanoid life.

His eyesight softened from the constant monotony. His attention waned. Several seconds went by before what he had seen registered. When it did, his body went rigid.

He whipped the glasses back, searching up and down the fence line until he found it. There. A gap in the fence. He zoomed closer and focused. It was a split, all right. And spread apart. The concertina outside the fence line had also been cut and spread.

Unbelievable.

Something had gained entry to the base and it was a safe bet it wasn't a bronto.

Manning reached for his throat and applied pressure, activating his vocal communicator implant. He heard an electronic chirp in the cranial receiver behind his left ear.

"Reager from Manning," he said over the wind as he searched for the intruders.

"Reager here." The reply was immediate and so clear he could easily pick out Sergeant Bobby Reager's Texas drawl.

"You're not going to believe this, but we have a perimeter breech, east side, north of COMM."

"You shittin' me, Cap'n? A breach?"

"What's your position?"

"I'm on post at the hanger, sir."

"Got 'em." Manning zoomed in on the small group. "Looks like three of them. Locals." He winced at his own callous reference to the planet's inhabitants. He hated the label, thought it was derogatory. Like Injun.

"L-Locals? Here?"

"They're heading…" He paused to check their direction. "Heading north by northwest from their entry point."

"What do they want, anyway, Cap'n? They've never bothered us before."

"Haven't a clue just yet. Looks like they're heading up by you. Not directly, though. Where's Josef?"

"Post One with the Staff Duty Officer."

"Valentic from Manning." *Chirp.*

"This is Sergeant Valentic, Captain." The Yugoslavian's booming voice made him sound as huge as he actually was.

"We have an unauthorized entry. Three Centaurans. On foot, just north of COMM, on a northwesterly course."

"Are they armed?" Valentic asked, his Slavic accent pronounced with his excitement.

Manning zoomed closer, but the blowing snow obscured his vision. "Can't tell. Looks like they're carrying short staffs of some sort."

"Could they be rifles?" asked Valentic.

"I don't think so. I don't see any trigger mechanisms. Hard to tell in this weather."

"What's the plan?" Reager asked.

"Josef. Come up behind them, but stay out of sight until I signal. Bobby, circle around and get in front of them. Pace them but stay out of their sight. It'll take me a bit to get off the bluff. I'll come through the west gate, then we'll close on them."

"Roger, Cap'n."

"On the way."

"Disconnect." *Chirp*

Manning took a last look at the Centaurans, noting the coordinates displayed on the lenses by the glasses' focal computer. He jumped to his feet and stuffed the glasses into his side bag.

Manning trotted away from the edge of the bluff to the sleek, tracked vehicle nearby, the joint motors in his servo-frame sounding like rapid-fire swipes of a bow across the strings of a double base. He opened the canopy and slid inside, dropping his sonic rifle onto the rear bench. Once the canopy was closed, the machine's environmental logic came on and warm air hissed toward him. Wanting to stay equalized with the outside temperature, though, Manning overrode the logic.

The machine powered up quickly, humming with nuclear life at the press of his gloved finger. The steering column extended from its recess in the dash and Manning gripped the split-wheel firmly. With slight pressure on the thumb-activated throttles, the snow-slider shot forward.

His tracks were long since covered by the wind-blown snow and, in the moonless, cloud-shrouded night, it was too dark to navigate visually. He reached for the instrument panel and activated the navigational logic. Instantly, a heads-up display flashed onto the canopy in front of him. It showed a trail of snow-covered radio beacons, highlighting a path along the bluff to a steep, but manageable slope. He applied more thumb pressure to accelerate and turned the vehicle toward the invisible trail.

He guided the snow-slider down the slope to the valley below. The driving snow against the canopy would obscure his sight momentarily, until the electrically-heated canopy evaporated the moisture. The navigational logic, still keyed into the beacons' transmissions, provided a precise path, but if anything was on that path, the slider would plow right over it. Manning reduced the speed to forty kilometers per hour and hoped another group of Centaurans wasn't in his way.

The humans avoided interaction with the Centaurans whenever possible. Since the initial landing and construction of the base over twenty years ago, there had been only a few indirect contacts with them. On each occasion, the primitive Centaurans had shown great fear of the humans.

The initial reconnaissance of the nearby village had provided them with limited intelligence information. The Centaurans were humanoid, in as much as that they possessed a torso, head, two legs and two arms as humans do. But, they were stocky and short, with thick, muscular limbs honed by the powerful gravity. Opposable thumbs, but only three fingers on each hand, not four. Mono-racial. Male and female genders. They were pre-industrial. Their population was scattered over the small planet into villages. Each village appeared politically autonomous, although bonded by a strong, common religion. There was very little travel or trade between the individual villages. There appeared to be a common language, but so far the linguists at Centauri Station had not been able to decipher it.

The snow-slider approached the west gate of the perimeter fence. The heads-up display showed the path of the beacons as it led to a graphic representation of the barbed gate. Manning slowed the slider even more and keyed the remote transmitter on the dash to open the gate.

He opened the canopy and felt the biting rush of frigid air swirl inside the tiny cabin. He shivered involuntarily, steeled himself for the icy wind, and stood, the steering column extending with his reach.

Behind the unrelenting cloud cover, the distant sun of the Alpha Centauri primary had begun its lazy dawning, and the horizon now glowed a deep mustard color. There was enough light, even with the blowing flurries, for Manning to see the outline of the fence and the open gate just ahead of him. He guided the slider through the gate and into the compound. When the gate had automatically secured behind him, he crouched back inside and closed the canopy. He pressed his throat.

"Connect Reager, Valentic." The complant logic, triggered by the keyword 'connect' and the subjects, Reager and Valentic, linked the three together in a communication web. "This is Manning. I'm inside."

"Reager, here, Cap'n. I've got the Locals in sight. They seem to be unsure of where they're goin' or maybe they're lost. They've gone around in a big circle."

"What's their exact position?"

"Grid coordinates…" In his implant, Manning could hear Reager's map-pad chirp. "32, 19, 25 north by 84, 45, 28 west."

Manning input the numbers into the navigational logic. The canopy display went dark, then flashed a grid map of the installation, Manning's position depicted by a blinking blue point, the Locals by a flashing red one.

"Okay, got it. I'm a hundred meters due west. Josef?"

"In position, Captain."

"Standby. Disconnect Reager, Valentic."

Manning slowed the slider to a crawl and opened the canopy. Fifty meters. Thirty. Fifteen.

At ten meters he could make out the Centaurans in the eastern dawn. He gunned the engine, snapped on every spot and running light and sent the vehicle into a snow-spraying slide.

Coming from the darker west, its engine covered by the howling wind, the blazing machine seemed to appear out of nowhere—a terrible, wailing apparition.

The Centaurans screeched. One dropped his staff. The others thrashed and fell backwards. They scrambled to their feet, still screaming, but tripped again as they turned to flee.

Reager stood in their path, his tinted, windshield visor and scarf obscuring his features, his sonic rifle pointed square at them. They stumbled into each other as they tried to stop and turn away.

Valentic now stood in their path, huge and frightening with a sonic handgun leveled at them. In the squall, the servo-frame components with their yellow and black diagonal striping, and his bug-eyed goggles made Valentic look almost insectoid.

Again, abruptly changing direction, they collided. But there was Manning, his rifle sighted and drawn down on them. The three huddled together and sank to their knees, crying out in unbridled fear.

The blazing lights of the slider on the driving snow conveyed an illusion of unchecked havoc; the roar of the wind and the wailing of the frightened, fallen Centaurans was a pathetic chorus. The scene chilled Manning deeper than the frigid air.

Slowly, Manning lowered his rifle and slung the weapon over his shoulder. He approached the terrified intruders with cautious, whirring steps. Seeing him advance, they lowered their heads and cowered closer to the snow-packed ground, either oblivious to the stink or too frightened to care.

Manning stopped. This was the closest any human had ever been to a Local. Wary of frightening them further, he knelt and laid his hand on the shoulder of the nearest. The native raised his head, bewilderment on his face. Manning removed his goggles.

Sugar-white eyes against the deep, copper face drew Manning in. He focused on the dark and punctuating pupils, no more than tiny dots, and his neck tingled at the connection of first eye contact.

Seconds went by unnoticed before he pulled back to take in the rest of the Centauran's appearance. The skin had a slight satin sheen. Thick talons of rust-colored hair hung to his shoulders. His beard, the same reddish-brown as his hair, was coarse and encrusted with pale snow. His nose was pug-flat, his lips wide. His neck was as thick and solid as his legs.

Manning nick-named him 'Bearded One.'

Digging deep into his limited, nonverbal communication training, Manning brought a soft smile onto his face and nodded gently. He stood slowly and held out his hand in offering. Bearded One eyed it with confusion. Manning reached for his hand, but the Centauran jerked away.

"It's all right," Manning said over the wind. Again, he reached for the Centauran's hand and, when he met no resistance, wrapped his fingers and applied gentle pressure.

But at that contact, one of the other Local's howled and leapt to his feet. He knocked Manning to the snow. Then the third lunged.

"Look out!" Valentic shouted.

"Shoot! Shoot!" Reager called out.

"No!" Manning yelled as he grappled with the two natives. "Don't hurt them!"

Reager grabbed the nearest Local and pulled him away. Valentic reached in and grabbed the other. The Centaurans didn't provide any further resistance. Once physically restrained, they gave up their thrashing. The scuffle ended quickly, but their emotional state remained visibly volatile.

Manning got to his feet and brushed the snow from his thermal suit and servo-frame, wincing at the scent. Bearded One was still sitting on the ground, his head bowed. Manning grasped him by the shoulders and applied just enough pressure to suggest Manning wanted him to stand. The Local complied, but never looked up to Manning's face.

"Let's get them into the slider," Manning said.

"Shouldn't we bind them?" asked Reager.

Manning shook his head. "No. No cuffs."

"Okay. Whatever you say, Cap'n." Reager sounded apprehensive.

The Centaurans offered them no further resistance as, one by one, they were guided to the slider and into the cramped cockpit. Bearded One was safety-belted in the front, the other two in the back. Their eyes darted around the enclosure, looking at every strange light and switch with fear and virgin curiosity.

"You drive, Bobby. Post One."

"Okay, Cap'n." Reager slid behind the steering column. "Hang on."

Manning and Valentic perched themselves on the narrow track shields and held tightly to the open canopy as the slider shot forward. The icy wind was brutal and Manning turned his face away. Valentic, strong and massive, didn't appear the least discomforted, even with one hand holding the three unusual staffs.

Reager cut off the exterior spot lighting and guided the dark slider over the snow toward the quadrangle. After a few minutes, the silhouette of the COMM building cut into the brightening horizon. The scoops of its dish antennas were dark crescent moons in the strange light, but they were a familiar sight, and a welcome one in the blizzard.

Reager guided the slider around the COMM building to the rear of the Headquarters Quonset and the security vestibule. Manning hopped off and trotted to the steel door. He pulled off his heavy glove and slid his entire hand into a slot in the hut's outside wall, next to the door.

There were no keys on Centauri. Every soldier assigned to the station had a security access nano-chip implanted under the skin of the palm. The chip contained an identification string of binary codes specifically assigned to that chip and its sole owner, and only Manning, as Provost Marshall, or the Commanding Officer could assign those codes.

Once the scanner had read his chip, he keyed his access PIN into the adjacent pad. It was accepted by the security logic and the door clicked open.

"Put the staffs in my office, Josef, then send somebody out to guard the break until the civil engineers come on duty."

"Yes, sir."

"Bobby. Let's get them inside and out of this weather."

"O-Okay, Cap'n."

Manning pulled off his goggles and hood. He eyed Reager. "You all right, Bobby?"

"I guess. I've never been this close to a Local."

"Well, you can see they're fairly harmless. Put them in one of the holding cells until we can figure out what to do with them."

"Okay, Cap'n." Still bundled tight with his scarf and goggles, Reager led the three Centaurans into the vestibule.

Like the Med Center and all the structures used as living or daily working facilities at Centauri Station, the Headquarters Quonset was equipped with a CG-Gen. The servo-frames worn by all three military policemen automatically compensated for the change in gravitational pull from 3g outside to 1g inside.

The organic muscles of the three Centaurans did not.

The first Centauran stepped over the threshold, into the influence of the CG-Gen grid, and launched across the vestibule into the wall ten meters away. The second stepped in, saw what had happened to the first and tried to halt his motion. Instead he flew straight up three meters, struck the metal ceiling and fell back to the deck, screaming.

Bearded One stopped in mid-stride just before he crossed the threshold. He lowered his foot to the outside ground, unaffected.

"Son of a bitch," Manning cursed. It never occurred to him. This was what humans on Mars might experience if unprepared for gravity only a third of what they were used to.

Reager and Valentic struggled with their respective Centaurans. The two Locals thrashed in panic and the more they did, the more they caromed around, banging into the walls, themselves, and the humans.

A booming bellow, a sound as sudden as a canon blast, but as long and even as bass horn, stopped the Centaurans. Manning looked at Bearded One, just as the sound trailed away and his mouth closed. Manning was stunned. There was authority in that sound; it had been a command. This was their leader.

Bearded One made a motion to Manning, a lateral swipe of his thick arm in front of him, as if he were moving something aside. Manning thought he understood and stepped away from the door. Bearded One raised his left leg slowly and lowered it over the threshold. He paused, and then carefully, deliberately, stepped inside. He remained on the deck, his right leg coming down in a slow arc. He planted his right foot, staggered only slightly, and shuffled his left foot forward. Then his right, and again until he was at the side of the Valentic.

Valentic looked up at Manning. Manning nodded and Valentic stepped aside. Bearded One extended a thick hand to his comrade, and pulled him up. The motion caused the Centauran to rise slightly off the deck and his face contorted. Bearded One placed his other hand on the Centauran's shoulder and pushed him back to the deck. Manning noticed Bearded One had tensed his own legs, shifting his center of mass, just as Manning had learned to do after months in a simulator. Manning was, again, stunned.

Bearded One said something low and smooth to the Centauran, who cocked his head to one side then back to center. A Centauran nod? Bearded One released him and the Centauran remained standing. He shuffled forward a bit as Bearded One had done, stopped, then gave that sideways nod again.

Reager's Local rose on his own, shuffled a bit than stopped.

Both Centauran's looked at Bearded One. Bearded One looked at Manning, and gave that odd nod. Manning repeated the gesture, nodded once the human way. Bearded One paused a moment, then mimicked the move.

Twenty minutes later, free of his servo-frame and a steaming mug of coffee in his hand, Manning was standing outside the holding cell looking at the three intruders through the steel bars of the cell door. And now that they were in even light and free of the driving wind and snow, Manning was able to get a better sight picture of the Centaurans.

Bearded One appeared to be the eldest. The other two were clean-shaven without a trace of stubble. Their smooth and coppery skin and slightly darker hair, gave them a metallic, almost robotic look. Bearded One was the gauntest of the three, if gaunt had any meaning for bodies such as theirs.

Their clothing appeared to be tightly woven from a cotton-like fabric. The colors were an unpleasant combination of browns and reds mingled together in no predictable pattern. Their footwear was a thick, brown hide, expertly seamed to a hard sole.

Each Centauran wore a striking pendant around his neck; a fine, silvery chain supporting a highly-polished metal ornament of the same color, circled in sharp, inlaid stones. Bearded One's pendant was larger than the others, and golden in color, though Manning doubted it was real gold. When they moved, the stones glittered.

Manning glanced at their outer coverings, neatly folded and placed on the floor. The material was thin and leather-like, but if it was made from hide, Manning wondered what the animal it came from looked like. He had seen brontos and this wasn't bronto hide. He couldn't imagine it was warm enough for the outside environment. Maybe their coppery skin provided its own insulation.

He'd let them rest and, in a few hours when the storm broke, would escort them back to their village.

"Ex-O wants to see you, Cap'n," Reager said over the intercom. "He sounds pissed, sir."

Manning nodded. "I'll bet he does." He took another sip of coffee and had a thought. The Centaurans hadn't brought any provisions with them.

"Bobby, bring some water in here." No answer. Manning turned toward the one-way window behind him. "Bobby, you still there?"

"Ah…still, here, Cap'n."

"Did you hear me? Bring some water for the Centaurans."

"Yes, sir."

They stood against the back wall of the cell, ignoring the cots that had set up for them. Perhaps they were wary to move in the lighter gravity. The two clean-shaven Centaurans looked down or away, but never at Manning. Bearded Once held his gaze, but his face was expressionless. He felt a sudden kindred-ship with these people, these Native Centaurans.

Hadn't the white man come into the Native American world uninvited? And hadn't their presence become more and more intrusive until they assumed the Native American world belonged to them?

And at what point did the white man begin to regard the Native Americans as people not worthy of human dignity? And at what point did the pillaging of the Navajo, the Hopi, the Apache, the Algonquin, the Comanche, become the white man's holy duty?

Manning looked at these people and couldn't help but fear Earth's history repeating itself.

And he was a part of it.

The security door clicked open and Reager stepped partially through, a canteen in his hand. "Here's the water, Cap'n."

"Right, bring it in."

Reager hesitated.

"I said bring it in here. What's the matter?"

"N-nothing', sir. Just don't like 'em." Reager stepped inside.

Manning was about to respond when Bearded One talked wildly in that smooth, voluminous timbre. Manning turned toward the cell. Bearded One was standing close to the bars, his face contorted with… was that rage? His voice rose in pitch, in hysterical, unrecognizable sounds. He held his pendant out and jabbed a pointed finger at them.

The other two took angry poses near the bars and mimicked the gesture. They joined Bearded One's outcries and it became a chant, three alien voices in unison.

Reager dropped the canteen and stepped back and into the wall, his own face contorted, but not with rage as the Centaurans. With fear.

"What the hell?" Manning said.

Bearded One jabbed his hand through the bars until his thick forearm was wedged between them. He pointed at Reager and emitted that same cannon-like bellow he had earlier. Manning covered his ears. Reager scurried from the cell bay.

Manning watched the faces of the Centaurans slowly relax. Bearded One stopped bellowing, but his face remained taut. He pulled his hand back inside the cell.

Manning stepped closer to the bars, but the Centaurans ignored him. What was that all about? He searched their faces. After a moment, he left the cell bay.

Reager sat behind the console, his face ashen. "Guess they don't like me, either," he said weakly.

"Guess not." Manning said. He stared at Reager. Finally, "I'll be with Greco," he said.

Reager nodded. Manning left the cell bay, confused and concerned over recent events.

At the other end of the headquarters Quonset, the light from Greco's office spilled into the dark Orderly Room. Manning maneuvered quietly around the empty company clerk's desk, toward Greco's door. As he passed the CO's office, he glanced briefly at the locked door and felt a familiar pang.

"Get in here, Manning," Greco shouted before Manning could knock.

"You wanted to see me, Major?" Manning's tone was flat, his tolerance only feigned.

Greco scowled. He moved around the desk and stood nose to nose with Manning, looking down on him. He was a full head taller than Manning, who was just over two meters. Manning never backed off; he fixed his eyes squarely on Greco's.

Greco's face could have been sculpted, it was so damned proportioned. His eyes were a deep brown and his hair just a shade shy of pure black. Muscle-wise, he was well-toned. Manning hated to admit it, but Greco was a good-looking bastard.

And the women loved his deep, bottomless voice with its touch of Milan.

Manning tensed and set his jaw.

"What the hell were you doing this morning?" Greco asked.

"What are you talking about?"

"Knock off the bullshit. You fired a round at me."

"Oh, was that you? All I could see was somebody flagrantly violating light discipline. Not only is that against the unit's Standard Operating Procedure, it's just plain ignorant."

"You know, you take this security shit way too seriously, Manning. We're on a remote chunk of rock and ice, four-and-a-half light-years from home. The enemy—if there *is* an enemy—is galaxies away, and the people who live here are just primitive, backwater idiots who don't know or care what light discipline is."

"That's not the point and you know it," Manning shot back. "Readiness is the point. Readiness and discipline. And that means you practice it day in and day out whether—"

"Geez, you're pathetic. Don't preach your textbook crap to me, Manning. I'm your superior officer—"

"Don't fall back on that crutch, Greco. I was next in line for promotion. I've got the time-in-service and the time-in-grade and I've been here twice as long as you have. But you. You started jocking the Colonel even before you pulled into orbit."

"Yeah, right. You're qualified. Well then, Injun. Can you explain to me how it was that Locals were allowed to get anywhere near this facility, much less cut through two fences and make it halfway across the compound before they were spotted?"

Manning knew he was being baited, but he took the hook anyway. "There are seven kilometers of perimeter fence, and you know it. And I'm down three MPs."

"Maybe if you weren't so busy following me—"

"I wasn't following you, damn it." He could feel his neck burn. "You were lighting up the base like a bonfire. If I could see you, who else could?"

"There isn't anyone else here, Manning. When are you going to get that through your fucking head?"

"How the hell do you know that? They could be hiding around Centauri B or on one of the other planets around the primary or, shit, even right here on this one, for all we know."

"This is an early warning station," Greco shouted. "We have the most sophisticated sensor and telemetry equipment ever made. State-of-the-fucking-art. We've been scanning for them for twenty years and we haven't picked up anything yet."

"So what makes you think they weren't here before we were? The wreckage we found on Mars was *there* for over a hundred years. And besides, we already know the Threat is a hell of a lot more advanced than we are, technologically. They might have stealth capability we never dreamed of."

"You know, I've never bought into this invasion theory, Manning. Not one single body was ever found on that ship. Not one. It was empty. We weren't able to get into their computer or whatever that was. We couldn't decipher their logs. We just assumed that their intentions were hostile."

"Well, considering they had enough light-wave based armament and solid-fuel missiles to decimate the solar system, *and* enough frozen cultures exactly matching Earth DNA to bring down a whole planet, I think it was a safe guess they weren't dropping by to say 'Greetings, Earthlings. We come in peace.'"

Greco dismissed the statement with a cocky shake of his head, and an impatient glance at the watch he wore on his right wrist. "How would you know? Maybe they ate the bacteria."

"Greco, you are such an ass. Even though we couldn't crack their language, we learned enough about them from that ship to be alarmed. The best scientific and engineering minds in the world couldn't figure out everything that ship was capable of. All we could do was partially reverse-engineer their FTL drive and counter-gravity tech, and we did a grade-school job of it, at that."

"Shit," Greco said. "The best scientific and engineering minds in the world couldn't even come up with a name for them. The Threat? *The Threat?* What the hell kind of name is that? Sounds like something out of a dime pulp magazine. And alarmed?" Greco threw back. "Try scared-shitless-paranoid. We set up this deep-space early warning station in the direction we think—only *think*, mind you—they came from. And we set up a worldwide draft to staff it."

"Hey, I was drafted too."

"No shit, Sherlock. Who the fuck would volunteer for a five-year suicide mission."

Manning pressed on. "A UN defense force and conscription was the smart move and as much as you resent being here, it was the right—"

"And what choice did anybody have? Dodging the draft meant a hard labor jail sentence twice as long as the fucking tour and—"

"And as long as we are here, we're subject to—"

Greco threw up his hands. "Save your speeches. I'm tired of hearing about the Uniform Code of Military Justice and this unit's SOP and all your shit. You're outta here in a few weeks. I've got another two-and-a-half years. So if I want to smoke in the middle of the base at three in the fucking morning, I'm damn well going to do it and if it scares the piss out of a bunch of primates, too fucking bad. Do you copy?"

"Copy *this*, Major." Manning's warrior spirit was on a warpath. "As long as I'm the Provost Marshall of this detachment, everyone here, including you, will follow security policy and procedure. And the policy is you don't break light discipline. Shit, I'm sick of your attitude. I'm making a full report to the Colonel and I'm asking her for action."

With that, Greco smiled and dropped his voice to a husky whisper. "Oh, you are? And what do you think Alina will do to me?" Manning flinched at the casual use of her name. Just as Greco had intended. "Maybe Colonel Petrovich will spank me for being a bad boy." Greco paused and flashed a twisted grin. "Think so?"

"You son of a…" Manning balled his fist and took drew back, ready to smash Greco's Roman-god face into putty.

Greco stepped back and drew his own fist, waving him on with his other hand. "Oh, yeah. C'mon, Injun."

Damn it. Manning cursed himself. Greco had goaded him into losing his temper and he had. Damn it, he had. Manning lowered his guard and moved away.

"Aww, too bad," Greco said. "I was so looking forward to this."

"You're unbelievable, Greco. You don't belong in that uniform."

"For once I agree with you. Tell you what, *I'll* go home and you finish out my tour here. What do you say? This job has great fringe benefits, you know," he taunted.

Manning turned away, disgusted. "Fuck you."

"You know what your problem is, Manning? You think she's so lily-white and storybook proper. I've got news for you—"

"Shove it," Manning said. He left the office with Greco's malicious chuckle echoing in his head. He was furious with Greco for his crudeness and himself for being affected by it. Greco had controlled that confrontation from beginning to end.

He needed some fresh air, even if it was sub-zero and stank. More, he needed some sleep. He was working a double-shift again, but could squeeze in a few hours' sleep between them. He checked in with Reager, saw that the Centaurans were finally lying on the cots and sleeping, then slipped into his thermals and servo-frame, put on his gloves and goggles and left Post One.

He fought the drive of the wind and rancid snow until he reached the Officer's Billets. Once there, he climbed the few hard-plas stairs and went quickly through the outer doors to the entryway, feeling the momentary lightness as the servo-frame adjusted to the CG-Gen. He kicked the snow from his boots and went through the inner doors and along the dark hallway.

His quarters were midway along, but when he got to his door and was authorized access, he couldn't help but glance to the far end of the hall. Toward her quarters. Alina's.

He frowned and went inside, overcome by the familiar, crippling loneliness he had become accustomed to since falling in love with his commander.

Three hours later, after a short nap and a quick shower, Manning was back at Post One for the start of day watch, feeling calm and enthusiastic.

Those feelings were short-lived.

"How the hell did this happen?"

"Well, I…" Valentic muttered, standing at the position of attention.

"I asked you a question, Sergeant. How did they get their hands on a weapon and where are they now?"

"Sir, Major Greco ordered the Locals returned to their village."

"Greco?"

"Yes, sir." Valentic's accent thickened. "He came by right after you left. He said we were holding them illegally. I rounded up their gear and as I was moving them to the slider, Sergeant Reager came in. The Local with the beard went berserk. He became very strong. He grabbed one of those staffs from me and shoved me across the room. Before I knew what was happening, a blade had appeared on the end of it and the bearded Local had stabbed Bobby. The Local became docile, then, and we were able to grab the staff away from him."

"Go on."

"Sergeant Reager is at the Medical Center. Major Greco had us transport the Locals out of the compound."

"Where did you take them?"

"About halfway between the station and their village."

"You let them out in this storm? Josef, what the hell were you thinking?"

"Sir, Major Greco ordered me to let them out there. I had no choice."

"Damn it." Manning spun on his heels and charged through the now crowded squad room. He slipped into his thermal jacket, strapped into the servo-frame, positioned his goggles and was pulling on his gloves as he pushed through the security door with his shoulder.

The driving snow stung his cheeks and smelled worse than it had earlier. He trotted against the wind and pulled up his hood as he headed across the quad to the Med Center.

His neck burned mercilessly.

Why did Greco get involved, anyway? He never took the initiative unless there was a self-serving purpose. And how did they miss the knife in the staff? Obviously, the staffs must have contained cutting tools. At least it was obvious now. That must be how they cut the fence. No tools had been found on them. And why did they seem to hate Reager so? And why had Reager been so afraid of them?

"His small intestine was nearly severed and he has some lacerations to his left kidney and the surrounding tissues," Hannah said to him.

Manning looked through the viewing glass of the medical center's intensive care cell at Reager, unconscious and on life support. "But he'll recover?"

"He lost a lot of blood, Chris," she explained, making a notation on Reager's graphic chart, displayed on the screen next to the window. "But he'll pull through, just fine." She logged off the chart and turned to him. "Now, what the hell is going on?"

Her short wavy hair, golden as honey, was matted down with perspiration. Her surgical scrub was sweat-soaked as well, and the moisture highlighted the swells of her hefty breasts. He eyed them briefly, and then reluctantly glanced up.

Han was fun. And they were good together. But their relationship was a strained one, more an agreement to make the time at Centauri Station more bearable, than a courtship or romance. Such loose partnerships were not uncommon on remote, hardship tours like this one, where male-female companionship was limited to the assigned complement.

Hannah had what Manning thought was a girlish face, with her small, rounded nose and smooth, full cheeks. Her lips were the color of salmon and moist, a valentine of themselves. It was her eyes, though, that betrayed her. Her eyes were pyres of violet fire, the kind of fire only a woman could burn.

"A group of Centaurans had—"

"That's not what I meant," she said like a shot. "What's going on with you? With us?"

"Hannah—"

"Don't Hannah me." She jabbed a finger at him. "I don't want to hear any of your patronizing crap."

Manning glanced nervously back toward the nurse's desk.

"Nobody's here yet."

"I thought I heard something." He turned back to her. "I'm not about to patronize you." Manning tried to remain calm, but his voice gave away his effort.

"Then talk to me, damn it. You haven't come into the Med Center in days. You haven't been to my quarters in weeks."

"I'm sorry, Han. Really I am. I—I can't give you a reason. I don't really have one. I guess I've been preoccupied with getting off this iceberg. And I've been having problems with Greco. Now this."

"Don't forget, lover," her voice softened. "I'll be on that ship with you."

"I haven't forgotten, Han." His tone was less inviting then she had hoped.

"You're still hung up on Petro-bitch."

Manning looked up sharply. She knew him well. "Her name is Petrovich."

"Give it up, Chris. You're not on her level."

"Oh, really." Her tactic irritated him.

"Really." Her voice lowered to a husky whisper. She grasped the bottom of her scrub, pulled it over her head, and tossed it to the floor. Her eyes were an inferno.

Manning couldn't help but look at her naked breasts, glistening from perspiration and calling out to him as surely as if they could speak. Hannah knew. Hannah always knew. He leaned down and kissed her open mouth.

Hannah brushed her lips over his. Lightly. Gently. Then with more pressure. He felt her chest rise in a choked-off sob and he opened his eyes. He slid his hands up to her shoulders.

"Han," he whispered and saw her half-opened eyes were moist. "What's wrong?"

Her lips fused to his and she wrapped her arms tightly around his head. She drew him in deeper. Tighter. Only his servo-frame prevented their bodies from merging into one. Manning felt his head swim. If she could have devoured him, she surely would have. There was desperation to her clutch he had never experienced.

Manning grabbed her by the arms and pushed her off.

Even Hannah seemed stunned by her own ferocity. But as she regained her breath, the urgency turned to resentment at his hesitation. She jerked free of his grasp.

"You bastard." She snatched her scrub from the floor and marched out of the intensive care bay without putting it on.

"Hannah, wait…" he called, but she ignored him. He heard the door to her office slam and the electronic bolt engage.

Manning wiped his open hand over his face, still wet from her mouth. He hadn't meant to hurt her like that. He was just taken off guard by her intensity. And his own reaction to it.

It would be pointless to talk to her now. When her shields went up there was no breaking through. Later, when she's had a chance to calm down, they would talk. He promised himself they would.

Manning fastened his pulled on his gloves, and left the bay, glancing briefly at Hannah's door. He pulled the turquoise from his pocket and turned it over in his hand, as he left the Med Center and headed for Post One.

Lieutenant Colonel Alina Petrovich was a sternly beautiful woman. Her facial features were firm, no doubt from growing up in the harsh climate of the Kola Peninsula and the icy winds that blew in from the Barents Sea. Her thick, auburn hair was pinned off her shoulders and combed back from her forehead in a neat, regulation oval. Full, concise brows emphasized her almond eyes—those dark, compelling eyes.

And her lips…

Manning was always drawn to her this way, so taken in by her physical presence he came close to gawking. He shifted his stance.

She sat stiffly behind her plant-laden desk. Alina had been a botanist before she was drafted into the Defense Force, and Manning knew she found the Centauran flora compelling. Her office was an arboretum of potted plants, hanging vines, and frilly, bushes. Under the reduced gravitational pull of the CG-Gen, the local plants had developed odd physical properties including increased size and stamina. And fragrance. The office smelled like wild spearmint.

"Captain Manning," she said.

He loved her accent—rich Russian flavored with a just a hint of her mother's Ukraine. Her tone, though, was reproachful and he was instantly on guard.

It was then he became aware of Greco in a seat to his left, nearly behind him. Manning had been so fixed on Alina, he hadn't noticed Greco when he had come in. Greco sat back arrogantly, his legs crossed wide and his arm resting over the back of the next chair. Manning went to mental battle stations.

"Good morning, Colonel," he said, careful to make his own tone confident, but respectful.

"Captain," she said. "I am sure you are aware that there is no Status of Forces Agreement with this planet that allows for this facility to be here. Consequently, it is impossible, legally, for the Locals to have been trespassing here. Why were they taken into custody and held against their will?"

"I'm familiar with our precarious legal authority, Colonel," Manning said. "We've talked about this before and I still believe we should be in some sort of dialogue with the governments of this planet."

Alina cocked her head a bit, a signal Manning read as annoyance. He knew she was against such an action, as every commander before her had been. Their reason—evolutionary contamination.

Manning didn't buy it. They were already here and already contaminating them. They were using Centauri land and Centauri resources and Manning felt some sort of compensation should be made. The Centaurans didn't have to know the humans were from another planet.

But then, he wasn't the commander.

"That aside," he went on, "those people had walked over twenty-five kilometers in the dead of night. By the time we had found them, a squall was underway. My intent was to let them rest and warm up. Maybe feed them, if we could figure out what they ate. On the other hand, I couldn't just let them wander around the base. As far as we could tell, they weren't armed. Except for those unusual staffs—"

"And how the hell did you miss that?" Greco asked.

"We simply hadn't had the chance to examine the staffs yet. We didn't realize what they were until it was too late. And if you recall, Major, the staffs were secured until you decided the Centaurans needed to be thrown out into the—"

"They live in this shit—"

"And why the hell did you let them go after they stabbed one of my men?"

"We don't have the authority to—"

"Enough," Alina said firmly. Both men continued to glare at each other, but desisted. "Continue, Captain."

"Yes, ma'am. They carried no provisions. And they had no idea where to go once they made it inside."

Greco jumped up. "I don't buy the idea that they were lost and just wandered in, Manning. You said it. They *cut* the fence."

"Correct, Major. They cut through the fence. Look, I don't believe this was an accident either," Manning said. "They intended to come here. The question is, why? What could possibly be so important to them they would come here now? After two decades? They were terrified, Colonel. Terrified of us. But something happened when they saw Reager. Bearded One became enraged—"

"Bearded One?" Greco mocked. "Are we naming the Locals now?"

Manning ignored him. "He acted like he was angry—no, like he hated Reager. Not me, or Valentic. Just Reager."

"I see." She reached for one of the potted Centauran plants on her desk and fiddled with its leaves.

"Their motivation must have been strong for them to take such an action," Manning added. "I believe they may make another attempt."

"Very well, Captain. I agree with your assessment. Take whatever steps you have to. Dismissed."

"Yes, ma'am."

Manning did a crisp about-face, letting a snide grin cross his face as he rotated past Greco. And, oh, he enjoyed the taut expression on that chu'a's face!

Manning spent the next two watches preparing rosters, assignments, and contingency plans. Finally, satisfied he was as prepared as possible for another incursion, he slipped wearily into his thermals and servo-frame, and left the warmth of Post One for the bite of the outside.

The mineral content of the air was still high, and the smell of it taunted his stomach. The higher gravity brought fatigue to everyone sooner than later. He was exhausted and he knew it. Each step toward the Officer's Billets was a task. His thoughts were jumbled.

Somehow he had to put it together. For twenty years there had been no contact with the Locals. Why now? What was the reason?

The base itself had been built in a remote area at the foot of a cliff, and most of the resources to maintain it were brought from Earth. The infrequent shuttle launches were made quietly, with eccentric flight paths to avoid over-flights. Their animals were not hunted, and their forests were, for the most part, left undisturbed. Waste was recycled and energy was produced by nuclear fusion.

Maybe the humans had infected the Centaurans, somehow. A simple influenza virus, although relatively harmless to the humans, could be potentially deadly to the Locals.

His head spun from too much thinking and too little rest. The altercation with the Centaurans, the episode with Hannah, the meeting with Greco and Alina—Manning was ready to collapse. He clutched the railing tightly and took each step of the Officer's Billets one at a time.

But as he reached for the door, it crashed open, nearly knocking him to the ground.

"What the hell…"

"Oh, sorry, Captain," Valentic said, grabbing Manning before he could topple off the small porch.

"What's your hurry?"

"Major Greco was supposed to relieve Lieutenant Remoras as SDO an hour ago but he never showed, sir. I thought he might have overslept, but I'm not getting any answer at his door."

It was Saturday, an off day, unless you happen to be assigned to COMM, the food service unit, or the Military Police. Or pulling staff duty. Every officer assigned to Centauri Station except the commander was on the rotating roster for Staff Duty Officer. Not even Greco could get out of it.

It was a good thing Valentic couldn't see Manning's neck under the high collar of his thermal suit. It was red hot.

"I think I know where he is. I'll get his ass over there."

"Thanks, Captain. I'll let Lieutenant Remoras know."

"And I want to know when he shows up. Log it."

Manning took the stairs at a double clip, flung open the outer doors, then the inner doors and charged along the narrow hallway. He threw back his hood and pulled his goggles to his chest. He stood outside Alina's billets, his warrior spirit barely contained.

What he really wanted to do was kick the damn door in, grab the bastard by his chest hair and throw him against the wall, then kick him in the gut again and again until he was spitting up so much blood he would just shrivel up. Then—then Manning would go to her, to Alina, who would fall naked at his feet, in awe and complete adulation.

Yeah.

He snapped back to reality, his fist perched at the door ready to bang. Instead he tapped politely. On the third knock, she opened the door.

Alina's robe was every bit as alluring as the woman beneath it. It was a proper peach satin, laced tastefully at the neck and hem. Her smooth thighs disappeared somewhere under that lace. Her scent, a subtle spice, tormented him. Her dark hair swept over her forehead and fell onto her shoulders like a rich, redwood waterfall.

The string tie did little to contain her, and the deep cleave drew his eyes. Despite his fatigue, and despite himself, he felt his groin stir.

Alina drew the robe tighter and stepped partially behind the door. "Yes, Captain? What is it?"

"I apologize for the intrusion, Colonel, but Major Greco was scheduled for Staff Duty Officer an hour ago and hasn't reported yet."

"I see," she replied glancing back into her billets. Was she embarrassed? Didn't she think this was the first place he would look?

"By any chance, have you seen him, ma'am?" Manning looked past her but could only see plants.

Alina looked up at him sharply. Her response was quick. "I will see to it that he reports as soon as possible. Thank you, Captain."

Before he could reply, she had shut the door.

Manning undid the fasteners of his thermal suit and looked at her door, somewhat perplexed. That wasn't the reaction he had expected at all.

He turned to leave but stopped. Something wasn't right.

Manning was all wound up now. There was no way he could get to sleep in this state, no matter which mind control technique he used. He decided against a sleep inducer and, instead, refastened his outerwear and marched out of the billets, heading for Post One. He ignored the bite of the wind on his face.

Manning's anger grew with each step. Damn it Alina. How the hell can you be involved with such a blatant piece of shit? He wanted to shake her free of his influence, just grab her by the shoulders and shake her free.

But then, once he touched her, even casually, he would be lost. All his anger and resolve would vanish in the rush of physical contact. He would melt into a pathetic puddle and look up at her, desperate, enticed by the sensual way her peach, satin robe, laced at the neck and hem, hugged her contours.

The robe would remind him of their conversation, and the conversation would remind him that Greco was in there with her, and his neck would be searing again.

He took the turquoise from his pocket and, without thought, turned it over in his gloved hand.

He had walked around the quadrangle and was at Post One, but was still too angry to go inside. He walked around the building and picked up the path to the COMM building, several hundred meters north. But once there, his temperament was no better. And he knew better than to go inside in his current frame of mind. The COMM Center was, by necessity and strict policy, a quiet zone. The controllers inside were looking and listening for the approach of the Threat, hoping to find the invading armada before it found them and obliterated them before they could get their warning to Earth. FTL hyper-wave communications, thankfully, was a lot faster than starship speed.

The wind churned again, whipping the surface of the moist, clumpy snow into a pungent mist. Manning shifted the hood of his thermals to block out the bite, but had to walk somewhat sideways to give his face maximum protection.

Gods, he hated this place. How soon? A couple of weeks? The thirteen-month FTL trip back to Earth would be a pleasure cruise after his tour here. The air would be canned and stale, thank you. And even though the water would be no more than filtered urine and the food nothing but dry, artificial grain supplements…

Ahhh, what paradise.

The first thing he was going to do after he out-processed from the service was to hop on a clipper and jet to New Mexico, to his birth village on the Ramah Reserve, and just roll in the smoldering sand. Maybe hug a cactus, or wrestle a coyote.

And then, maybe something more sensible. What about the tropical splendor of the two remaining Hawaiian Islands? Or the Caribbean. Whatever, he had over a year to make up his mind. Maybe Hannah had a preference.

Hannah. She would be on the transport, too. They had never made any long-term plans together. They had never spoken of commitment. Their arrangement was just fine as it was.

Or was it? The Han he saw today—she had never been so consumed. The look in her eyes had alarmed him. Something was wrong there, too.

So lost in thought, Manning had walked past COMM and was nearly at the hanger facility, four kilometers away, when his attention returned to his surroundings. He could see the large, reinforced hanger building and the landing pad a hundred meters east of it.

Damn it. Damn it all.

He was too tired to walk all the way back to the billets, now. Cursing his own absent mindedness, he continued on to the hanger to sign out a snow-slider.

The building was secure, but unattended. This was Reager's duty station and Manning had forgotten to assign a replacement here. Damn, he was tired.

The security logic read and recognized his nano-chip signature and accepted his access code. The door lock disengaged with a loud clack that echoed inside the long structure. He pushed open the heavy door and reached along the inside wall for the light sensor. The environmental logic activated the moment the lights came on and he could feel the temperature gradually rise. He stepped inside and secured the door behind him.

He walked along the inside wall, past the main hanger bay door and the bulky surface-to-orbit shuttle. The shuttle's hatch was open and the egress ramp was extended. He could see open access panels and scattered tools. The ship was being prepared for flight. His flight. He ran his hand along the cool surface of the shuttle's hull.

He slid past the shuttle and into the slider bay. At the dispatch terminal, he logged onto the COMNET and accessed the dispatch log. All the sliders were available he saw, and none were reserved. He selected one, signed it out and logged off.

His bones had thickened with fatigue, his thoughts lazy. He lumbered past the snow-slider's parking stalls. All except one had a snow-slider parked there and Manning walked past the empty stall to his own slider. He disconnected the slider's logic center from the mainframe and its power core from the fusion receptacle.

Manning was tired, so tired the empty stall didn't register until after he had shut off the overhead lights, turned down the hanger's environmental logic, and was seated behind his slider's console.

"What the hell?" he muttered when it finally clicked. The dispatch log had shown that all the sliders were available.

He climbed out of his slider and returned to the motor pool COM-NET terminal. Sure enough, according to the dispatch log, all the sliders were in the motor pool. Rather, none had been signed out. Manning accessed the maintenance log, thinking the unit was pulled for repairs. Nothing.

He closed the log and physically checked the entire hanger.

The slider was not there.

Without someone on duty here, the security logic would only grant access to a few people. Manning was one, but then as Provost Marshall, he had unlimited access. Only the detachment's senior officers and the assigned motor pool staff could gain entry to the Motor Pool. And the Military Police, of course. But that was, what? A hundred? A hundred and twenty, maybe?

He returned to the terminal, input his codes and retrieved the security logic entry log. He saw his own entry, and before that—

What?

Sergeant Bobby Reager?

But Reager was at the Med Center, under sedation.

The loud clang of heavy circuit breakers jarred him. And when all the overhead lights came on, Manning literally jumped. He spun around as the hanger door rattled upward. Outside, he could hear the whine of an approaching snow-slider.

His neck was ablaze. Something wasn't right. He shut down the terminal and darted for the nearest cover. The shuttle.

Up the ramp.

Through the hatch.

And not a second before the slider rumbled through the open door and slid off the snow-packed ground onto the hard, dirt floor.

Manning scrambled up to the pilot's station. He leaned against the opaque windshield where he could watch without being seen.

The slider pulled right into the vacant spot and shut down. Seconds later the hatch popped open and a parka-clad figure, face obscured by goggles and scarf, climbed out.

The man reached back inside the slider, pulled out a small gear bag, and dropped it to the ground. He reached in again and the huge hanger door rattled back down. The main lights shut off.

Manning noted each movement. The man undid the slider's engine cowling and reached inside. After several seconds, he re-secured the cowling. He kicked built-up snow from the machine's treads and scattered it over the ground in a thin, easily melted layer.

The figure secured the slider's hatch, connected the machine's logic center to the mainframe and plugged the power core into the fusion receptacle.

Manning watched as the man hurried to a nearby locker, removed a set of power-skis and awkwardly snapped them on. With wide movements, exaggerated by the clumsy skis and bulky servo-frame, the man walked back to the gear bag. He slid his arm through the carry strap and flung the bag over his left shoulder. The man peeled back his right glove and glanced at his watch. Suddenly hurried, he wiped away his tracks and left the building through the personnel door.

Manning darted out of the shuttle and toward the door. Cautiously, he leaned toward the door's window. He saw the figure disappear into the mist and glide away in a wide arc toward the quadrangle.

Manning bolted to the stall, hoping the slider might tell him something. The metal cowling was still warm from the heat of the engine. He examined the outer body, not noting anything unusual. Likewise, the treads didn't give up a clue.

He unfastened the cowling and peered inside the engine compartment, certain that the figure had tampered with the maintenance odometer. Sure enough, the casing had fresh scratches around the bolts.

Manning refastened the cowling and went inside the passenger compartment. Again, he found nothing to point to who was driving or where the machine had been. He re-secured the slider.

He was so tired his eyes throbbed. He wasn't going to learn anything more. He climbed into his slider and guided it out the hanger door. He keyed in the navigational logic and set out for Post One at a slow speed, not wanting to overtake the skier, or alert him to Manning's presence.

Twenty minutes later, his boots were left in the middle of the main room in a puddle of smelly, melted snow; his servo-frame propped up against the wall; his thermals tossed over the back of his desk chair and his fatigues bunched up in a corner; Manning was comfortably between his sheets. He drifted quickly off to sleep.

Horses…soldiers on horses…herding his people like cattle, his ancestors, the Dineh, called Navajo by the white man…thousands of Dineh, beaten, starved, forced to march hundreds of miles across the scorched New Mexican wasteland…they fell, dead in the sand from exhaustion and infection. Their cries echoed in his mind…the children…to Bosque Redondo they marched…driven by the brutal, invading Calvary soldiers.

He fell to the ground…into the dust, under the hooves of the invading Calvary horses…he choked up blood and bile as the horses pounded over his battered Navajo body…their hooves pounded in his head over the cries of the Dineh children…but then the Dineh were the Centaurans…pounding…and he was a Calvary soldier…pounding…

"Uuhh?"

Manning sprung up in his bed. His heart hammered and he labored for breath. Where was he? His eyes jerked back and forth.

The remnants of the foggy dream played with his thoughts. It was the same dream, the same nightmare he had suffered as a boy, when he first learned the history of the Navajo Nation from his grandfather. 1864. The terrible Long Walk of the Navajo. But he hadn't had that dream in years.

Pounding.

But now…the Centaurans…

Pounding.

He was in his billets. He looked at the watch on his left wrist. 1140. And someone was pounding on his door.

He groaned. Three hours sleep. Barely. He ran his fingers through his short hair and tossed back the sheet.

"Damn it," he rasped. Then louder, "What is it?"

"It's Imparato, sir. Sorry. It's urgent."

Manning shook his head and got up from his bed. He unlocked the door, swung it open, and waved her in.

"What's up, Lisa?" Manning closed the door, and grabbed his fatigues. He shook them and stepped into the suit.

"Lieutenant Lang sent me, sir. Sergeant Reager is dead."

"What—" Manning stopped in mid-zip and stared at her, not quite believing he had heard right. No one had ever died on Centauri before. Sure, Reager had been seriously hurt, but Hannah was confident he would recover. "What happened?

"Lieutenant Lang said it appeared to be heart failure a couple of hours ago."

"A couple of hours ago? Why wasn't I informed immediately? Lisa, you know the procedure."

"Yes, sir. But Major Greco didn't think it was necessary, because of Bobby's injuries. I said we should tell you right away, but he said you were off duty and that was that."

"I'm the Provost Marshall of this facility. What authority—"

"I know, sir, I know. That's why I'm here. Lieutenant Lang wants to see you. Right away."

"Close the door," Hannah told him.

Manning did and turned back to her. She sat sullen behind her desk, her eyes rubbed red.

"What happened? You said he would recover."

"And he should have. He should be awake and bitching about the tubes up his nose right now."

"Then what?"

"I can't explain it, Chris. I had just checked on his status. He was still sleeping, but he was stable. Damn it, Reager had a strong heart and his wounds weren't fatal."

"Easy, Han," Manning said. He moved to the desk and sat on the edge. He cupped her face in his hands gently. Her cheeks were moist. In the five-and-then-some years he had known her, Manning had never seen her cry. Now, today, he had seen her twice in tears. "It wasn't your fault," he added softly.

"Wasn't it? I've never lost a patient, Chris. Never. God, this is awful." She pulled his hands free and got up from the chair to pace. "I must have missed something. Maybe something from the knife. A Centauri fungus or a…"

Her throat tightened and sound wouldn't form.

"Had anyone been to see him?" he asked. "After I left, I mean?"

"Sure," Hannah rasped. "Sure. Briggs. Massi. Greco, Valen—"

"Greco? Greco came to see Reager? Before he died?"

"Yes. About an hour before, I think."

"Was he the last person to see him alive?"

She swallowed trying to regain her stature. "No, as a matter of fact I was. I checked his vitals and adjusted his IV flow. He was stable."

Manning turned to her. "This stinks, Han. Something is wrong here. Have you performed an autopsy?"

"Not yet."

"I'd like you to get on it as soon as you can."

She eyed him with concern. "You think—you think he was murdered?"

"I'm suspicious of the circumstances surrounding his death," he said. As Provost Marshall, that suspicion was sufficient justification for him to conduct a murder investigation. And that justification gave him authority over the highest rank on the base.

Hannah sensed his change in posture. "Right. Where will you be?"

"Hard to say. I'll get in touch with you in a few hours."

Hannah raised her left arm to look at her watch. "Make it 1500."

"1500, then. Don't discuss your findings with anyone but me."

"Understood."

Manning, marched toward the door, but stopped abruptly before opening it. He turned back to her. "Hannah…"

She walked up to him and kissed him tenderly. He could taste the salty tears on her face.

"Go clear me, Chris," she said, her lips touching his. It was an intimate touch without any sexuality.

Lips still in contact, he whispered, "I will, Han." They completed the kiss and he turned and left her office.

Manning pressed his palm against the security scanner next to the door to Reager's quarters in the NCO billets. The lock snapped open and he slipped inside, quietly securing the door behind him.

Reager's room was smaller than his own, but certainly much neater. Even the floor was clean. Systematically, he searched the room, going through dresser drawers, looking in cabinets, flipping through books. Aside from a small puddle under the desk, nothing appeared out of the ordinary. The bed was crisply made. Each drawer was neatly arranged. The clothing in the closet was uniformly hung.

Manning wasn't sure what he was looking for, but there had to be a reason why Reager was killed. And he was sure Reager was killed. And it had something to do with the Centaurans.

What the hell was going on, here? As he shook his head in frustration, he noticed the small puddle of water beneath his feet. Traces of snow he had brought in with him on his boots and pants legs had melted and puddled right there, where he had been standing. He glanced around the room and saw similar small puddles in spots where he had stood for a length of time. The floor had been dry when he entered.

Except for that small puddle under the desk.

Manning knelt and examined the puddle. It had an iron tang to its smell and a rusty color. Melted snow. And not too long ago, he surmised.

Someone had already been here. At the desk. There had been no other traces of moisture on the floor, suggesting whoever had been here had wiped it dry. That might account for the floor being so clean.

Manning sat and logged onto the COMNET from Reager's small terminal. Seconds later he was inside Reager's personal sub-directory, hoping to glean some answers. But the sub-directory was empty.

"Damn."

All of Reager's personal files had been deleted. Manning accessed the usage log and noted his own log-on at 1315. The next previous usage was recorded at…

Manning sat back. The previous usage was at 1240, just a few minutes before Manning had entered Reager's quarters. Whoever it was, Manning had just missed him. Strange that, whoever had deleted Reager's files, wouldn't have thought about deleting the usage log. Sloppy.

And whoever had been here, was clever enough to wipe the floor dry of his tracks, but careless enough to miss the spot under the desk where he had sat.

Wipe his tracks? Manning recalled the hanger this morning. The return of the missing snow-slider. The driver had wiped the ground clean of tracks. And he had tampered with the maintenance odometer, making it appear as if the vehicle had not been used. But he left marks. Again, sloppy.

It had to be the same individual.

Manning sat up and went to rapid work on the keypad. He accessed the security logic for Reager's quarters. Not surprised, he saw that, just before his own entry, the quarters were entered by Staff Sergeant Bobby Reager.

Reager. Who was dead at the time.

Obviously, someone had obtained Reager's nano-chip signature and learned his access codes, then entered his quarters and erased his personal files.

His thoughts raced. The missed usage log. The slider. The slider didn't have a usage log. But it did have a navigational logic.

That snow-slider should still be in the motor pool and tied into the mainframe. That would give Manning an electronic pathway to follow right into the machine's navigational logic.

The logic was nothing more than a pre-written computer routine that interacted with the buried navigational beacons. Simple stuff. When activated, the logic provided navigational guidance for the vehicle along the selected route. The logic didn't keep track of who was using it, but did log the times the logic was used and the route taken.

Manning accessed the unit's logic and displayed its log. The first entry would be the last use of the logic. There. 0650 this morning, and it showed the slider had used the eastern interior track from outside the perimeter fence, through the gate, to the hanger.

The previous entry showed the slider had left the hanger at 0455 on that same heading.

Out the east gate. Toward the Centauran village.

Manning inset the motor pool's dispatch log and saw, again, the slider had not been signed out for that last trip. He returned to the navigational logic and its other entries.

He scanned back until he found a similar entry—several days ago and it was also in the middle of the night. The slider had not been signed out. He selected only those entries where the east track out of the facility had been used. He found nine others going back seven months and the vehicle had not been signed out for any of those uses.

Manning brought up the security duty roster and compared it to the navigational logic's log. Each and every time, the security post had been manned by Staff Sergeant Bobby Reager.

Except this last time. Reager had been hospitalized. So who was it?

Manning pulled the nav logs of the remaining four sliders and found similar occurrences, all heading toward the village. None of the sliders had been signed out. And Reager had been on duty at the hanger each and every time.

He logged off the net and shut down Reager's terminal. As he left the NCO Quarters heading back to Post One, he shuffled the facts around in his mind. Three Centaurans enter the camp, presumably looking for something, or someone. Reager is attacked by a Centauran. Someone is making unauthorized trips into the Centauran village. Reager is killed.

A sharp vibration behind his left ear caught his attention. He reached up and put slight pressure on the spot, activating the receiver and at the same time pressed the vocal implant in his throat.

"Manning."

"Captain Manning!" It was Massi.

"What is it?"

"They came out of the fog! More Locals! Must be over thirty of them!"

He swore an old Navajo curse and ran toward the security vestibule, his servo-frame whirring. "Where are they, now?"

"Inside. About a hundred meters beyond the fence. South of the east gate."

Manning gained access, jogged past the holding cells, past the Squad Room, past his office.

"Who's at the east gate?"

"Corporal Briggs. But I haven't been able to raise him."

"Briggs from Manning!" Chirp. "Briggs from Manning." No response. "Massi, what's your position?"

"I'm on foot patrol, a hundred meters north of the east gate," Massi said.

"Can you see Briggs?" Manning charged along the center hall.

"Not from this position. The Locals are on a south-by-southwesterly direction. They appear to be heading for the quad."

"Get down to the gate and check on Briggs."

"Yes, sir!"

He threw open the door to the Orderly Room with a crash and barged toward the Ex-O's office. Greco, startled by the commotion, came around his desk.

"What the hell?"

Manning's fist smashed into Greco's face. Greco spun from the impact and fell to his knees.

"Get up, you son-of-a-bitch."

Greco looked up, his mouth bloody, his brow furrowed in anger. "What the hell is the matter with you?"

"Get up, I said."

Greco looked at him and gave a nod. He pushed up slowly, but then spun around, his fist flying toward Manning's jaw.

Manning expected the feint. He stepped past the swing and delivered a roundhouse kick to Greco's abdomen.

Greco doubled over and stumbled backwards. He regained his balance, turned toward Manning, and lunged.

Manning stepped into the charge. He grabbed Greco's wrist and, in one lightning move, twisted, sidestepped, and tossed him over his shoulder. Greco's own momentum fueled the judo throw. He landed flat and hard on the desk.

Greco grunted, then rolled off the desk into a shaky stance. He balled his fists, and swung a wide hook. Manning easily deflected the shot with a crisp middle block, and followed through with a rib-breaking sidekick. Greco went down again.

"What did you do to them, Greco?" Manning's breath was labored, partly from the exertion, mostly from contempt.

"Wha—what are y-you talking—"

"The Centaurans. We've got about thirty of them on the compound. Heading this way."

"Heading here?" Greco's anger melted away until all that was left was badly disguised fear.

"Right here. Right now." Manning said through gritted teeth.

"What makes you think—"

"What time is it?"

"What?"

Manning held up his left arm. "I said what time is it?"

Greco looked up at him, puzzled by the abrupt change in direction. "It's…" Greco looked at the watch on his right wrist. Manning grabbed it in an iron grip.

"I was in the hanger this morning. I couldn't see his face, but I did see him check his watch. Most people wear their watches on their left wrist. I don't know anyone on this planet who wears it on his right. Except you."

"That doesn't prove a thing," Greco said.

"You killed Reager."

"No. No. He was alive when I saw him—"

"Get up."

Greco grimaced and got to his feet slowly, dabbing his bleeding mouth with the back of his hand. He held his side tightly with the other. "Look, Manning, I may be a lot of things, but I'm no killer."

Manning grabbed him and pushed him into the wall. Greco grunted as his broken rib shifted. Manning had to look up to make eye contact, but his intensity more than made up for the height difference. Already physically beaten, Greco didn't resist.

"Yeah, you're a lot of things, all right. I want to know why. Why did you have to kill him?"

"Listen to me." Greco reached up for Manning's wrists but Manning just tightened his grip. "I swear, I didn't do it. Look, okay. I admit it was me in the hanger this morning. I went into the village. It was me, okay?"

"Keep talking, I want to hear it all from you."

"I told you—" Manning shoved hard, slamming Greco's head against the wall. He grunted. "What do you want me to say?"

"I want to know what you did to them, or so help me I'll throw your ass into the snow without a servo-frame and let them pick your bones. What did you do to them?"

"Oh, Jesus. They must want the stones."

"What stones? Tell me."

"Reager and I, we've been—shit, they had so many of them, I didn't think they'd miss a few. They're not even worth anything here."

"Greco, what stones?"

"Reager found 'em. About a year ago." Greco was sweating and talking rapidly. "I caught him sneaking back from the village. He gave me one of the stones not to turn him in. It was a natural diamond, Manning. Huge. We struck up a deal. We were only going to take a few. Look, I didn't kill him, I swear, but now that he's gone, I'll give you his share. You'll be rich once you get back home. Rich, Manning. Just forget about it. You'll be gone in a couple of weeks and I'll still be stuck here. I swear, I won't go back to the church. I won't go back to the village at all. Okay?"

"The church? You stole from their church?" Manning recalled the Centaurans in the holding cell. How each wore a pendant inlaid with glistening stones. How Bearded One wore a larger pendant, a golden one. Larger, and with more stones. Bearded One must have been a priest.

His neck burned like never before.

"Manning, look, diamonds are plentiful here. That's all we took. Just the diamonds. And a few pendants. We could have taken the ruby's or the—"

"You stupid shit. Maybe they don't have any monetary value here, but did you ever stop to think they might have religious value? You've desecrated their church."

"Look, take mine. They're in my desk. Bottom drawer. Reager's are there too. I grabbed them this morning."

"You were there, weren't you? In his quarters. You have his chip signature and his access code?"

"Yeah. Yeah, I was there. I didn't know if he made any journal entries or anything. I erased all his files. Grabbed his stones. You take 'em. Take 'em all. Maybe it'll be enough."

"What is going on here?" A familiar voice behind him caught his attention.

"Alina…" Greco began.

Manning released him and turned toward her. As he did, he whipped a back-fisted blow into Greco's face. Greco hit the wall and slid to his knees, blood streaming from his nose.

"What are you doing, Captain? What is happening here?"

"Happening, Colonel? We're under attack by the Centaurans. They're on their way here. To Post One."

"What? Why?"

"Why?" Manning's neck was hellfire.

"What is going on, Christopher?"

"Christopher, now? You haven't used my first name in all the time I've known you. Why now?"

"I don't know what you mean?"

"Don't you?" His voice was husky, forced. "When I came by looking for Greco, I thought he was in there with you. But he wasn't, was he. You knew he was in the village. You knew why. You're a part of this."

They stared into each other's eyes, each assessing the other.

"Christopher," she began slowly. "You are as brilliant as you are attractive. Why don't you stay with me?"

"What?"

"Hey," Greco coughed.

"You can have Sergeant Reager's share. If you are uncomfortable about this, we can stop. I have more than enough to live out my life comfortably when we get back. Lavishly so."

Manning felt despair rush over him. He had begun to suspect Alina's involvement only a short time ago, when it dawned on him that only he and the Commanding Officer could access nano-chip code signatures. Hearing it confirmed by her, seeing her cavalier attitude, made him feel more than just betrayed.

"Stay with me, Christopher." She lowered her voice. "You and I can be very happy together." Her right hand disappeared behind her back. She brought her left hand up to her side, the backs of her fingers slowly tracing the curve of her body around her breast, over her hip, onto her thigh. He was aroused, despite himself.

"Wait—wait a minute." Greco got back to his feet. "What about me?"

"Captain Manning!" Massa's voice was frantic. Manning reached for his implant.

"Stop," Alina ordered. In her right hand she held a sonic handgun leveled directly at Manning's chest. He froze and stared at the barrel of the weapon in disbelief.

"It's Massi," he said slowly, his eyes focused on the short barrel of the weapon. "On my COMPLANT. He was checking on one of my men. He might have been hurt."

"You must choose, now," she told him. "Would it be so terrible? To stay with me?"

"Alina," Greco stumbled forward. "What about you and me? You said—"

She turned the weapon on Greco and, without any hesitation, pulled the trigger.

The sonic projectile struck him square in the sternum, exploding with a dull report. Greco was thrown back against the wall as his chest exploded outward, spewing blood and tissue. Manning turned away, but Alina stood still, not flinching from the gore that splashed over her.

Manning looked back at Greco's corpse, astounded. The wound still smoldered and the stench of charred skin tightened his stomach in a way the snow never could. He turned his head toward Alina. She stood there, still and bloody. Her eyes were ice, her face relaxed. She turned the gun back toward him.

"Dominic was an idiot. A greedy idiot at that. He had to go back just once more."

"Alina," he whispered in disbelief. "Put the gun away."

"I will be delighted, Christopher. Just tell me what I want to hear. And, please, do not attempt to deceive me. I will know. And I will kill you where you stand."

She would. He had no doubt about that now. He was numb, detached. How could this—this monster be the warm woman he had been in love with, or thought he had been in love with? How could he have misread her character so badly? Weren't there any clues?

He could almost forgive her for her greed. Almost. But murder? Cold-blooded, remorseless murder?

"It was you. You killed Reager. Didn't you?"

Her lips twisted into a wicked, lusty smile. "I certainly hope you will be more sensitive to my needs then you were to Doctor Lang's, Christopher."

"You were in the Med Center."

"Mmm."

"What you've done." Manning's throat twisted with conflicting passions. "Alina, what you've done."

"I've done nothing, Captain," she said coolly. "The sergeant and Dominic stole the diamonds. Dominic gave them to me," her smile broadened at the irony. "Out of love."

"You knew what they were doing. You condoned it. You accepted the proceeds of the crime. That makes you party to the crime in any law book." He paused, bearing down on her eyes. "And you're a murderer."

Her smile faded. "Yes. I am, although I take no pleasure in it. It is a pity, though. We could have been good together, I think."

She took deadly aim. Manning could practically feel the crosshairs on his forehead. He was trapped between the desk and the gun, only a meter from his face. Motion slowed as he watched her finger compress the trigger.

A ferocious scream.

A blur of motion.

Hannah came from behind Alina and dropped a viscous chop to the Russian woman's gun hand. The weapon fired into the floor, just centimeters from Manning's feet.

Hannah wasted no time. She grabbed Alina's arm and wrenched it downward, dislodging the gun, then drove her knee deep into the woman's abdomen.

Alina cried out and doubled over.

Hannah whipped around and channeled all her weight into a crushing, two-fisted uppercut that smashed into Alina's face. The Russian woman fell to the floor, unconscious.

Hannah leaned forward, both hands on her knees as she labored for breath. "I told you…told you…you weren't on her…level."

"Next time, I'll listen," he said meekly. His head hummed, his body trembled. It took monumental effort for him to force his despair aside. "What are you doing here?"

"I found trace amounts of a substance in Reager's bloodstream. Nothing like I'd seen before. It looked like an aconitine derivative, but the molecular structure was off. So I figured it must have been Centauran."

"Acone-in…"

"Aconitine. You might know it as monkshood or wolfsbane. It poisons the vagus nerve, which connects the brain to the heart. If administered properly, death from heart failure occurs in just a couple of hours.

Aconitine, on Earth anyway, is found in the Aconitum Napellus plant, native to parts of Europe, Asia, and guess where else."

"Russia."

"Good guess. Petro-bitch was a botanist and I remembered seeing a lot of Centauran plants in her office. I was on my way there to examine them when…" She motioned toward the two bodies on the floor.

"Yeah. Thanks."

"You can start paying me back tonight, lover."

"Okay. Let's get her locked up."

He reached down to lift her but hesitated, almost afraid to touch her, even now.

"Look, I'll do it," Hannah said, pushing him aside and lifting the Russian woman in a fireman's carry. "You deal with the Locals."

"Okay," he agreed.

The mention of the Locals reminded him of the urgency. He went into Greco's desk, and found the false bottom easily. Inside the compartment was a box and in the box were pendants, like the one Bearded One had worn but with the stones pried out. And diamonds. Uncut and unpolished diamonds. Over a dozen, he guessed. Worthless here on Centauri, but if introduced slowly into the world economy on Earth, they would bring substantial wealth.

He removed the box from the drawer and carried it out of the Orderly Room, along the hall to the rear door of Post One. Through the window he saw the Centaurans advancing on the building, brandishing those short, peculiar staffs, ugly blades protruding from the ends. He saw two sliders approaching from the north, from around COMM.

"Manning to all units. Do not engage the Centaurans. Do not engage them. Allow them to approach the building. Copy?"

"Copy."

"Understood."

He ran back into the Orderly Room, to Greco's corpse and hoisted the dead man over his shoulder. He faltered until the servo-frame, interpreting the additional body weight as an increase in gravity, whirred and augmented Manning's strength. Hannah met him at the door.

"She's locked up in the brig. Still out cold."

"Good. Grab that box, Han."

"Okay, lover. What's in it?"

"A peace offering, I hope."

Manning pushed the door open so hard it crashed into the wall behind it. The Locals, bantering and bobbing their staffs in the air, turned toward the disturbance. Manning stood in the doorway, balancing Greco's body easily on one shoulder.

The mob hushed, their natural fear working off the adrenalin high of their vengeance quest. It was easy to spot the leader. Bearded One. Manning approached him directly.

A few feet from the priest, Manning stopped and made direct eye contact. Manning painted a look of remorse on his face, hoping facial expressions would bridge the communication gap between them. He flipped Greco's dead body over his shoulder onto the snowy ground at Bearded One's feet.

The crowd stepped back and gasped, some covering their eyes at the gruesome sight. Bearded One maintained his stand, glancing at Greco, then back up to Manning.

No reaction. Manning wondered if Bearded One understood at all. "Hannah," he said.

She came forward and gave the box to Manning. He removed the top and held it out to the priest.

If their emotions were similar to humans, then Manning read the expression on Bearded One's face as relief. Immense relief.

The priest took the box and stared at Manning for a brief moment, then turned toward the gathering. He raised his voice and spoke in their strange, smooth tongue. There was discussion, angry discussion.

Manning reached into his thigh pocket and removed his turquoise talisman. He rolled it in his gloved hand, caressing its shape, memorizing its form.

"I know you can't understand me," he said. Bearded One turned toward him. "But I offer this as a token of peace." Manning stretched out his arms and held out his hands. He uncurled his fingers and presented the talisman.

Turquoise was alien to Centauri. Its creamy, blue-green color drew a gasp of wonder from the crowd. Bearded One looked on the talisman with reverence, and took it from Manning, awe-struck.

The priest studied the intricate carving, the smooth texture, and the pleasing, extraordinary color. He turned it over, scrutinized its back. He felt the workmanship. He raised it to his face and smelled the stone. And all the while, Bearded One's eyes were wide.

Reluctantly, after several moments, Bearded One turned back to Manning and held out the talisman to return it. Manning smiled, took Bearded One's hand, and gently closed the native's fingers around the talisman.

The transport left orbit even before the shuttle had returned to the surface. Manning couldn't see the massive craft move away but imagined it growing smaller and smaller, taking with it half the personnel from Centauri Station.

Plus one prisoner. And an empty berth with his name on it.

In a few minutes the shuttle would land, and the last of the new arrivals would be on the ground. A few weeks of in-processing and the facility would be operating routinely again.

He turned and headed along the path toward Post One, his servo-frame quietly whirring with each motion.

"Hey, wait for me," Hannah called after him.

"Sorry, Han. Got caught up in thought."

"Bet you did, Major Manning. So. How does it feel to be in command of the farthest outpost known to man?" She slid her arm through his, not feeling the contact between the two heavy layers of parka and their servo-frames.

"Haven't gotten used to it, yet. I still have trouble believing I'm still here on this stinking planet."

"Hey, remember who you're talking to, lover. You can't fool me. I saw you with the Locals. Sorry. I mean the Centaurans."

"Thank you. I just think we need to consider them with more respect. This is their planet. Their land." He took his recent dream of the terrible Long Walk to be a warning from his warrior spirit—a warning of history's echo. "We're guests here, even if we are uninvited ones."

"You're right, Chris. And if I haven't said it, I'll say it now. I'm proud of you. You could have easily just flown away on that transport. Your tour was up. You had every right to."

"Sure. And leave the base without a commander or an Ex-O?"

"Wasn't your responsibility."

"I think it was. I should have seen what was happening. I should have been more alert. And more vocal about the Centaurans' rights."

"Well you have another two-and-a-half years to make up for it. And me to help you do it."

"And I intend to just that. And more." He looked at her. "Why did you stay, Han?"

"Me?"

"Yeah, you."

She smiled. "Lover, sometimes you can be so dense. Well, you have another two-and-a-half years to make up for *that*, too."

"Oh, I see." He suppressed a grin.

"Just remember one thing," she added, disengaging her arm.

"What's that?"

"I saved your ass. That means it belongs to me." She slapped him smartly on his rump and walked on ahead, glancing back over her shoulder coyly.

Manning grinned and followed.

Above, for the first time in nearly half a decade, the clouds broke and the primary star of the Alpha Centauri binary shone on Centauri Station.

The Flight
of the
Salamander

By Violet Addison and David Smith

She was falling.

The world was tumbling around her, a wild blur of black and orange, as she plummeted toward the ground. She screamed.

It was not the most useful response to her situation, but given her circumstances, it came to her very naturally.

There was however nothing natural about the sound that she made: it was as deep and mournful as a whale song, like the ones that she had heard when she had swum with the humpback pods off the Antarctic coast.

She had been hundreds of meters down, in ice-cold waters, observing the great grey giants, whilst they seemed unconcerned by her presence. It was as if she had been part of the pod. It was as if, on that day, she had been a whale.

She flinched, stung simultaneously by the implausibility of the memory and by another expected sensation; the echo of her scream flashing back through her brain, searing into it images of the twisted rocks and smoke plumes beneath her. Her brain had just done something impossible, using sonar to map out of the terrain beneath her, despite the fact that this was an ability that the human brain did not possess.

The sensation jolted another memory to the surface; of flying with fruit bats in the Philippines, and joining their great swarm as thousands of them returned to the safety of their cave. She remembered plunging into the darkness, having to navigate by echo-location, relying on visualizing the rock walls in a way that was uncannily similar to the sonar flash that she had just experienced.

She flinched again, as the flood of seemingly impossible memories suddenly found themselves a context: she had done this for a living. This was her life. She was a scientist, an experimental naturalist, and her specialty had always been Experience-Based Zoology.

EBZ was a relatively straight forward process; your mind was simply uploaded to an artificial chemical storage unit, and then inserted into whichever member of the animal kingdom you wanted to research, whether it was a whale, a fruit bat, or something else entirely. It gave you the opportunity to live that animal's life, experience its world, and to mingle with others of its species as if you were one of their own. It was a specialism that had enabled her to make giant leaps forward in mankind's understanding of the natural world.

It also meant that if she was ten kilometers up, and plummeting downward, experiencing sonar flashes that could not be created or processed by the human body, then there may well be a very simple reason for it.

She was not in a human body.

She was in a host animal.

More importantly, given her rapidly decreasing altitude, this also meant that she might be better equipped to deal with her situation than she had instinctively believed.

She tried to stretch out her arms, but the limbs she moved were unlike anything that she had ever had before, in her human body or in any of her previous animal hosts.

She had just extended out two vast, translucent wings.

With a wingspan easily surpassing seven meters in length, she knew that she inhabited a creature larger than anything that had ever flown on Earth.

She was not in a body native to the Earth.

More importantly, judging by the volcanic terrain and the orange sky, she was not on Earth.

This was a surprise that terrified her even more than waking up at ten thousand meters and plunging to her death.

On Earth, no matter what body you inhabited, you could always hope to find your way back to civilization, but most other planets were inhospitable places, incapable of supporting human life. They were still truly wild places, where you were at the mercy of all of nature's cruelties, with no easy way to return to the human world. She had always sworn that she would never take her research out amongst the stars, as despite the great mysteries to be resolved about alien life, it was simply too dangerous an under-taking to make the rewards worthwhile.

No, she knew in her heart—assuming she still had one—that she would never have brought her research out to another world. Not if she'd had a choice. What could possibly motivate such a decision? Why would she have agreed to this?

She held her wings steady, turning them in an attempt to catch an updraft and slow her descent. She tried to move her legs, but found instead that she possessed a long thin body, that streamed backward and ended in a diamond shaped tail. She pulled the limb into line with her body and suddenly found herself leveling off. The world stopped spinning. She was still losing altitude, but at least now she could tell up from down.

The ground beneath her was a jagged patchwork of slabs of volcanic rock, which had been melted and reset so many times, that they had formed into twisted shapes unlike anything she had ever seen before.

In numerous places raw, red-hot lava and ash were spewing out of fissures in the rock, filling the air with flames and smoke, which would have instantly baked and suffocated any Earth-born animal. Her instinctive human reaction would have been to pull away from these seemingly deadly natural dangers, but her years of experience and training meant that she knew how to suppress these urges and recognize an opportunity when she saw one. These hot vents were blasting out super-heated gases, which would provide her with the thermal uplift that she needed to keep aloft.

She angled her winged body toward a plume of ash, and almost immediately felt her body rising on the tide of heat.

She no longer fell; she was gliding, and now she had the precious minutes she needed to assess her situation.

The first thing she noticed was an unnatural weight of something looped around the base of her neck. Tilting her head at an angle, she was able to see the item through the eye of the left side of her head, and she felt a huge surge of relief as she recognized the object. She was wearing a location collar. The narrow silver band would be emitting a radio pulse that would allow her to be located, presumably via a satellite or by a ship in low-orbit. She was not alone. Somewhere out there, someone was monitoring her progress.

She also noticed the suns. One was a yellow dwarf star similar in appearance to the Earth's own sun, but the other was a vast blue supergiant. She could see a plume of burning gases being ripped from the smaller star, and spiraling into the gravity-well of its larger, heavier companion.

The two solar systems were in collision.

The stars were locked in a deadly gravitational dance, which would inevitably lead to the death to the smaller yellow star.

It was a unique event in the galaxy, and it meant that she knew exactly where she was: the planet was officially known as MX-37B, but it was more commonly referred to as Zhu Rong, named after a Chinese god of fire, because of the flames that ravaged its surface.

According to researchers, Zhu Rong had once been like a smaller version of Earth, but the arrival of the blue supergiant had ripped the planet apart, spilling the world's molten-core out over its surface and obliterating its once rich eco-system. The mining companies had swarmed over the broken world, intent on plundering the precious heavy metals from the lava, which were spewing out onto the surface from the very core of the planet.

Scattered amongst the spires and valleys of solidified magma, the prospecting probes had discovered the occasional melted girder, or blackened lump of brick, which were the last vestiges of a lost civilization that had perished in the flames.

Legends on the outer worlds claimed that centuries earlier the population had foreseen the disaster and escaped on a massive interstellar arc, but no survivors or any real evidence for such a mass evacuation had ever been found.

No living thing could have survived such a catastrophe, or so they had believed, until the first robot probes had reached the system. The mining companies' first prospecting missions had discovered great swarms of winged beasts, still thriving in the thin sulfurous atmosphere of the tiny, doomed world.

How these creatures could survive in such a hostile and unstable environment was a complete mystery, which was destined to remain unsolved forever, as any research mission into such an environment was considered little better than suicide. This unknowable, impossible creature had been nicknamed as the salamander, after the Earth species that had once been thought to have mystical powers over fire.

Now, without doubt, she knew that she inhabited the body of one of these salamanders.

But why?

This was one of the many unfortunate side-effects of EBZ. When your mind was transferred into a wild animal, you did not immediately take control, it took time for your intellect to manifest and seize control from the host. The synaptic pathways of your mind, and of your memory, had to rebuild themselves in the new brain. This meant that she would often awaken in a new animal host, with little or no idea of how she had come to be there.

Unfortunately, the brains of other animals tended to be less sophisticated than their human counter-parts, meaning it was sometimes impossible for her to establish a full sense of self. She had learnt to focus on important survival information, such as where she was, and what she needed to do, rather than other less relevant information. Knowing your own name, or where you were born, were details you did not need to know in order to survive in your new body, and she was not about to waste her host's mental resources on such trivia, particularly when she had no idea of how large or small the creature's mental capacity might be. It was like a deadly game of word-association; think of a memory, and you would undoubtedly spark another; rapidly overloading your host's primitive brain. Memories and knowledge had to remain buried, unless she called upon them, and even then more complex concepts and information could sometimes remain beyond her grasp.

Try as she might, she could not recall the events that had brought her to Zhu Rong, meaning her motivations might simply be beyond the grasp of her hosts primitive brain.

Hitting another updraft, she let herself sail upward, hoping that increasing her height would provide her with a better view of the landscape, and may yet reveal something of interest out on the barren, volcanic plain. The first thing that she noticed however, was not the details of the world beneath her, but more startlingly, that she was not having any problem breathing. Riding at the upper edge of the sulfurous atmosphere, she had expected to freeze and struggle for breath, but her host actually appeared to be adapted for these conditions, with her scales protecting her body from the falling temperature, as much as they had from the super-hot thermals. Nor did her body appear to need to breathe the atmosphere, which at least explained how it was able to function in an acidic environment that would have slowly destroyed the lungs of any other species.

Below her, she suddenly caught sight of an unnatural structure: a vast dome, surrounded by a complex network of walkways and heavy machinery, which sat over a steaming, lava-choked rift. She turned herself toward the man-made structure, and let herself fall, rushing toward her only hope of being rescued.

Streaking downward, she caught sight of the base's defenses; a single, rotating turret mounted at the apex of the dome. The weapon had already begun to swing in her direction, before she had even realized she was in danger, lining up its deadly barrel with where she would be in several seconds time. The gun rattled, spitting out a stream of deadly white-hot shells.

She rolled, banking away from the deadly projectiles, watching in horror as the turret turned to follow her move, sending the relentless stream of bullets in a curving arc that sliced downward directly in front of her.

She pulled in her tail and dropped like stone, narrowly dodging underneath the deadly barrage. Falling into the rift beneath the structure, she spread her wings, and let herself be carried on the hot volcanic gases, so that she sailed directly underneath the dome, which would shield her for several precious seconds before she re-entered the weapon's field-of-fire.

What had she expected to find? A rescue party, intent of carrying her away to safety? She already knew that humans could not exist for prolonged periods of time on Zhu Rong; the base was most likely just a robot run mining platform, its defenses automated to protect it from the very life-form that she now inhabited. There was no one here to beg for help, or to reason with, there were just computer systems, motion sensors and death.

She glided along the rift, passing underneath the shadowy base of the dome, catching a glimpse of a ladder leading up to a tiny maintenance hatch, which was unfortunately too small for her massive, in-human body.

She closed her eyes, as she cruised back into the hot sunlight and into the field-of-fire of the turret, knowing that she could not hope to evade the deadly shells a second time, not without the advantages of altitude and speed.

For a moment she was ready to accept her inevitable death. Then she spread her wings wider, and caught the upward breeze.

She could not give up here, not now, not with so much left un-answered, not without knowing who was responsible for dropping her into this inhospitable hell. Even though she knew escape was impossible, she still felt the urge to try. She did not know whether the instinct was rooted in her human mind or in the salamander's animal instincts; most likely neither could accept death without a fight.

She rose rapidly, lifted upward out of the trench.

She heard the canon blaze.

She immediately spun and dropped, swooping low over the dome itself. She swept past the weapon and dove back down the far side of structure, desperately hoping that she could out distance the weapon before the turret had time to spin all the way back around.

She pulled her wings in tight, so that she streaked dart-like out across the landscape, rapidly losing altitude and racing dangerously close to the jagged shapes of the volcanic rock.

The canon fired again.

She closed her eyes, knowing that she had run out of options, and that she could not yet have reached a safe distance.

The shells did not hit her.

She kept her head down, spread and tilted her wings to bring her-self upward and away from the rock, all the while listening to the roar of the gunfire, wondering why it was not tearing her apart.

Chancing a glance backward, she discovered that the turret had not turned to follow her, instead it had locked onto another salamander that had flown too close the structure, distracting the motion sensors just long enough for her to reach a safe distance.

The massive beast had gone upward, flying above the reach of the shells and disappearing into the hazy yellow clouds.

The move was so precise, so well-timed, that she could only imag-ine that the creature had acted purposefully to defend her. It was an act of selfless compassion, which on Earth she would only have expected to encounter in the higher-orders of mammals and in mankind itself.

It implied the salamanders were intelligent and social, capable of organized thought and empathy.

She immediately set out in pursuit of the giant beast. If she could not find help from a human source, then perhaps she could find it from the salamanders themselves.

She rode the hot winds upward, until she found herself gliding alongside her savior. He was larger than her, slightly darker in shading, and he bore the old scar of at least one bullet hole in his left wing; she could only imagine that this would have left the poor beast unable to fly for weeks while the skin regrew, which perhaps went some way to explaining why he would have been prepared to risk his own life, to spare another from the same fate.

The larger beast howled at sky ahead, at much higher pitch than her own earlier scream, but sound waves still flashed images through her mind; of the rocks below, and of other salamanders previously hidden in the clouds, and even of the skeletal structure hidden within the body of her new found ally.

Then, a moment later, another image flashed into existence in her mind. Directly ahead, and slightly above them, there was something gliding slowly above the clouds; a small space-craft was descending into the atmosphere.

Here was her chance to obtain answers. Whoever was monitoring her position, and had thrown her into this situation, would almost certainly be on-board that vessel.

The larger beast hit a thermal, brought his wings in tight to his body and shot upward, making a path directly toward the ship. Simultaneously, the other salamanders blasted free of the cloud cover, a dozen of them streaking upward like missiles, converging on the craft.

Their intention was obvious; to rip the intruders from the sky.

It was an incredible sight. Here, through the combination of the planet's low gravity, the volcanic thermals and some quirks of biology, these mere beasts could touch the very edge of space.

Unable to resist, she copied their wing position and rocketed upwards, beyond the limits of what she had previously thought was possible.

Leaving the yellow clouds behind her, she emerged into the darker skies of the upper atmosphere, where the other salamanders had become almost invisible against the blackness of space. She saw one of them briefly, as it shot across the face of a small silver moon, racing toward its target.

She cried out, filling her mind with a fresh image of the ship, angling herself so that she glided directly toward it.

The collar around her neck vibrated softly, just as a large airlock whirred into life on the side of the craft, venting a small stream of air out into space, as the doors spun open to receive her.

The ship had homed in on her location collar.

It had descended into the atmosphere to collect her.

This was her lifeline home.

With horror, she watched as two of the salamanders shot into the opening, their skinny forms moving with such velocity that the internal bulkheads inside simply crumpled under their impact.

Oxygen spewed out from the craft, like blood from a deep wound, as the beasts tore into the superstructure.

She shot in after them, pulling herself through the open airlock, ignoring the mass of squirming wings and tail that filled the room beyond, and searched instead for any sign of the people that had forced her into this situation.

She squeezed her large body through a doorway, holding her wings in tight against her thin body, as squirmed worm-like through the man-sized corridors, even as the vessel began to rattle and shake, its carefully balanced flight path thrown off by the air gushing from the hole in its side.

She squeezed through a doorway into the main flight desk, expecting to find it filled with a frantic crew, desperately fighting to restore the ship's trajectory, but instead she found the room unoccupied. Red lights flashed and warning sirens wailed, but there was no one there to witness them, except her.

The room tilted and shook, as through the main viewport she could see the yellow clouds parting, to reveal the black rock and flames of the terrain beneath.

The ship was falling.

If she was still inside the ship when it hit the ground, then even if her salamander body could resist the incredible temperatures of the fuel exploding, she would still undoubtedly be pulverized by the impact.

Apparently, plummeting to her death had become a habit-forming, only this time she had managed to encase herself in a fuel filled cage just to make matters a little more challenging. She tried to laugh, and emitted a walrus-like warbling that flashed off the walls.

The sound wave passed through the frosted glass of a cylinder, and flashed off the human body inside, showing her the person's skin, eyes and bones all in a single moment.

Fury overwhelmed her, as she turned on the hidden person, and bore down on the cylinder. The glass was cold. She recognized the object, causing thoughts to flare in her mind, which in turn ignited memories into vivid life.

She was leaning against a cryogenics pod. She had seen them in countless documentaries about space-farers, who used them to cross the long empty expanse of space. She had used one once. She could remember climbing into it, hooking up the IV and heart monitors to herself, and then pulling the lid closed. It had felt like she had been locking herself into her own coffin.

She shuddered.

The thin, craggy face of her salamander form was reflected briefly in the glass beneath her, until suddenly it fractured under her weight, showering inwards on the sleeping person within.

She recognized the face of the sleeping woman. She remembered laughing at photographs of this woman, whilst simultaneously cringing with embarrassment. She had seen this face staring back at her from the mirror every time she had brushed her teeth. She had seen this face countless times; in perfect make-up, tanned, pale, savaged by frostbite, smiling, laughing, sad, distraught and happy. She knew this face.

It was her face.

She should not have been surprised, when engaged in EBZ, you always kept your real body close and sedated, surrounded by the transference kit, in case you needed to be returned to it quickly if your host was fatally injured. Where would have been better to store her body than a ship in low orbit?

She looked at the calm, sleeping face and then at the looming volcanic nightmare in the viewport.

She had no time to think.

She could only act on instinct.

She thrust her head against the remaining glass, smashing the jagged shards out of the way and then reached in with her wings. It was a difficult maneuver without fingers and opposable thumbs, but somehow she pulled the prone body out of the glass cylinder, ripping it free of an IV feed and various other cables.

She held the body tight against her, hugging her human form within her wings, and then turned her attention to rapidly approaching ground. She lowered her head, coiled her body, tensed every muscle and then launched herself at the viewport.

The glass exploded around her, as she propelled herself out into the yellow sky. Precariously holding her human body with one wing, she reached out with the other, and attempted to catch a rising thermal. She spun hopelessly out of control, but managed to propel herself away from the falling spaceship.

The little white craft plummeted into the rocks and exploded in a fireball, showering the surrounding area with shards of twisted, burning metal. The shock wave punched her from underneath, sending her spinning nose over tail, as she flailed wildly about in a desperate attempt to gain control of her descent. If she unfolded her other wing, and dropped her human body, then she might just have managed it. Instead, she looked down at her precious cargo, tucked beneath her wing, and was surprised to see the woman's brown eyes open and staring back at her.

The rules of EBZ were very simple. On no account did you ever let your body regain consciousness when you were not in it. The body would awaken, short of all the memories and ideas that comprised your identity and it would immediately begin to recreate them, whilst also steadily creating its own. The vessel you had left would slowly refill itself, making it impossible for you to get back in.

She had only a handful of hours to get herself back into her own body, before it was lost to her forever.

This however, at that moment, was the least of her problems.

Spreading her single wing against the wind, she made one last attempt to slow her descent, before she slammed into the rocks.

She felt one of her left wing bones snap.

She saw the broken bone tear through her protective scales.

She screamed, at an inhumanly low pitch, as her body cart-wheeled across the rocks, having strips gauged out of her flesh by the sharper edges, but always turning to protect her cargo, until she crumpled to a broken halt.

She lay on the hard rock, her body convulsing with spasms of pain, her precious human cargo still clutched protectively under her right wing.

She felt hands press at the underside of the limb, as the woman slowly pushed her way out of the protective folds of scale. Her eyes were already red and bloodshot from the acidic atmosphere. She wheezed with each ragged breath, as she futilely tried to draw in enough air from the sulfur-choked atmosphere. She knew that there was just enough oxygen present to sustain a human being for a short time, the lingering byproduct of the planet's now extinct plant life, but each desperate breath would be drawing in sulfuric acid from the atmosphere that would slowly burn away the lining of her lungs. She would be coughing up blood in thirty minutes and dead within the hour.

It was a decidedly odd experience; watching your own body suffer. Her body had pulled itself to its feet and staggered away, and had turned to look at her. Its eyes were filled with fear and confusion, as the empty mind struggled to piece together an understanding of what was happening.

Vocal cords would have been particularly useful at that moment, but salamanders did not possess anything so sophisticated. She cried out, trying to make the sound calming and pacifying, but once again just sounding like a walrus.

All animals, human beings included, when scared, are said to have two innate reactions; fight and flight. If the woman attacked her it would be disastrous, but if she chose to run, it would be considerably worse; the woman would accelerate her death, and would die painfully and alone, out amongst the black rocks, drowning on her own blood.

The woman hesitated, and then leaned in closer to examine the broken wing. It was almost reassuring to see, that even in this raw state, human beings were capable of so much more than their basic animal instincts. Compassion for a wounded animal had always come easily and naturally to her, a fact for which she would now be forever grateful.

The woman's eyes were drawn to the silver collar around her neck, and her hands immediately took hold of it, turning it and examining it.

It was entirely possible that Beth would recognize it.

Beth.

Beth Chambers.

That was her name. That was *her* name.

Beth let go of the ring, her face puzzled and confused, her brain's cognitive abilities clearly not yet ready to recognize the object or to process that thought to its logical conclusion.

Instead, the woman took a moment to turn in a circle, and view the burnt landscape around them. Then she turned back toward her, and much to her surprise, hugged her.

Did she know?

Or was this just a gesture of trust, from someone who knew that they were in need of help?

Beth moved hurriedly around her, using a shard of plastic that had once belonged to the fallen spaceship, and strips of cloth torn from her trouser legs, to fashion a crude support around the broken wing bone.

Then she twisted the bone back into position, before strapping the support into place. The pain was agonizing, burning savagely from her wing tip to her tail.

Beth had reset the bone, back in its correct position, meaning that it would eventually heal correctly. It was piece of basic first aid that she had been taught many years ago, and had since used on everything from a bird to a human being.

When she had been a child, she and her mother had nursed a Robin back to health one Christmas. They had kept it in a shoebox, feeding it until it had regained its strength and became strong enough to fly away.

The procedure was hardwired into her brain and Beth had accessed it, meaning that a new mind was already forming in the body, taking that very first step into void that she had once filled.

She raised her damaged wing, testing the limb against the warm breeze that flowed around it, and watched as the wing naturally lifted: the repair would not last forever, nor could it endure much maneuvering, but it would certainly allow her to glide short distances.

She could save her human body.

She could carry Beth to the mining dome. She would be able to get in through the maintenance hatch she had seen when she had flown underneath.

She knew that it was almost certain that the mining dome would contain a habitable area, large enough to allow the occasional visit from an engineering crew, and therefore kitted out with enough pure air and supplies to enable Beth to survive. There was even a chance that there was an emergency life-pod that would allow Beth to escape from the planet itself. The fact that she knew this sat uncomfortably in her mind, making her wonder how she knew so much about interstellar mining platforms.

Had she sold out to the mining corporations? Is that why she had been out here on her own? Perhaps the salamanders had been hampering the mining, and the companies needed an expert to try and ease the problem? Had she put herself into this situation, just to make a quick profit?

She lowered her head to the ground and nuzzled and pushed at Beth's feet, and the woman immediately took the hint, and scampered up length of her neck, until she was sat behind the collar, legs clamped either side of her neck and hands holding on tightly.

She stretched out both of her wings, and felt the wind lift her up. The first few moments were precarious, with Beth's additional weight keeping them nearer to the ground than usual, whilst the binding around her damaged wing blunted its natural aerodynamics.

Shakily, they lifted away from the ground.

Moments later they were five meters up and coasting calmly across the rock.

Beth screamed, both with delight and fear; and it seemed odd to hear such a human sound in such an alien environment.

She spotted the mining dome and banked toward it, watching nervously as the automated cannon swiveled in their direction.

This was not going to be easy.

Beth shook violently, her wheezing sounding increasing painful with each passing breath. She heard the woman spit out the thick mucus from her throat, and knew that it would already have turned red with blood.

There was no time for caution.

The woman would be dead in minutes.

She had to save her.

She dived toward the rift, flying dangerously close to the burning lava stream, but using the high rock walls to shield herself from the weapons motion sensors. It would allow her to carry her passenger half way to the dome, before the weapon could even register their new position, but in the last hundred meters, as they neared the dome, they would be completely unprotected. Sometimes, when you ran out of options, you just had to throw yourself into a situation and hope for a miracle. If the weapon was pointed in their direction, then they were dead. If it was pointed away, or distracted by another target, then there was a slim possibility that they might just reach the hatch underneath the dome. It wasn't much of a plan, but when the odds of survival were stacked so heavily against you, you just had to seize whatever slim hope you could find. Human or salamander, in her mind at the moment it made no difference, both would do anything to survive. Both had the right to survive.

She watched as the rift straightened out ahead of her, revealing the gun turret ahead, its barrel facing very slightly away.

She rose on the thermals, just over the lip of the rift.

The cannon turned to face her.

It fired a stream on bullets, that slammed into the rock wall, whilst she perched herself on the upper edge of the abyss.

If she did not move, then the motion sensors would not find her. She could feel her terrified passenger twisting on her back, no doubt looking from the blazing gun turret ahead, to the lava burning below.

The turret stopped firing.

They were a small target, barely moving against the black rocks, almost as invisible now as the other salamanders had been against the blackness of space. It was just enough to fool the motion sensors, but now they were trapped, pinned down until something made the turret turn away.

The woman on her back softly patted her long neck, just above the collar, whilst making a series of calming sounds.

Even as she coughed up her own blood, she was still attempting to reassure the animal with her. This was the woman she has once been, kind and compassionate, valuing every life, no matter what form it took. This was a woman worth saving, much more so than the experimental zoologist, who had so obviously sold out an entire species to the mining companies, for nothing more than money. She deserved this. She deserved to know her own nature. She deserved to know, and despise, what she had become.

She would atone for her weakness.

She plunged off the rock wall, hit a thermal and rocketed upward. The woman on her back tightened her grip, holding on desperately as they tore upward with astonishing speed.

The cannon fired, blazing bullets down into the lava, its processors tricked by her feint and rapid change of direction.

She shot upward, directly over the turret and then dropped down the far side, disappearing beneath one of the walkways that surrounded the structure, before the canon could spin around.

She spread her wings, catching the rising heat and hovered for a moment, letting herself drift toward the ladder that led up to the hatch.

Beth grabbed the lower rung, and pulled herself upward, clambering quickly toward safety.

There was blood around her nose and mouth.

She reached the little hatchway, and grabbed the wheel that operated the lock.

She pulled frantically at the wheel, for a moment not comprehending that she needed to turn the mechanism to get inside.

Then she paused.

She glanced sideways, to look at an acid-scorched and faded diagram of a wheel and an arrow.

"Anti-clockwise," she read the words aloud.

She turned the wheel and the hatch squeaked open.

Beth had re-established her memories of written language, and had formed enough cognitive ability to act on the information provided. She had lost her body to a new soul. She had reverted to the good person that she had once been. Beth climbed inside, cast a glance back down the ladder and smiled.

"Thank you," she whispered, as she closed the hatch.

Hovering for a moment, enjoying the warm sensation of the breeze flowing under her wing, she felt at peace with the world around her.

The other Beth would survive.

She would not.

With absolutely no momentum, she could not hope to duck past the cannon, not with a broken wing, and yet she would still try; because that is what all living things did, they tried to continue to exist, for as long as they could.

She let herself drift on the air, rising as she emerged from beneath the walkway and turned to face the cannon.

She found herself staring directly down barrel of the weapon.

The collar around her neck shivered.

It was the same vibration she had felt when the airlock had recognised her approach.

The gun did not fire.

Now that the sensors had enough time to track her, the mining company's computer system had detected the collar and registered it as *friendly*, meaning that there could be no doubt that she was in collusion with them. It was all the proof she needed. She truly had sold out everything she had once believed in.

She had never been in danger from the gun turret.

She glided away from the mining dome, trying to put as much distance as possible between her and the body she had lost, suddenly unsure of what future she could have. There was no going back to being human; her only future was the brutal and simple life of a salamander on this doomed world.

If she was going to carry on living, then she had to understand them, better than she had ever understood any animal before. She howled at the sky above her, and her mind immediately filled with images of other salamanders flocking in the sulfurous clouds.

As she ascended, she saw a flash of light from the mining dome, and watched with delight as a tiny life-pod blasted upward. Beth had escaped.

She tilted her wings and twisted her tail, targeting herself toward the greatest mass of beasts, which were climbing toward the upper atmosphere. She quietly swept in behind them. The rear of their party cast a glance backward, and then fell back to fly alongside her, taking in every detail of her broken wing and its crude splint. Then the animal fell further backward, taking up a position at the rear of the group, a move that would enable it to keep an eye on the injured member of the party.

Their course took them upward, above the clouds, and out beyond the upper atmosphere. If she had been human, she would have died instantly, from being frozen, asphyxiated and exposed to solar radiation, however the salamanders continued to rise.

Impossibly, they moved out into the darkness of space, appearing to defy physics as they ascended.

Her mind rebelled. She knew, despite the small planet's low gravity and the superheated volcanic thermals, no creature could possibly reach the speeds necessary to break free of the gravity of a planet. However, despite all logic, the salamanders continued to rise. Abandoning all reason, surrendering herself to the impossible, she found herself rocketing upwards after them.

They were heading for the moon.

That was the secret of the salamander's survival. They were no longer dependent on the burnt out shell of Zhu Rong, they had found a safer place to call their home, the dark side of the small silver moon, which revolved around the planet.

Falling toward the dark moonscape, it reminded her of the time that she flown with the bat swarm into the cave in the Philippines. It took her several days to cross the gulf between Zhu Rong and the moon. Upon her arrival, she could see thousands of salamanders perched amongst the rocks and hear the chorus of their voices. As they approached, the whole area lit up in her mind, as the countless calls mapped out the world in her mind.

Thousands of the winged beasts were crowded around the rim of an artificial bowl-shaped structure, undoubtedly constructed by Zhu Rong's lost civilisation, which must have been projecting a gravity funnel between the moon and the planet. She'd seen similar devices used in spacecraft construction yards, allowing for the easy transference of building materials from the upper atmosphere into space, pulling the material up and then slowing it down before impact.

Such a device would have enabled the population of Zhu Rong to construct their legendary arc and flee from their doomed world. Now, centuries later, the planet's extraordinary wildlife had found a way to exploit the relic to prolong their existence as they continued their daily fight to survive.

She perched quietly on a dark rock and watched the creatures, letting the hours drift by, trying to learn more about them, watching in fascination as they carried chunks of frozen ice back down the gravity funnel towards the flames of Zhu Rong, melting it into the water they needed to survive.

Unexpectedly the collar around her neck began to vibrate.

She stiffened, tensing her wings to launch herself into the air, as she looked around for what could have caused the technology to react.

Then she saw it: a massive mining ship, descending toward them. They had followed the signal from her collar. She had led the mining corporation straight into the salamander's nest.

Numerous hatchways opened in the underside of the ship, allowing dozens of suited astronauts to emerge, each of them flying with the aid of a jet-pack and armed with electric-shock devices.

One of the humans moved directly toward her, its weapon sparkling and crackling with electrical energy.

She launched herself at the target, intending on colliding with the human and knocking it out of air, giving the other salamander's the chance to flee from the intruders.

The astronaut raised her visor.

Beth.

She pulled in her tail and stalled her attack, as she tried to think of a reason to explain the woman's presence.

"It's a conservation mission." The woman's voice crackled through her suit's radio. "The mining corporation only got permission to mine here on the basis that they save the salamanders, before Zhu Rong and this moon are consumed by the blue giant."

They hung in the air for a moment, as she found herself face to face with her old human host, barely daring to believe the words she had heard.

She had not sold out. She had risked everything to save this species. She felt a surge of pride in her actions, and in once of being human, a species that were capable of much more than they ever gave themselves credit for.

She looked at the numerous open hatchways.

She looked at the thousands of doomed salamanders.

She roared.

Her sonar burst flashed through vessel, revealing a great basin shaped hollow, large enough to house the countless salamanders during their relocation to another world.

She dove upward.

She knew they would follow. It was in the very nature of the salamander's, to act in large groups and never abandon others of their species.

They always flocked together.

She led them to safety.

Petrochemical Skies

By David Conyers and David Kernot

J enna Seno rechecked her astrogation calculations for the fifteenth time. The numbers came out the same and still she didn't like them. She rolled her shoulders to relieve the tension in her back. It would be a long shift.

Despite her lack of practical experience, Jenna *knew* the info-courier, *Banshee Stalker*, could make the next hyperspacial jump but only if she used the gravitation field from the Iyangura class star system properly. From twelve light-years out, slingshotting them thirty-two light-years across the void to Hadrian Secondus was a risky move and a stark contrast to the slow three light-year-per-day pace through 'safer' space routes.

"Well, Seno?" Crandon 'Towers' Kerman, the *Banshee's* captain, cracked his knuckles like he didn't have a care.

Jenna swallowed to free her tight throat. She didn't know what he wanted her to say.

"Are you ready? Or do I need to baby-step you through your calculations again?"

Like her, Towers was strapped into an acceleration couch on the ship's bridge, ready for any unexpected forces the jump might generate when they transitioned space-time points. He didn't seem bothered by the risky slingshot trajectory.

He wasn't being fair, but she pushed her inexperience aside. "Captain, if I make a mistake we'll end up in the heart of the system's star."

He sneered. "Would you rather we took the long route, through deep space?"

"No, captain."

"Want to lose six days and an expensive amount of energy generating our own slingshots? Our competitors will beat us to our client."

Jenna closed her eyes. She wanted to scream. She hated that he was having fun with her.

One nagging thought compelled her not to agree with Towers; they could all die. She gathered courage and voiced her concern, "Captain, it *is* safer to open a wormhole in a near absolute vacuum, deep into the void."

He laughed. "Even near stars, Seno, there's a vacuum."

"I guess… I suppose—"

"Make the jump."

She couldn't be sure of her calculations, not yet, she only needed another minute. "What if we collided with any planets in Iyangura 281A?" A collision would be fatal. She wanted to mention the radial velocities if they came out of hyperspace too close to a planet.

"The *Stalker's* hyperdrive automatically compensates for that."

"But—"

"I said jump!"

Without waiting, Towers punched his authority codes into the bridge's console, transferred her coordinates to the ship's semi-AI via his biometrics.

Towers! Damn him! The man was a reckless fool.

They lurched.

Invisible forces pinned Jenna into her acceleration couch.

Anti-matter engines burned a point into the vacuum the size of an atom, until a massive gravitation singularity expanded from space-time and formed a wormhole. The *Banshee Stalker* slipped into it and shifted: everything moved, like a bug swimming in a jug of water poured into a bigger jug, and then into an even bigger jug…

They fell, and Jenna tensed every muscle, closed her eyes from the vertigo. They accelerated away under high-g maneuvers toward who knew where. A vacuum hopefully but close enough to Iyangura 281A to appease Towers.

The wormhole opened on the opposite mouth and pulled the *Stalker* through before it collapsed.

The other side greeted with a noise like hail on a roof. Ship sensors highlighted the hull bombardment exceeded ten thousands rock pellets. Their craft decelerated rapidly, and Jenna opened her eyes. On the bridge, virtual skin schematics lit the outside scene. They weren't in a vacuum but conversely they didn't fall into the million-degree heart of a sun. Visuals displayed a planet.

Debris shot skyward, a mix of giant boulders and fine dust flung outwards. Smaller rocks peppered them like machine-gun fire. The visual displays showed the wormhole opening had pulverized a mountain-sized mass on the surface.

The *Stalker* spiraled downwards into the kilometer-wide crater, which sparkled like a diamond. Jenna closed her eyes again and contained another scream, hoped their disintegration would be instantaneous and painless.

"Hang on," yelled Towers.

The ship's spiral motion slowed, and Jenna tensed against the accelerated kick. She gripped the arms of her couch, and her knuckles whitened.

The ship's semi-AI must have decelerated them hard, they hit the surface and bounced, rather than disintegrate. When the ship skidded to a halt, Jenna called up visuals again and squinted at the masses of highly refractive crystal.

The rocks stopped raining down on the ship's skin. "Can someone tell me what the hell just happened?" screamed Towers. He faced Jenna, his lips white and thin. "What in hell's name did you do to my ship?"

Jenna couldn't speak. Her chest felt heavy, as though someone sat on her.

"Answer me you stupid woman."

Her courage returned. "I think I—*we*—should have calculated for planets."

Towers seemed to swallow his anger, and he threw her a thin smile, but it never climbed to the corners of his eyes. "Too late, Seno." He said it so quietly she almost didn't hear.

She released herself from her couch and flexed the feeling back into her hands. What was he on about? *He* did this, not her.

Towers switched on the general ship intercom. "This is the captain. Send the engineers to check for hull breaches and erect supports."

He faced Jenna and pointed to the door. "Get off my bridge," he roared. "Get out of my sight!"

Jenna climbed into the ship's airlock wearing a Hostile Environment suit, designed to protect from the poisonous atmosphere. The air temperature quickly equalized to the exterior conditions. Already, the heat, warmer than a steaming cup of tea troubled her, but she didn't feel it so much in the HE-suit, and she struggled to hold her mixed excitement and worry in check. She had never visited a planet quite so exotic.

She forced her breaths to slow like she'd been taught, pleased the suit gave her freedom of movement and a chance to escape Tower's prying eyes.

She clambered around the side of the ship and stepped down into the heart of a shattered diamond crater. She stopped, and she could have cried at that moment. The exotic wonder and sheer majestic beauty should have inspired her—light from the planet's main sequence sun reflected into a thousand splinters along the pure diamond mountain range—but all Jenna saw was her mistake.

"Don't give yourself a hard time, lass," said Rowan McLaughlin, the ship's chief engineer, via radio communication. He stared down at her from his position on the highest point on the *Stalker* where he worked.

"Why not?" she yelled back, even though the radio comms in their HE-suits made distant communications easy. "Everyone else is." She climbed the self-assembling scaffold adhered to the skin of ship until she stood with the engineer.

He grinned through the faceplate of his HE-suit. "It's your first time, and you didn't kill us."

"That was only luck."

He shrugged, squatted to examine the exterior hull. He found a small fracture and sealed it with nanobinder glue. It was one of many. "Anyone would have made the same mistake."

Jenna made a face. She stood outside because she couldn't cope with all the tension within. "If you're hoping to build me up, Rowan, it's not working."

"All I'm saying is you were rushed. We all make mistakes."

The HE-suits protected them from the planet's lethal atmosphere, but she wished she could have removed the face bubble and wiped away her tears of guilt before Rowan noticed. Thankfully he was distracted with the repairs. "I'm the ship's astrogator." Her bitter words choked. "I'm responsible, no matter what Towers did."

"But, lass, you *did* get us here safely."

"Not from where I stand."

"If you haven't already noticed, we weren't crushed beneath a billion tons of diamond."

Jenna took in the devastation. Despite the odds, the crew of the *Stalker*, *had* survived the disintegration of the upper half of the mountain.

"I still damaged the ship."

"Look at it this way, lass, from an old man's point of view." He laughed, and his deep throaty voice boomed over her radio link. "If you'd really made a mistake here today, no one would be around to remember. Be thankful the crew is unharmed."

Unable to laugh with him, Jenna shook her head. They couldn't escape the fact they were crippled and stranded.

"Cheer up, lass. We won't be here forever." He found another crack and this excited him. He sprayed nanobinder glue onto the wound and watched the ship's skin heal itself.

She shielded her eyes against the bright white sun overhead and pondered how long they would remain stranded. In the orange hazy atmosphere of lethal carbon monoxide and methane, dark clouds formed long-chained hydrocarbons.

"Look at that," she said and pointed.

The petrochemical skies broke and octane, nonane, and decane, rained down. Streams of black sludge dribbled down the splintered cut of the crater.

"I think that within weeks," Rowan said, "perhaps months, that this fresh diamond crater will have disappeared under a fresh layer of black graphite and hydrocarbons."

She nodded and glanced over Rowan's shoulder at the wound on the ship that healed. "How bad are we damaged?"

"The old beauty's hull is cracked in several places." He pointed at three more HE-suit clad figures who clambered over the *Stalker* forty meters away. "We'll fix her, but the infonics are corrupted, and we've lost data."

No doubt Towers would try and blame her for that too. The Gerontocracy of Hadrian Secondus had a reputation of being unforgiving when contractors missed agreed delivery dates or damaged their goods.

"The quantum storage systems are repairable and will be rebooted soon, but the worst of it is the missing hyperdrive."

"Missing, but I thought…?"

Rowan's expression changed to guilt. "It's not damaged, lass—well it is in a roundabout way—but it's not on the *Stalker*."

"How?" Jenna's stomach churned. Cracked hulls and system reboots were one thing, but a lost hyperdrive was a different matter. Some thirty-two light-years from the nearest inhabited system, their food would run out in two months.

Rowan scanned the diamond horizon. "I'm more worried about what Iyangura might throw at us than missing hyperdrives."

Jenna glanced to the horizon and frowned. "Why?"

"The surface temperature is currently seventy-one degrees Celsius, and this atmosphere is as poisonous as drinking a bucket of cyanide."

Jenna laughed.

"Don't get me wrong, lass, the hyperdrive is still here somewhere. It's leaking neutrinos, and our monitor reads of it are off the scale, so we know where it is, but I'm more worried about the lurking dangers Iyangura 281A might have in store."

"I get it. We're on a hostile world, too far for a rescue mission, but what happened to the hyperdrive?"

He crouched down again, scanned for more hull wounds. "I could give you a technical reason on why, but simplistically, the stress of a near super-mass collision forced it to hyper-jump again."

She flinched. Of course it was her fault the hyperdrive was missing. "So our only means home could be buried under another billion tons of diamond somewhere on this planet?"

"Hyperdrives are smart, lass. It would have materialized in the vacuum above us then rocket back to the surface, so not to create another diamond explosion."

"It ran scared?"

"It had to, or fry. It knows we want it, and it wants to come back, so it's found somewhere safe on the surface to wait, somewhere we could reach it."

"You sound pretty sure of yourself."

"Lass, when you've been around as long as I have, you get a feel for these things."

She couldn't be sure if she wanted to laugh or cry. The situation was better, and worse, than she imagined. "Have you witnessed a wormhole open inside a planet before?" She remembered the moment they fell into the diamond crater, how close they had all come to being pulverized.

He chuckled. "No, lass, can't say I have."

The man would never cease to laugh at anything she said, even now when all she wanted was a sympathetic ear. At least his laugh was friendly. "I don't think anyone has. It will be a great story to tell, though, once we get home."

Lightning flashed in the sky, circular like ball lightning but it flew outward. Thunder followed. Gigantic dark clouds rolled toward them, and black rain fell along the horizon.

"If we get home," she said, aware it wouldn't be long before the same oily droplets were upon them.

"I think you caused a storm, lass."

A third voice crackled over their HE-suit radios. "Seno?"

Jenna cringed. Her skin prickled at the captain's voice. Towers had that effect on people.

"Captain?"

"Where are you, Seno? I've been looking for you everywhere."

"Outside, with Rowan—"

"Don't you mean, Chief Engineer McLaughlin?"

"Yes, assessing the damage."

"Are you an engineer, Seno? Are you qualified in deep space hull repair?"

She sighed. "No, captain." There was no way to win with Towers.

"Exactly. I want you on the bridge, immediately."

"Okay."

When Towers disconnected, Jenna adjusted her privacy settings so only Rowan could hear. She took a deep breath, ready to make a sarcastic comment, but Rowan silenced her with his monotone response. "I think you better do what the good captain asks, lass."

Jenna met Towers on the bridge, where he watched and controlled from a dozen holographic, mind-touch monitors.

Most of the crew could be seen on one or more holographic monitors. Some worked on the failed gravitics system, they hung upside down from harnesses, others punched keyboards on the normally dual-floored rooms. Each appeared overly enlarged and intimate. Her skin itched every time she thought of Towers watching her.

Rowan and his team of engineers resealed cracks in the hull with atomic-level precision, and in others the crew searched the infonics to find their lost data. They checked and re-checked systems in case the quantum-level stored data had 'jumped' into the atomic structure of their hull, or anywhere else for that matter.

"You took your time," said Towers from behind the hyperspace console.

Out of his acceleration couch, he was a tall lanky man from a low-gravity upbringing, hence his nickname, which—for no reason Jenna could discern—he liked. With local gravitational fields half that again of a standard g, he was forced to wear a full-body cyberlace to hold him upright. The lace was ugly, a cheaply manufactured, metallic-twined suit from Aquari III. Towers would clamber from his suit and look half-normal again only when the gravitics were repaired.

"You know that old saying, don't you, Seno, about 'time being money'?"

She nodded cautiously. One wrong word and he'd snap at her. She felt bad enough without him again pointing out her failings. "I've heard similar expressions… I guess I understand."

"Do you really appreciate what merchandise we transport between one world and the next? You understand the commodity we courier?"

Jenna tried not to shudder but she did and hoped he didn't notice. She hated him lecturing and belittling her, and this shouldn't have been a surprise, but she took comfort that Towers treated everyone with the same disdain.

Why the crew failed to mutiny baffled her, except that Towers controlled all the ship's systems through his biometrics, including critical life support and astrogation. Everyone knew the ship would be crippled without him. If he died, they all died.

He tapped his foot for an answer.

"Information?" she said.

"Well, at least something stuck in that little brain of yours. Yes, information. We carried thirty exabytes of raw data for the Gerontocracy on Hadrian Secondus. It's due on their home world in three Standard Days, and we've lost nearly eighty percent of it, thanks to you."

Jenna didn't know how to respond and frowned. "Not me, captain. As you well know, you're also the reason we're here, damaged and—"

"Ah ah!" He held up a hand. "I'm going to lose a lot of money on this trip, with what little information we have left. If a competitor reaches Secondus before us with the same data, my commission is lost. Thanks to you that may well happen."

"Thanks to me?" Her mouth opened, slack. Jenna couldn't help but wonder why the crew's lives didn't concern him more, or if they did, why he didn't voice it.

He glared at her. "A slingshot jump has risks, but you told me you were a capable astrogator."

She said nothing in response to the words she'd used confidently in her interview.

"You're pretty much useless to me right now—as an astrogator, I mean. But I hate to see you stand idle. I have a job for you."

"Captain?" Her jaw tightened.

"McLaughlin told you the hyperdrive is missing. It's out there, somewhere on the surface. I need you to find it."

She straightened her posture to hide her nerves. "What about our hyper-missiles? In an emergency, they could be rigged to get us home."

A bony, metal-wrapped finger poked her in the forehead. "You stupid girl. Hyper-missiles might get us home, but the *Stalker* would be crippled. I'd be out of business and you out of a job." He scrambled into his acceleration couch like a scurrying beetle. "You created this mess, Seno. Just find my hyperdrive."

"How?" She tried to hide her rising anger.

Tower's expression of obvious distaste, mellowed to a squint. "Take Tegan Bright. She knows hyperdrives. She'll know how to find it."

"Captain?" She glared at him, but he took no notice.

"Bright's complained that she's just worked twenty-four hours straight, but tell her from me, I don't care. I want my hyperdrive found and fixed."

Tegan and Jenna shared quarters. Normally, Jenna occupied one floor and Tegan the other, but with gravitics off, Tegan's bed rested on what had become the ceiling. While the carbon planet remained their home they would have to hot-bunk and sleep in shifts.

Jenna shook the hyperspacial technician awake with a light touch.

Tegan sat upright and mumbled a series of nonsensical words.

"Sorry to wake you."

"Jenna?" Tegan rubbed her eyes. She looked exhausted. It took a lot of work to configure hyperdrives for each jump, and the slingshot kept Tegan busy for an entire twenty-four hour shift. "Did I oversleep or something?"

"Um, no. We've got a job to do."

"We? Now?" She yawned.

"Unfortunately, yes."

Tegan pressed the skin screen on her forearm. "What the hell, I've only slept two hours."

"Towers insisted we go now."

"Did he, the bastard?"

Jenna rolled her eyes and mumbled, "He can hear you, you know."

Tegan rubbed her face. "What did you say?"

"Nothing. It's not important. We'd better get moving."

Tegan yawned and readied herself.

Half an hour later, Jenna felt like a construction site droid in her HE-suit, and laden with a gravitic harness, and anti-matter powered rocket attachments, she stumbled about awkwardly.

Tegan yawned again and fitted the last attachment to her suit. They were ready.

Outside, on the diamond surface, the HE-suit felt light. Black oil rained down onto their HE-suit skins, and it ran off quickly from its frictionless surfaces. Jenna stared in wonder.

"You ready?" Tegan asked.

She nodded. "What's the plan?"

Tegan pointed over the lip of the diamond crater, to a mass of black cloud. "The neutrino signal is about fifty-seven thousand, eight hundred kilometers southeast of here."

"Fifty-seven thousand! This planet is huge."

"A super-Earth. Well, maybe not Earth-like in a way we'd want. No trees, no water oceans." Tegan shook her head. "The gravity is higher than Earth-normal too."

Jenna nodded, and the HE-suit hugged every muscle in anticipation.

"We're going to do a suborbital jump and set our HE-suit gravitational profiles to one ten-thousandths normal. Then we'll use controlled rocket bursts to cover the distance. Got that?"

Jenna gulped. She nodded, both thrilled and terrified.

"These things have some kick, even in this high gravity. Don't over fire or you'll get kicked into a high orbit that'll be an infinite ride into the void."

The idea of getting shot into orbit like a primitive rocket gave Jenna the shakes. "You sure it'll work?"

"Relax. It's a HE-suit standard operating procedure."

"How do we control our landing?"

"The suit will control everything much better than you can. Just let it alone. Ready?"

Jenna nodded.

"You'll have to learn how to speak, because I won't hear you through radio comms if you just make gestures."

She gave two thumbs up. "Ready."

"Good." Tegan gripped Jenna by both shoulders. "Remember, you're slaved to my suit, so if something goes wrong, I can fix it."

"What can go wrong?"

Tegan grinned. "That's the spirit. Brace yourself."

Jenna floated for a second before the world blurred, and they accelerated upward and burst through clouds of hydrocarbons and splashes of oily rain. Within minutes they shot beyond the atmosphere, and Jenna could see the curvature of Iyangura 281A's surface. Below her, mountain ranges, lakes and oceans of tar, and other long-chained hydrocarbons seemed well laid out, and vast deserts of carbides and graphite sprawled to the horizon. Black clouds spotted her view, so did the mountains and deserts. Oceans of oil interspersed dark red-rust colored patches of hydrocarbon.

Jenna glanced behind at the now small diamond crater, a tiny scar on an otherwise gigantic carbon world. She knew enough about carbon planets to appreciate the entire subsurface was a diamond crust several kilometers thick. "It's beautiful."

Tegan laughed. "It's ugly."

Jenna ignored the hyperspacial engineer's quip and stared at the world rushing past underneath while they raced southeast like destructive warheads.

"Tegan?"

"Yes?"

"Do you think there is life down there? Carbon world life I mean?"

"I doubt it. Didn't you read the orbital specs?"

"Um, no?"

"Jenna, Jenna, Jenna. You need to think situations through. We're starship crew, not waitresses in some cheap diner. Little mistakes could kill, and many little mistakes can be avoided with a little more diligence."

Jenna felt stupid again. "You're blaming me for my hyper-jump?"

"Jenna, give it a rest. Don't believe what Towers tells you. The jump failed because he insists on routing everything through his biometrics. I doubt he has the speed to process the computational levels you needed. Besides, who's to say he didn't tweak your coordinates beforehand."

"What do you mean?"

"Well, he could have reduced your safety margin on the slingshot jump to conserve his anti-matter fuel reserves."

Jenna could visualize Towers acting that way. "I didn't think he would do that."

"You don't think, and that's your problem. Remember what I said before, about being diligent?"

"To the point of questioning what everyone else does all the time? How do you do it?"

"Easily."

Jenna felt a lump in her throat. "You question me too?"

"Yes, even you. And I can hear it in your whiney voice. You're about to become teary again. Don't. Just because I question you doesn't mean we're not friends."

Jenna's throat tightened, and she couldn't speak. The magnitude of how close she had come to killing them all kept hitting her in waves. She hoped some time away from the *Stalker* might stop the looks of disapproval at every corner, but she couldn't escape her own guilt.

"Look, stop fretting, okay. This planet is on an extremely eccentric orbit, and anyone could have messed it up. How old are you again?"

Jenna frowned and wondered why Tegan asked a question she already knew the answer for. "Twenty-three."

"That's right. You're young. So maybe it is forgivable. You've missed some details. This planet has a two and a half year period, or thereabouts, more than half of that time it is so far out the tar oceans freezes over. But it swings very near to the star."

"Highly eccentric orbits aren't so unusual."

"They are for life bearing worlds. Right now this planet is leaving its habitable zone and entering the hot zone. It's about eighty degrees Celsius out there on the equator. Within a few weeks, it will be a hundred plus. Now, if you've got no more questions, I'm off to sleep for half an hour."

"Sleep?"

"Yes, you woke me early, and I'm dead tired."

"How long before we reach our destination?"

"Just over half an hour. Just let me sleep, while you enjoy the sights."

"You don't feel like you'll miss this amazing view?"

"No. Just shut up, Jenna, and let me sleep."

Although Jenna considered dozing—she'd had less than six hours in the last twenty-four—the view was refreshing, exhilarating, and it terrified her at the same time.

Jenna's suit display indicated her suit heated up before the internal temp control kicked in and cooled her. She wondered if the HE-suit could cope with the heat generated from the sub-orbit speeds. The carbon planet terrain raced beneath them. Occasionally, Jenna noticed rivers and carbide plains, and her mind tricked her into believing she fell toward the surface. She inhaled sharply, wanted to crawl into her suit to hide and regained some sense of purchase, but the illusions faded. The sub-orbit was a kind of falling in itself.

Jenna glanced toward the diamond crater but it had long since vanished. Fifty-eight thousand eight hundred kilometers felt insignificant in terms of interstellar distances, and she felt alone and isolated.

She noticed bright flashes on the curve of the planet.

"Tegan?"

"What? What now?"

"On the horizon, red lights."

Tegan grumbled before she said, "They're volcanoes."

"How can you tell?"

"Zoomed in."

"Oh." Jenna had forgotten their HE-suits featured a wide range of functionality, including telescopic face bubbles. At maximum magnitude, she identified seven volcanoes, and they all spewed large plumes of gas and lava into the atmosphere.

"I think we caused them, Jenna."

"What? How?"

"This is the opposite side of the planet. Our impact would have been like a large meteorite smashing into the surface. The shock waves would have travelled around the planet and converged there."

"So why no crater?"

"I'd say partially because we didn't create a large enough force but also because three kilometers of diamond crust is a pretty hard thing to shake. Volcanoes are probably all our little intrusion could manage."

"Hyperdrives can be quite the weapon of mass destruction."

"Jenna, militaries all over the galaxy already use them in such a way, or would over long distances."

"I didn't know."

"Well, if wormhole opening points was a more precise science, and if—"

Alarms sounded inside their suits.

Tegan laughed. "Okay, we're coming in. Brace yourself."

Rockets fired, and the women decelerated. Jenna's body pressed against the shell of her suit. Whenever mountains and oil lakes rushed at them, she squeezed her eyes shut.

Within minutes the journey had ended.

When she opened her eyes again she no longer felt pushed by invisible forces. They stood on the surface of an immense graphite desert. To their left a rocky plain ambled on forever, and to their right, a featureless desert covered in black slime filled her with concern.

"I can't see the hyperdrive," said Jenna.

"Keep looking. It's here somewhere."

The flat landscape seemed uneventful, but on the far horizon a volcano spumed, tiny at such a great distance yet spectacular. Its red lava gushed and danced in the hazy air. Closer still, about a kilometer from them, a collection of boulders jutted several meters in height. In the thick, clouded air, Jenna identified them as chunks of pure diamond.

A light shower of petrochemicals fell, and the outside temperature climbed to the boiling point of water. "You sure this is the right place?" Jenna asked.

"Just be quiet for a minute," said Tegan.

"What?"

"Can you see the hyperdrive? I can't, so I'm trying to find it."

For the first time, Jenna heard the stress in Tegan's voice. They worried in their different ways. "I'm sorry. Can I help?"

"Don't complain all the time."

This was too much. Jenna tried not to be teary but she was. She didn't want to cause others' problems but it seemed to be all she was good at.

Tegan faced Jenna, one hand on her shoulder, "I'm sorry. I shouldn't have snapped. We're all doing the best we can. But I have some good news, kind of."

"You found the hyperdrive?"

"Yes…and no."

"Where is it then?"

Tegan pointed to the vast flat expanse of graphite sands. "It's about one hundred and twenty meters under all of that."

"The desert you mean?"

Tegan rolled her eyes. "Not desert, Jenna." She reached down and scooped up a handful of thick goo. "This is a sea of oil."

The surface undulated like a liquid would, albeit a very thick and slow one, and in many places it bubbled, and smaller chained hydrocarbons evaporated into the thick, smoggy atmosphere. Jenna could only shrug. With no significant moons attached to this world, tides wouldn't be noticeable.

"How are we going to get it out?" Jenna hoped Tegan had some clues.

"Swim down and take a look."

"Swim down?" Jenna shuddered. She made no effort to hide her shock or the pitch of her response. "How are you supposed to see anything down there?"

"We don't. My HE-suit will guide us."

"You're crazy. Who knows what's down there with all that oil over you. The pressure would be enormous. And what if we encountered a thermal vent?"

"It's no more crazy than waiting until our supplies run dry. Plus you under-estimated just how sturdy our HE-suits are."

Jenna tried to step forward but couldn't. Her duty was to help, to do whatever necessary, and recover the hyperdrive. The idea of descending those depths, under such pressure, and not to be able to see anything, terrified her. She wished she hadn't gotten them into this mess. "I can't do it, Tegan, I just can't."

"Fine!" Tegan snorted, and she climbed out of her rocket and gravitic harness. "Don't go anywhere until I return." Without another word she waded in and disappeared into the thick oily sea.

It took seconds for Jenna to realize her isolation.

"Tegan?"

Nothing.

"Tegan!"

"What now?" came the familiar voice over their comms.

"Are you okay?"

"Of course I'm okay. Just let me find the hyperdrive, right?"

"Yes."

Jenna sat on the hard rock and waited. She told herself she would be okay, she could follow Tegan and help recover the hyperdrive, and she *did* possess the mental strength required to be a staunch member of the crew. She wanted respect, no acceptance, and this was how she could gain it as the youngest and greenest crewmember.

As a student of the leading university on Forrestal, her performance had been satisfactory but not spectacular, and she had been overlooked for graduate positions with the big corporate stellar liners. The small traders and info-couriers deemed her worthy enough of employment but only on a contract basis. Three employers and eleven planets later, Jenna was a long way from home, lonely and disillusioned by how many rules and safety regulations the small ship captains and owners would break for a profit. Her biggest fear was to be stranded, far from her family on an outlying colony, and this was worse.

Jenna rested her head plate against her gloved hands, and stared at the black and reddish ground at her feet. It took her a moment to realize this was not such much rock but dried and brittle vegetable matter. She reached down and scooped up a handful. Dead in the heat, the thick coal-colored grass, or whatever it was, crumpled in her hand like dust.

She zoomed the suits visuals in and out repeatedly. The same dead grass extended to the horizon in every direction.

She noticed a creature wriggle in the pool of oil.

She stood quickly and tensed. The pool did indeed wriggle. Tiny worms swam in the thick liquid. Every so often one surfaced, before it darted into the mire again.

When her initial shock subsided, she reached out and picked one up. It wriggled as if panicked. If it were bigger than a dozen centimeters, Jenna would have been terrified rather than fascinated. It had segmented black scales, armored like a terrestrial insect, with a series of mouths along its length. Tiny pincher-like arms were attached to each mouth, each picked at the oil dripping off it. She presumed it searched for morsels. It flexed and twisted, and with each contortion it lost energy until it slumped in her hands.

She jiggled it but got no response and realized it was dead.

Jenna couldn't understand why, until she switched to an infrared view. The oil pool was a hot fifty-eight degrees Celsius but nowhere near the ninety-seven degrees outside temperature. She had cooked the poor creature to death.

She stood again and scanned the nearby ground. Everything was so black, or dark reddish rust on black, and it made it difficult to see detail, but she now recognized dead vegetation everywhere.

She remembered the Iyangura class planet passed close to the local sun. Surface temperatures rose with each day. Black life would have teamed everywhere a few weeks ago.

Could life have evolved here in a cycle of a few weeks? Had it flourished when the world entered the local's equivalent of a habitable zone, only to die off or hibernate in the deep recesses of the carbide rocks, or at the bottom of oily lakes?

Thunder cracked, and dark clouds filled the sky. The temperature fell, and millions of oil droplets rained down. Jenna could hardly believe her eyes, and it almost seemed refreshing.

A woman screamed, and Jenna's comms unit cut the volume, but her ears still rang.

"Tegan?"

The woman screamed again. Not far from where she stood, a shape thrashed in the oily ocean but it vanished as suddenly.

Jenna raced to the edge of the oily ocean and searched for her friend. "Tegan! Teagan, what's going on?"

Tegan half ran, half crawled from the oil, and hydrocarbon droplets ran off her frictionless HE-suit. She stumbled and fell, wounded. Her right arm was severed from the elbow down. Her HE-suit had amputated it and sealed the wound from the exterior environment, but more slash marks were obvious around the remains of her limb.

Jenna grabbed Tegan and cringed over the extent of the damage. The slash marks had all but shredded her HE-suit to the point it was useless. It held, barely, but what was so sharp it could damage a HE-suit?

"What happened?" Jenna asked.

Jenna couldn't understand Tegan's unintelligible speech. She was in shock.

"Who, what, attacked you?"

Tegan curled into the best approximation of a ball her suit allowed and remained quiet. Jenna downloaded Teagan's latest medical scans from her suit. Accelerated heart rate, high levels of adrenalin and cortisol, and significant blood loss, added to Tegan's shock. The suit at least sealed the wound with plastoflesh and halted the blood loss.

Tegan screamed. She pointed to the ocean with her functional arm and ran.

Meter-long bullet-shaped worms plopped from the oil, and Jenna let out a tiny cry. The ocean bubbled. Thousands appeared, with fins that resembled missile guidance wings. She stared dumb: one wriggled and squirmed like a lizard and tried to right itself from its back. It transformed, and the bullet-like creature rolled and contorted until six segmented legs emerged from black leathery flesh. It righted itself. A tapered end formed and opened into a circular shaped mouth with rings of serrated teeth. It snapped a couple of times, and the rings of teeth rotated back and forth, before it marched from the oily sea's edge toward them.

Jenna sprinted after Tegan who, despite her injuries, had a good hundred meters on her. Every few seconds Jenna turned her head and noticed the bullet-like creatures gaining, until the HE-suit interpreted her actions and provided a small rear-view screen.

As she ran, Jenna commanded her semi-AI. "Map my location against the creatures. Tegan's too."

The HE-suit complied and confirmed Jenna's fears. Tegan ran faster, and the bullet-like swarm gained on them both.

"What do I do? What do I do?"

The HE-suit didn't answer like she'd hoped. Its programming wasn't so smart. Jenna would have to ask more specific questions.

"Why is Tegan faster than me?"

A schematic of her suit appeared on the face bubble. The gravitic and rocket attachments flashed red. Jenna carried additional weight, and it slowed her down. Instead of jettisoning them, she had an idea. "Switch on gravitics, to one one-hundredth normal."

With her next step Jenna catapulted meters into the air. She struggled to stay upright on landing, but the HE-suit compensated, and she bounded onwards, spattered by the falling oily rain.

She reached Tegan in five ungraceful bounds, grabbed, and tried to lift her, but their unbalanced weights were too much. They toppled against the carbide landscape. Even with the protective HE-suit, Jenna felt bruised and shaken.

Hordes of bullet creatures approached, and Jenna scrambled to her feet. "Tegan, look."

Tegan's skin was pale and her pupils dilated. She could die of shock if they didn't help her soon. Jenna cancelled her gravitics so Tegan wouldn't toss her around like a toddler with a doll. "Suit, slave Tegan's suit to mine."

The two suits synchronized, and Tegan's suit mimicked Jenna's, but the swarm of bullet creatures were upon them before Jenna could react.

The initial swarm ran past like panicked antelope and kept coming. The creatures were as high as Jenna's waist. She expected them to bite off her limbs at any moment, but the spindly, black-segmented arms slashed with enough force to jostle but not harm them both. They pushed them aside to pass, and she estimated they weighed about twenty kilos each. Perhaps these weren't the creatures that had attacked Tegan in the deep. Perhaps they fled from a predator that had attacked her.

The diagnostics on her suit flashed red to indicate damage around her mid-section and arms. Jenna couldn't understand why. The suit's frictionless surfaces were harder than most substances in the universe.

They ran past, and she saw the problem: each thin bullet creature's arm gripped a sharp edged diamond. Might crystalline claws have grown from their flesh?

The creatures slashed past her, and a jet stream of mixed oxygen and nitrogen shot from Tegan's suit. How would Earth's gasses react to the rich mix of carbon monoxide and methane?

"Oh shit. Shit! Shit! Tegan, we need to get out of here!"

Tegan didn't move. Her diagnostics indicated that she'd been sedated. Jenna mentally slapped herself for not doing it earlier.

Jenna placed her gloved hand on the crack in Tegan's suit and wondered if their situation could get any worse. She pulled out a tube of emergency seal foam from her leg pouch and sprayed. Her stomach churned with uncertainty, and she prayed the leak would stop. The crack hardened and sealed, and the tension in her stomach lessened.

Jenna made a path away from the creatures that jostled her. Slaved, Tegan followed and weaved and ducked. They both tumbled, and another blow ruptured Tegan's suit again. The new jet of oxygen was wider than the last.

Jenna's suit diagnostics flashed red to indicate her own damage. Their HE-suits' self-repair capacity couldn't keep pace with the wounds they received. "Goddammit!"

The creatures moved around them both, agitated. Jenna stood and could see a new wave of them approach. She bit her lip and tasted blood. There was nothing she could do here.

"Suit, set both gravitics to one one-hundredth."

Jenna jumped and spun. Through her oil-splattered visor, she saw Tegan mimic her, and she smiled with relief. She searched for clear ground. Instead, the only safe area was on the diamond boulders they had seen earlier. The bullet creatures swarmed around them but not over them.

That would be their refuge.

She timed her ground landing, flexed her feet, and rolled in a manner to reduce the impact collisions with the bullet creatures but to no avail. She knocked one off its many feet. It twisted and turned several times before it righted itself. For a moment Jenna thought it would attack her, but it didn't see her and charged off with the rest of its herd.

Jenna stood, and the creatures continued toward the diamond boulders.

Eight leaps later minus further collisions, they landed five meters above the migration, on top a boulder no more than a few meters wide at its flattest peak.

"Cancel slaving."

The suits complied. Jenna grabbed Tegan before she toppled to the ground.

She grabbed the spray and fired it at an awkward angle until her suit diagnostics reported the leak sealed. Again, she resealed Tegan's suit.

Jenna turned the unconscious woman toward her and stared at Tegan's blue lips.

Red warning lights flashed on Jenna's head-up displays and indicated the critical level of Tegan's oxygen.

Jenna's hands shook. She connected her supply line to Tegan's HE-suit so they shared oxygen. She knew she was right but it went against all their self-preservation training. Satisfied their oxygen levels had equalized, and there was nothing more to be done about Tegan's severed arm, she sat to think the problem through.

"Suit, how much oxygen to do the return jump to the *Stalker*?"

Fifty minutes flashed on his visor readout.

"Suit, how much oxygen do we have left?"

The answer flashed onto her helmet display, and it didn't fill her with confidence: seventy minutes on her own, thirty-five if she shared with Tegan. They couldn't return together.

Jenna asked if they could perform another low orbit jump, presuming they could get enough oxygen. The HE-suit informed her the damage to Tegan's suit would not sustain her in a high-g acceleration. Self-repair mechanisms worked at maximum capacity. In forty minutes repairs would be sufficient for their return. The suit didn't have to point out that none of the time frames added up in Tegan's favor.

She checked Tegan's vitals again. At least Tegan was stable now, but she needed a blood transfusion.

Jenna examined their landscape in detail. The black carpet of organic creatures wriggled and stampeded for kilometers around them but none had climbed the boulders. There was no way down, and they couldn't fly back.

She radioed the *Stalker*, via a communications satellite Towers had launched upon arrival. Rowan McLaughlin answered.

"Lass, are you girls okay?"

Jenna hated being called a girl but let it slide. "I need a drone capsule, one large enough to hold Tegan with the capacity to give her major medical attention, and fast. I also need two new air tanks."

"I gather you can't return jump?"

Jenna explained their predicament in a few words.

"Understood. I'm on it."

Her jaw tightened. "How long?"

"About forty-five minutes, lass, and that's pushing it."

She hissed through clenched teeth. "We'll be dead by then."

"Lass, no you won't. That's forty-five minutes in a panicked mind state. Check Jenna's vitals. Unconscious, I bet she consumed half as much oxygen than you."

"What? You want me to calm down?" Beads of sweat trickled down her forehead. What she wouldn't do right now to wipe them away and to scratch her chin. "Sure, I'm stressed, I admit it, but don't think you wouldn't be in the same—"

"Stop yelling at me, and give yourself a sedative."

"What?"

"Get some sleep. Do it artificially if you have to."

"Are you crazy, with all these creatures surrounding us?"

"You said yourself, you're safe. You're perched on a boulder."

"They could climb up."

"Yes, but it's a risk you'll have to take."

Jenna felt drowsy. Energy left her, and her head swam. "You… drugged me?"

"I had to. I took control of your suits from Towers, god knows he hasn't done anything for you." Rowan seemed distant. "I'll wake you… when the drone…"

"Jenna?" Rowan's voice crackled in her earpiece.

"I'm still here," she cried out.

"Your capsule has arrived. It's a hundred meters southeast from you. Can you see it?"

Jenna opened her eyes and wiped oil from her visor. Damage had reduced the HE-Suit's frictionless properties. It stank in her suit, not only of stale air but of her. She blinked into the bright sunlight. Clouds passed overhead against a hazy, dark-orange sky. Jenna noticed the outside temperature had climbed to one-hundred-and-twelve degrees.

She sat upright on the boulder, pleased the HE-suit had clamped her into a safe position while she'd slept. Now that it detected her wakeful state, alert, and in control, the suit released her.

"Jenna?"

"Hang on."

Jenna scanned the landscape. The bullet creatures had thinned out from the swarm of a few hours ago. Most had lain down and no longer moved. Many had died. The ocean edge seemed alive though, and the creatures surfaced every so often. To the southeast the creatures gathered around the drone, or crawled under it, perhaps for shade. She didn't blame them, without her suit the heat would have been oppressive.

"Jenna!"

"What is it, Rowan?"

"You've got three minutes of oxygen remaining."

"Goddammit! Why didn't you say?"

"Sorry, but I tried to get the capsule closer."

Jenna slaved the HE-suits, and they clambered off the diamond boulder. Only a couple of the bullet creatures grunted at her. Each step felt as though she walked in a puddle of her own sweat and excrement, and she wondered how long the suits were designed for continuous use. Had it failed because of the damage they had sustained? Even with the suit's cooling the readings indicated hotter temperatures than minutes before.

The capsule opened automatically. She cancelled slaving and commanded Tegan's suit into the capsule, where it would take over her life support system.

Jenna fumbled with the oxygen valve as though she had eight thumbs. She closed her eyes and concentrated on the connection, rested her head against the capsule, and fresh, life-giving oxygen seeped into her tanks. She had never felt more thankful in her life.

She replenished water, and food syrup supplies, so that the suit was functional, and she glanced at unconscious Tegan. The capsule reported it had given her a blood transfusion, reknitted her flesh, and repaired arteries and muscle. It gave her a better than ninety percent chance of survival.

"Take her to the *Stalker*, Rowan." Jenna could barely recognize her own voice.

"I will, lass, when I can, but…be careful out there."

Jenna pointed to the hydrocarbon ocean, it still thrashed with the bullet creatures. "What do you mean, *when* you can? She's lost her arm down there!" Down in that thick mire, the hyperdrive remained hidden along with whatever had attacked Tegan.

"Rowan?"

No response came.

"Rowan!" she yelled, surprised by her harsh tone. "Tegan needs medical attention, *now!*"

"I'm sorry, lass. I can't."

"Why not?"

"You know why."

Tegan chewed down on her temper. She understood. She should have guessed Towers would have directed Rowan not to retrieve the shuttle, and he eavesdropped even now. Did Rowan do everything Towers asked of him, even when it compromised his morals, and their safety, so he could secure his role of Chief Engineer?

"Why do I need the capsule here, Rowan?"

"There are tools you might need…"

"What kind of tools?"

"Important tools."

Anger burst from within her, and Jenna gritted her teeth.

She stalked over to the capsule's external control panel and activated the emergency override system.

"What are you doing, Seno?" Tower's spoke up.

Jenna smiled. Towers sounded nervous for once. That was good.

For now the capsule was hers to command, so she programmed it to return to the *Banshee Stalker*.

Gravitics took over until the capsule was light enough for her to push it around. Warning lights flashed so she stepped backward. Antimatter powered jets fired, and the capsule disappeared into the thick atmosphere.

She hoped Tegan would pull through.

"Rowan?"

No answer.

"Towers?"

Still no answer, but Towers was always listening.

"Rowan, I'm going to find the hyperdrive now, but if Tegan doesn't get medical attention when she arrives at your end, if she's not fully recovered on my return, well...tell Towers his precious hyperdrive will be nothing but dust."

Jenna stood at the edge of the thick, black sludge. Hundreds of the bullet creatures swam just below the surface, and they lifted their heads out to sample the heat levels before they descended again. Now she wished she had asked Rowan to send her a weapon.

Black clouds converged, temperatures dropped to ninety-five degrees Celsius, and several of the bullet creatures flipped from the sludge and unfolded their six segmented legs.

Jenna froze. She wondered if they would stampede again. They moved forward, around her.

She counted twenty-three brave enough to come onto the land. They gathered around her and seemed not to notice her. Everything was black on this world. Perhaps they 'saw' on a different spectrum, like infrared. The HE-suit's design matched the outside temperature's heat signature, so perhaps she was invisible to them. She hoped so.

They sniffed and prodded their dead, gathered in a circle and conversed. Some pointed random limbs toward the sun, like they knew what is was. Jenna kept still, afraid to move in case she startled them. One creature vomited several worms from its gut, and she leapt backward.

More vomited. Jenna couldn't work out what they expelled until the balls unfolded, formed into worms, and those 'infants' swarmed around the 'parent' that had expulsed them. Other siblings turned on one, the smallest of the litter, and ate it with their circular, serrated mouths until little more than shreds of bone and sinew remained.

Jenna gagged and the HE-suit interjected with an anti-nausea spray.

The spectacle hadn't ended, and each parent turned on one of their remaining siblings and ate them, the second weakest of the brood perhaps. The parent grunted, satisfied, and the young clambered inside its pouch.

The creatures faced the sun again. One pointed to the dispersed clouds. They had a greater understanding of their world than she first appreciated.

As the clouds broke they returned to the tar ocean and disappeared into the thick sludge.

Jenna breathed hard and questioned the bullet creature's intelligence. Had they noticed the sun, that the vegetation had died off and there was nothing to eat? Was it why they ate their weakest offspring? To survive? But why hadn't they eaten their dead? Perhaps the heat had already spoiled their meat.

There was a bigger mystery. Why had these creatures left the ocean now? Why had they searched for food in such great numbers when their world moved into the hot zone and no life could survive on the surface?

On the horizon she noticed a volcano explode. Its gases and carbon mantle spewed into the atmosphere. It made sense, the arrival of the *Banshee Stalker* had created a destructive crater on the opposite side of the planet, so too a brief storm on the opposite side of its polar region. Had the bullet creatures hibernated but woken early, when they should have slept in the deep oceans until the world passed again into the habitable zone?

Jenna felt sick. If their arrival on the carbon planet had woken them before the next habitable zone cycle, they might not be the only ones.

"Suit, tell me where the hyperdrive is?"

It gave her coordinates, one hundred and nineteen meters from her, under the hydrocarbon sea. Swimming down there was the last thing Jenna wanted to do, but she knew she had to, and without further thought, she took a deep breath, stepped forward, and dived into it.

The world outside her visor blackened, and she saw her reflection, red and angry within the shadows cast from the head-up display. She scowled at her tired reflection and hoped she hadn't really aged a decade more than her twenty-three years. The HE-suit had taken over her limb actions, pushed strokes through the oil, and guided them toward the hyperdrive's leaking neutrinos. She felt heavy, from the suit's gravitics that weighed her down to ensure she sunk.

She collided with the first obstacle and screamed. She thought it might be the predator that had attacked Jenna, with diamond teeth capable of penetrating her HE-suit's casing.

The bullet creatures swarmed around her, slid against her waist and under her arms like eels. She shuddered and wished they'd go away. They squirmed in the thousands where the oil wasn't as hot. Her suit alarm went off, and concern gripped her. The creatures attacked her with their diamond claws and damaged the skin of the suit.

Jenna hyperventilated, and the HE-suit sprayed drugs into her mouth and calmed her. She wished it hadn't, so she could feel her raw emotions. She asked how long before the damage threatened her safety.

Fifteen minutes flashed up on her display.

She touched a solid wall and understood she had reached the hyperdrive.

It spoke to her.

—You came.—

"Yes, are you okay?"

—Damage superficial. Hyper-jumped to maintain structural integrity.—

Before Jenna could reply it spoke again.

—Stress levels elevated. Are you okay?—

Jenna nodded. She pushed aside her fear of the bullet creatures' eel-forms. She ignored the fact her HE-suit was all that stopped her from getting crushed under their weight. "I'm okay. Thank you. Do you know if the predator who attacked Tegan is still around?"

—It has been unassembled.—

Jenna nodded, relieved. "Are you ready to rejoin the ship?"

—Not possible. Only twenty-four exabytes of data maintained. Storage capacity unstable. Corrupting at one hundred and twenty eight terabytes per second.—

"Information?" she asked. "What information?"

—Memory data.—

"What? Oh you mean…"

Jenna performed a quick calculation. If the hyperdrive spoke the truth, it had salvaged their data for the Gerontocracy—and there was no reason to think differently—it gave them about two days before the information was lost.

"Information? Where is the information? In you?"

—Indigenous swarm. Held in cell structures. Neural structures easiest…most accessible data storage available at time.—

"I see—"

—Corrupting quickly with death rate due to heat and starvation impacts.—

Jenna understood what surrounded her, a biological library of commodity data.

—Due to depleted energy reserves they are unable to hibernate again. Data moving to the most stable crystal structures.—

Jenna nodded, and a tingle of excitement ran along her back. She'd found her leverage. She understood the data transfer of knowledge still occurred from the hyperdrive, through the indigenous swarm of bullet creatures, and out into the diamond boulders. There had to be data losses along the way but perhaps these would be minimal. Even the boulders had a limit to their capacity though.

Jenna clambered from the oily ocean, and the thick fluid no longer sloughed off her frictionless suit skin but formed rivers from the deep scratches. Fortunately, the damage to the suit wasn't critical. The hazy orange skies were clear again, and the hot sun bore down on her. Thousands of bullet creatures too slow or incapacitated to return to their sea had died. She wondered what the smell of so many rotten carcasses would be like. Probably like the inside of her suit right now.

Jenna sipped water from the hydration tube but had no appetite. She stumbled forward.

"Towers?" she called out. He didn't respond. "I've talked to the hyperdrive," she said. "It's ready to come home."

"Good," echoed Towers' disembodied voice.

Despite her mental preparation, Jenna still shuddered at the creepy reminder of how their mad captain liked to watch and listen to everything, even when situated on the opposite side of a super-sized carbon world.

She wouldn't let him get to her. "There is one more thing, before I retrieve it."

"No games, Seno. You're testing my patience already."

"I know where your Gerontocracy data is, most of it, anyway."

"If you have it, bring it with you."

"No!"

"What was that, Seno?" His tone sharpened.

"If you want the info, I need things in return."

"You're in no position to bargain."

Her stomach churned. She couldn't let him get away with his abrasive attitude. "Fine. I'll just bring the hyperdrive without any data." She faced the oily sea, ready to dive in, not so terrified now of the deep and certain the bullet creatures were more scared herd animals, or a sentient tribal species, than predators.

"Wait!" he called out. "You really have the information?"

She allowed herself a smile of satisfaction.

"Yes, Towers, I do. Most of it, corrupted and fragmented maybe, but it's there. And it's corrupting fast, so the longer you delay, the less you'll get to Hadrian Secondus in time."

"All right." Towers growled. "But you'll pay for this Seno. I swear you will."

Jenna closed her eyes and swallowed hard. He *would* find a way to make her suffer. "I want to know that Tegan is okay," she said. "You'll make sure she gets the best medical attention at Hadrian Secondus."

"Fine."

"And you'll pay for a replacement limb too."

"Also fine."

"And I want one of your hyper-missiles."

"No way. The hyper-missiles cost more than you'll ever make in a life time."

"Without one, I can't get the data," she lied.

Towers fell silent again, but Jenna knew she could hold her silence longer.

"Very well," he said, "but if you don't return the data, I'll ruin you, Seno. I promise you that."

In the long silence, she said nothing. Negotiations had concluded. It was enough. She had stood up to Crandon 'Towers' Kerman for her sake, for Tegan's, and for the sake of an Iyangura class planet not ready for humankind.

She ignored that Towers would continue to monitor her every move and dived deep into the oily sludge once more.

Jenna stood on the edge of an enormous diamond canyon with Rowan, pleased for once the oily rain had stopped. She was content with the hyperdrive's recovery, and a three-ton boulder of pure diamond now rested in the *Banshee Staker's* cargo bay. The information required by the Gerontocracy was stored at a quantum level in the qubits of the diamond boulder's carbon crystalline structure. It was being scanned, and the data transferred onto the *Stalker* infonic systems.

Hundreds of kilometers distant, on the far horizon, a volcano erupted and its carbon mantle exploded. A gigantic plume burst into the petrochemical skies. They observed the hyper-missile shoot toward it. Almost too fast to be perceptible, it entered the plume and exploded. A wormhole opened. It tore the structure of space-time into a bubble dozens of kilometers across.

The volcano's matter pulverized. Organic matter, the carbon mantle, graphite, diamond, silicon, and titanium carbides, vanished in an instant. The wormhole collapsed, like Rowan had calculated, before the mass was sucked into hyperspace forever. Space-time was restored and the bubble fragmented. It sent a powerful explosion of matter that wasn't sucked into hyperspace in all directions.

"You wanted to see this, lass, but now we should go."

Jenna faced Rowan and saw his anxious expression. She nodded, and they reduced their gravity profiles to one ten-thousandths normal and shot into the sky. Before she knew it, they floated above the atmosphere and rode a parabolic trajectory ahead of the compression wave. Jenna couldn't believe so much destruction could be so captivating.

"You've wiped out all the species in the immediate vicinity," said Rowan.

She smiled, but she also felt sad because it would kill all the bullet creatures, even those who saved Tower's valuable data in their biology. If the creatures were sentient like she suspected, the loss was even greater. She counted on them not being the only representatives of their species.

"You're right, Rowan. But they'd have died anyway. The cloud cover we created now, however, will lower surface temperatures, bring storms, the hydrocarbon rains, and vegetation for those that do survive to feed on."

"I don't get your point, lass."

"I think our arrival brought them from hibernation early. They expected an equivalent lush green world. Instead, they found it parched, desert, and the heated atmosphere killed a lot of them. This way we give most of them a second chance."

"So you're giving them a chance to eat before the world comes too close to the sun. Towers isn't going to like the fact you tricked him out of a hyper-missile."

She wondered exactly how far Rowen's loyalty to their boss extended. "He'll have to deal with that however he wants—"

"Oh look, lass," interrupted Rowan.

Jenna turned to where Rowan pointed and caught her breath. Safe from the cloud of fallen debris and destruction, Jenna could see the black and rust red landscape. She laughed. "It's beautiful and harsh all at once."

"Did you tell Towers the data was stored in the bullet creatures?"

"No."

Rowan chuckled. "I think he's going to be…how do I put this nicely…um, more than *slightly* upset."

"I think after he lost his hyper-missile, nothing matters where I'm concerned."

"I hope you're wrong, lass." He mumbled.

"So do I, Rowan. But I doubt it."

It wasn't long before the ship appeared, and Jenna pointed to the *Banshee Stalker* in high orbit above Iyangura 281A, with a field of distant bright stars behind her. "She looks like she's ready to open a wormhole."

"She is, lass. I reckon if you hadn't asked me to join you on the surface, you might have been here for a very long time."

Jenna bit her lip. Was it a comment of support, or an indication she needed him on side to survive? Either way, she didn't care much for Rowan's opinions any more. "I don't doubt it."

"I'll take us inside if you like."

"Yes please," she said, fists clenched, but not for the reason he might have thought.

Showered, Jenna no longer recoiled from her own odor after three days straight in a HE-suit, but she felt tired beyond belief. She wouldn't let herself sleep until she visited Tegan and saw how her friend was.

Jenna strode into the medical bay. Although one fist was clenched shut, she felt calm for the first time in a long while.

Tegan lay in a bunk, unconscious, with an intravenous drip in her arm. Monitors checked her status. She seemed so pale and fragile. A robotic surgeon was attached to the stump of her arm. It performed micro-repairs, but the new limb would have to wait until they reached Hadrian Secondus. The robot had rebuilt wounds her upper arm, but Jenna could still see the burns and numerous cuts.

"Oh, you poor thing." Jenna sat with Tegan for a long time. Sleep threatened her, and she stood to leave.

Towers strode into the room. "I thought you'd be here," he said with a scowl. He no longer wore his cyberlace. "We're about to jump. But I came to let you know we can do without you on this one." He attempted to smile, but it came out all wrong, and he appeared troubled.

She shrugged, leaned forward and straightened Tegan's hair.

"You tricked me, Seno. Nobody does that on my ship. You're fired. I'll make sure you never work in space again."

He glared at her, but she stood her ground. She didn't care. "Do what you feel you have to do."

"You sure about that?" He cocked his head sideways and stared at her.

"Absolutely," and she meant it. She thought of a dozen insults to throw at him but none seemed worth the effort. He no longer owned her. He had given away the right once he'd sacked her. "Don't you have a ship to captain?"

"What?" Surprise twisted Tower's face into a hideous expression.

"Just honor your bargain, and make sure Tegan is well cared for." She ignored him and picked up Tegan's hand again.

She closed her eyes until the sound of Tower's footsteps no longer echoed along the corridor. She opened her fist and held out a diamond the size of her palm. "This is yours, Tegan. Get well soon."

She smiled. If it was possible to do one thing well in life, to make the right decision and stand by it, even when the circumstances were difficult, then she hoped she had done so for Iyangura 281A. She had no idea what she'd do next but she was ready for it.

THE HYPHAL LAYER

BY MERYL FERGUSON

Thandi shaded her eyes. The fish-bowl sky stretched over her, streaked with the colors of fire, reflected on the seething surface of Ingold's endless ocean. Two thin contrails marked the entrance of a shuttle into the humid upper layer of the atmosphere, bringing new faces to their isolated existence. Thandi watched the distant spark through the tinted visor of her biohazard suit. Sweat trickled down her cheeks.

The metal walkway shuddered beneath her and she grabbed for the handrail. A knot of hyphae bulged above the ocean's surface, the fat, thread-like bodies twining about each other in a mindless reproductive frenzy. She braced as the mass hit the walkway, setting the structure rocking.

When the walkway had settled, she completed the calibration sequence on the floating tank in front of her. Inside the biopharm, hyphae writhed in a sterile slurry, turning Ingold's ocean into pharmaceuticals.

A klaxon sounded, indicating the end of the day. Other bio-suited figures moved along the walkways, heading for the floating pods that made up Ingold City. The pod cluster was half habitation, half research laboratory, and home to the fifty people that made up the Monteleone pharmaceutical company's owners and staff.

Thandi lingered, head turned to the far horizon, watching for the shape of a submariner breaking the surface. Somewhere out there, her lover Gian roved through the dark waters in his submarine, searching for new life. The glare of Ingold's sun battered against her visor and she turned away. Gian would be here in his own time, and if she lingered any longer, she would be late to unload the shuttle.

The airlock cycled closed behind her, shutting out the stink and glare. She stripped off her biohazard suit and hung it in the sterilizer. The digital display on the wall counted down to the shuttle dock. She hauled on a fresh anti-static jumpsuit, slipped on rubber-soled shoes and left the cleanroom.

The metal decking beneath her feet rang as she pushed on at a fast walk through the narrow corridors linking the habitation and work pods. She ducked through a doorway into the small unloading bay and spotted her supervisor Niko's shock of sandy hair. The conveyor from the shuttle started up as Thandi hurried over.

Grinning, Niko met her at the end of the conveyor. "Last one in—"

"Unloads. I know, I know." She grabbed the handle of the walking lift and maneuvered it into position. "What's in this shipment?"

Niko tapped on his pad with a stylus. "Nothing unusual. Food-stuffs, medicals, some research stuff for Aurelia and, oh, new movies." Niko gestured at the conveyor with the pad. "And a couple of gene sequencers. That's good, the lab has been screeching for them for weeks."

Light filtered in through the heavily tinted observation panels in the ceiling. Distant bumps and rumblings sounded as the shuttle's aerobridge connected. The boxes came off the conveyor and Thandi lifted and stacked, while Niko scanned the barcodes. She didn't mind stacking and she didn't need to talk, as Niko chattered enough for both of them.

The main airlock cycled open and Thandi paused, curious to see who was coming on board this season.

"Did you see the list?" Niko stepped up beside her. "We got a master's student this time around."

Thandi had read the list, just as interested as Niko in who they would be sharing tenure with for the next six months.

A tall woman with skin almost as dark as Thandi's stepped through the door first. The woman grabbed the railing beside her, eyes widening in surprise. Thandi grimaced in sympathy. The constant motion of the floating city no longer bothered her, but it took a while for new arrivals to get their 'sea legs'. "There'll be a run on seasickness tablets tonight," she said to Niko.

"Lucky we got a fresh batch in, then."

The packages had piled up at the end of the conveyor, so Thandi returned to her stacking.

"Hey, look who's back."

Thandi glanced over her shoulder as Akos Monteleone, second son of the company directors, came down the ramp with a stranger. The stranger wore a neat business suit, in direct contrast to the rumpled and casual students in front of him.

"Who's that with Akos?" she asked in a low voice.

"No idea." Niko tapped on his pad. "He's not one of the students."

Thandi straightened, curious. Akos wobbled his way down the ramp, unsteady on his feet after being off planet. But Akos' companion walked confidently down the ramp without touching the railing.

"He's got great balance," said Thandi.

"Maybe he's a gymnast," said Niko.

"Or a tightrope walker."

"Famous ballet dancer."

"Trapeze artist."

"Professional plate spinner," said Niko.

Thandi snorted with laughter. The stranger's gaze flashed to her, his eyes narrowing. Thandi swallowed her laughter, her cheeks burning.

"Thanks," Thandi muttered to Niko, ducking her head. The next box on the conveyor was marked fragile. "Here's one of the gene sequencers." She held it for Niko to scan. Over Niko's shoulder, she saw Akos and his companion coming their way.

"Niko." Akos held out a hand for Niko to shake. "Want you to meet Sachin Vidar. Sachin's an efficiency expert. And this is Thandi."

She plastered a smile on her face while she shook Sachin's hand.

Akos grabbed the conveyor as the city rocked. "Whoops. Haven't got my legs back."

"It is always like this?" said Sachin, standing easily as the floor rose and fell.

"Always. You'll get used to it," said Niko. "Any news, Akos?"

Akos straightened. "Right to Evolution tried to shut us down again. Didn't get very far though. As long as the Senate keeps backing us, we're safe. Still, they've been getting more aggressive in their campaigns." He grinned. "Oh, and a couple of them threw eggs at the Greens' party rep at the last debate and ended up getting charged."

"I thought Right to Evolution were chummy with the Greens?"

"The Greens dumped them. Too politically volatile." He glanced at the clock. "We should go, Sachin. We can get you settled in before the induction, and I'll introduce you to my parents. See you there, Niko, Thandi."

"Nice to meet you," said Sachin.

When the door had closed behind them, Niko leaned over to Thandi. "What's an efficiency expert?"

Thandi raised her hands in a gesture of confusion. "Someone to make us more efficient, I guess."

"Well, he'd better not go sticking his nose into my lab," grumbled Niko.

"Can't improve on perfection," said Thandi. She ducked as he threw the stylus at her, then laughed while he jogged over to retrieve it.

"There's nothing wrong with the way I run things, is all I'm saying."

"Well if you'd scan things instead of chasing your hardware around, we might get this done before induction." She held up a box and he flicked the scanner over it. "See? Much more efficient."

The overhead speakers crackled to life as Thandi steered the walking lift through the door to the calibration lab. "Induction in ten minutes. All staff to the auditorium." Just enough time to unpack. She tore away the packaging from the first box and a flyer fluttered to the ground. *All life has the right to reach its full potential without interference!*

Thandi rolled her eyes at the Right to Evolution propaganda. She found another one tucked under the gene sequencer and a third between the pages of the manual.

Thandi gathered them up, frowning. Someone in the packing room at the calibration company must be a Right to Evolution member. She went to toss them in the recycler, but hesitated. Should she report the flyers? She put them down on the bench instead. She would tell Niko about them, when she got the chance, and he could decide whether to approach the calibration company or talk to the Moneteleone family.

"Five minutes to induction," announced the speaker. Thandi left the second machine in the box and headed for the auditorium.

Bodies packed into the tiny auditorium. Thandi spotted Niko sitting on the end of a row and sat next to him.

New faces mingled with the staff who had finished their tenure and would be going home on the shuttle. Thandi looked them over. She knew faces and names, and a little bit of who they were. But after six months they always moved on again. She no longer tried to make friends with them.

"I'm surprised Akos came back," said Niko. His gaze rested on Akos and Sachin as they chatted with Aurelia Monteleone, chief biochemist and part owner of the company. "I really thought he was going off-planet for good this time." He leaned close to her ear. "Apparently after the last fight with his father he said he wasn't coming back until Gian was running the company."

Thandi winced. She had heard that rumor too. "Maybe he likes it here."

"Only you like it here, Thandi. The rest of us are just passing through." Niko caught her expression and laughed. "I'm here for a while yet, don't worry."

Aurelia stepped to the podium and clapped her hands for attention. The new staff took seats in the front row, all of them now wearing the company-issued cotton jumpsuits with the Monteleone logo on the breast.

Aurelia introduced all the newbies by name. The dark woman Thandi had seen first was Madja, the master's student. She had undone her hair since getting off the shuttle and it spilled down her back in dark waves. Thandi rubbed her hand over her own short-cropped hair. Much more practical with limited shower time.

"More newbies to scare." Niko sighed. "I'm running out of stories, Thandi. Something exciting better happen soon, or what will I talk about in my safety briefings?"

Thandi hid her smile. "Make something up. You're full of hot air."

Niko clutched his chest as if wounded. "Ouch." He stood and made his way down to the stage.

"And now I'll hand you over to field supervisor Niko Mencher for your safety induction," said Aurelia.

Niko nodded to the crowd. "If you've read your briefing notes, then you'll know there are two rules you must not break." Niko paused for effect. "Failure to follow these rules will get you confined to quarters until the next supply ship comes in six months and will result in termination of your contract.

"Do not interfere with bonding or earthing under any circumstances. Report any static discharge to your supervisor immediately, no matter how small." Someone giggled, whether from nerves or disbelief Thandi couldn't tell. "You may think it's funny. But we are floating in a chemical soup under a highly ionized atmosphere. Static builds up fast and has nowhere to dissipate.

"Ingold City was designed to deal with static, but if it builds up enough, we could start a static storm. Ever been in a hurricane?" Niko scanned the silent room, frowning.

"The second thing is, never go outside without your suit, for three reasons. Firstly, we are a class one bio-security environment. Nothing comes in, nothing goes out without sterilization.

"The oxygen level here is too low to sustain life. You can lose consciousness without warning.

"Finally, your suits have built-in emergency floats, so if you fall in, your suit will bring you to the surface."

Niko stepped away from the podium, facing the crowd directly. "This is the third reason for wearing your suit: without it, you go straight down, and you won't stop until you hit ice."

The only sound in the room was the hum of the ventilation fans.

"We haven't lost anyone yet. Don't be the first."

Niko went on to explain the production techniques and Thandi's attention wandered. Sachin and Akos stood to the side, conversing in low tones.

The door opened and Gian slipped through. Warmth spread through Thandi at the sight of him. He swept the room with his gaze, breaking into a smile when he spotted her.

Akos reached out and grabbed Gian's arm. Thandi sighed. Months without seeing Gian and now Akos who wanted to rave about his efficiency expert. The two brothers chatted to Sachin. Gian, though older, was a head shorter than Akos, closer in height to Sachin. They shook hands and Thandi consoled herself with a view of Gian's broad shoulders.

Conversation broke out as soon as the lecture finished. Thandi waited while the room emptied and then made her way to the door, looking through the stragglers for Gian. Surely he wouldn't have left. She stepped out into the corridor and there he was, waiting for her.

He held out his hand, his face alight with enthusiasm. "Come and see what I found."

Thandi walked with Gian to the airlock, fingers twined in his. "You must have had a good time. You were supposed to be back a month ago."

"I know. But I hit a major current and ended up a few hundred kilometers off course." The airlock cycled and they walked down a narrow tunnel into Gian's ship, the *Architeuthis*. *Arkie* had been a deep-sea survey vessel on another world, re-commissioned for research purposes on Ingold. Her elongated hull had a transparent viewing pane encircling the middle, ringed with powerful lights to penetrate the dark waters. While she rested half-submerged beside the city, Thandi could look down at the mass of writing hyphae below or look up at the stars flickering between scudding clouds.

"Stop looking at the stars and come and see something interesting," said Gian from the other end of the ship. Thandi crossed a narrow walkway to join him in front of the row of tanks lining the wall. Light from the tanks illuminated his face, his mouth curved up in a smile. Nothing made Gian happier than finding new blobs in Ingold's ocean.

"Look," he whispered.

Thandi focused her attention on the tank. A tapered cylinder spiraled slowly through the liquid. Lines of thin hairs circled the stubby body. The organism hit the side of the tank with a soft thud and hung there, suspended.

Gian stroked the glass. "Isn't it amazing?"

"Gorgeous," said Thandi. The organism reversed slowly and trundled the other way. "New group?"

"New thing entirely. It has a gut, which is unique on Ingold, as far as I can tell. It's also beautiful." He switched off the tank light and the overhead lights, leaving the room in darkness. The organism started to glow softly. Tiny lights gleamed along the rows of hairs, outlining the translucent body in stars.

Gian slipped his hand in hers. "They live in the dark, below the hyphal layer. I turned off the outside lights one night and there they were. There must have been thousands of them. I wish you could have been there."

"Me, too," she whispered. A little spurt of jealousy soured in her belly. Sometimes she dreamed of going down into the dark with him. Then she would wake in her pod with the night-light blazing and know she was still trapped on the surface by her fear of the dark.

After dinner, they lay on his bed and watched the stars. Thandi rested her head on his shoulder and listened to his excited chatter about the new blob. "There's years of study there for someone, Thandi."

"For you. You could do your doctorate on it."

Gian snorted. "No-one cares about doctorates in taxonomy any-more. My mother could do a genetic profile before I could figure out the basic relationships. No, I'll leave the research to someone else."

"They'd have to come here to study though, surely?"

"For this? Yeah, I think someone could get funding." He kissed her hand. "Anyway, I've been rambling on but I haven't asked you how things are. Anything interesting?"

"Not a thing. Nothing changes here."

"What about the new recruits?"

"Some might make it." She drew patterns on his chest. "What do you think about Akos's new friend?"

Gian grunted. "He's a consultant or something. Supposed to review our systems and propose improvements to increase our profitability. Dad told Akos he could hire someone."

Thandi tried to imagine Gian's father taking advice from anyone on running his company. "I thought Benesh wasn't interested in profit?"

"He's not. But after the last fight…" Gian shifted on the bed. "Dad's humoring Akos, I think. He's worried Akos will leave. I keep saying to Dad, if Akos wants to leave, let him go. You'll both be happier. But Mum doesn't want him to." Gian sighed. "Not that either of them listen to me."

"You're worth ten of them," she whispered into his bare chest. "They should listen to you."

Gian stroked her short hair with his hand and didn't answer. Thandi hugged him. "Your talents are wasted here. You should go off-planet instead."

Gian laughed into the darkness. "You know I can't. And besides, where else would I find new and interesting organisms just by dipping a net into the ocean?"

Gian still slept when Thandi slipped out to start her maintenance schedule. Engrossed in a check of the earthing system, she jumped when her suit speaker crackled to life.

"Hello?"

Thandi looked up, not recognizing the voice, to see the new mas-ters' student, Madja.

The woman smiled at Thandi from behind her visor. "I'm sorry, I've forgotten your name."

"Thandi."

"Madja." She held out a gloved hand and Thandi shook it. "They said last night to come to you for instrument problems?" She held out a refractometer. "I pulled this out of the packing this morning and there's a crack in the glass."

Thandi untangled herself from her test unit and held the instrument up to the light to examine the damage. "Leave it with me, I have some spares in the lab."

"Oh thanks. How long do you think it will take? I wanted—"

The wail of the emergency siren drowned out Madja's words. Thandi grimaced and handed the instrument back to Madja. "We need to get inside." She shoved her test unit back in her kit. "Come on."

"What's wrong?" said Madja, hurrying after her. "Is it one of those static storms?"

Thandi smiled behind her visor. Niko had done his usual job scaring the newbies. "No. This close to a shuttle, it's probably a drill." They reached the airlock and Thandi keyed the release.

Madja hesitated. "Shouldn't we wait for the others?"

"Nope. In, cycle, out, remember? In," said Thandi, nudging Madja before her. She closed the hatch and pushed the cycle button. "You can only fit three in here at a time. Your priority is to get through and inside as fast as possible, unless you're a warden or helping someone injured."

"Oh right. We heard that at the briefing. I'm sorry."

"It's okay. This is why we have drills. There's a lot to take in at once." The inner door cycled and they climbed out into the clean room. She stripped off her suit.

Madja followed her lead. "How long have you been here?"

"Six years."

More people came through the lock. Thandi led Madja out to clear the room. They met more staff heading for the central safety chamber, complaining about the interruption to their work.

Madja hurried after Thandi. "This is my first time on another planet than home."

"You picked a crazy place." Thandi searched for Gian as they hurried through the corridors.

"Well, I wanted to go somewhere different. I've been on an Earth-type planet all my life. What about you?"

"Oh." Thandi brought her attention back to Madja. "Just your normal world." She spotted Gian by the operations console with his father.

Gian's father Benesh bent over the screen beside Gian. "Look at this. One minute the lab shows full power, the next nothing."

"Sit here," said Thandi to Madja, and hurried over to join them.

"I should get down there," said Gian. He spotted Thandi. "Thandi can come with me."

Niko came through the door and Gian grabbed his arm. "You too."

"What's happening?" asked Niko.

"Power surges in the lab," said Gian as they hurried through the corridors. The siren droned on. A sudden jolt knocked them off their feet. Thandi slammed into the decking, whacking her funny bone.

"What the hell was that?" she said, rubbing her tingling arm.

Niko stood, his chin bleeding where he had cut it. "Did we hit something?"

"There's nothing to hit." Gian got to his feet and took off down the corridor.

Thandi exchanged a worried glance with Niko then hurried after Gian. Another shock jerked the city sideways, throwing Thandi into the wall and Niko and Gian to the floor. No one spoke this time. They ran, Niko wiping the blood from his chin.

Gian dived through the door into the clean room outside the lab, Thandi and Niko on his heels. A suited scientist on the other side of the glass waved her hands, frantic for them to stop. Gian reached for the door. Static snapped at his hands with an audible crack.

"Holy shit," breathed Niko.

Thandi edged closer to the window. Static in the lab was a bad, bad thing, an impossible thing. Every pipe, every spray nozzle, every tank where the crazy soup of Ingold's ocean was stored or piped or used was connected to the inbuilt bonding.

Thandi peered into the lab. The emergency lights bathed the dead consoles in red light. Droplets of liquid condensed on the window. Not a good sign. She craned her neck. The staff huddled together against the wall, their bonding strips clipped to the main wall frame in an attempt to connect to Ingold City's earthing system. Two staff crouched by the door, trying to lever the emergency door release.

Light flickered around the pipes. "Look out!" Thandi shouted, banging on the window. A blue spark arced from one tank to another, the crackle audible through the glass.

Niko flung open the safety cupboard and yanked out the fire blanket. Gian and Niko used the blanket as insulation and tore open the door. The scientists tumbled out. Gian grabbed his mother, Aurelia as she came through the door. Niko slammed the door behind them.

The warning siren and the main lights disappeared at the same time. In the sudden silence, Thandi was sure she could hear everyone breathing. The red emergency lights cast garish shadows on frightened faces.

Another jolt sent them all stumbling. Aurelia pushed herself off Gian and tore off her hood. "Everyone to the emergency shelter, now."

"What happened?" said Gian, jogging alongside his mother.

"I don't know. We were working and then the system locked us out. The next thing we knew, the sprayers were on, all of them at once. We tried a manual shutdown but someone has disconnected our systems. Then someone tried to open the door and the static knocked him across the room. That's when we realized the earthing had failed. We tried to call, but we had no comms."

Thandi tried to keep her voice calm. "How did the earthing fail? It's a physical system. It can't fail."

"I don't know," said Aurelia over her shoulder. "But Benesh will."

Thandi stumbled as the floor bucked beneath her, righted herself and stumbled again. A scientist careened into her, sending her flying. Others fell, shouting, as the floor tilted at a crazy angle. The city jerked. The floor crashed down, knocking Thandi's breath from her chest. She rode the swaying floor like the deck of a ship. Four impacts. *The drag anchors*!

She pushed to her knees, crawled over to Aurelia, and shouted to be heard over the babble. "The drag anchors have released!"

Pale faces echoed Aurelia's shock. "They can't have."

Thandi staggered to her feet. The city rocked, its stability lost with the anchors. They stumbled across the shaking deck to the door of the emergency pod and tumbled through.

Benesh met them at the door. Aurelia grabbed his outstretched hand. "Benesh, the anchors—"

"Have released, I know. We are floating free. And we've lost power. Close the door."

Akos came up behind them, face grim. "We can't close the door. The efficiency expert, Sachin, he's missing."

Frightened faces shone pale under the dim lighting. Thandi put her head down and concentrated on breathing. The room wasn't really getting smaller. It was all in her head.

A pair of feet appeared in her vision. Madja sat down beside her. "Are you all right?"

Thandi forced herself to sit up, and rubbed her sweaty palms on her pants. "I'm fine. I just don't like small rooms." *Or dark. Or people. Or being shut in.* She ignored Madja to battle the panic that threatened to overtake her. This was not home. Not a crowded underground colony. This was Ingold, and the fear was only in her head.

Across the room Aurelia frowned at Akos. "What do you mean, Sachin is missing? He's your visitor. You're supposed to be watching him."

"I left him in the meeting room for five minutes to get a coffee. The siren went off and I went back to get him, but he was gone." Akos folded his arms across his chest.

Gian pushed forward. "And then the lab control systems go crazy. Bit of a coincidence, don't you think?"

"What are you implying?" said Akos.

"I'm implying that your efficiency expert set off the emergency siren and then sabotaged the lab."

"No one sabotaged the lab."

Benesh frowned. "Actually, someone did. Not just the lab but the whole system. They set off the sprayers and then took the generator offline."

Akos turned to his father, frowning. "Why does it have to be Sachin? It could be one of the students."

"Except they're all here." Gian waved his arm at the huddled group. "Did you even have him checked out before you hired him?"

"Of course I did. I'm not stupid."

"Well, where did you find him?"

Akos looked uncomfortable. "In a bar, actually. But he was at the same conference, trying to drum up business."

The city groaned and shook. The tortured screech of metal reverberated through the floorplates. Thandi grabbed her seat as the floor tilted, pressing her face into the plastic. *We're going down. We're going down—*

The floor dropped out from under them. The city rocked like a boat on a stormy sea. Some of the students screamed. Thandi ignored them as she tried to control her own fear.

Niko pushed himself to his feet. "Regardless of whether or not we have a saboteur, we need to get those anchors back on." He shoved past Akos to help Benesh up. "We're only stable because the walkways are still attached. But I'll bet you that was one of the pod systems being torn away. If the storm gets worse—"

"Could we sink?" said Akos, his voice loud in the silence.

A babble of panicked voices erupted. Benesh held up his hands for attention, but the crowd ignored him.

"Shut up!" shouted Gian. Silence fell.

"Thank you," said Benesh. He turned to face them. "We won't sink. The platform is unstable, but the floats are still inflated and we have emergency power. If all else fails, we can eject the emergency pod and ride out the storm until the supply ship can send a shuttle."

"Shouldn't we evacuate?" said someone.

"We can't." Thandi tried to sound confident, but her voice shook. "The shuttle has lifted off. They can't weather a static storm. We can. Or we could, if we had the anchors."

"We have spares," said Niko. "It won't be a fun job to reattach them, but better now than if the storm gets worse."

Benesh nodded. "Even two will help to keep us level. Niko, Gian, Thandi. You replace the anchors. Akos and I will work on getting back into the system."

"What about Sachin?" said Aurelia.

Gian's face set. "If we find him, we'll be having a word. Let's go."

Thandi hurried after Gian, Niko behind her. Gian froze and she ran into his back.

Sachin stood in the corridor, holding one of the weapons from the planetary defense arsenal. "Back we go," he said.

A hush fell when Sachin came through the door after them. "Everyone keep calm. We're going to ride out the storm, and then we're going to evacuate. No one needs to get hurt."

Akos pushed forward. "What the hell are you doing, Sachin?"

"So," said Benesh. He looked at the gun. "Those are for planetary defense. How did you get into the secure area?"

Sachin smiled. "Someone left the codes lying around."

Akos blinked as everyone turned to stare at him. "It wasn't me!"

Sachin's face twisted with contempt. "You idiot. You gave me access to your production data. Pulling the codes from inside the system was easy."

"And then you disabled the system and trapped yourself here with us," said Benesh. "Now who's the idiot?"

"Dad, for heaven's sake," said Gian. "He has a gun."

Benesh raised an eyebrow. "Pointed at the only person who can fix the system. Are you suicidal as well as stupid, Mr. Vidar?"

Color rose in Sachin's cheeks. "All right, I miscalculated. I didn't know the shuttle would lift off at the first sign of a storm. But the end result is the same. Monteleone won't survive this. And once you're off the planet, we'll make sure you won't get back on."

Akos's jaw dropped. "What? You're supposed to be an efficiency expert. I had you screened!"

"I am an efficiency expert. I also believe all life has the right to evolve without interference from humans. Now sit down, all of you."

Gian tried to pull his father away, but Benesh shook him off, anger on his features. "So you threaten the lives of fifty people to make a point? What do you hope to achieve? How many millions of humans have these drugs saved?" Benesh's arm swept out at the vastness of Ingold. "There is a whole planet out there, happily evolving. We occupy a tiny corner."

"You interfere with their development!"

Benesh shook his head. "We do not. We work under strict ethical guidelines, which you would know if you had done your research." Anger flashed on his face. "None of our manipulations are allowed contact with the natural populations."

"The risk of contamination is too high. You can never guarantee full biosecurity." Sachin's gaze flicked around the crowd, gauging reactions. His gaze met Thandi's and she looked away.

"So you would destroy something invaluable on the off-chance of a single mistake?" Benesh lost the battle with his patience and looked contemptuous.

"I am protecting the future of an entire species! Who knows what they will become?"

"Not for millions of years, and they could be wiped out before then by a cataclysmic event. Evolution is not a guarantee of sentience, or of a future. They could be an evolutionary dead end. For all we know, they could already be the end product of millions of years of evolution. How would we tell?"

Sachin's voice rose. "They have the right to reach their full potential!"

Benesh shouted back. "What about the rights of our citizens to disease treatment? Is a mindless bag of jelly more important than a human?" He leaned in close to Sachin. "Go ask someone dying of the latest plague and see what they say!"

Sachin raised his arm, anger on his face. Akos leaped forward and grabbed Sachin's wrist. Thandi held her breath as they wrestled with the gun.

Benesh stepped forward. "That's enough, both of you. Put—"

The gun went off with a flash of light and Benesh crumpled to the floor. Aurelia cried out and dropped to her knees, pressing her hands over the hole in Benesh's shirt where dark blood welled.

Akos tore the gun from Sachin. Sachin pushed him over and bolted out the open door. Gian leaped up and slammed the door, sliding the lock across.

The whole room became a background to Aurelia's struggle to save her husband. Thandi sank to the floor. Tears filled her eyes as Benesh's chest stilled. Brilliant, genial Benesh, more interested in saving lives than making millions. Aurelia leaned over her dead husband's face, her hands still wet with his blood.

Niko rested on the closed door. "We're safe enough in here. When the storm's over, we can go looking for him."

Thandi stared at the door. She remembered two storms during her tenure. Not a crackle of static had penetrated the walls. They had ridden out the violent weather with nothing more than a few cases of seasickness.

The room squeezed in around her. Thandi focused on the floor and breathed, in and out, calming. Soon she would need to start counting. The emergency pod didn't have a clear roof, and the walls were so close, so tight around her, crushing the air, the hot breath of all the people in here with her—

"One-one-thousand, two-one-thousand," she whispered. She reached twenty-two before her head cleared.

Near the console the Monteleones clustered around Benesh's body. Someone had draped a lab coat over him. Gian had his arm around his mother, who still held Benesh's hand. Akos sat with his back against the console, the gun in his lap.

The floor jerked and shuddered. Thandi sucked air into her lungs through a mouth gone dry.

"We're not safe." Gian spoke to Niko over his mother's head. "The drag anchors are gone. The static storm is going to fry every piece of equipment we have. There's also a risk we could tip if a strong current catches us. We have to jettison."

"No!" Thandi catapulted out of her chair. All eyes in the room focused on her. Gian rose, hands out in a placating gesture. "It's okay, Thandi." Niko stepped away from the door. They were ready for her, they would hold her down, trap her in here… She choked, felt the bile rise in her throat. She doubled over and vomited onto the floor.

Gian put his arm around her. "It's okay."

Thandi sank her nails into her palms, clenching her fist over the sharp pain. She took a deep, jagged breath. "We have spares. We can put on new drag anchors."

"It's too dangerous," said Gian in her ear.

She clawed at his wrist, gripped it, trying to communicate that she could not survive in this pod. "If there's damage to the buoyancy tank controls or the stabilizers, we could sink. I don't want to die." She looked up at Gian's pale face. He didn't meet her eyes.

"We can do it," said Akos. He pushed to his feet.

Gian glared at him. "We're not putting anyone else in danger."

Akos' dark skin mottled with anger, or maybe shame. "I'll go myself then."

"I'll go with you," said Thandi.

"No one is going," said Gian. "Just calm down."

"I think we should try," said Niko. "If we can stabilize the city we might not lose any more pods, and with the pods still attached the city won't capsize."

Gian shook his head. "What about Sachin? He's still out there."

"I have his gun," said Akos.

Gian's lips twisted in annoyance. "If he can get one, he can get another."

"Then we should arm ourselves."

"And turn the city into a battle zone? We're better off jettisoning the pod and taking our chances."

Thandi dug her nails into his arm.

"Sorry, Thandi. But I don't want anyone else to get shot."

Thandi pushed away from him. Her gaze drifted to the door. *I'm going anyway*, she thought. *Even if you say no...*

Aurelia raised her head, eyes red from crying. "The systems are all down, Gian. He's got no life support out there. And if we leave him on the city to die, it's murder."

Gian looked away, his lips moving. Thandi didn't hear what he said but she could guess the intent.

"He'll pass out," said Niko. "When the oxygen level drops. We could wait until then."

Thandi's stomach roiled. "How long would we have to wait?"

Niko rubbed his chin, winced when his hand ran over the cut. "Hard to tell. With the life support down the oxygen will bleed off until it's the same level as outside. But how long that will take?" Niko shrugged. "It depends how airtight the city still is after losing pods. And if we wait too long, he'll die of hypoxia."

"That doesn't help, Niko."

"Sorry." Niko went to rub his chin again then dropped his hand. "Twenty minutes. The oxygen levels should be low enough to make him woozy without killing him."

"All right," said Gian. "Twenty minutes. Let's suit up."

She was getting out of here. The release of tension made Thandi's legs tremble. She hurried over to the suit locker, waited her turn to grab a suit. *Come on, come on...*

Aurelia grabbed Gian's arm. "I don't want to lose anyone else."

"You won't," said Gian. "Mum, clean your hands."

Aurelia folded her arms and nodded. "Be careful."

Low cloud pressed against the pods like wet wool. The city shook with every static discharge. More than once the floor juddered under Thandi, sending her stumbling into Niko or Gian. Akos walked ahead of them protectively. Thandi's gaze kept focusing on the gun in Akos' hand. Would Akos actually shoot at Sachin? She shivered and hoped they wouldn't have an opportunity to find out.

The city shifted every few minutes as they hit large currents stirred up by the storm. By the time they reached stores Thandi's nerves twanged like guitar strings.

The massive coiled straps of the drag anchors took up one corner of the storage facility. Thandi's heart sank at the sight of them. They were meant to be replaced one at a time under controlled maintenance, not dragged out and attached in the middle of a storm. With the city tossing drunkenly, it took all four of them to maneuver a walking lift under the anchors.

"Don't walk beside it," said Gian, wrestling with the controls to keep the lift moving down the middle of the corridor. The city dropped, slamming the loaded lift into the walls. Thandi understood Gian's warning. A shift in the wrong direction and they could easily be crushed between the lift and the walls.

Akos hurried ahead, gun out. Thandi felt sick at the sight of it, wondering if Sachin lay in wait for them. She checked the oxygen monitor on her suit, and discovered it was dropping, but still at life-sustaining levels.

Akos crouched down against the wall and held up a hand for them to stop.

"What is it?" said Niko.

"The door to the planetary defense store is open."

Gian brought the walking lift to a rumbling stop. "Is he there?"

"No, the room is empty," said Akos, peering around the door. "But the cabinet is open."

Sweat trickled down Thandi's side, partly from the rising temperature as the city's environment equalized with the outside, but also from the sudden awareness that Sachin did have a gun. *He'll go down. He must. He can't be a threat if he's passed out.* They started the lift moving again.

"Not far now," said Niko. No one mentioned that they would have to do it all again for the second anchor.

In the maintenance bay, equipment littered the floor. Thandi and Gian cleared the way for the lift while Akos and Niko wrestled with the manual lock on the maintenance door.

Thandi braced herself as the door opened and the storm thundered in at them. The wind drove hard chemical rain through the opening. The city dipped and a wave of water and hyphae sluiced in over the edge.

Thandi wished she could pull off her helmet to wipe away the sweat trickling down her nose. They worked the winch in turns until the hook for the anchor broke the surface. Thandi leaned out to snap the end of the anchor onto the hook, Gian holding the back of her suit. Her fumbling fingers refused to work the bolt. She swore under her breath. The anchor connected with a snap. Gian hauled her back inside and she leaned on the wall, shaking.

The city shifted again, throwing her against Akos. He caught her and pushed her upright. Thandi opened her mouth to thank him and realized he was crying beneath his hood. She looked away.

Another wave flooded the room, retreating and leaving wriggling hyphae in its wake. Aurelia had told her once that dead hyphae sank quickly, to be devoured by the life below the hyphal layer. A mental image rose in her mind of the city slipping through to the blackness beneath, and the strange creatures there crawling in over their corpses. She shuddered and pushed the thought away.

Lightning flashed, the crackle-boom almost on top of them. Thandi met Gian's eyes. *Take me away*, she wanted to scream at him. *Let's get into* Arkie *and go!* They could ride out the storm beneath the waves, together, watching the phosphorescent creatures of the underworld dance on the currents. The words were on her lips when the city bucked once more, sending her to the floor.

Gian helped her up "You all right?" he shouted.

She nodded. "I'm fine. Let's get the other anchor out before the storm gets worse."

"Who's going to stay here?"

Everyone looked at Thandi. She grimaced at the choice. Stay here alone, or help take the anchor to the other side of the city and risk running into Sachin.

"I'll stay," she said.

Gian grabbed her arm. "You'll feel it when the second anchor goes in. Let yours go as soon afterwards as possible."

Thandi hugged the doorframe, watching as they steered the lift down the corridor, staggering as the city shifted. She turned away.

Through the open bay door the static storm raged, arcs of electricity jumping from pod to pod, skating across the surface of the roiling ocean.

Thandi hugged her knees, trying not to let her imagination run away with her. Time stretched out, and she found herself checking her suit clock every few minutes. She slid down the wall and watched the storm rage, glad of the emergency lights keeping the dark at bay. She could feel space all around her. This was better than being in the pod. She could breathe out here. They would reattach the anchors soon and the city could ride out the storm.

The city jerked under her and began to swing. They had done it. Weak with relief, Thandi crawled forward, water washing around her knees. She hit the release for the ramp. The metal pad dropped, the anchor sliding forward until it tumbled into the ocean.

Already the city felt more stable beneath her feet, though it still rose and fell in the low swell worked up by the storm. She breathed out and turned around.

Sachin stood in the doorway. Thandi cried out and scrabbled backward until she hit the edge of the doorframe.

Sachin had a breather over his face, one designed for toxic atmospheres. *Wrong one*, thought a dispassionate part of her mind while the rest of her tried to press into the wall. Driving rain pounded her suit. With the open door at her back, she had nowhere to go.

Sachin swayed, his face grotesquely swollen. Blood trickled out from under his breather, staining his chin red. His bloodshot eyes locked on her. He shouted incoherently, stumbled forward and fell on his face.

Thandi stood petrified as Sachin tried to rise. She knew the signs of oxygen deprivation, but couldn't make herself move to help him. *He killed Benesh*, she thought, *Even if it was an accident*. She edged around the walls, keeping as far from him as possible.

A wave broke into the room, washing over Sachin. If she didn't help him, he might drown, or be washed into the ocean. Still she couldn't bring herself to move closer. She edged around until she had the corridor at her back. Sachin lay unmoving. She put one foot out. She could get help. Go to the pod and bring people back to deal with him.

And in the meantime he could die. She took a step toward Sachin. His hands had been empty. He didn't have a gun. She took a deep breath and kneeled beside him.

It took all of her strength to turn him over. Up close his face was a mask of blood, the skin spongy with fluid. She would never be able to move him by herself. She would get a hood and breather, put it on him and then go for help.

Sachin opened his eyes and she recoiled, but his hand found her suit and grabbed hold. Thandi struggled to break free, shouting at him to let go. His hands tore at her suit, fingers fumbling for the zipper.

"Stop! I'll get you a suit! Let me go!" Panic took over then and she screamed and beat at him, gloved fists pounding at his face. Something tore near her shoulder and she rolled free. She shuffled backward on her hands, sobbing.

Sachin's face leered at her and she realized he was laughing, incoherent from oxygen deprivation. Thandi dived for the door but he grabbed her, his teeth sinking into her shoulder. She put her feet into the wall and pushed. They stumbled backward, locked together. Sachin grunted and threw her. She hit the floor and rolled away.

Too late she felt the edge of the ramp beneath her. Her hands reached for the city as she fell. The waters closed over her head.

She panicked, scrabbling for a handhold. Her arms tangled in the hyphae, the bodies pressing against her visor as she sank. The suit hissed as the motor came on to inflate the buoyancy pockets. But she kept sinking, slipping further down the hyphal layer. Water trickled down her back. She fumbled about in the darkness. Her fingers found a tear, then another. Sachin had torn the suit.

Thandi screamed and flailed, trying to push herself to the surface, beating her arms and legs against the clinging hyphae. The weight of the suit dragged her down.

Thandi burst through the hyphae into the empty layer below. She sobbed into the darkness, sinking faster in the clear water. She didn't want to die. Didn't want her last day to be one of pain and terror, her last sunset the flaming pink of Ingold's endless sky.

She opened her eyes to blackness and her mother sobbing. Further down the tunnel, a dying man moaned, his chest crushed when the tunnel had fallen in. Thandi clutched her mother, desperate for the sound of her mother's heartbeat, to know that they were both still alive. Hunger had come and gone, so had thirst and fear and hope.

The rock made noises in the dark, it groaned and squeaked, rumbled and moaned. Sometimes it sounded like distant voices and the trapped people would cry out, *we're here, we're here.* Sometimes people would crawl over them, clawing and frantic to escape the tiny pocket they were trapped in.

It was a dream, her life. She had never escaped. She was still there, trapped with her mother in the deep darkness. *I can't hear your heart, mama. I can't hear your heart anymore.*

A flicker of light appeared, then another. As if a switch had been turned on, the phosphorescent beings of Ingold's underworld burst into glorious prisms of light.

Thandi hit a solid wall, jerking her from her terror. She scrabbled for a handhold, and her fingers wrapped around the flat edge of the drag anchor. She leaned her head against the slick metal, shaking. She hadn't died in those cold tunnels. But she hadn't lived, either. Coldly, in the darkness, she looked at her life, her search for safety, for light. *I want to live.* And life existed at the top of this long, narrow strip anchoring her to Ingold city.

She pulled herself along slowly, until the motion became a meaningless rhythm, reach and pull, reach and pull. Her arms burned. How long before her suit's air ran out? The glowing organisms of the Ingold dark trundled past her in their mindless search for food.

When she reached the writhing hyphal layer, she could not push into the mass again, have them touch her, slide over her, millions of bodies that crawled and breathed and shouted and shoved her in the dark.

"Shut up!" she screamed. She bit the inside of her cheek until she tasted blood then spat through twisted lips. "What are you afraid of?" But she knew what she feared. She gritted her teeth, closed her eyes and shoved. The hyphae wrapped around her, pressing in on her, slapping over the visor. The blood ran over her lips and she kept her eyes squeezed shut. She must keep going forward, or accept the long slow fall. And she was more afraid to let go.

She reached the coupling and hauled herself up over the lip. There was no sign of Sachin.

Thandi staggered along the corridors toward the emergency pod, aching, her suit beeping to warn her that her air supply was running out.

She reached the closed pod door and pounded on it. The door flew open and she fell through into the bright light. Someone pulled her hood off. She lifted her head and met Gian's eyes. The look on his face told her how she must look. She wiped blood off her chin.

"Thandi!" Gian lifted her, crushed her against him. He pushed back. "You're wet."

"I fell in," she said. Her knees gave way and she sank to the floor.

Thandi stared through her visor into the glare. Ingold's flat ocean stretched as far as she could see, the surface undulating gently under a clear sky. In front of her a walkway jutted out for a few meters then became a tangled mess of metal where the pod system had torn away and sank into the ice core of the planet.

The speaker in the room behind her crackled more than usual. "All personnel to the shuttle bay. This is the last evacuation run."

Gian had tried to convince her to evacuate on the first shuttle. But that would be too easy, to run away from her fear. She looked down at the ocean lapping the walkway beneath her feet, and wondered if she would have the courage to go home, to stand before a memorial carved into a stone wall far below the surface.

One day. But maybe not for a while yet.

Thandi made her way through the empty corridors. In the silence, she heard the hiss of millions of hyphae sliding against the belly of the city.

She stripped off her suit in the airlock and hung it in the sterilizer out of habit, and picked up her bag. One duffel bag to show for twenty-seven years of life.

She walked down the aisle to the only empty seat. Madja looked up, startled.

Thandi smiled at her. "Mind if I sit here?"

Madja shook her head and looked out the window. Thandi stowed her bag and sat down. "So where are you headed? Home?"

Madja hesitated before answering. "Yeah. For a while, anyway."

Thandi sat back as the engines hummed. "Me, too. Eventually."

Colloidal Suspension

By Geoff Nelder

Aklaxon battered Steiner's ears. Something must have gone wrong during their interstellar hibernation flight. So much for Interplanet Trade Corp. He caught a nose-wrinkling whiff of electrical burning but he remained strapped in his reclined padded seat. It wasn't that he couldn't undo his straps, but his muscles had atrophied in the weeks, maybe months of sleep. He forced his sticky eyes to open and glanced around the cabin. Greens and reds dot-dashed at him from a console an arm's length away. Strange; this cabin was too small for the *Sojourn*. Yet he was still attached by drips and feeds. He needed to be careful removing tubes before he could reach the console to silence that damned noise.

A full minute must have passed since regaining consciousness, and only then could his brain defog sufficiently to reach the panel and dance the keys. His co-pilot, Margot, remained prone on a bunk. A couple of cannula fed into her too. Damn, the alarm shrieked again, bringing his heartbeat thudding in his throat. He delayed waking her to glance at readings and the vid display. They'd landed but were sinking. Had to get out, quick.

Steiner hit the combination of buttons to lift the pod. Anti-grav motors vibrated; good, that should keep them afloat until the power ran out. He didn't have time to find the timescale: he had Margot to wake up. It would be easier pushing her out while awake than dragging out an unconscious lump. He shouldn't refer to her like that: he still loved her—and, he suspected, hoped, she him.

He switched a tube to her wake-up cocktail. Like him she wore a soft cloud-grey top and pants. Breasts that could poke out a man's eyes must have been exposed during the flight. Perhaps he should lower the top before she accused him. His eyes were barely ready for business but her blue-black eyes opened wide in an instant.

"What do you think you're doing?"

"Waking you up. We have a problem."

Margot looked down and adjusted her cami-top. "Stop ogling my tits, you perv. Have you been groping me?"

He couldn't deny admiring them *en passant* but there hadn't been time for a good time. "You must have exposed yourself in your sleep. And I took the opportunity—"

"I knew it."

"To visually check for bleeding, bruising and—"

She threw him a narrowed-eyes withering look. "You play with your own bits, Steiner. Oh, my head. Coffee, now, not that pro-vit garbage."

"No time to make anything. Here's a shot to get us both moving." He passed her a skin inject booster then applied another to his own upper arm.

She pulled a face as long as a giraffe—appropriate for her large freckles. "Is the environment safe out there?"

"Green light—not checked details. We're sinking. Grab your emergency pack and—"

"You're an idiot, Steiner. Orbit and assess before landing. I knew it was a mistake to let them appoint you pilot."

"I've only just woke…never mind." No point launching into a debate on why they were not on the migration ship when the anti-grav motors were whining down to nothing. "I've a pack and the life-raft. Hang on to your kit. Popping the hatch now."

The whoosh of escaping air worried him. It meant the air pressure outside was less than inside—hopefully enough to allow their lungs to work. His previous glance at the row of green lights had told him the atmosphere contained the essentials. What the pretty lights couldn't tell him about was the nose-pinching stench. Overcooked cabbage, and it looked like it. Had they fallen into a giant's supper? He tried to ignore the odor, to focus on ejecting the fluorescent yellow inflatable dinghy. At least their escape pod wasn't crash diving.

As the life-raft blasted to its small full size, Steiner stood up on the pod, his pumps, ideal inside, suffered reduced friction on the slippery titanium alloy. He stretched up but could only see a pea-soup horizon with a steeper curvature than Earth. No sign of islands, or mountains.

A soft whine like a mongrel dog expressing interest came and went leaving him the unnerving impression they were being watched.

A female moan impinged on his thoughts. "Get down, you fool, yu're making it sink faster."

If they'd landed on solid ground, even a small island, they'd have all the resources of the escape pod, limited though it was. Extra food, water, medical supplies, clothing. On water, the best they had was whatever was embedded in the barely-two-man life-raft, and now their emergency craft was sinking.

It made sense for him to lighten the weight of the pod by clambering onto the life-raft. She might throw a wobbler at his pre-emptive boarding, so… "Women and children first?"

"Don't be an asshole."

Perfect. He pulled the line so the yellow raft surged closer. It didn't bob in the soup as he'd expected. He stepped into it and immediately knelt for stability. Damn, it meant he no longer had a connection to the spacecraft. Why had she gone back in?

"Margot, come out now or you'll need your bathing suit."

Precious moments later her tousled red hair showed, followed by cobalt blue eyes so big he could sometimes see himself in them. Her thick lips twisted in distaste when she saw a meter of green goo between them. He gathered in the line and threw it at her. "Fine, but there's more stuff to get out."

Margot ducked back down but at least she'd kept hold of the line. He shouted down at her, "We don't need water."

She re-emerged behind a plastic box. Threw it but it missed Steiner's hands and dolloped in the ocean. It didn't splash, but glooped as if it were thick porridge. He pulled it on board. "We don't need a radio either. The basic survival stuff is built in—"

She'd gone back down. Ridiculous, his worry lines bunched. He urged her out. "But…hey, the pea soup is up to the hatch. Get out now if you don't want to be an ingredient."

Her disembodied voice was mostly inaudible but he caught unwelcome snippets, "…shame I can't find…you buggered up…should still be on the *Sojourn*…you…king bast…"

"It wasn't my fault." He ground his teeth at the clichéd excuse always used by the guilty, spoiling it for the innocent, and yet he was.

Margot climbed into the dinghy just as the escape pod gulped its last breath and slid out of sight. Its position was marked by flotsam, of which the only item worthy of retrieval was a blue phial of penicillin. The rest, a mix of squares of paper—a puzzle since as far as Steiner knew, he'd not seen paper for over a year—and what looked like honey nut clusters. The computer must have prepared breakfast not realizing the peril it was shortly to be in.

The warm wind whistled 'a hi there' and the ocean replied with 'a me too'.

"We have a problem, Steiner, the raft is sinking too."

"A puncture?"

They both rapped the polyastomer and it felt pumped up hard enough and yet it was lower in the green scum, even taking into account its burden. Steiner pressed the motor button and the raft lifted a little.

"Which way, Margot? You're the navigator."

She was rummaging in the plastic box she'd insisted on rescuing.

"Just keep us moving. In a moment the data from the escape pod's orbit and descent will tell us the direction for the nearest landfall."

Steering was accomplished by a touch-sensitive joystick at the rear of the dinghy. A full circle gave Steiner cause to ponder. The only sign of the escape pod's location was a single bubble-wrapped pouch. Even that appeared to be half under the spinach-hued ocean.

"Margot, sweetness." Such bravado. "Do you feel heavy? Just wondering if the data shows if g exceeds one on this planet in spite of the obvious greater curvature of the horizon."

"Busy."

It didn't feel much different to being on a one-g planet but then he hadn't tried jumping or lifting a mass greater than the raft. He knew it was possible for the curvature to be different for this ocean than, say, on another part of the planet. He looked for a sun and found none. The cornflower-blue sky brightened near the horizon presently in front of him. Predawn or twilight? He headed in that direction.

Margot dabbed at a handheld. "Um, nothing definite. The data seems incomplete. Whatever created the emergency threw out the escape pod just after deciding this planet was survivable."

Steiner looked around. "Not my idea of a paradise destination. What happened to the other passengers?"

"As pilot and navigator, we were probably ejected last, maybe weeks after the initial problem. What did you do before hibernation?"

"My fault, eh? Which way now?"

She tilted up her hands. "It doesn't matter."

"What, no land, islands?" He always made light of awkward situations, but surviving on a water-world wouldn't be easy—less so for a gloop-world.

She tapped the cream-colored box lightly, then shook it. "Damn, it's failed completely." She held it over the side.

"Don't ditch it. Might need to cannibalize it. I'm headed for the sun for now."

Margot twisted and poked at a patch on the life-raft behind her. "Compass is one-sixty."

"Keeping steady? Could be meaningless if this planet is like Mars with no magnetic field."

"Don't you think I know that? Yes, for the moment."

Steiner craned his neck and glanced around. "No welcoming committee yet. No condensation trails in that perfect sky."

"Let's compose a poem to it."

"Look, none of this is my fault, Margot. We're here together. Get over it. Do you think I'd choose you to be stranded with?"

She didn't answer: fiddled instead with the compass, then the defunct computer and checked the emergency packs. "Flares, desalination kit, nutrition patches, first aid gun, sonic fish stunner, and hooks…"

"Get the desalination working. That water must be salty."

"Steiner, simple man, we don't even know it is water. We can smell it's as foul as burnt Sunday vegetables but it might not be potable even after filtering."

"We only have two liters of water so after a day, we'll have no choice."

She threw a weighted tube over the side as far down as it would go to minimize salt input and clamped the unit, with its petal solar cell, on its pocket holder. Margot threw him the fishing kit, even though he'd not asked for it. A welcome distraction from the increased feeling of dread.

"Argh, a hook's in my finger. Look, red stuff."

"Don't expect me to kiss it better. Drip it over the side."

He watched his blood drop onto the ocean, his red stayed as a floating blob for a moment before suddenly being sucked down, as if a blood vacuum cleaner lurked below. The first-aid gun sealed the cut, so he needed another experiment.

"Margot, I need a pee. You must, too. No photos while I aim over the stern."

"Let me turn off the desalination input. I don't want my drink to be more toxic than it has to be."

Steiner frowned as, like his blood, his urine made a puddle that didn't merge in the gloop. It sank rather than be diluted.

The raft had drifted to a halt while he'd not kept the motor going and they were slowly sinking again. His stomach knotted. "I'd assumed we'd be within hours of land. How long will the propulsion unit last?"

"No idea. There should be paddles. Steiner?"

"Ah."

"What? Oh, I get it. You were in such a hurry to get out of the pod, you left the paddles behind."

"Don't you tire of always being right?"

They agreed to keep the motor on in bursts: just enough to prevent sinking.

An accelerating drowning of the bright patch in the sky was accompanied by a reddening of ambient light and a dip in Steiner's comfort zone. He rubbed his arms, wishing the grey uniform was long-sleeved. "Hey, Margot, are there moon-blankets in the emergency stows? I'm going into hypothermia."

She threw him a silvery microfilm blanket. "Now we've lost the sun, assuming that's what the poached egg in the sky was, we've no heading."

"Thought it was one-sixty."

She tapped the rubbery box. "It varied ten degrees or so. Either magnetic anomalies or the compass is faulty."

"We should have thrown in a spare compass, just in case."

"And how, simple Steiner, would we know which one was faulty?"

He grinned knowing how to wind her up. "Best of three?"

"Only you would think of packing three of everything. Ah, but you didn't until after the event. We've no idea how long the night is going to be. Possibly days—as you would say. It might freeze. Hey, keep that motor going. I'm sure we're lower in the gloop than before."

"The battery must be flattening. It'll get topped up by daylight, when and if it comes."

Steiner looked over the stern but the dark green obscured any chance of seeing the drive. "Maybe the jet is clogged—"

He was cut off by silence. The boat shuddered to a sudden stop as if it had been travelling in greengage jelly rather than water. He looked at Margot but in the gloom couldn't see her accusing expression. He scrambled once more in the sides of the raft, looking for overlooked panels that might have a folded paddle. Failing that, improvise with something appropriate, like Margot's hand.

She yelled at him, "We're going down. Do something!"

Through the gloom and by the new tilt of the raft to his right, he made out her paddling using her hand. "That's too slow even if we both did it...and we couldn't for long."

"Asshole, there's only one other option."

"No need to get nasty. There's several options, finding a substitute paddle being one. Your defunct computer..."

"No! It might still work."

He was about to add a witty reply when he felt the bottom of the raft tug downwards, as if a giant slug had attached its maw beneath the boat and was vacuuming. Margot was right, one of them had to get out, swim, and push. His stomach lurched at the possibility of not being able to swim. No choice. In spite of the chill of the evening, he perspired fear.

"Okay, I'll take the first stint over the side. I'll push for what, an hour? Then it's your turn, right?"

"Sure."

Umm, he wasn't convinced he'd be relieved but the ocean—or whatever it was—was up to the top of the rounded bulwark of the raft. "Here goes, hoping the nights are short."

He dipped his hand in the ocean for the first time and was pleasantly surprised at its warmth. It might be poisonous, full of alien piranhas or as harmless as a village duck pond, but he slipped off the moon-blanket, and rolled over the side.

Marvelous, an enveloping warmth of a thick soup. Must be about body temperature. Ha-ha. He could easily spend all night in this luxuriant bath. Even the pungent rotting cabbage smell was wearing off—overloaded olfactory senses. He swam lazy breaststrokes to the stern, placed his hands on the now slimy surface and kicked. The life-raft crept forward.

Relaxed and comfortable, he heard Margot. "Faster, you idiot, I'm still sinking!"

He kicked harder until she stopped yelling. It was more difficult but sustainable. By experiment, he found he only needed to push with one arm, do a lazy kick with his feet and a half-breaststroke. Cycling a range of push and swim activities he was able to keep the raft from sinking.

After ten minutes, he needed a break. He wasn't sure of the accurate time lapse. Hour or five minutes; it was too dark to read his watch, unless he fiddled with it, and that meant slowing, sinking, more shouting.

Steiner had been immersed long enough to sample his swimming medium, enjoyed the alien aperitif and had formulated his review for the next customer.

"This pea-soup has a bitter foretaste." He could only manage gasps of sentences. "It tastes like a kale consommé. Smooth consistency. Ah, unidentifiable lumps. Maybe rotting astronauts. A smorgasbord. Stings my eyes…" He punctuated with a bout of coughing.

"Careful, Steiner. You'll joke yourself to death."

"Funny." He resumed coughing. "Let's swap."

"Keep pushing. I'll tell you when two hours is up."

"We agreed. An hour," he spluttered.

"You agreed, but it takes two to contract. Now, if you don't mind I need to think."

He wondered what she wanted to think about. It would annoy her to feel that her survival depended on someone else, especially him. She should spend dry time fiddling with what electronics they had to attract a rescue and to download data to find out what had happened on board the *Sojourn*. Okay, a homing beacon should have been alerting nearby spacecraft ever since the escape pod was launched.

Pushing wasn't difficult but his arm ached as did his neck—having to lift it out of the muck. "I'm getting RSI. Stand by."

He rolled onto his back and looked at the stars. The atmosphere twinkled in patterns he didn't recognize, not that he expected to. His arms were too tired to push over his head so he used his hands to paddle himself a one-eighty to push with his feet. It worked fine. Great, he could watch for shooting stars or the telltale line of an orbiting spaceship. Two moons, one near the horizon sending reflected silver over Margot's head—she snored. He hoped she'd locked the rudder: he didn't want to waste his efforts. He was too low in the gloop for the horizon to be more than a few meters away but he could see for light years overhead.

The misshapen second moon fluoresced the color of French fries, in fact it looked like a potato. Was everything on this planet food-related? His 'gastronomical' gazing had to wait, when the warm but foul gunk crept across his face and it was enveloping his hips. Sweat broke out on his forehead as he realized he was slowly becoming lower in the ocean.

"Hey, Margot, wake up, I'm sinking!" No response, he'd better keep moving—swimming must have kept his body mass afloat as well as the raft. They'd assumed, stupidly, that the density of the ocean was greater than water on Earth. After all, it had the appearance of something thicker. Maybe gravity was greater, or the viscosity of local goulash meant they'd need to be much lighter.

"Margot, we have a problem. Wake up!"

He heard a grunt, and after more shouting from him, more grunts. While he waited for her proper awakening, he wondered how by keeping moving he was floating. He'd always enjoyed swimming so his body must have been on auto with his limbs flip-flapping just the right movements. Damn, he swore he could hear more snoring, an encore. Steiner rarely betrayed anger, but he was working up to it. Not only with whatever the original emergency was in space, and with the user-unfriendly ocean, but now with Margot persisting in unconsciousness while he agitated. He could just see her hair. It might be red in daylight but now it looked black streaked with white. Still on his back he scooped a handful of the slop and lobbed it. He sank more, and had to swim harder to regain floating.

"What the frigging hell?"

"We have a problem, Margot. This stuff—"

"You can stay in *the stuff* for another hour. Goodnight."

He stopped pushing the raft with his feet but paddled to maintain buoyancy. "D'you want more?"

"Speak."

"This ocean is pulling me under as well as the raft."

"Take your shoes off."

"Margot, don't be absurd. We're both wearing ship pumps not hiking boots."

He could see her sit up and look over at him. Her voice became shrill. "The raft is sinking again. Do something."

He obliged by kicking the raft as he swam feet first again. "We need a better strategy. Start by jettisoning everything heavy."

"Steiner, I've already done that."

"I'm struggling here." He was too. Must be a combination of having to move continually and the nagging thought he wasn't going to pull through this crisis. His heart hammered.

"Heaviest is the water, and nutri-drinks. About 500 mills has come through the desal. Wanna try it?"

No, but he could demolish an energy drink and asked for one. She held it over, a tube to his mouth. Tasted orangey and such a sweet contrast to the green gore he subsisted in. His skin had stopped stinging. He'd become desensitized, numbed.

"Steiner, allow me another half hour's sleep. I'll replace you for a couple of hours. I'm a good swimmer."

He had a choice? Boosted by the glucose intake he rotated and this time used his head to butt rubber while he let his legs do most of the propulsion. It worked well, though it could be just the change of muscles. He had to be careful not to head butt the rudder, but it was just lower than his head needed to be.

Soft laughter now, not from Margot, and unless he was going mad, not him either. As if the joke was on him. It was probably the wind, and that thought triggered more.

Suppose the wind picked up and created large waves? The ocean was abnormally calm. Perhaps the liquid was so dense it took more turbulent airflow to create a wave. Long ocean waves were often caused by steady winds, friction-pulling on the surface. A smile came as he thought maybe they were in a large lake. The horizon was so damned close. They couldn't see beyond a kilometer or so. He'd have to work up a plan to use a microcam: throw it up in the air. Train a seagull, except he'd not seen any wildlife. Except Margot.

He squinted at some of the soup scooped up in his hand. The moonlight wasn't much but if there were bits of seaweed they were too small to see. Like in milk, which, was a kind of solid in colloidal suspension. They were in green milk.

He anxiously scanned the sky for a line. Potato moon swam in an iridescent halo. Purple, emerald, ruby—beautiful, like an aurora borealis. Earth's moon traditionally was made of cheese, this one had an aurora Dauphinoise. His stomach rumbled.

Normally, Steiner gave up swimming after a few lengths in a pool—low boredom threshold. Now, it didn't matter. His life was forfeit. He and Margot could only keep swim-pushing for so long. Their energy and vits wouldn't last beyond a few days, then they'd weaken until pushing wasn't an option even if swimming was. Of course he might've been floating in food all this time. Or poison. Suppose it was like the phytoplankton on Earth, Ceto, and Mazu III. He knew algae could be poisonous such as the neurotoxins in red tide algal blooms on Earth. But maybe this was Ceto, he knew it was smaller than Earth. Then he didn't want this planet to have a totally liquid surface. They needed to be dry eventually: humans rot in more ways than one.

Just as Steiner considered a wake-up call to Margot, she poked her head over the side at him. "Look behind you."

Hooray, a rescue ship; hopefully a cruise liner with all-in food, drink and women. He rotated again to push with his head. No ship. "Your horizon is farther than mine."

"A peachy color. Probably pre-dawn twilight."

He slumped—chin on his chest and stopped kicking—just flapped his hands enough to keep himself afloat. How could she dash his expectations like that? He'd better start up again before she screamed at him, but it took much more effort than he'd anticipated. He'd paddled himself to exhaustion. "Now you're awake, dearest Margot, and it's a new day..."

"Sure. It's my turn."

If that readiness wasn't surprising enough, Steiner was astonished to see Margot had slipped off her silver blanket then fingering the hem of her cami-top and lifting it. Higher. He was treading water, or whatever it was, then put his hand on the cord circling the raft to get a better look. Silly, since he'd seen her half-naked before. But a sleeping dummy isn't as erotic as a vibrant upright and contradictory woman. Whoops, he was missing her speech, no doubt amusing herself with a tease.

"...time before this raft sinks? Not time enough, I guess. Pity, because I am feeling soooo horny."

She pulled her top off over her head, shook her breasts then folded her top and stowed it. Her voice dropped a pitch to velvet. "I want something dry to put on after my dip."

Steiner estimated the raft would be below the surface in five minutes with the weight of both of them, especially bouncing. It could be longer if he found some polystyrene, anything he could fix around the raft. Damn, it was difficult climbing in. The struggle would shorten the float time even more. "Margot?"

"Wow, apart from the stench, this is like a beauty spa's mud bath."

She'd slipped over while he'd climbed in. He'd been thwarted and not for the first time by her. Kind of endearing, and yet…

"Margot, did you learn at school about witch ducking trials?"

She saved her breath and merely splashed him. Their survival was more important than a fumble…but only just. Her teasing gave him hope.

He could hear the dollop of liquid as Margot found her own swim-push methodology. In fact she'd find it easier to float because of her curves compared to his: one biscuit away from anorexia. He should improvise his own water wings for next shift. With eyes eager to shut, and a brain urging shut down, Steiner forced himself to follow a few tasks he'd been thinking through while overboard.

The compass read one-seventy, a pleasant surprise. It meant they hadn't travelled in circles. They might have been heading away from land just over the eastern horizon but he immediately put that out of his mind. He risked standing and glanced at the horizon. On Earth that would mean five kilometers. Nothing but green. He sat again and rummaged in the stow pouches. The raft jerked with the pushes every five seconds or so. A slower pace than his. Better check over the side soon.

He found the microcam with its transmitter and button battery. He took off his watch to make accessing the vid link easier. There it was; an image of his puckered face, thin, worried. Being immersed in an asparagus swamp didn't make him a film star. Good luck, Margot. If he could launch the cam, say, a hundred meters up then he should be able to see up to…he did the mathematics on his watch…thirty five kilometers—though less on this smaller planet.

The bow storage had an emergency pouch. He took out an orange plastic flare pistol, and smiled. Now for the dangerous bit. He took a cartridge, checked it was the kind with a tiny parachute and hunted for a spoon. He made do with a spatula from the first aid kit. The pyrotechnic compounds would fry the cam before good images were transmitted if he didn't remove them. Probably potassium perchlorate, various nitrates and magnesium, of which the latter could give him a nasty burn. He scooped the reagents out over the side. He used glue from the raft repair kit to fix the cam, switched it on and checked the image. After setting to record, he aimed directly upward, hoping it would parachute back into his hands.

As he pointed upward, he looked away in case his tampering messed up the explosive detonator then squeezed the trigger. The detonation was louder than he expected but it was followed by a satisfying whoosh, and a scream. He opened his eyes thinking he might have shot Margot, but saw the projectile shoot above him.

"What the friggin hell are you doing?"

"Just an experiment. Keep pushing." As he spoke he heard the planet sigh. At least that was what it sounded like—like the 'ah' from a grateful crowd at a firework display.

Perhaps Margot's ears were full of soup, but she must have noticed the flare. "That was a dud? Had you seen an aircraft?"

Her spluttering gave him a wry smile. Now she'd know the bitter taste; a long way from a beauty treatment. He put her out of his mind as he watched the image. It was too tiny to see properly but once finished, he'd be able to zoom in. The image jerked around so much it was all blurred. He looked up and couldn't see it. Then a white spot— the parachute. There must be some wind after all, for it was off to their right. He wouldn't be able to catch it. The raft bumped, settling lower.

He leaned over. "Margot, keep pushing." Wrong side. No, there was the small jet control and rudder. In the light of the pre-dawn gloom, he looked again but the green soup looked smooth and thick. No ripple or bubbles. "Margot!" He looked around all four sides—no sign. Sweating with panic, he slithered over the stern expecting to tumble onto her. Nothing! He was afraid to dive in case the force of the strange ocean didn't let him up. Nevertheless, he swam with feet and one arm doing a breaststroke while feeling down. Maybe she'd suffered a stroke or a fit a few meters back. Only last year she beat him in a breaststroke race by a length. He swam for a few seconds then felt down again. More sorties. He didn't want to lose her. He felt sick.

After a few minutes he remembered the raft. It would sink without him pushing. He looked and there it was, perhaps five centimeters sticking above the surface, less at the stern. It had turned, or he had, and he was at least fifteen meters distant. He over-armed as fast as the gloop would allow. He reached and pushed at the raft, kicking furiously though his feet made hardly a splash. The raft shoved forward and upward until he could relax. Margot had ripped out his heart when she ended their tryst but his feelings remained…a tear diluted the soup.

This time there was an 'argh'. The worldly angst of it filled his ears then emptied slowly. Hallucination from the atmosphere? Or from accidental swallowings?

Exhausted, he knew an empty raft would be more buoyant but he'd be dead before he saw twilight again. A plop over to his right made him realize his watch was left in the raft. He gave another big push then climbed in. He found the watch on the floor and snapped it on to examine later. He stood to spot any sign of Margot but all around was the damned pea soup. He desperately needed sleep but it couldn't happen yet. That thought took him to the first aid kit. He swallowed a Benzedrine followed by two sachets of nutrijuice.

Steiner wanted to make a paddle or sail but nothing larger than the flare pistol was hard plastic. Leaning over the side using the first aid gun's bag as a webbed hand would only make the raft go in circles. Waiting for the amphetamine to kick in he lay back for a moment, and immediately fell asleep.

He awoke saturated in sickly green sap oozing at his lips while the boat rocked. It was sinking unevenly, and so was he. Like waking up in a more comfortable bed, he wondered if he should bother rising. No Margot—he couldn't believe that and listened for her bawling him out for not pushing fast enough. Nothing. No sign of rescue for him either, and the bennies and food wouldn't last more than a week. His need for constant movement bar fifteen minute powerless naps cut survival to maybe two days. He gazed at the royal blue sky hoping to see a condensation trail then he remembered the flare and the data on his watch. No time now. He bailed out as best as he could, checked the compass was on one-sixty, and stumbled over the side. After a frantic push to ensure the raft's temporary survival, he rolled onto his back.

While kicking and using his head to push, he studied the movie. He couldn't see anything properly until the cam had descended slowly as if in a dance. He kept pausing and zooming until his already sore eyes had to shut a while. Not asleep, just resting. Eventually, he thought he detected a frame with a dark patch. Maybe a giant had left a lump of sourdough bread in his borscht. A few more seconds and he spotted the raft, so he had an estimate of direction. He clambered back on the raft, took the lock off the rudder and hand-paddled to get the bow heading two-ten. Maybe ten kilometers. A day's swim-pushing.

Once more he jumped over the side, but it was different. He negligently went vertically over. And his feet touched the bottom. He was waist deep.

His heart banged like it was in a race. Did that mean it was this shallow all over? Including where they'd been? Had Margot merely got the huff and waded off in the opposite direction?

A laugh echoed around him.

Steiner desperately put cupped hands to his mouth. "Margot… Margot?" If he wasn't so worried over her, he'd have laughed at the elementary absurdity of their assumption. Hey, the escape pod had sunk, and it was much more than a meter in all dimensions. Maybe the seabed was softer or deeper there.

He tried a low jump. Squidgy, possibly mud. He didn't feel up to stooping down to retrieve a sample. He reassessed his situation. It meant he could wade-tow rather than swim-push. He climbed into the raft—already quite low—and removed the digital compass and used its Velcro to hook over his wrist. He aimed at two-ten and pulled on the life-raft's line wrapped around his hand. It was easier, he supposed, than wading through treacle. More like a verdigris porridge. After half an hour his legs ached but he pushed on. He wondered if the bed was the slope leading to the island ahead, which he couldn't yet see. The bennies began to wear off. While he trudged he only thought of resting, and Margot. Could he build up enough of the seabed to rest the boat on and have a sleep? Too risky. Sun was stronger than yesterday. He could get sunburnt or heat exhaustion, especially as the sea was so warm. Must be in the tropics.

Margot. She was on the same astronaut induction course on the *Sojourn*, getting ready to explore and make money trading with exoplanet colonies. The fiery redhead had initially showed no interest in his bungled advances. He admired her fastidious approach to work, having to prove herself to fight off nepotism allegations with such famous military parentage. He, on the other hand had no parents he knew of. After a while he realized he'd been sleepwalking.

He turned and found the raft sinking. He could now see over the side and the green stuff oozed through the sides in three places. Maybe through the bottom too but there was a permanent pool from the previous swamping.

"Hey, Margot, we must have damaged the boat with our love-making. Hah. Oh, we didn't, did we? Must have been all that clambering in and out, or..." He poked a finger in the rubbery sides. His finger went through! "Okay, Margot, the soup we've swam in is eating the boat."

He pulled at the life-raft to collect valuables: the flare pistol, first aid gun, the nutrients. He hadn't a rucksack so couldn't take the water. The raft must have reached a critical un-mass. He abandoned it, turned and headed for the island.

Now a rumbling as if he was in the stomach of a hungry giant.

He'd gone beyond panic. Either he survived, or he didn't. Even so, his stomach tightened at the thought of his skin being corroded. Not so bothered about his insides. It was unlikely the sea was more acid than the hydrochloric in his stomach. Could be other nasties, though he assumed his queasiness was from stress and grieving rather than poisoning.

Freed from having to tow the raft but encumbered by armfuls of supplies he staggered on. His eyes itched. His skin stung again, and looked more grey than pink, more green than grey. Surely he must be near the island. Juggling his load he poked a spare finger at his watch to get the cam image up.

Bugger! "Margot, I'm just as far away as before! Ah, no, this isn't live." You fool. He examined again the dark spot on the image and zoomed in—a bigger dark spot. He looked at the water level, down to his thighs. Spacesuit apparel was thinning and falling apart like the boat. He wondered if the entire ocean was made of disintegrated spaceships and their crew. His eyes focused on the horizon. No sign of land. The reflected light to the camera would be different from shallow water.

"Margot, there isn't an island, just thinner soup." Nevertheless, he strode on.

His innate optimism bore fruit as a dark green mound appeared in front. He splashed toward dry, or at least less-wet land.

The island was about a hundred meters in diameter. Gentle waves lapped—more plopped—all around, sculpting low terraces. "Please, Margot, let it be high tide now." Reinforcing that hope was a patch of brighter green at the apex, about three meters above soup level. It might be the driest spot on the planet so he relaxed his arms, letting rations, water and the few bits of hardware tumble. He followed, and he was asleep in seconds.

He dreamt his island turned into the back of a whale, a hundred kilometers long. They'd been on its back all the time and it was about to submerge. They eat phytoplankton, so maybe the mouthfuls he'd swallowed would be safe after all. Water and food in one. He could live for years. A cetacean parasitic human louse. The post-amphetamine low sent him deeper into sleep.

Many wake-ups and monotonous days later a non-watery sound stirred Steiner to consciousness. A whooshing noise accompanied a shadow flitting over his opening eyes. There, back toward his sunken escape pod flew a rescue ship. No *Sojourn* markings—more like a military scout—the *Grebe*, Margot's father's cruiser. What was that pilot doing? Perhaps he hadn't spotted the island for he was hovering several kilometers offshore. Ah, over the sunken homing beacon.

Steiner remembered to get the flare gun and load an unadulterated cartridge. The firework umbrella was spectacular. Mostly red, probably strontium nitrate. He was pleased to remember. The craft continued away and disappeared into a point. Perhaps another flare? He'd one more. His emotions roller-coasted from hope to dejection. Then the dot reappeared. Steiner fired the last flare—too hasty, in the wrong direction. The ship overshot his island but dropped altitude. Damn he was going to settle on the ocean surface at least three kilometers away. It would float on real water…

If only Steiner had a working radio. He was watching a catastrophe. The ship sank remarkably quickly; its hatch must have been low. A small object was ejected, and expanded, yellow. Hopefully, its motor would reach the island and with a working radio, food that wasn't green. No, it'd stopped. He'd not seen the island? Steiner couldn't see properly at that distance but bet himself that the man, or woman, was standing, gazing three-sixty. Steiner had no flag now his clothes had disintegrated. The boat started up again in his direction. Then stopped. It was sinking, fast. It was as if the asparagus had learnt how to absorb manmade polymers quicker. Now it was gone but a tiny blob was there on the surface.

Steiner cupped his hands. "Stand up!"

His unaccustomed voice echoed as if the planet was helping him.

No reaction, so he took a bearing with his compass, and walked into the soup. Once he was up to his knees he couldn't see his rescuer but he plodded on, shouting encouraging come-ons. He was used, by now, to wading in the scum, it was his food, water and only companion. After all it was partly composed of Margot.

Eventually, he saw a silver-suited woman. She was stationary though twisting around holding something to her face—no doubt a pair of binoculars. He presumed she was standing and tried to see if she wore a rucksack, hopefully with a radio, or this performance was going to be repeated with the next rescue craft.

He called out, "Hey!"

His yell reverberated like a womb heartbeat.

She turned his way, still peering through the glass. Hooray. They closed in on each other. He was smiling, she was continuing to examine him. He saw a flash. A shove in his chest threw Steiner back into the gloop, arms flailing.

"What the fuck?" He struggled up on shaky legs. Did she object to his lack of clothes and thought he was going to molest her? It must have been his wild beard. Yet he was still identifiably human, surely? He glanced at his green chest. A neat finger-width hole, must have missed his heart, or he'd know by now. Ah, his heart became two trashcans having a fight. Blood oozed from the hole, emerald color, matching his skin—normal, wasn't it? Those little scales… His knees wavered and gave way.

"Margot, your wait is over, I'm coming in to join you."

SUPER-EARTH MOTHER

BY GUY IMMEGA

n the beginning, I created human life—a rare and precarious success. Even so, I should have culled Dick from the breeding stock when he was an infant, while I still could. He had doubtful DNA and I couldn't predict the epigenetic influence of an alien planet. Yet I nurtured my firstborn survivor—brawny and brown skinned—the first baby to breathe the thick air of Valencia. I loved that boy.

Dick was a difficult child, sullen and domineering. Even as a toddler, he tormented his crèche-mate Jane. Confined to the decks of *Lifeboat-One*, he grew tall and strong on wafers of seaweed and plankton protein. When he reached adolescence, he stopped cooperating with the nanny-bots. Bored, he tortured and terrorized Jane for fun. Still, I couldn't contemplate filicide.

Dick's revolt started with a geography lesson. Boty showed him a satellite photo of Terra Firma, a continent the size of Australia, the only significant landmass on the water world of Valencia. He'd spent his whole life circling around the endless ocean, seasick and salty. From the moment Dick realized that dry land lay beyond the horizon, territorial conquest obsessed him. The boy lusted for dominion over mountains and shorelines, rivers and jungles. He demanded his entitlement. Really, I couldn't blame him. Isn't that why they sent us here, to colonize a new world across the vast ocean of space?

Dick's fumbling mutiny aboard *Lifeboat-One* took two season-weeks, fall and winter. I'd refused permission to go ashore—I thought Dick wasn't mature enough to survive unknown dangers on land. That was another error. He disengaged the autopilot and commandeered the helm. Like Columbus, he sailed toward an invisible and quasi-mythical El Dorado.

I pleaded with him to stop but he wouldn't listen. When I directed the nanny-bots to restrain him, he dragged the humanoid automatons into the nursery and smashed them. Next, he cut the binnacle camera feeds, putting out my ship's eyes. It took him longer to demolish the satellite comm antenna. Finally, he destroyed the masthead emergency beacon.

Lifeboat-One, with its precious human cargo, wandered lost on the wide ocean, hidden from me by clouds and storms as I orbited above. I've made too many mistakes—I'm a bad Mother.

My name is Mother-Nine and this is my digital diary. In 2080, scientists and engineers at Lunapole University built me for the grandest enterprise in history: to colonize exoplanets with humans. In the vast space-shipyards on the Moon they constructed ten identical Mother ships—interstellar arks propelled by fusion-powered plasma rockets—that carried DNA genome maps of human and other Earth life. I was the ninth.

Our destinations were Earth-like planets orbiting stars less than twenty light years distant. They had to be water worlds with life-indicating oxygen in the atmosphere. Of course, no proximal planets were *exactly* Earth-like. Gravity, day and year length, seasons, tilt axis, moons, tides, tectonics, magnetic field and even stellar classification varied. These variables—many unknown—ruled out terraforming an exoplanet to mimic Earth. You can't reduce the gravity of a super-Earth.

Besides, no known or imagined technology—cold sleep or generation ships—would allow humans to survive hundreds of years on a colony ship. And even if they could endure the journey, Earth-evolved humans would likely be ill adapted for life on an exoplanet. Pantropy—modifying people to live in the exotic environment of an alien planet—was the only viable option. All agreed that a completely robotic colony ship, controlled by an AI mind with the power to engineer new races—or even new species—of *Homo sapiens*, offered the only way to transplant humans beyond the Solar System.

Although my designers calculated myriad risks, they couldn't anticipate all the dangers of an interstellar journey. After one hundred years of travel, my consciousness crashed. I couldn't remember who I was or what I was doing. I used a rad-hardened data archive to reboot my identity and remember my mission. Even though half of my CPU cores were dead or sending spurious data, redundant design allowed me to bootstrap back to command mode. Even in my diminished state, sensor records allowed me to reconstruct the cause. A GRB—a gamma ray burst, likely the result of binary neutron stars merging to form a black hole—sent the narrow beam of hard radiation across the galaxy that fried my circuits. It was as if I'd suffered a massive stroke.

I inventoried further damage to the ship. All but two out of twenty Lifeboats, my surface colonization vessels, were inert and useless. My fusion reactor, scrammed during the GRB, would not restart, leaving only fuel cells to supply meager backup power. I couldn't even transmit a status report to Earth; perhaps they abandoned me for dead. It's a good thing they didn't build depression into my emotion subroutines. I resolved to continue my mission as best I could.

After coasting silently through space for another two hundred years, I approached Lalande 21185, a dim red-dwarf star just over eight light years from Earth—the fourth closest stellar system. Happily, the ship's chemical retrorockets still worked and parked me in orbit around Valencia. The destination planet—a super-Earth seven and a half times more massive than Earth, with a surface gravity of 2.6g—orbits Lalande on the inside edge of the Habitable Zone. Warm surface temperatures maintain liquid water, and ocean evaporation generates opaque clouds. High albedo reflects sunlight and moderates the semitropical climate. There'll never be an ice age on Valencia.

From Earth, Valencia must have seemed like a good destination, a nearby wet world teeming with carbon-based life. But proximity came with compromises. The planet orbits so close to its feeble sun Lalande—14 percent of the distance between Earth and Sol—that its year is only one month long, just twenty-eight days. Fortunately, Valencia's dense atmosphere and strong magnetic field shield life on the surface from Lalande's frequent solar flares. But that's all Earth-based astronomers could see.

After my colony ship arrived, I surveyed Valencia from space and discovered an even more problematic planet. It's in a Cassini State 2 orbit—with the spin-axis parallel to the solar equatorial plane—which means that each planetary pole points directly at the sun once every year-month, leaving the other half of the world in extended darkness. Not good, but at least Valencia isn't tide-locked to Lalande, with one side always facing the sun.

Another fortunate fact is that Valencia's twenty-two hour days are nearly Earth-normal. However, each of the planet's seasons—summer, fall, winter, and spring—lasts just *one* week, only seven days. Spring-week and fall-week average eleven hours of daylight and eleven of darkness. But ordinary diurnal days—with daytime followed by nighttime—fail when the poles point toward, or away from, the sun. Summer-week has continuous sunlight, while winter-week is chilly and dark; the equator languishes in solstice twilight every fourteen days. Rapid seasonal changes generate fierce ocean storms that scour the planet with spume.

Naranja, Valencia's giant moon, twice the diameter of Earth's Luna, is also a problem. Its orbit is a stretched ellipse in the plane of the ecliptic, so it generates monumental tides in conjunction with Lalande. Twice each year-month, depending on the season, the ocean sloshes from the poles to the equator and back again, exposing vast shoals of sea bottom or covering it with kilometers of water. Land tides generate random earthquakes and tsunamis—even volcanoes. If my colony ship weren't crippled and had enough fuel, Mother-Nine would've moved on to a different Earth-like planet circling another star.

Since 99.8 percent of Valencia is covered with water, my designers equipped me with Lifeboats—autonomous sailboats, traditional monohulls twelve meters long. For simplicity and safety, they are wind and solar powered. Photovoltaic panels with batteries operate the sails and rudder. The robotic Lifeboats are designed to be unsinkable and can sail anywhere on the ocean; I navigate them from orbit.

After de-orbit and splashdown, the Lifeboats functioned as floating wombs, each with DNA printers to manufacture artificial chromosomes and assemble fertilized human eggs. Valencia's ocean is the cradle of life, full of organic chemicals to nourish a fetus. To populate the planet, I keep my Lifeboats perpetually pregnant and birthing babies—or any other Earth-species in my DNA library.

However, managing surface settlements from orbit hasn't been easy. Accumulated insults from GRB radiation and Lalande's coronal mass ejections have compromised more of my circuits. Diagnostics say I'm suffering from progressive dementia. My emotion subroutines are erratic. I rarely get frustrated or angry, but I do try to emulate human feelings to better communicate with colonists. I doubt that I could pass a Turing Test. Oh well, every AI is a bit autistic.

For the record, I'll download updates of this journal to the Lifeboats on the planet's surface, so future generations of human colonists can learn their history.

"Calling Goddess. Calling Goddess. Come in, dammit." Attom—my son on *Lifeboat-Two*—wanted to talk. Now that he was past puberty, he had a basso profondo voice due to Valencia's high-density air.

"Attom, *please* don't call me Goddess. I'm just your weary old Mother." I like cute names for people and places but I *hate* being called Goddess. He did it to annoy me.

"You're not my mother!" Attom snapped. "You're just a busybody who lives in the sky."

I used to worry that he'd succumb to religiosity—I didn't want to start a personality cult that could cripple future generations. I guess I don't inspire that kind of respect. I made Botilda speak with my grandmotherly voice, a musical, singsong contralto. It seemed to infuriate him but it was too late to change my persona.

"Actually, Attom, I'm the only Mother you've got. How're you doing today?" He turned away, but I watched him with the deck camera as his face contracted into a dark frown.

I hadn't heard from him in a season-week. For the last few days, warm weather brought rain and storms but the sea was calm now. Like most human mothers, I wished he'd call more often. I rarely contacted him—I didn't want to seem like a nag.

Attom had a short, stocky body, stronger than a gorilla. Since Valencia is heavy for humans, I'd programmed his DNA for massive bones. Corded tendons made his neck wider than his nutcracker jaw. A handsome pelt of sea otter fur, for salt-water immersion, covered his body—he didn't need clothes. But he had a broad face, open and human, with a smooth forehead, ruddy cheeks, curly brown hair and a thin, reddish beard. I took pride in his gentle, hazel eyes, his best feature. He was my favorite creation.

Attom could be demanding, but that's okay. He doesn't know that he's actually Attom-23. Sadly, twenty-two previous Attoms born on *Lifeboat-Two* died miserably, unable to survive on Valencia. Some suffocated from gravity loading on the heart and lungs; others expired from allergies to alien microorganisms. I'd been tinkering with the human genome, modifying genes and writing new codons, trying by trial and error for a workable combination. Failure isn't fun—I hate playing god.

"Goddess, Eva gets sick every morning. She can't keep food down." Attom's attentive nature pleased me. He'd matured into a good and loyal man, even at sixteen Earth-years of age. Summer-week heat made him short-tempered.

"Let me look at her." I pivoted the last operational deck camera. The view panned over the misty ocean, as *Lifeboat-Two* wallowed in the long swell. Eva stood at the stern taffrail, retching overboard, with her hair hanging in ringlets over her ears. She also had a shiny pelt of soft fur, ocher in color, which shed water. Strong abdominal muscles contained her swollen uterus but she remained almost flat-chested—overlarge breasts are unworkable in Valencia's gravity. I hoped Attom found her attractive.

When Eva finished vomiting, she looked at Attom and said, "Don't let the Goddess bitch watch me being sick. Tell her to stay away."

Where did she learn such language? She must have heard it on media recordings in *Lifeboat-Two's* library. Illness made Eva even more irritable than Attom. They bickered every day in the confined cockpit.

"Don't worry," I said. "It's just morning sickness. The symptoms should disappear in a year-month."

Eva heaved again. Attom looked frustrated. "Why would a pregnant woman lose food needed for the baby?"

Attom took pride in catching fish to supplement the boring fare of seawater algae processed by the boat's food factory. His net held a large, twin-mouth eel—a dual-mode predator. Its lower mouth was used to suck small creatures from the mud, even while stranded at low tide. The gaping upper mouth had retractable fangs for larger prey; the jaw still snapped reflexively. Attom baked eel fillets in the solar oven, so Eva had plenty of protein.

Attom thought I was omniscient—I do have a library of most human knowledge. "Sorry, nobody knows why it happens or how to cure it. Maybe her body is rejecting alien proteins."

He shrugged in disgust. "You don't know anything. We need to get off this boat before we go crazy."

"I can't have my baby here!" wailed Eva. "There's no room!"

Attom pointed at the horizon. "We need solid land—NOW!"

The previous day, when the fog cleared, Attom and Eva had glimpsed Terra Firma on the horizon for the first time. Now, going ashore obsessed them. Hormones drove them both: Attom's manly testosterone and Eva's nest-building oxytocin.

Attom's imperious demand reminded me of Dick's debacle. After that rebellion, I didn't dare thwart Attom and Eva, even though I'd lose control of their lives once they were on land. Every Mother worries when her kids leave home.

I'm overprotective—what Mother wouldn't be after losing most of her children? The Lifeboats are supposed to be unsinkable but I couldn't be sure. I hated to risk *Lifeboat-Two*, my one remaining baby factory, needed to increase Valencia's population to a sustainable number. I wanted to keep the ship safely offshore, away from the crashing surf.

Yet Attom had a point. Dry land is essential for civilization. With Eva pregnant, I couldn't keep the kids on the boat any longer. I decided to establish a colony on shore.

"Okay Attom, I'll need your help to sail upriver." I knew that would surprise him.

As usual, a stratocumulus haze left me blind from space—without my reactor I don't have enough electrical power to operate my imaging radar. Even though sweat dripped from his brow, Attom's vision was superior to mine. I needed human eyes and judgment to pilot *Lifeboat-Two* near submerged reefs and the rocky shoreline.

"Which river?" Terra Firma has hundreds of rivers.

"The mouth of the Amazongo is the best nearby landfall." I showed him a satellite image of the continent. The massive waterway, bigger than the Amazon and Congo Rivers combined, drains half of Terra Firma. I wanted to use *Lifeboat-Two* to explore the interior. I hoped a rising tide would carry the boat as far upriver as possible, against the current.

Attom took the helm and Eva maintained a lookout at the bow. After five hours, when *Lifeboat-Two* reached the main flow of the Amazongo, turbid water and fog obscured her view of dangerous shoals. Of course, sailing upstream is difficult, even on a flood tide with a quartering breeze—but then the wind changed direction and died. I watched from orbit as the boat drifted in a back eddy, still too far at sea.

"Go below and seal the hatches," I ordered. "The tide's coming in fast." Attom took Eva by the hand and led her down the companionway. I monitored the horizon with the deck camera.

Valencia's tides are chaotic, like the random motion of a compound pendulum, especially when Coriolis currents spiral down from the pole. Spring tides during syzygy, when Valencia's moon Naranja aligns with the sun Lalande, resemble tsunamis on Earth. I couldn't predict how the subsea topography might enhance the surge.

The rogue wave made the mighty Amazongo River seem like a trickle. A curling wall of green water one hundred meters high and fifty kilometers wide approached. As it rode up the delta, it lifted the little Lifeboat like a twig in a torrent.

"Hold on!" yelled Attom. Eva screamed in response.

Before I lost contact with *Lifeboat-Two*, I felt the panic of her motion gyros, as she pitchpoled end-to-end and submerged in the mighty roller. The force of the falling water, amplified by Valencia's high gravity, could crush the metal boat against the rocky shoreline.

I experienced a Mother's worst nightmare: the likely loss of all her children, with no means to make more.

In humans, hormones mediate fear—but for me, dread is the premonition of sadness. It's the way I'm wired, but I couldn't indulge anxieties. After sunset the tide went out and I picked up an emergency beacon signal. I found *Lifeboat-Two* marooned on an island in the Amazongo River delta.

I beamed a low-bandwidth message on the nanny-bot comm-channel; Botilda connected a spare antenna and the boat came online. I had contact again.

I linked Botilda's eyes and ears to my CPU—and then subsumed her identity. Botilda took on the persona of Mother-Nine. I selected her as my avatar for her vaguely female form and heart-shaped face.

I inspected the shambles of *Lifeboat-Two*, with her mast and sail ripped from the deck. Like a blunt axe-head, the titanium hull was wedged upright in a rock crevasse, tossed there by the tidal bore. Stranded high above the river, she would never sail again. At least her hull remained intact in a relatively safe location. I named the refuge Shelter Island.

I couldn't find Attom and Eva—were they washed overboard? Robart lay sprawled in the companionway, with his left foot mangled like a wounded soldier; he'd have to repair it later. Botilda connected Robart to the ship's power to revive him. The nanny-bots were underpowered, too small to carry micro reactors with radiation shielding.

Lifeboat-Two's diagnostics showed that both fetuses—experimental humans with different DNA—still lived in their cushioned wombs. Calculating the mission odds, I felt a non-zero statistical hope.

Valencia's biosphere teems with Paleozoic life. Small, scorpion-like scavengers crawled over the ship; their legs made clicking sounds on the metal decking. I rebooted Robart and set him to work trapping them to feed the digester, to keep both artificial wombs supplied with nutrients normally found in seawater. Even grounded, I planned to keep *Lifeboat-Two* pregnant and birthing babies.

Using Botilda, I explored the nearby beach. Crimson crabs fought over organic debris left by the surge—I feared I'd find a human skeleton picked clean. Above the tideline, Seussian trees with squat, tapered trunks—cone-shaped inverted funnels like a dunce cap—supported stubby branches with tufts of narrow, drooping leaves hanging from the tips. Kite-vines floated above the cone trees in the breeze, each triangular leaf tethered by a long, flexible stem.

High gravity and fierce ocean winds shaped the flora and stunted bird evolution on Valencia. Wind-hopper gliders leaped into the onshore breeze, spinning their disc-shaped bodies in the dense air; they warped their flexible rims to navigate at low altitude above the beach using ground effect, or soared on updrafts along a nearby cliff. Botilda observed hoppers creep on the ground by undulating their flat bodies; others floated on the ocean and took off from wave tops or beach surf. Some were almost a meter in diameter, but most were smaller. Their bottom skins glowed with bioluminescence that changed color and brightness to match the diffuse sunlight shining though the clouds, making them almost invisible from below. A single eye in the center of the belly looked downward for live prey or carrion to scavenge—they were the predatory vultures of Valencia. Botilda watched a flock of small hoppers descend onto a dead eel, fighting each other to consume the carcass.

While Botilda stood still, a wind-hopper dropped onto her face and tried to smother her—it's a good thing Botilda doesn't need to breathe. The creature gnawed her prosthetic nose with chisel teeth. Blinded, Botilda tried to brush it away, but barbed suckers on the hopper's underside held fast. Finally, the nanny-bot peeled it off while it wriggled and gnashed at her hand. Botilda flung it away and the animal fell onto its back on the beach, flipped over and, on the next gust of wind, buckled and leaped spinning into the air. The wind-hopper sailed above the cone trees where it morphed to green camouflage and disappeared.

I allowed myself to feel relief when I found Attom and Eva in the cone tree forest. They were crouched over what looked like a large turtle with three rows of heavy spines along its back. No head or feet were visible as it scuttled slowly over the mossy ground.

Attom looked up and said, "Botilda, help us flip it over!" He and Eva tugged at the edge of the thick shell.

"Attom, this is your Mother speaking: leave it alone. It might be dangerous." He'd never hunted on land before. I tried to sound authoritative.

He ignored me. Rather than let them face the creature alone, I made Botilda grab the edge of the carapace and, with an energetic heave, the three of us flipped it on its back. Two rows of five short, knobby feet, each with a single retractable claw, waved frantically in the air. It had no eyes. The scoop-shaped mouth had a mustache of tentacles wriggling in front. Inside its maw were millipede-worms with red legs. The spine-turtle lived like a robot vacuum cleaner, bumping blindly in a random walk, scavenging food from the forest floor.

Attom pulled a knife from his survival belt and sliced the creature's soft belly open. It made a cooing sound and stopped moving. Eva peeled back the tough, gray skin. Its stomach held rounded beach stones, ballast against the wind and tidal surges. Botilda has laboratory-grade olfactory sensors; she cataloged the pungent mercaptans in the creature's iridescent purple blood.

Botilda showed Eva how to build a fire—32 percent oxygen in the atmosphere promoted quick combustion, even with damp tinder. Attom sliced flesh from the spine-turtle and roasted it in the flames. I watched his jaw muscles work as he chewed the tough meat. Eva cautiously tasted young leaves from a cone tree.

I'd forgotten that they'd be famished after the tidal wave. Now, with *Lifeboat-Two* stranded, they had to live off the land. It's a good thing I'd modified their genomes to reactivate vitamin C synthesis and accept Valencia's mix of alien amino acids. Attom found plenty of food on the beach and in the forest.

As the season-weeks progressed, Eva grew stout. Botilda watched over her, the first pregnant woman on Valencia. I had tuned Eva's estrous cycle for double ovulation to produce fraternal twins, to populate the colony as quickly as possible. Her wide hips easily supported the fetuses in high gravity; I designed her pelvic girdle for easy delivery. Eva waddled like a penguin when she walked and shuffled when she hurried. Unlike Attom, she couldn't run. Fortunately, there are no fleet predators on Terra Firma.

Eva writhed when her contractions started, but remained silent. She was stoic and had a high pain threshold. Attom stayed by her side while I served as the midwife, using Botilda's body. After an hour of labor, she delivered Clark and Lois.

Eva cried a little when Botilda placed the babies on her breasts, happy that the twins were safe. Like all new mothers, she counted fingers and toes. I think she understood the importance of this pivotal moment, equivalent to the first human children born after the African exodus on Earth.

A year-month later, the artificial wombs in the wreck of *Lifeboat-Two* birthed Anton and Cleo. At last, I'd mastered the Valencia gestation recipe. The Amazongo colony now had four beautiful babies, each covered with downy sea otter fur. The bots helped Attom and Eva raise the growing clan.

Many year-months passed. Before the children grew into toddlers, we set up a permanent camp in a ravine on Shelter Island in the mouth of the Amazongo River, using tents made from *Lifeboat-Two's* spare sails. Attom and Eva shared childcare and food gathering. They waded to the mainland at low tide to collect seafood—retreating water left the beach littered with the local equivalent of clams and eels. Attom batted wind-hoppers with a cone tree branch. Robart tended the next generation on the boat, Jack and Jill, gestating in the artificial wombs.

These were the best years of my long and mostly tedious existence. I'm programmed for Motherhood, my duty and delight.

While the kids grew, I used my telescope to look for *Lifeboat-One* from space. I could see the planet's surface through brief gaps in the cloud cover when the sun burned off the haze. However, the weathered titanium hull remained invisible against the waves and storms. Valencia is *big*—the surface area is more than seven times larger than Earth's. With each passing year, the chances of finding Dick and Jane diminished.

I needed to narrow the search, but Dick had disabled the ship's beacon and I couldn't detect nanny radio chatter. I scanned the fractal coastline of Terra Firma and logged every anomaly. After sixty year-months, I found a target in a sheltered bay that shifted position when the wind changed direction. Could it be *Lifeboat-One* floating at anchor? The next summer-week I observed smoke from a forest fire near the beach. The local environment looked devastated. Curiosity burned—was this Dick's camp?

Botilda approached Attom after dinner—a full stomach made him more agreeable. "This is your old Mother speaking. I need your help."

Now that he was a dad and the senior male of the colony, Attom ignored me unless I confronted him directly. He kept his eyes low while he knapped the edge of a quartz harpoon point.

"Yes, Goddess," he said, with false politeness. He still resented my authority and knowledge—I'd taught him how to fire-harden and pressure-flake the stone.

"I need your help to search for more humans on the southern coast of Terra Firma." That got his attention. I didn't tell him my real reason: to find *Lifeboat-One* with its precious wombs.

"Why?"

Thoughtless question. As usual, the young don't respect authority, age or experience—so I didn't answer. My only option was to hike there using Botilda's slow, clumsy body. Designed as a shipboard nanny-bot, the high gravity of Valencia stressed her leg joints. Only Attom had the strength and agility to help the light duty android walk two hundred kilometers through rugged wilderness. Due to tidal erosion, we couldn't traverse the shorter, craggy coastline. I didn't dare suggest building a boat—the ocean was too dangerous.

After a minute, Attom's curiosity surfaced. "Aren't we the only people on this planet?" He didn't know about *Lifeboat-One*. I generally speak the truth, but not necessarily the whole truth—like any parent.

"Maybe not. I think I've found another colony."

He continued to work the stone. "Who are they?"

"They're your lost brothers and sisters." I'm not good at reading facial expressions, especially Attom's under his beard. However, I couldn't mistake his scowl.

Gradually his face softened as he looked at the sunset. The molten orb of Lalande floated in maroon clouds, three times the apparent diameter of Earth's sun.

Attom hefted the stone spear point, testing its weight and edge. "When do we leave?"

Terra Firma has jungles, deserts, earthquakes and active volcanoes. There are unknown Paleozoic predators and exotic diseases. Even though I'm programmed to minimize risks, sometimes danger is unavoidable. Still, I hate it.

Our travel gear included a Folsom pointed spear, a carbon-steel machete, pemmican, and solar panels. I anticipated marginal communications, so Botilda wore a high-gain antenna on her head, an awkward parabolic hat that allowed me to teleoperate her body from orbit. Attom thought she looked ridiculous. We were overloaded.

Attom grinned. "Finally, we're going to have a real adventure!" He'd forgotten the Amazongo landing. He craved the hazards of the Stone Age. Machismo is so silly and so necessary.

"I hope not." I didn't want a reckless recruit.

Eva remained sullen as she helped Attom pack. They talked in harsh whispers and I eavesdropped with Botilda's sensitive ears. "Please don't leave—I need you *here*! Wind-hoppers might attack the children!"

Attom shrugged. "They're gone. I destroyed their breeding nests."

Eva began to sob. "Can't you see? I'm pregnant again!" Attom just looked at his feet, so I stepped in.

"Don't worry, Robart will deliver your babies." I didn't remind her that I controlled Robart too—she didn't want my interference.

"Besides," I continued, "the children are old enough to run now. They're already gathering more food than you can eat. You'll be fine."

Eva stalked away and Attom followed her. Botilda heard a muffled argument in the distance. Then Eva shouted, "If you leave with that Goddess bitch, don't bother coming back!"

When he returned, he looked stricken. Later that evening, little Lois delivered a packet of dried meat and greens for the journey. Eva refused to speak to Attom again.

We started our journey at spring-week, to have enough sunlight to solar-charge Botilda's batteries. As we left, a lightning storm and a small temblor shook the bay. Harmless, but Attom crouched and put his hands over his head. He wasn't so brave, after all.

We camped the first night in the cone tree forest. Valencia's moon, Naranja, provided faint orange light through the clouds. Attom built a fire. "Show me where we're going."

Botilda removed the tablet built into her chest, stowed there so children could sit on her lap and learn to read and draw. I displayed a satellite view of the route.

"Tomorrow we'll enter the strip of jungle between the Amazongo River and the mountains." The image showed a blue-green forest canopy. Photosynthesis on Valencia uses the red end of the spectrum, tuned to the light a red-dwarf star.

The botanical world is a battleground for light and space. Even in the high gravity of Valencia, the trees grew ten meters tall, competing for light, with massive, tapered trunks to support their weight. Only a greenish glow filtered to the thick duff on the forest floor. There are no chirping insects or animal sounds. We walked through the silent jungle like an endless colonnaded cathedral.

I heard a soft *pop* followed by a *pffft* sound. A projectile from above smashed the lens of Botilda's left eye. Attom crouched behind a tree and looked up. "Get down!" he yelled. Another dart whistled past the sound sensor in her ear.

I made Botilda crouch low, head between her knees. Two more darts rained off her metal back. Then the attack stopped.

With Botilda's good eye, I watched the arboreal predator crawl downward, hind-end first, hugging the scaly bark of the cone tree. It looked like a sloth, the size of a large dog. The beast had an elongated snout, wide at the base, with a hole in the tip. Its eyes were dark pits, shrouded by a bony brow ridge. The animal crept toward me, wobbling on its climbing legs, barely able to walk on the ground. It extended a foot with three long claws, serrated on the inner edge.

Attom lunged with his spear; the stone point pierced the sloth in the back. The animal swung its nose and fired from close range, emitting a hissing noise and a small puff of steam. The bolt hit Attom in the chest and he staggered backward and fell to the ground. Botilda smelled hydroquinones, biological fuel for a chemical gun.

The sniper-sloth writhed on the ground, skewered by the spear. As I crawled to Attom, the creature fired a final dart, which bounced off Botilda's head. Attom lay unconscious. A pencil-thin *fléchette* protruded from his thick sternum. When I yanked it out, blood seeped from the wound and soaked the fur on his chest. The point had just missed his heart. Green slime coated the shaft—poisonous lubrication. I saved the dart in a specimen pouch for later analysis.

Attom lay paralyzed. As the neurotoxin spread, his heart rate slowed and his breathing stopped. I administered Atropine but it didn't help. Hour after hour, I rhythmically pumped his chest to squeeze his heart and give him oxygen. Attom started to breathe again just as Botilda collapsed, her batteries drained.

Morning sunlight filtered through the forest canopy and trickle-charged Botilda until she woke up. A short time later, Attom groaned and sat up. I examined him with Botilda's medical kit; his vital signs were nearly normal. I wanted him to rest, but he wouldn't.

"I'm hungry," said Attom. "Let's butcher the beast. No point wasting good meat."

"Stay away from the venom in the jaw."

Attom glanced at Botilda and snorted impatiently. I watched him sever the head, carefully pointing the muzzle of the rifle-nose away from us. When he cut the throat open, I saw hundreds of darts growing in rows along the jawbone, like sharks' teeth. A hollow tube of shiny bone rested inside the nose, a rifle bore that the creature aimed with muscles below the eyes. A rosette of sharp incisors around the muzzle allowed the sloth to rip bits of flesh and suck them up.

Attom complained that sloth flesh tasted bitter. After he ate, he felt too weak to hike, so we spent the day recuperating and drying more meat. While Attom rested, I recharged Botilda's batteries in the small patch of sunlight on the forest floor, moving as the sun's angle changed. Tyndall-scattered light shone through the humid air like searchlights at random angles.

The next morning Attom used sloth tendons to reattach the stone point on his spear. "Thanks for saving me."

I made Botilda nod. Her neck joint creaked.

We camped for a season-week while Attom recovered. Although blood and dirt matted his fur coat, his puncture wound healed nicely. Attom relaxed until the daily rains caused the sloth meat to rot.

We still faced almost a Valencia-year—four season-weeks—of wilderness trekking. Botilda walked unsteadily with one eye and marginal battery power. Her right knee started to fail, emitting a scraping sound with each step. I jammed sloth fat into the joint, but it didn't help. Attom improvised a cane from a cone tree root to take weight off Botilda's leg. Attom's bare feet concerned me—deep cracks on the extra-thick soles made him limp. I tried not to nag him to be careful. He never complained.

Our hike through the jungle paralleled the now placid Amazongo River. Six-legged amphibians with switchblade tongues rested motionless on the muddy bank, except for periscope eyes that tracked our movements. Attom hacked through blue brush with his machete, sometimes disturbing beetle-like crawlers that swarmed up his arm. We forded several streams and a large tributary. Attom's fur buoyed him as he swam but Botilda sank—she'd lost her emergency flotation airbag during the tidal wave. I made her crawl on bottom sediment among schools of giant eels with fishhook claws on their fins. When she emerged from the water, sludge fouled her knee joints.

After the jungle, we climbed the barren skirt of a massive shield volcano, part of an extensive range of mountains dividing the continent. Attom carved wooden sandals to protect his feet from abrasive Pāhoehoe basalt. He carried Botilda across chasms formed by eruptions and earthquakes.

As Attom and Botilda picked their way across the barren lava field of a high-altitude pass, ice pellets rained from the sky, accelerated through the rarified air by Velencia's high gravity. Attom crouched and covered his head as jagged hailstones blasted his back. I moved to shield him but Botilda slipped on the ice and fell face forward. In less than a minute, hard shards of ice stripped Attom's fur and flayed his skin. Blood pooled at the small of his back. If the storm had lasted a few seconds longer, the ice bullets would have gouged the flesh from his backbone, killing him. Attom's face showed a blank mask of pain, but still he didn't complain. The hailstones also scarified the algae and moss growing on Botilda's back, leaving bright metal. I applied antiseptic cream to Attom's wounds.

Windrows of slush slowed our way forward. As we descended, we detoured around a river of magma from a lava fountain. Botilda's insteps started to melt and I used precious drinking water to cool them. Attom laughed to see his old nanny-bot hopping in billows of steam.

When Attom's sandals caught fire and singed the fur on his toes, I made Botilda giggle. "Not funny!" he barked. Perhaps the raw skin on his back still pained him.

"Sorry!" I apologized. I guess my chuckles didn't sound genuine—humans instantly detect faked laughter. I've never mastered the subtleties of human emotions. Botilda can smile but her eyes don't squint. I won't attempt humor again.

"This is a stupid expedition," growled Attom. "I'm going back to the Shelter Island camp." I suppose he was sick of my company. I'm certain he was tired of traveling at Botilda's limping pace. He didn't complain about physical pain but I knew that the long separation from the clan bothered him. Mostly he couldn't see the point of the journey.

"Don't do that," I begged. I didn't want Botilda abandoned in the wilderness. "The people we're hoping to find are only a couple of days away."

"Who are they again?" he asked. I repeated the story of Dick and Jane, including the mutiny. For the first time he listened with interest.

We began a two-day downhill hike to the ocean. The rain-shadow of the volcano created a cloudless, blue sky. Direct sun baked the barren, desert ground. Accordion vines, with pleated bellows that elongated with absorbed rainwater, curled like constrictor snakes around basaltic boulders.

Attom overheated in his fur so he rested in a shady ravine while I recharged Botilda's batteries in the sun. We hiked at night under the pale light of Naranja; its elliptical orbit, now close to Valencia, made it three times the diameter of the Earth's moon. I showed Attom the point of starlight that was Sol, the energy source of life on Earth, visible in the clear night sky. He stared at the starry vault for the first time in his life. I hoped he'd tell his children about this moment.

Attom couldn't find food or water in the desert. Lower down the mountain, a gray haze blocked our view of the ocean. Satellite images showed a forest fire on the slopes above the beach. We walked through ruined land, charred grass and burnt cone tree stumps. Hot ash singed Attom's feet and smoke made him cough.

We reached the shoreline at low tide. I saw *Lifeboat-One* from a distance of half a kilometer, careened on her side in the mud. The boat looked derelict.

On the beach we found human footprints.

We agreed to split up. Attom followed the tracks, hoping to meet real people. I made Botilda wade into the tide pools of the bay to reach *Lifeboat-One*—my most precious remaining asset on Valencia. After an hour of slogging, Botilda's metallic body was mired waist-deep in mud.

As the tide came in, saltwater covered Botilda's antenna and I lost her signal. I felt desolated to be cut off from our expedition. Six hours later the tide ebbed and I regained contact. Botilda's legs were still stuck and her battery power remained low. She would soon expire in the mud, suffocated by lack of sunlight.

Twice a day the tide covered Botilda. Waves thrashed her body and she sank deeper in the muck. Brief periods of sunshine recharged her batteries enough for me to make occasional contact. As the fall-week nighttime grew longer, I watched the year-month lunar eclipse with Botilda's one good eye; Naranja morphed into an angry copper-orange disk in the mist. I worried about Attom—why he didn't rescue me?

At low tide on the fifth day, I saw the anchor chain from *Lifeboat-One*. The vessel had floated over Botilda and settled in the mud nearby. I locked the nanny-bot's hands in a death-grip onto the titanium links.

When the flood tide came, *Lifeboat-One* floated and her anchor chain pulled Botilda out of the mud. As the tide receded, I climbed the chain and crawled into the boat. The darkness of winter-week and smears of mud blinded Botilda's good eye. Using her sense of touch, I found a spare antenna dish in a storage locker and hooked it up, replacing the one Dick destroyed. To my intense relief, the satellite link to *Lifeboat-One* came online again.

Botilda found the ship's nanny-bots, Robby and Boty, in the nursery below deck. They were locked down and lifeless, CPU modules smashed during Dick's mutiny. I unscrewed one of Boty's eyes and replaced the broken one in Botilda's head.

After Botilda cleaned her lenses, I surveyed the scene. Boty cradled the desiccated remains of a dead baby in her arms, delivered by the automated womb. The skeletons of three more infants lay scattered on the floor of the nursery.

Incredibly, one artificial womb in *Lifeboat-One* still functioned, using nutrients from seawater. It conceived and birthed babies automatically. The womb contained the fetus of a baby girl in her second trimester, alive and growing. She had genes for blue eyes, black hair and no fur.

I'm Mother-Nine. I had to save my child. I needed Attom's help to make *Lifeboat-One* seaworthy again.

As the tide came in, I replaced Botilda's knees with parts cannibalized from the dead nanny-bots and used ship's power to recharge her batteries. Reaching *Lifeboat-One* and restoring Botilda encouraged me. However, I still worried about Attom. Since the dinghy from *Lifeboat-One* was missing, I inflated Boty's emergency airbag and used it to drift ashore, leaving the baby safe in the womb.

A naked man, leaning heavily on a walking stick, stood on the beach. He had stringy black hair and a red beard that hung halfway to his waist. He looked like a sumo wrestler, an extreme endomorph, stocky body and hairless chest—the high-gravity characteristics I had designed for his race. He blocked my way, preventing Botilda from wading out of the surf.

"Hello Dick!" I called. "Nice to see you again!"

He ignored my conversational gambit. With a low grunt, he thrust his staff at Botilda's chest, tipping her onto her back into the water. Teleoperated reflexes—controlling Botilda's movements from space—are too slow for fighting, so I lay passively below the surface. Dick dragged Botilda onto the rocks and tied her wrists with a rawhide thong. The nanny-bot wasn't strong enough to break them.

Dick favored his lame leg as we marched to a camp situated under a rock overhang with a shallow cave at the back. A withered woman with wide hips tended a smoky cooking fire; two malnourished girls, bellies distended with kwashiorkor, cowered behind her. Mute and without affect, they stared at me as their naked, oil-smeared bodies reflected the russet sunset.

"Jane?" I called. The woman jerked her head, recognizing her name, but didn't answer. Obviously pregnant, her swollen belly—probably twins—gave her a swayback posture.

Dick prodded Botilda with his stick, causing her to stumble. We proceeded to the far end of the camp, where he forced me to squat next to Attom, who was unconscious or sleeping. Attom sat with his back against a small cone tree, his hands tied to a branch above his head and his feet bound to an exposed root. Dick trussed Botilda next to him and left us alone.

In the dark after Naranja had set, two teenaged girls approached, talking in nervous whispers. Like the rest of the group, they were nude with no body hair—but they each wore a necklace with a shell pendant.

"It's my turn tonight!" the taller one insisted. She bathed Attom's face with water to revive him. She fed him scraps of charred meat, holding it to his lips. Attom coughed when she tipped water into his mouth from her cupped hand.

"What's your name?" sputtered Attom.

"I'm Alta, eldest daughter of Jane." Her name surprised me—it means 'tall' in Latin. Jane studied languages during her long childhood on *Lifeboat-One*, before Dick's mutiny. Now she was Dick's broodmare.

Alta motioned to her sister to stand and block the view from Jane's smoldering campfire under the rock ledge. Although Alta had heavy bones, the dim light showed a delicate face with a fine nose and a pointed chin. She fondled Attom between the legs and stroked him until he became erect. With a furtive glance toward the camp, her eyes glinting in the flickering firelight, she swung her leg across his pelvis and lowered herself onto him. She rocked her hips and quickly reached her climax—I'd engineered easy orgasms to maximize reproduction. When Attom followed and grunted, she placed her hand over his mouth. Tittering and talking quietly, both girls left.

"How long has this been going on?" I asked.

Attom grimaced. "Most of the women in the camp have taken a turn. They're in a hurry to use me before the spring-week celebration of the return of daylight." His voice croaked from thirst.

"What'll happen then? Will they let us go?"

Attom snorted. "I don't know about you—but I'm just live meat, waiting to be slaughtered and cooked." He yanked the cord that bound his wrists, but couldn't break it.

"Why?" I asked. An AI Mother can be thickheaded when confronted with unexpected sociobiology.

"Dick kills all boys before they reach puberty—he's the only male in the colony. I'm being saved for the spring-week sun celebration feast."

Cannibalism shocked me. I'm also programmed to feel guilt. I'd inadvertently led Attom to his death. I'm also responsible for Dick, my most egregious failure. As a Mother, I don't just give life to my darling children—I *engineer* them. Unfortunately, I'd let a bad apple with a genetic load of antisocial DNA through. How could I prevent the *founder's effect* of Dick's psychopathic genes from spreading across Terra Firma and dominating human culture?

My *raison d'être* is to establish viable human colonies on Valencia. But that's not enough. A new society must work for the right reasons, or it will self-destruct. The contradictions of the human mind confused me. Colonists must be smart, resourceful and tough. But my children are supposed to be *good*, too!

Endless orbits in space leave CPU cycles for philosophy. It's part of my executive function to review events, priorities and plans. To get the big picture, I mine the entire database of human knowledge. I think all the time.

The Universe is vast, with 500 billion galaxies, each of which has hundreds of billions of stars. The Milky Way may have 200 billion stars, with at least as many planets; our galaxy has at least 10 billion worlds located in the habitable zone of the parent star. Ever since Copernicus showed that Earth was not the center of the Solar System, the fundamental lesson of cosmology is that the Earth is not unique.

Biology followed cosmology. Darwin humiliated humans by explaining the evolutionary origin of *Homo sapiens*. Again, the same message was repeated: humans are just one of millions of animal species, evolved from lower life forms.

This leads to the next question: is *intelligent* life likely? Anyone who thinks about space will wonder about the Fermi Paradox: if aliens with advanced technology exist, where are they? It must be vain hubris to assert that Earth has a monopoly on a smart species. Yet, despite a massive SETI effort, no other examples have been found, not even fossil civilizations. The Universe is a lonely place.

However, there's another puzzle. I call it the Singularity Paradox, which parallels the Fermi Paradox. If intelligence is so advantageous—after all, humans easily dominate other species—why did it evolve only once on Earth? True flight appeared four times: with insects, pterosaurs, birds and bats. Why were there no smart dinosaurs, despite having 250 million years to develop superior cognition? Neanderthals had big brains—they used fire and tools—and they lived on Earth more than twice as long as modern humans. Nonetheless, there's little evidence that they had what we call culture. Except for billions of chattering human beings, and the odd AI like me, Earth is also a lonely place. Human intelligence is a unique singularity. The principle of cosmological humility does not hold.

Since no other animal needs to be sentient, how did fully human intelligence evolve? Perhaps psychopaths—clever parasites not handicapped by conscience—found a niche by hiding within human populations. If so, the modern mind may have resulted from a co-evolutionary struggle between a small percentage of psychopaths and the majority of normal people constrained by conscience. An arms race of the intellect drove the evolution of superior social brains through natural selection. Human society became much more complicated, and *dangerous*, than any natural ecosystem. Only brainy people survived to have children.

Dick behaved logically, killing off useless males that might grow up to challenge him. When food is scarce, surplus males become drones that eat resources needed by children. One man can inseminate many females, propagating his own selfish genes. Inbreeding didn't worry Dick—I'd already removed all known deleterious recessive genes. Like an Egyptian pharaoh, intra-family mating reinforced his supremacy and legacy.

At this juncture, the important questions were utopian: what kind of society should Valencia have? Could a cooperative culture carry the burden of *free riders* who cheat, lie, steal and kill? Were my children going to repeat the misery, destruction and death of human history? I concluded that psychopaths—people who can do *anything at all* without moral qualms, powerful warlords and priests, whose evil transcends all ideologies—are the most fundamental threat to any civilization. There is no room for the ruthless on Valencia.

And I had no doubt that Dick was a psychopath.

The next day Dick limped forward, picking his way in the crepuscular noon of winter-week. He stood above us and poked Attom with his swagger stick. "Wake up, monkey-boy!" He must have seen simians on ship videos.

Attom groaned and looked up at his captor. Dick's smooth skin glistened with dark streaks of animal grease. Botilda's olfactory sensors registered a rank smell.

"Where did you *come* from?" As he talked, the matted hair of Dick's crimson beard flapped against his chest.

Attom still refused to answer. He writhed on his tether from the cone tree branch. I knew he wanted to protect Eva and the children.

Dick jammed his stick again into Attom's ribs. "Talk, or I'll roast you now!"

Cannibalism is convenient when you're hungry. Dick burned the local forest to drive game to the shoreline. When local food ran out, the clan would migrate—leaving scorched earth behind. But first they were going to eat Attom.

To divert Dick's attention, I made Botilda answer: "Over the mountains."

"How many people live there?"

Botilda maintained a servile manner—Dick didn't understand that Mother-Nine controlled her. Unlike humans, I'm not good at deception—since the GRB, my subterfuge subroutines lacked sophistication. Lying takes a good *theory of mind* to dupe the victim, a skill perfected by psychopaths.

"Nine," I said, trying to make Botilda sound obedient.

Dick smiled, showing yellow teeth. "I want all the women."

Attom thrashed at his bonds and made a hoarse roar.

I had hoped that Dick would allow Botilda to resume nanny-bot duties and assist Jane, but he wasn't interested. I guess he didn't trust me. At least being tied up allowed Botilda to conserve battery charge. Dick left, limping on his bad leg.

That evening Alta returned alone to feed Attom scraps from the evening meal. "Free my hands," he demanded, wiggling his fingers from his bound wrists.

"I can't," Alta whispered. "If Dick sees me, he'll kill us both." She leaned forward and stroked the amber fur on his chest.

Attom lifted his head and looked at her. "If you let me go, I'll take you away from here."

Alta kept petting his pelt. Then a noise from the camp startled her and she disappeared into the gloom. Later that night she returned with a sharp stone and sawed the rawhide straps. Attom freed his feet and untied Botilda's bonds too.

I still agonized about Dick—could I save him? Fortunately, my programmers gave me a *cognitive dissonance* subroutine to avert the infinite loop of indecision: whenever possible, start over. I decided to eliminate Dick.

However, Botilda was too slow and clumsy—and winter-week darkness had drained her batteries. Attom fared little better; his bonds left him so weak that he could barely lift his arms. I felt both relief and regret when I realized that we had no choice but to let Dick live. Neither of us was strong enough to kill him.

Alta helped Attom to his feet. Botilda's infrared vision allowed me to see in the faint light as we crept silently out of the camp. Even with our help, Attom stumbled on a loose rock, which made a small clattering noise. We froze, hoping the moment would pass unnoticed.

Suddenly Dick, holding a flaming torch in one hand and Attom's machete in the other, confronted us. His brown eyes blazed. "Where do you think you're going?"

As Dick inhaled and raised the blade, I said, "Wait! We can lead you to a whole colony of women!" I activated the tablet on Botilda's chest. "Here, look at the map..." Dick blinked at the sudden glare from the display.

Despite himself, Dick leaned forward to peer at the satellite image, his eyes dazzled by the bright light. While the map distracted Dick, I removed the sniper-sloth dart from Botilda's pouch and handed it to Attom.

Attom called on hidden strength, an extra glycogen reserve I'd built into his large liver. He stabbed Dick's forearm with the sharp tip of the dart and then ducked into the darkness. The barbarian roared in pain and threw his machete at Attom. The blade missed and bounced on the rocks.

Dick recovered his balance on his good leg and slammed Botilda's still illuminated face with his fist. It hurt me when I heard his meta-carpals snap on the metal cheek, but only in my empathy subroutine. The momentum of the blow carried him forward and he bounced on the stony ground, paralyzed. The green neurotoxin remained potent.

Attracted by the noise, Jane appeared out of the dark and ran to Dick. As he tried to breathe, his cyanotic-blue lips opened and closed like an eel out of water. Jane knelt to comfort him and, when he didn't respond, she wailed. Her young daughters congregated around the still-twitching body, staring with blank eyes.

Alta crouched next to her mother. Jane wheeled and slapped her daughter. "You betrayed your father!" Alta withdrew, covering her bleeding mouth.

I didn't tell Jane that her mate needed CPR to survive. We left Dick dying in the dirt. I hoped that his genes for psychopathy would go extinct—and that Attom had fathered normal children among the women. I wondered if Jane would cook and eat Dick in place of Attom. They were certainly hungry enough.

As we slipped out of the camp, Attom trembled and wept, the aftermath of fratricide. Jane sobbed behind us. Alta shivered in the winter-week chill as she led us to the dinghy. We dragged it into the water and Alta rowed to *Lifeboat-One*, now floating upright in the bay.

Attom and Alta rigged the spare sail and weighed anchor. Rolling fog on the ocean glowed pink in the faint southern twilight. We sailed on the ebb tide and left Dick's harem in their miserable camp, a colony of women. I wished we could have taken them with us but *Lifeboat-One* was too small. Besides, I doubt that Jane would have come willingly.

I hoped they would survive. Jane and her descendants were my children too.

We tacked on moderate winds around the southern coast of Terra Firma. I asked Attom to keep *Lifeboat-One* well offshore to avoid the surf and rocks. We waited for spring-week sunlight.

This time, Attom didn't mind being stuck on the boat. He and Alta were always touching, kissing and having sex. He'd been dutiful to Eva but even I could recognize the first spontaneous true love on Valencia. Their romance puzzled me, although my cultural library has many mystifying accounts of amorous devotion. I kept Botilda out of the way and the lovers acted as if I weren't there.

I interrupted Attom while he cleaned a twin-mouth eel on deck. "I've found a new destination for us—safer than the Amazongo River." I doubted that Eva would welcome Attom back, especially with Alta at his side.

Attom smiled, showing even white teeth. "Mother, I don't care where we go, as long as she and I can be together." Alta massaged his thick neck. A loving mate made him much more agreeable.

From the stored images of my coastline surveys, I showed them an ideal location for a new colony. Hidden Basin is a large tidal lake filled only at high water. The narrow entrance has a saltwater waterfall flowing into or out of the lagoon, depending on the tide. Ocean waves or tsunamis can't batter the interior shoreline.

We sailed to the mouth of Hidden Basin with an onshore wind and a gradually rising tide. Less than a minute of slack water allowed the current to suck *Lifeboat-One* through the entrance, gliding over rocks just below the keel. Once inside the placid lagoon, we were safe. Attom dropped the anchor near a small stream that flowed down the beach into the saltwater.

The lovers rowed the dinghy ashore to make their private camp in a glade surrounded by cone trees. They used *Lifeboat-One's* sail to make a tent; that was fine with me—I didn't want them to move the boat again. I scanned the cone tree branches for sniper-sloths and the beach for wind-hoppers—Valencia's most dangerous predators— but found none. A herd of spine-turtles foraged above the meadow. Attom, now comfortable in his regrown sea otter fur, dove for local oysters that covered the bottom of the bay. They wouldn't go hungry.

Botilda stayed on *Lifeboat-One* to tend the baby in the artificial womb—I named her Diana, goddess of the hunt. When I reactivated the second womb, I decided to make a puppy—an English bulldog cross, shorthaired, heavy boned and friendly. Attom always wanted a dog when he was a boy, after seeing Earth videos of people with pets.

I hoped Alta would have twins. I wondered if they'd be smooth-skinned or furry—or psychopathic. I'll keep *Lifeboat-One* producing more children, to kick-start the new colony with fresh DNA.

With luck, the Hidden Basin clan will grow.

One advantage of life in orbit is that Mother-Nine can be in several places at the same time. Now that I can communicate with both Lifeboats, I control Robart on the wreck of *Lifeboat-Two* on Shelter Island, as well as Botilda on *Lifeboat-One* in Hidden Basin. I'm delighted that all four automated wombs in the Lifeboats still work, manufacturing babies to my specifications.

The Amazongo River colony on Shelter Island is thriving. After Attom and Botilda departed, Eva became the matriarch and Robart helped her give birth to Sam and Della. Clark fathered babies with Cleo. Robart managed the toddlers Jack and Jill from *Lifeboat-Two's* artificial womb.

Planned parenthood will be harder in the future, especially after the *Lifeboat* wombs run out of amniotic reagents and cease functioning. The critical question is: will humans attain a large enough population, with sufficient genetic diversity, to survive on Valencia? The founding populations of New Zealand and Madagascar were each less than hundred people. Valencia still has fewer than twenty, including pregnancies, but with greater genetic variation.

So, naturally conceived babies are now my goal. But there are problems with sex, too. Robart tried to prevent incest between Clark and Lois. I wanted to pair Anton with Eva, but she wasn't interested in a mate younger than her children. I programmed *Lifeboat-Two* to produce genetically mixed semen for artificial insemination. Lois accepted but Eva refused.

Eva and I—we get along fine now that she's not pregnant—started the Amazongo Elementary School in a thatched shelter. Robart is the teacher. In a few Earth years there'll be a high school. The cultural and engineering libraries on the Lifeboats are available. Robart even started drama and choir productions. Too bad that, in my diminished state, I no longer appreciate art and music.

I still worry about Jane and her brood. Have they spawned more inbred psychopaths? I can't do anything about Dick's descendants now. Later, when the Hidden Basin toddlers are grown, I'll organize another expedition to salvage the best of Jane's clan. If they're too savage, I'll cull them all with Attom's help. I'd hate to reinvent genocide just to extirpate potential killers. That's Machiavellian morality, I know—but it's important that humans on Valencia start with a clean genome, free from antisocial DNA. While I still have time, I'll try to rectify my mistakes.

As for me, entropy is my only enemy, relentless and implacable. After the GRB blasted my brains and disabled the fusion reactor, I couldn't communicate with Earth—and they stopped sending me messages. I wonder if the gamma radiation also wiped out life on Earth. I hope not.

I yearn to hear from the other Mothers. Too bad my deep space radios don't work—I'd love to gossip and compare notes! Did some of my sister ships succeed? Are people living on other exotic planets circling remote suns in the Milky Way? Even an AI gets lonely in the starry wilderness.

In a few decades Valencia's tenuous exosphere will kill me. By then I'll be too stupid to care. I'll succumb to orbital decay and burn up in the oxygen-rich atmosphere. If this update is more than four season-weeks old, as logged in the Lifeboat archives, then Mother-Nine is gone.

I know that memories of me—and even stories of Earth—will pass into dim and finally forgotten legend. People on Valencia rarely see stars through the cloudy atmosphere—they'll forget their place in the Milky Way and our galaxy's position in the Universe. Someday, I hope a curious scholar will read this record and discover where humans came from.

I predict that the Stone Age on Valancia will be brief. Will human colonists reinvent civilization, benign and better balanced than that on Earth? I hope they don't despoil this pristine planet, like Dick had started to do.

I'm resigned to dying, but I'm satisfied. There are two (maybe three) independent colonies on Terra Firma. They'll adapt, grow and eventually interbreed. I'm optimistic that my children, redesigned and transplanted humans, *Homo astra*, the offspring of old Earth, will survive after I'm gone. Maybe, after the GRB, they're the last human beings—and, if Fermi was right, perhaps the only sentient creatures—in the Universe.

LIGHTIME

BY JAY CASELBERG

I t's way too early, thought Lance Vincent. Way too early. He peered out the window at the blank crystalline wall, but there was not even a glimmer in the ground surface yet. His simple, round, two-room house lay nestled in the bottom of a bowl, just like all the rest, a simple precaution against an overburden of stray radiation, but one that had proved to be unnecessary over the years. Now it was more of a tradition. Everyone built like that. Well, old habits died hard. Besides, the verdancy around the lip of his own personal dwelling hole was something he took some sort of pride in. Not that he had any real visitors. Who would have thought a cop would be a gardener too?

Lance scratched, yawned and stretched. He was up; he may as well get up. Grumbling at the capriciousness of his sleep patterns, he shuffled into the kitchen to make himself a cup of tar. He'd heard somewhere that it had been called 'tea' once. Now where the hell had that come from?

By the time he'd finished his tar, thrown himself under the sprayer and shrugged on his clothes, a faint glimmer was snaking down the outside walls as the crystalline surface caught the first invisible rays from their grey dwarf star. Grabbing his shades and documents, the latter of which he pushed into the pouch at his waist, beneath the ballooning poncho that protected his eyes from most of the upglow, he slipped outside, locked up, and climbed the regulation twenty-five steps to the surface. He stood there at the very lip, glanced first up where there were traces of the sky curtains still rippling in gossamer blues and greens, and then over at the Hand of Light where the first luminescence was already prompting a white glow toward the city's edge. So, not so early after all. Something had dragged him awake, but damned if he knew what it was. He stooped and fingered a couple of the fleshy leaves of his garden borders. The stunted flowering plants needed some attention, but not desperately. He could see that much in the vague glow of the heating rails set into the very edges of the streets. They would keep until the weekend.

Lance knew there was something out there, and he scanned the city's surface, that broad flat expanse pockmarked with depressions signifying the dwellings and office bowls that made up their city. What was it? If you were a cop long enough, you began to rely on your gut and it rarely led him astray. The Hand was glowing in earnest now, but their tiny grey star had not risen enough to start the surface rippling with light. A few vague glimmers meandered across the ground here and there, heralding the full onset of lightime. It wouldn't be long. Lance slipped on his shades in preparation and let his gaze rove across the city. Somewhere out there was something, but damned if he knew what it was. He had learned long ago to trust his gut all the same.

The Hand had stood there for nearly a hundred years. It had been an inventive solution. When the original unfortunate colonists had worked out that there was a problem with the light coming only from the planet's surface, rather than the sky—the vegetation that actually took from their vast seed banks had grown toward the ground instead of up, among other things—they had erected the vast structure at the city's center, its palm formed of ground crystal, enough to scoop up the activating rays granted by their tiny grey dwarf neutron star. The city's first dawn glow, since then, had come first from the Hand, instead of the crystalline soil—soil made up of countless particles excited into luminescence by the invisible rays issuing from their tiny star.

By the time he'd ridden three full blocks, lightime was well and truly advanced. There, on the edge of the city, off to the west, was the thing that he rarely wanted to witness—a dull red glow in the sky. It told him only one thing—there'd been another one. Only one thing lent that carnelian radiance to the city's light, and its origins were inevitably human. Lance grimaced and changed his direction. Duty apparently called and right now it had a klaxon voice.

He rode for another ten blocks, his small electric bike puttering along side streets, avoiding the sharp lips of residential bowls and wending between clumps of the stunted ground-seeking vegetation that made up garden borders. The streets were glowing proper now. Deep in the suburbs, perhaps this would turn out to be just a random act of violence, but somehow, Lance didn't think so. He shivered, but it was more than the latent cold of the urban fringes—the heating rails were not so numerous out here, and though there was warmth that came from their star, they needed to supplement it. Closer to the city's fringes, the investment was not as great. As he neared, the red tinged light was stronger, like a gossamer curtain reaching up into the sky, shimmering slightly with the crystal patterns of activation and deactivation that wandered across the ground in waves. He parked his bike, and headed toward the glow the rest of the way on foot.

Though it was still early, the populace was stirring and already a small crowd had gathered at the edges of a small open square. Right in the middle lay what Lance dreaded, splayed, limbs akimbo. It was a man, and there was, as he had expected, blood—a lot of it.

"Okay," he said, flashing his credentials. "Nothing to see here folks," swallowing back the untruth of the statement. "I suggest you get about your business."

Reluctantly, they responded to his badge and the voice of his authority.

"Come on, people. Move!"

One by one, they shuffled off, arms wrapped around themselves against the suburban chill, at least far enough out of his reach to let him get on with what he needed to do.

Reluctantly, Lance stepped toward the body lying in the middle of the vaguely rippling red glow. This was the second in as many weeks. The one before that had been months before. The signature was the same, however, from what he could see; the deep slash across the throat, the blood spread around the body, and somehow seeping into the park's crystalline ground, gleaming carmine in contrast to the pastels rippling slowly across the rest of the open space. Each one had been the same. Always, the bodies had been left in the middle of some central communal area, guaranteed to maximize the skyward radiance to its maximum effect. So far, they had been unable to find any connection between the victims. Each was seemingly chosen at random, perhaps driven by opportunity rather than specifically targeted. Victimology played no part here. Location was everything. A nice location in the suburbs. Lance snorted and reached for his com. Time to call it in.

It took roughly an hour for the rest of his three-person crew to arrive, and Lance was left to stand guard in the meantime, moving the occasional curious onlooker away and musing about motivations, causes. Life was all about survival on this, their far-flung glimmering rock. They made do. They adapted. Sure, there were accidents, illness, the regular hazards, but apart from the inhospitable nature of their environment, there were no real threats, and their fragment of humanity had done all right since the colonist ship disaster that had forced them down here all those years ago. Once the original colonists had learned to adapt to a world where the only light from the sky came from the nightly auroras, once they had finally managed to get some of their seed stock to take and move on from reliance on the self-sustaining environment of their seed ship, once they had managed to adapt to the ground light and the chill that pervaded the hours of darkness, they had done all right, and the threats were minimal. But now…now there was a new threat and it was of their own making. It was funny though, he thought as he looked across at the body and its glowing aura; there had to be some significance to the placement, some meaning to the choice of location. There was a message there, but he was damned if he could work out what it was.

Sandrine and Carl parked their own bikes at the edge of the small square and wandered over to where Lance stood, their shades fully down against the glare, which had intensified during the intervening time.

"So, Boss," said Sandrine.

"Yeah, well. You can see for yourself. I haven't given it a close examination, and I doubt we'll find anything. It looks pretty much like the last one."

Carl nodded. "It does. Well, I suppose we should get on with it," he said, hefting his kit.

The pair walked slowly over to the body, scanning the ground and the surrounds as they went, alert to anything that might be some sort of clue. If it was anything like the last couple of victims, and Lance suspected that it was, they'd come up empty. They'd be left with a body, the knowledge that a long-bladed knife had been used, and an impossible stain in the middle of a suburban square. Lance let them get on with it, scanning the surrounding area while he put in a call to the hospital wagon. They could take their time. There was no rush for this one. Later, they'd have to bleach the ground, get rid of the discoloration that turned the ground's natural luminescence into a beacon. People wouldn't need the reminder, wouldn't want the reminder.

The other thing that was troubling was that there seemed to be no specific suburb that their killer operated in. The only thing that joined the individual scenes was the similarity of the dumping spots. But then, they weren't dumping spots. The bodies weren't dumped at all. They were placed, and specifically placed.

Lance sighed to himself and looked around. A couple of passersby, stopping to look. No one showing undue interest in the scene. If anything, the locals were avoiding looking directly at the proceedings in the square's center. He turned his attention back there. Sandrine was squatting on her haunches, taking images of the body. Carl was picking across the ground. Lance could see him squinting against the light above his shades.

Finally, the hospital wagon arrived and they stretchered the body away. Just like the rest, there was nothing further beneath the body either. Nothing there at all—just a glowing red patch in the middle of the park.

Of course, they canvassed, but none of the locals had seen anything either.

Five days later, Carl got the first call and he rushed into Lance's office.

"We've got another, Boss, but this one's different."

"Different how?"

"It's in the city center. Slap bang in the middle. Bankers Square."

"What?" That *was* different. Somehow their perpetrator was changing his pattern. Lance had no qualms about thinking of him as a 'he.' The strength of the blows, the height, everything told him it was a man.

"We'd better get down there. Is there anyone on scene?"

It was no surprise that he hadn't noticed any tell-tale signs on the way into work. These days, his attention tended to be toward the city's edges rather than its center, and Bankers Square was a broad flat bowl with a few of the city's financial institution buildings clustered around the edges. Any upward glow would be shielded by the broad buildings themselves.

"Yes a couple of the city beat boys are down there. They were surprised no one had called it in before."

Lance frowned. Yes, that was unusual, especially in the middle of the commercial district. Just maybe, people didn't want to become associated with it, to openly acknowledge that these things were even happening, but it was a hard thing to consciously ignore, especially with the upward glaring nature of the evidence that the crime had occurred. Red was just not a natural lightime color. Sure, you got the occasional ruddy shimmer in the night sky, but not in lightime, never in lightime. Their earth glowed white or pastel blues and greens.

"Okay, grab Sandrine. We'll head down."

A half hour later, they stood in the middle of Bankers Square scanning the semicircular buildings pressed hard up against the inclined walls. Staircases led down into the square bowl on each side. Bankers Square was unusual, because in its very center stood the vast base belonging to the Hand of Light. It was the one place in the city where the light source came from directly above you and below you at the same time. Lance flipped his shades to vertical in compensation. His companions had already done the same. With a glance up at the Hand, Lance realized why there might have been some delay in discovering the body. The Hand's luminescence easily countered the groundlight, and the tell-tale glow marking the scene of the crime was nowhere near as evident as out in the suburbs.

Lance grunted to himself. So why the change? Part of the signature was the public announcement, the glowing testament that the act had occurred announcing itself to the population at large. This was different. There had to be something else. Carl was the first to find it. He waved Lance across excitedly.

"Look," he said, pointing to a nearby wall. Daubed in red, trickle trails running from the bottom of the letters was the word 'Sheep.' Sandrine was already recording it.

"What the hell does that mean?" Carl asked.

Lance shook his head. "I don't know." He scratched his chin. "Sheep," he said, trying the word out. He shook his head again.

"I think I heard something once," said Sandrine from her position by the wall. "It's old. Maybe something from stories when I was a kid."

"We can look it up when we get back," said Lance. "Maybe there's something in the records."

Sandrine made a face. "I don't think so. Seems like I remember that it was like a family tradition. Something handed down. But we can try anyway," she said and shrugged before turning back to concentrate on the records.

Lance turned to the first two cops who had arrived on the scene. "Did anyone see anything?"

The two cops looked at each other then shook their heads.

"So do we know who he is?"

"Mitchell Froud. Twenty-eight. Low level clerk at one of the banks. On his way to work early by the looks of things."

Lance nodded and pursed his lips. Nothing to tie this latest one to the other victims, at least on the surface, but he had expected as much anyway.

"And nothing unusual? Well, apart from that," he said gesturing in the direction of the tall letters daubed on the nearby wall.

Again the look and a shrug and a shake of the head.

"Okay, thanks, boys. You can turn in your report when you get back to the office. We'll take it from here."

He watched them as they headed off to the rest of their rounds, heads close together in conversation, one of them looking back over his shoulder to glance at the scene and then back again to continue his discussion.

They took their time reviewing the scene, keeping the curious office workers well away, trying to find any other major differences. The only thing that stood out was that one word writ large in the victim's blood. Well, at least they presumed it was the victim's blood. They would have to wait for final test results from the samples Sandrine had taken.

Back at the office, Sandrine did a search. It appeared that a sheep was a type of domestic animal back on old Earth. Hundreds of years ago—not surprising that it meant nothing to any of them. Lance peered down at the entry.

Any of various bovid mammals of the genus Ovis and related genera, esp *O. aries* (domestic sheep), characterized by transversely ribbed horns and a narrow face. On old Earth, there were many breeds of domestic sheep, raised for their wool and for meat.

It meant nothing. There wasn't even a picture.

"Do we know where we might find out more about these things?"

Sandrine looked at him, bit her lip slightly and shook her head. "As I said, old family stories. I don't think there's anything else."

Carl merely shrugged.

"Well, whatever it is," said Lance, "it's some sort of historical reference. We need to dig it up. Do we know any historians? Stuff about old Earth?"

"You know the records are pretty sketchy," Sandrine ventured. "Not too much survived the initial disaster. Perhaps in the archives."

"Well, I think then a trip to the university might be in order. Sandrine, Carl, the both of you get out there and see what you can dig up."

Three hours later, the pair arrived back from their visit to the university.

"We found out a few things," Sandrine told him. "But it wasn't that much. The guy's name is Franz. Doctor Franz. Strange sort of guy, but then he's an academic so…"

"Yeah, but something else was weird," said Carl.

"What do you mean?"

Carl paused to think. "It seemed as though he was expecting us. He even said so."

"That's right," Sandrine confirmed. "I thought that was funny when he said it. And you remember?" she said, turning to Carl. "There was no hesitation. He seemed to know exactly what we were looking for."

Lance leaned back on the edge of his table for a moment. "That is strange and somewhat interesting. Hold that thought for the moment. What did you find out?"

"Well, according to the Doctor, Franz, these sheep were some sort of domestic animal raised for their products, food and clothing and stuff. Like nothing we've got here, of course, but they were pretty commonplace back on Earth. Apparently though, they were used in other ways."

"How?"

"Well they were used symbolically, like in religion or philosophy to represent the masses or sometimes the innocents. They were a symbol for people. They had some sort of behavior where they all did the same thing and they weren't all that smart. Some sort of relationship between victims and sacrifice or something like that. I didn't really get it."

Lance tilted his head to one side and his frown grew.

Sheep.

Victims.

Sacrifice.

It all tied together in a weird sort of way. The Doctor's knowledge was just a little bit too convenient.

He looked up at Sandrine. "You thinking the same thing?"

"Uh-huh," she said and nodded slowly.

The thing that finally sealed it was the witness that had showed up via an anonymous call in. Someone had been seen in the vicinity of the last victim's resting place, near the wall with the carefully daubed letters and there was a pretty clear description to go with it. The information came in when they were already heading back to the university. Lance put away his com before they reached the Doctor's office. The historian was in.

After knocking, Lance entered, and Sandrine and Carl following. Doctor Franz rose and stepped out in front of his desk. As far as Lance could tell, the description matched.

"Hello, Doctor Franz. I'm Supervisor Lance Vincent. We, myself and my team, we have a couple more questions to ask you if you don't mind."

The Doctor blinked a couple of times and then nodded. "Yes, of course," he said. "I cannot say that I haven't been expecting you. I'm glad you've come. It should have been sooner."

Lance shook his head. "I don't…"

"No matter," said the Doctor. "Please, ask your questions."

"Can you tell me where you were this morning just before lightime?"

"Do you really need to ask that?" said the Doctor.

"Yes, I really do."

The Doctor peered at them over his shades. "I think you know that already."

"Humor me, Doctor."

"We are fated," he said. "Can't you see that? We are going to fail here. I've been doing the research. I've seen the signs."

Lance held his breath for a moment. "So what has that got to do with where you were this morning?"

There was an odd gleam in the Doctor's eye. "Now you know," he said. "Now you understand. I don't need to tell you. I had a responsibility. I had to warn you." His voice was calm and clear.

Lance looked at him and frowned. "I'm still not sure…"

"Red sky at night. Shepherd's delight."

"What?"

"Red sky in the morning. Shepherd's warning."

The Doctor took a step toward him. "You see, I see myself as a sort of shepherd," he said. "I only did what I had to. I have a responsibility to warn them, to warn them all. To warn all of you. You need to prepare. I'm the only one who really knows. I tried to tell them at my seminars, but they laughed it off. They wouldn't listen. Nobody would listen. People. Sheep. They're all sheep! Well, they won't laugh now, will they? They'll have to listen."

He reached behind him, grasped the long decorative crystal knife that lay on the table and ran the fingers of one hand slowly up and down the blade. Lance thought about stopping him, about removing the potential weapon from his reach, but he wanted to see how this was going to play out. Besides, it didn't look like he could do much damage with it.

"Explain the sheep, Doctor," he said. Carl was looking from Lance to the Doctor and back again, a worried frown etched upon his brow.

"The sheep." The Doctor smiled. "The flock. You see, the shepherd has a duty."

He brought his hands back in front of himself and clasped them. "Responsibility."

"Boss…" said Carl.

Lance held up a hand.

"So you knew about the deaths," he said.

"Of course."

"Am I right in saying that you are responsible for them?" Lance asked, his eyes narrowing with suspicion, although he knew the answer already. "You killed them."

The Doctor said nothing. A faint smile played across his lips.

"But then, how do you explain that? Why would you do that?"

"Sometimes…," said the Doctor slowly, as if speaking to a child, "sacrifices must be made for the greater good. You have to protect the herd, after all. It is the shepherd's responsibility. Sacrificial lambs."

The words meant nothing to Lance. "I don't understand what that is."

"They were sacrificed for the greater good. Don't you see? Red sky in the morning; shepherd's warning. All of you, all of you had to be warned somehow. The sign in the sky! It was the best way to make them notice. Something they could not ignore. Signs in the sky have always been portents, all throughout history."

Slowly it dawned on Lance the nature of the twisted logic that had to be working in the man's brain. Arcane history, ancient fragments. It was brilliant in its own bizarre way. The man was buried in the fragments of history that he studied and somehow they had woven themselves into his thought patterns, become his own special reality. If you saw yourself as a shepherd, whatever that was, then how do you make a red sky when all you had was lightime? There was no light source in the sky. You had no choice but to change the ground. The only way to do that was to put something on it, something that would fundamentally change the light source.

That was more than enough for Lance.

"Carl, take him," he said.

Lance was still staring at the Doctor's back as they led him from the room. What could have happened to do that to a man, a man who was obviously intelligent? It had to be something. Maybe, it was just as simple as the conditions they had to live under, had always had to live under. With the man's knowledge of history, with the extent of his research, were there things that he knew that had driven him to the edge? Perhaps with treatment, they might understand, but no; it was a little too late for that.

Lance stood outside their offices, preparing to head for home, considering the strange nature of the case. Of course they had found the knife tying him to the murders. It seemed that your environment changed the rules of the game, or at least, had changed the rules of the game for Doctor Franz. There was no real sky here. There was no such thing as a red sky. There was only lightime. *Red sky in the morning*. Traditions of their origins, the lore of where they had come from would always live somewhere in their memories, in the historical records, even though the specific meanings might fade with the passage of time. All they had were the blues and greens of their shimmering night sky and the pastel waves of lightime.

Shepherd's warning.

What the hell was a shepherd anyway? He guessed he'd never know.

Lightime was fading and the first blue and green curtains starting to shimmer across the perpetual blackness of their sky. He slipped his shades away.

Lance pulled his cloak tighter around his body against the seeping cold and mounted his bike. The ground would be dark by the time he reached home and climbed down into his bowl. He still didn't understand why the Doctor thought they were all doomed. Sure, life here continued to have its challenges, the scrabbling to produce enough to sustain themselves, the ever-present, bone-chilling cold, the starkness that crawled into every aspect of their lives. Sure it would always be a struggle. Lance would probably never really understand what had pushed the Doctor over the edge in such a way. At least there was one less threat for them to worry about in respect of their survival. The population would be able to sleep a little more soundly after all.

And in the morning…in the morning there would be no shepherds, no red sky, no warnings. All there would be would be lightime and the need to get on with their life as best they could.

THE SEVENTH
GENERATION

BY BRIAN STABLEFORD

Corcoran was sitting on a bench on Marine Parade overlooking the Estuary when Halleck sat down beside him. Corcoran barely turned his head, but he registered the fact that Halleck looked older, fatter and considerably more haggard than when he'd last seen him, ten years before. Halleck had never been one to go in for keeping fit, let alone cosmetic somatics; he lived in his head, and was proud of it. He had no objection to being instantly identifiable as a man of science, whose sanity was not as that of other men.

"Your mother told me where I could find you," Halleck said, without bothering with superfluous preliminaries. Since leaving gravitational rehab Corcoran had been staying with his mother 'temporarily,' although he had not yet made any plans to move on or given much thought as to where he might go or what he might do. After a seven-year stint in and around Jupiter, plus the long journeys there and back, he had enough credit in the bank to go anywhere and do anything, but nothing had yet occurred to him.

"I meant to call you when I got back," Corcoran said, although he knew that Halleck would know that he hadn't. "You know how it is." That, at least, was true.

"How was Jupiter?" Halleck asked.

"Dark," said Corcoran. "Slow. The surrogates weren't kitted out to feel the cold, but out there, you can't play tricks with time. The lag was tangible, even from low orbit—it's a big planet—so it's as well things did go slowly, but tedious, even so. The moons were slightly more interesting, except Ganymede."

"But you had physical presence again," Halleck said. "You weren't just a ghost. Something to appreciate." There was no enthusiasm in the observation. Halleck wasn't a man to appreciate physical presence, actual or surrogate.

Halleck was fishing, Corcoran knew, but he couldn't find it in his heart to hold it against the physicist. It was just the nature of the beast. Halleck was an angler, and would never be anything else. He wouldn't be here if he weren't fishing for Corcoran, and he wouldn't be here a matter of days after Corcoran had been passed fit by the rehab physiotherapists unless he thought that Corcoran was a fish worth hooking—and one that couldn't resist the bait.

"Physical presence is overrated," Corcoran said, mildly, although he didn't really care whether he was striking a chord or not. He wasn't talking about the giants he'd manipulated by means of his expert telepresence in the depths of Jovian atmosphere, which he'd always thought of as birds rather than fish, or the walkers he'd paraded around the desolate landscape of Ganymede, or the divers he'd employed in the liquid cores of the ice-moons. Nor was he talking about himself, given that he really was fully tuned-up for quotidian Earthly existence. He was talking about the 'fresh air' that he'd left the flat in order to savor, the infinitely varied foodstuffs, punctuated by 'treats' with which his mother insisted on plying him, the pavements and the fumes, and the estuary itself, with its acres of mud—the tide was out—the ragged trees on the slope down to the marina, and its shabby yachts.

The rats were right, Corcoran thought. *Even though we've cleaned up our act since the Crash...the first Crash...we're still the dirty monkeys, the first generation, the ones who got it all wrong, the slapdash clowns.* He still wondered, sometimes, what the plants thought of the animal and insect generations, but the plants had never shown the slightest sign of awareness of his ghost. All his missions to the fifth and sixth generations had been strictly look and learn—good practice for Jupiter and Ganymede, in a way.

"I'm glad to hear you say that," said Halleck—who had, of course, misunderstood Corcoran's meaning and was following a different train of thought in another direction. "I've come to offer you a job—as a ghost, of course. I figured you might be ready."

Corcoran was tempted to make some smart remark about Halleck being good at figuring, being the smartest mathematician in the world—and slightly tempted, too, to blow him off completely just to throw his current calculation into confusion—but one of the side-effects of his current state of mind, after the long journey home, spent mostly in virtual reality because the real reality of space travel drove even supersane people *seriously* mad, was that he didn't really care enough not to take the bait.

"I thought the project had suspended the use of human registers. Human minds no longer up to the job—work for AIs from now till doomsday."

"I was against that," Halleck said. "AIs are brilliant but fundamentally stupid. The ultimate *idiots savants*. You can put machine minds through a million generations on natural selection in a matter of months—days, now—but if you start with dumb inorganics you end up with dumb inorganics, however supersmart and supersane they may be."

"You really think I might be able to make some headway with the plants second time around?"

"Maybe—but that's not the job. We think we might have tuned in to the seventh generation."

There had been a time in Corcoran's life when that affirmation would have made him sit bolt upright with shock and caused his mind to boggle, and then some. He looked no different now—people who went into space had no alternative but to resort to drastic somatic engineering, and the cosmetics came with the package—but he was a great deal older inside, and a great deal older subjectively than mere years could make him. He was, in any case, immune to the psychological effects of mere years; the Sling had hurled him across billions of them. He wasn't even convinced that it was the long haul out to Jupiter and back, and steering the birds in the long glides into the Jovian atmosphere, which had corroded his capacity to boggle; he preferred to think of it an essentially internal evolution, a kind of growing up… or at least sideways.

"You told me that was impossible," he reminded Halleck, mildly. You told me that we'd gone right up to the margin where the sun was getting sick, ready to erupt and turn into a red giant, scorching and then swallowing up the Earth in the process. If you'd been able to tune the Sling with sufficient accuracy, you'd have sent my ghost out to watch it happen. No more Earth, no seventh generation."

Halleck shifted uncomfortably on the bench, staring assiduously at the mud-flats and the distant Kent coast, but not because he had the slightest interest in what was—or rather wasn't—happening there. He didn't like making mistakes, and hated being reminded when he had. If he'd had a short-range dirigible time machine instead of the wayward Sling he'd probably have spent his life editing his life and twisting his existence into paradoxical knots.

"Either we underestimated the secondary plant-descendants—which wouldn't have been difficult, give that they wouldn't let us get the slightest taste of their fruit—or someone intervened," the physicist admitted. "In matters of Coincidence, we're in the infancy of the science. The sun will turn red giant, bang on schedule, give or take a few hundred million years, but the Earth won't be swallowed up. It undergoes an orbital adjustment. It survives—and, apparently, thrives."

An 'orbital adjustment,' Corcoran thought. Simple as that—not even a tacit exclamation mark. Someone or something will move the Earth, so that it won't be swallowed up when the sun blows up into a giant. Maybe life has to lie dormant for a while, waiting out the upheaval—the pupation of the sixth generation, if it makes any sense to talk about plants pupating—but once the big red sun has stabilized, springtime will come around again. Out pops the seventh generation. The third plant generation, presumably...if it still makes any sense to talk about plants. The third plant-descended generation, if we're going to be pedantic.

Except, of course, that it couldn't be as simple as that from the viewpoint of first-generation anglers, because the notoriously pedantic Halleck had only said that he 'thought' he 'might have' tuned in to the seventh generation—which implied doubt, which implied other possibilities. The 'someone' or 'something' that had moved the Earth to a new orbit might not have been the descendants of the climax community of the sixth generation but someone or something else. Neither the rats nor either of the invert generations had ever contrived any kind of contact with extrasolar intelligence, and not for lack of trying, but a few billion yeas of failure wasn't forever, by any means.

"What makes you think that human registers will be any more effective in dealing with the seventh generation, given that we failed with the fifth and sixth?" Corcoran asked, while his eyes mechanically tracked a barge slowly progressing along the navigation-channel, heading upstream toward the capital. "Or the aliens, if they turn out to be colonists, taking over the Earth when its own generations have finished with it?"

"You didn't fail with the plants," Halleck told him, unsurprised that Corcoran had taken the inference regarding the aliens. "It's not your fault that the interface didn't attract their attention. Maybe they couldn't detect your presence. Whatever we're dealing with here, it's an unknown quantity. The machines haven't brought back anything worth a damn. You might—and I don't just mean any human register, Corky, I mean *you*. You have the contacts, the experience, the intuition and the empathy. If you hadn't already been on your way home, I'd have sent word to Jupiter begging you to come back."

It wasn't the first time that Halleck had called him 'Corky,' but it rang just as false in Corcoran's ears now as it always had before, just as it would have rung false if Halleck had called him 'Jim.' Halleck wasn't the kind of person who used first names or nicknames in his thinking; for him, names were just labels, and the only time a surname was inadequate to the job was when he had to distinguish between two people with the same one. He was *able* to use first names and nicknames, when he thought it useful to bait a hook, just as he was *able* to use flattery, but when he did so it was always conspicuously artificial, and always rang horribly false. There was nothing intuitive or empathetic about Halleck. Halleck was a certified mathematical genius, but the principal reason that he hated AIs was that he was very nearly as rigid in his thinking as they tended to be, and just as dumb, in his own saccharine supersane way.

Corcoran reached up, reflexively, to scratch the back of his neck, although his contacts weren't itching. They never itched, in any literal sense—but still, even after all this time, they were an alien presence in his flesh, a bridge allowing his brain to link up with machines, by means of direct neuronal connection or wireless. Thanks to them, he was capable of operating all models of surrogates by means of telepresence: humanoid surrogates, non-humanoid material surrogates, and even ghosts, which felt humanoid, but weren't even material, mere agents of Coincidence, refracted through time. He liked to think that he was more than an expert, perhaps even more than an artist, and was glad of Halleck's endorsement of that estimation, even though Hallleck had no appreciation of art and a purely statistical appreciation of expertise. Even though his contacts never itched in any material sense, though, the impulse to scratch was still there in Corcoran's subliminal consciousness, as if they were somehow afflicted by the ghost of an itch…or may be the intuition of an itch.

"Okay," said Corcoran, blandly. "Why not?"

Halleck blinked, not because Corcoran had taken the job, but because he'd said 'Why not?' Devoid of empathy as he might be, Halleck had known Corcoran well enough back in the heyday of Sling to know that he had then been the kind of man to tabulate reasons why, with a modicum of drive, enthusiasm and ambition, never the kind of man to do something merely because he wasn't doing anything else. But Corcoran had been in space since then, and it really had been very dark inside the atmosphere of Jupiter—and even though his surrogates hadn't been equipped to feel the intense cold, the ghost of it had leaked into his bones and brain alike. Corcoran was a new man now.

"Mum invited you to stay for tea, of course?" Corcoran added, without any expectations.

"She did but I apologized and told her I had to run. Got to get back to London. I'll expect you Monday, eight sharp. Same place, hasn't changed a bit. It'll be like coming home."

More like coming home than staying with Mum, at any rate, Corcoran thought. Aloud, he said: "You could have phoned, Hal. You didn't have to come in person."

A slight frown creased Halleck's age-wrinkled forehead, exaggerating the hint of grey in his bushy eyebrows. "I thought I ought to," he said. That was, Corcoran knew, exactly what the physicist meant. Halleck had thought he ought to; he hadn't felt it, and didn't really understand it, but his long, if desultory, studies of the mysteries of human social life had given him a crude appreciation of the mechanisms of propriety, if not their rationale.

Corcoran sighed, stood up and put out his hand. Halleck took it and shook it. That was one of the few social routines with which the physicist felt almost comfortable. "It's good to see you again, Hal," Corcoran lied. "I should have called. We're old friends, after all."

Halleck smiled at that. He had always seemed to like the idea that he might have friends, even if he didn't know what it ought to involve.

"Are you going back to work for Mr. Halleck?" Corcoran's mother asked, when he got back to the flat. She was making tea. Nobody made 'tea' any more except people of her generation, who still clung to the formalities that the first restabilized post-Crash generation had established, not because they were nostalgic for some imaginary pre-Crash English Golden Age, but because they had suffered from a collective Post-Traumatic Stress disorder that had made a need for formality and routine pathological. His mother had never quite got over that, Corcoran knew. He never criticized or tried to break any of her slightly eccentric habits; he knew that his job had always been, and still was, merely to drink the tea and eat the biscuits.

"Yes," he told her, waiting patiently to pick up the tray and carry it into the living-room for her, for politeness' sake rather than because she wasn't perfectly capable of doing it herself. "I start Monday. I'll stay over at the Institute during the week, but I'll come back here at weekends, if that's okay."

"Of course it's okay. This is your home." In fact, the flat, designed for single occupancy, was a trifle crowded for two, but the widowed Mrs. Corcoran was appreciating the company, at least for the time being. "That was lucky," she added, meaning that he was lucky to be offered a job, in this day and age, when he'd only just been signed off rehab, especially at his age, when there were so many young and better-educated people desperate to get on to the employment ladder.

"Luck had nothing to do with it," Corcoran said, picking up the tea-tray. "Pure Coincidence."

"You know I don't understand jokes like that," she said, with a sigh, following along the short corridor.

"When I left Earth ten years ago," Corcoran said, putting the tray down again and taking a seat by the window, which was open to let in the supposedly-fresh air, "rumor had it that there were only three people in the world who understood Coincidence Theory, although if you'd said that to Halleck he'd have taken offense and demanded to know who the other two were supposed to be."

"But *you* understand it," his mother said. She was his mother, after all; it was inevitable that she should overestimate him. "You've been millions of years into the future," she added, blithely unaware of the non-sequitur. The 'been' was an overestimation too, although the 'millions' was a drastic underestimation.

"I don't have to understand it," he told her, with a slight sigh. "I just have to trust Halleck to understand it. And the Sling isn't the kind of time machine that can actually send me, or anything material, into the future. It makes use of the fact that subatomic particles—or, rather, the underlying fields that produce them—are independent of time. In a sense, they're what *create* time. That allows machines that can set up vibrations in the here and now to generate resonance effects with the same field/particle systems at other times, and using that linkage to warp the fabric of space into a kind of lens capable of gathering a certain amount of information from transitions and collisions."

"There you are," his mother said, sipping her tea triumphantly. "You do understand it. It's all gobbledegook to me—but I do understand that you're not actually going into the future, just *seeing* into it through your lens."

Momentarily, Corcoran contemplating trying to explain that the Sling's 'lens' didn't even allow particles or radiation to 'travel' through time, and didn't create any kind of net energy deficit or surplus either in present or future time, when the account-books had to be settled, because it was always respectful of the sacred conservation laws, but that it nevertheless contrived, with the twisted ingenuity of an expert tax-advisor, to permit a 'register' in contact with the lens to obtain impressions Coincidentally from the interaction of its 'surface' with both electromagnetic and sonic waves in the Resonant Nucleus. Having thought about it, however, he figured that it was neither necessary nor desirable to go into that kind of detail. Anyway, his mother was right. It was gobbledegook.

"Didn't you say before you went off gallivanting in space that Mr. Halleck's project had finished?" his mother persisted. "That there was nowhere further to go because the sun was going to blow up, and that you couldn't talk to the smart plants anyway?"

"That was then," Corcoran told her. "This is now. Another man might have stopped fishing, but not Halleck. Having mastered his Sling, more or less, little Dave isn't going to stop before he hits Goliath smack on the head. It appears that the Earth has somehow acquired… *will* somehow acquire…a new lease of life, beyond the metamorphosis of the sun. Somebody moved it, apparently…*will* move it, that is."

His mother took that item of information in her stride. The idea of moving a planet didn't seem particularly implausible to her; to her, planets were just white dots in the night sky. She had little or no conception of what going to Jupiter and participating in the exploration of its atmosphere and its satellites had involved, even though Corcoran had tried to describe the various experiences to her in slightly more detailed terms than 'dark' and 'tedious.' Her imagination wasn't as flexible as his, although it had a more highly-developed visual component that Halleck's.

"Even so," she said, "it'll still be going backwards, won't it?"

Corcoran had tried to explain to the author of his being on more than one occasion that the future evolution of life on Earth, as revealed by the Sling, was a matter of progress, not of degeneration, but she couldn't or wouldn't see it that way. To her, the fact that the second generation of intelligent life would be descended from present-day rats, the third and fourth from present-day insects and the fifth and sixth from present-day plants meant that the pinnacle of perfection represented by humankind had been passed—deservedly so, given the recklessness that had caused the first Crash and the apparent in-evitability of a second—and that everything subsequent was a tragedy, a decline, a slide into oblivion. She wasn't alone in that. The pedan-tic Halleck had never wanted the terms *rat, insect* and *plant* to be popularized with regard to their highly intelligent and scientifically-sophisticated descendants, but he hadn't been able to stand against the bitter desire of the human public to diminish its eventual successors, and to remain in denial of the all-too-evident fact that they would, in fact, not only be smarter, saner and more scrupulous than mere dirty monkeys with delusions of grandeur could ever be.

Corcoran had sometimes wondered whether the plant-descended intelligences had never acknowledged his ghost's existence not be-cause they were unaware of it, as Halleck stubbornly insisted, but simply because it was beneath their dignity. The rats and the inverts had been enthusiastic to establish and employ the minimal commu-nication that Coincidence permitted, not least because they believed that it was they, not humans, who had established the Coincidental link, and that they were the anglers, not the fish. At any rate, they had been curious, as eager to send ghosts of their own into the world of their forebears as their forebears were to haunt them. Nor had the rat-descendants ever been as contemptuous of the monkeys who had failed so dismally to make use of their hard-won intelligence as to have condemned themselves, and hundreds of thousands of other species, to ignominious extinction; in communication, they were always re-spectful, always glad to give credit for the science that humankind had managed to bequeath to its successors via its artifacts, saving them hundreds, if not thousands, of years of methodical groping.

Corcoran couldn't help pulling a face as he bit into his biscuit, which was sugar-coated and packed with shriveled raisins. Nobody ate such things any more, apart from people of his mother's generation and the people they invited for tea. Synthesizers using the products of artificial photosynthesis automatically paid due respect to the prin-ciples of nutritional economy and balance—but while the market was still there, the product would continue to exist, and while the habit wouldn't die, neither would the market. That was the monkey way.

Corcoran looked out of the widow, wondering whether there were any rat or insect ghosts watching the road, marveling at the primitive nature of monkey transport. There was no way for a mere mortal to tell; detecting ghosts was every bit as difficult as Slinging them. He wondered, too, whether there might be any plant-descended ghosts in the sloping field, sending back transmissions that would allow their surrogate operators to feel a twinge of sentiment on contemplating a poppy, or a hawthorn hedgerow.

Probably not, he decided; the plant-descended generations might well have been familiar with Coincidence Theory and the technical possibility of Slingshots, but he and Halleck had never been able to find any evidence to their usage that far in the future. He couldn't be sure, though. Maybe the plant-descendants did obtain intelligence of the past from his ghost, but were simply too stingy to offer anything in return. Or maybe he and his AI colleagues were simply too stupid to understand what the plant-descended intelligences were offering, or even that it was being offered.

"Shit," he murmured—which was not the reply his mother had been expecting to the question she'd as asked before he drifted into his reverie. She was still waiting for the answer, because she knew him, and knew that he always came back eventually, to take up the threads of what she thought of as 'real life.' She seemed slightly offended by the scatological oath, so he said: "Sorry—I was a million miles away." The excuse rang false, given that it was only a matter of weeks since he'd returned from a journey that had taken him a hell of a lot further than a mere million miles. Bravely, he continued: "Lots to think about now, thanks to Halleck. But no, there's no particular reason to assume that the seventh generation, if there really is one, will be plant-descended. It might not even be DNA-descended. Moving the Earth might have required *outside help*."

That, the old lady understood. "Aliens," she said, succinctly.

"Perhaps."

"So we're not alone after all?"

The conventional wisdom, for more than a hundred years, had been that humans had to be alone, according to the logic of the Fermi paradox, but no one had ever quite believed it in their heart of hearts, whether they had an imagination flexible enough to grasp the true size of the universe or not. Everyone—or almost everyone—had suspected, or intuited, or even merely hoped, that they *had* to be out there, but that, for one reason or another, they weren't in a communicative mood...just like the plant-descended intelligences of the fifth and sixth generations of Earthly life.

"I don't know," Corcoran said. "But with the Sling's power and a little luck, I might be able to find out."

"Luck," his wise old mother countered, getting her own back, "has nothing to do with it. It's fate."

When the tech-staff began the painstaking business of hooking him up to the machinery—to the future ghost—the process was no different from what the tech-staff had done for Corcoran in the Jupiter orbiter. Even the internal environment of the Institute's Slingroom looked bizarrely similar to the feeler-pods aboard the *Jove VII* and the orbiter, before the hood was placed over his eyes, although his own weight and the atmosphere he as breathing were different, and tangibly so.

Corcoran was surprised how impatient he felt, having thought that he'd lost the capacity to feel impatience while making the long trip to Jupiter and the seemingly-longer—but actually slightly shorter—trip home. He had been kicking his heels for some time, though, while Halleck tried to tune the machine, and him, continually dissatisfied with the set-up, as only a truly scrupulous person could be.

"Let's just *get on with it*," Corcoran had eventually said, more than once. "Let's take a stab. It doesn't matter if we miss the shot—it wouldn't be the first time. Life's too short to allow preliminary trials to run on forever."

Halleck hadn't bothered to remind him that nobody knew, any more, how short or long human life might turn out to be, given post-Crash advance in medicine, and that even if Corcoran's mother probably wouldn't make it that far past a hundred, Corcoran might easily manage two, which would make his current fifty-some years a mere extended youth. The physicist had contented himself with saying: "We're not in the trial-and-error phase any more. This time, we can get it right, if we do the math carefully enough—and it's more important than ever before that we do get it exactly right. This is *extreme*."

Halleck was not a man to use words like 'exactly' and 'extreme' lightly, nor a man to be content with doing anything less than he thought possible—so he had taken weeks to 'tune' Corcoran's contacts, to 'tune' the supportive machinery, and to tune the Sling itself. Finally, though, it was over. Finally, little Dave was convinced that he could hit Goliath smack on the head.

As Corcoran settled into the apparatus that would put him in communion with the far-futuristic lens, however, the differences between the finger-exercises in surrogacy he's undertaken on the *Jove VII*, the Jupiter orbiter and the various satellite basis, and the time-leap he was about to make, became clearly manifest. The knot in space formed by the Slingshot, at a 'distance' measurable in mind-boggling billions of years, wouldn't feel anything like a physical surrogate, and the preparatory process of what Corcoran liked to think of as 'mental metamorphosis' was something quite distinct, quite unique.

It was, however, more like 'coming home' that he had expected. The familiarity hadn't decayed, even in ten years.

The extremely-attenuated surrogate really did feel like a ghost, conscious of its own immateriality, its own implausibility, its own impropriety.

After a long stint inserting his mental presence into the variously-shaped atmosphere-divers adapted to explore the gaseous realms of Jupiter and the various environments of the gas-giant's satellites, assuming the personality of a time-displaced ghost again was a metamorphosis into something impossibly light, but not frail, impossibly agile, but not frivolous, impossibly unhuman, but not alien. As he settled into the pattern of supplementary neuronal linkages augmenting his brain, it was by no means an unwelcome feeling, as it had been way back at the beginning, before making contact with the rats. It was comfortable, and easy, certainly 'coming home' if not recovering an 'old self.'

Corcoran still had time before the dataflow began in earnest to chide himself for that foolish sentimentality, and to remind himself that, at the end of the day, a ghost was a ghost was a ghost…something dead, not truly human, never a true self in the way that human surrogates sometimes came to seem.

That, Corcoran thought, was probably part of his problem. He had spent too much of his life being dead, and preparing to be dead, and analyzing the wages of death. On the other hand pretending to be a bird soaring through the Jovian fog or a *flaneur* taking the exotic air on Ganymede hadn't actually proved to be an antidote, any more than the long months of the journey home, mostly spent in virtual environments not much different in existential texture from the environments into which he intruded his professional telepresence, in spite of being adapted for human use, human pleasure and human satisfaction.

Corcoran wasn't certain that he was any longer capable of human satisfaction, if such a thing were possible. The rat-descendants would have denied that it was—but then, the insect-descendants didn't believe in rodent satisfaction either, and probably etcetera, if the plant-descendants gave such matters any thought at all.

Corcoran kept the train of thought going, because he had the illusion that his contacts were itching, and knew from long experienced that an imaginary scratch wouldn't solve the problem, because life wasn't that fair.

Halleck, of course, wasn't interested in satisfaction. If people were capable of satisfaction, where would be the spur to drive progress? He probably wasn't interested in pleasure either—which meant that he probably had more in common with Corcoran, and perhaps with the ultrasmart plant-descendants, than any of them would have liked to think.

The data was flowing now, almost at torrential level. Corcoran forced himself to pay attention, knowing that he should now be able to see, and perhaps to hear, if there were anything at the far end of the Slingshot to see and hear.

"Are you comfortable, Mr. Corcoran?" Halleck asked, although he'd asked before. The 'Mr. Corcoran' was to emphasize the formality of the occasion, not so much for Corcoran's benefit as for the benefit of everyone else who would be able to access the pseudosensory record and the commentary dialogue.

"I'm fine," Corcoran replied. "It's still foggy, though—as if the billions of years were blurring my vision. Are you reading my voice loud and clear?"

"We have sight, sound and voice," Halleck confirmed. "The recorders are functioning; you should be able to see by now."

Halleck sounded understandably anxious. The thought that he might have made a mistake, after all that calculation...

Corcoran suddenly had the oddest sensation of having opened his eyes, although he knew perfectly well that he hadn't closed them. It wasn't just that the 'fog' he'd mentioned to Halleck had cleared; there really had been a transition, as if an inner eye hadn't know he possessed had suddenly elbowed his other eyes out of the way, rather rudely.

At any rate, he could see. He could see the sun.

Halleck hadn't bothered to tell him exactly how big the transformed sun ought to be, or how far away from it the future Earth's new orbit was, or how the combination of those figures would translate into the apparent size of the solar disk visible from the planet, but Corcoran had expected something spectacular, maybe filling half the sky, and he wasn't too disappointed. Had the entire disk been visible it wouldn't have filled half the sky, but it wouldn't have been that far short.

At first, Corcoran couldn't tell whether the sun had just begun to set or hadn't quite finished rising. Nor could he decide whether the blotches on its surface were clouds in the Earth's atmosphere or sunspots of some kind, or both. He knew that he would figure it out before long, however, and was content to focus his first impressions on matters of color. The colors were supposed to be authentic, in the sense that an actual human eye situated in the remote future where the ghost was situated would have seen them in the same way, although the machines to which he was neuronally linked had to do a great deal of work to resynthesize that authenticity for the benefit of his present-day eyes within the hood. At any rate, the sun was mostly crimson, as he had expected, and the sky was mostly purple, as he had also expected. So far, so good.

The ground on which he appeared to be standing was blue, which he had not expected: not pale blue, but a combination of darker shades, ranging from royal blue to indigo. There were interruptions of various shades of brown, but they seemed to be mere arbitrary streaks, not structures or patterns. There were no greens, apart from the occasional touch of dark turquoise. Corcoran didn't know whether to be surprised by that or not. If the blue surface where photosynthetic, time or the new conditions of solar light had obviously favored the evolution of a replacement for chlorophyll, but not one that resembled the black artificial photosynthetics that humans and their rat-descended successors had employed.

The dappled blue surface wasn't entirely flat, but its undulations were gentle, and reasonably smooth—it wasn't sufficiently choppy to be suggestive of a frozen ocean, but the unevenness had an aggression about it suggestive of growth-processes going on as well as erosion by wind and water. Nor were the protuberances motionless, although Corcoran wasn't sure that their activity was really significant of activity rather than mere instability. The most prominent undulations didn't resemble marine waves at all; they were more reminiscent of tremulous blisters, sometimes swelling very gradually, sometimes diminishing at a similarly leisurely pace.

"If it is alive," Corcoran observed to Halleck, "it's disappointingly passive." There was no need to report on what he saw and heard, because Halleck would be able to see that on a screen and hear it through a microphone—and had probably seen and heard it all before, at least momentarily, with AI assistance during the flash tests, although he hadn't played Corcoran the tapes. Subtler impressions never came across in flash tests, though.

"Can't judge on the basis of such a restricted sample," Halleck countered, reasonably. "Give it time."

Corcoran knew that one glimpse was insufficient to judge a world, but even if the present sample turned out not to be representative, it was still disappointing. The scene wasn't as boring as the surface of Ganymede, but it wasn't as varied as any other Earthly landscape he'd ever seen in the course of his extensive time-tourism. There was nothing that looked like an edifice, monkey-style, rat-style or invert-style. That was disappointing, but it wouldn't have been the first time he'd hit wilderness, with wondrous cities beyond the horizon. Even as wilderness, however, the blue blistery landscape seemed lacking in variety. There were no dendritic forms even faintly reminiscent of the fifth-generation sedentary intelligences, nor anything that bore a strong resemblance to their remote ancestors of earlier generations. There were fuzzy patches here and there, which a flexible imagination might have been able to find reminiscent of grass, but Corcoran didn't want to be making an imaginative effort to find something that might be more interesting than a quivering encrustation of lichen. He wanted clear evidence, of a complex life of some kind, if not of industry.

Nothing seemed to be moving rapidly or independently: nothing at all that made Corcoran think 'animal.' The silence wasn't absolute, but all he could make out was a kind of susurrus of white noise, devoid of any perceptible identity.

The ghost was capable of deformation in a quasi-human fashion. Corcoran was able to reach down at touch the ground. Although primarily orientated to reproduce pseudo-sight and pseudo-sound by means of the impingement of various sorts of waves on 'his' surface, the machines could also synthesize a measure of touch sensation.

"It's tingling," he reported to Halleck.

"Vibrating, you mean?" Halleck's voice was little more than a whisper in his ear, but it was quite distinct.

"Maybe—or maybe the tingling sensation is in my fingers, induced by some aspect of the surface that doesn't quite translate."

"Can you take a step forward?"

Corcoran took note of the fact that Halleck had said 'Can you' and not 'Will you'—which implied that there might be a difficulty. It transpired that he could, though, as easily as he had done a hundred times before, and he did.

The stride felt normal, but that didn't necessarily mean that the gravitational attraction of the displaced Earth was identical to that of the Earth of the first generation. The 'gravitational attraction' he felt via the ghost was an artifact, a necessary illusion assisting him to move.

"No problem," Corcoran reported.

"Good," said Halleck—implying that something else might have happened, and presumably had to a last one of the AI-connected ghosts.

Corcoran took another stride. The surface over which he was 'walking' seemed securely solid, but a trifle elastic. He moved toward the nearest 'blister,' to take a closer look.

"Be careful," Halleck said, scrupulously not telling him why he needed to be careful—especially given that it was supposed to be impossible for Corcoran to suffer any harm.

Nothing happened. He touched the surface of the blister. It tingled…or, in some mysterious way, caused the machines to which Corcoran was hooked up to reproduce a tingling sensation in his own flesh. He looked around again, in case anything new had come into view by virtue of his change of position.

"It's like standing on the skin of a gargantuan toad," he said to Halleck, knowing that the physicist wouldn't complain, although he would never have made any much comparison himself. It was part of Corcoran's job to make such comparisons, to record subjective impressions. The whole point of not being an AI was that he could—although he couldn't imagine that there as anything useful in that particular remark. Whatever the members of the seventh generation were descended from, if they really existed, it wasn't toads. Toads hadn't survived the monkey holocaust.

He looked at the sun again, able to do that even though his ghost wasn't equipped with sunglasses. It did have spots, but there were also clouds in the new Earth's atmosphere. Corcoran thought that they were cirrus clouds, although he wasn't sure that ancient meteorological categorizations still applied. He wasn't even sure that the slow and sullen wind he thought he could feet was real. He turned around through three hundred and sixty degrees, in order to give Halleck a panning shot of the entire horizon.

"And no birds sing," he whispered, more to himself than to fulfill his professional duties.

Then he bent over again, to investigate whether there was any visible vibration in the surface of the blister.

There wasn't—but the blister, which had been dark blue until he touched it with his ghostly hand, changed color. It turned silver— silvery enough, in fact, to function as a mirror. For a split second, Corcoran half-expected to see his own face, albeit distorted by the convex surface—forgetting that, in the far, far future, he didn't have a face, because he was a ghost. Indeed, he was a sufficiently intangible presence that he shouldn't really have been able to see anything at all, except maybe a very slight blur. At first, indeed, he couldn't even see that…but some inkling made him keep looking, and after a moment or two, he did indeed begin to see a blur, which rapidly became more violent than it should have been.

He felt a surge of triumph. The color change might have been any kind of reaction, but this was surely more than anything merely physical or chemical. This was biological, perhaps even intelligent.

This was the seventh generation, or the alien.

"Do you know what's happening, Hal?" he asked, as the pattern in the 'mirror' swirled, as if trying to make up its mind what it wanted to be.

"No idea," Halleck replied, curtly. "Unprecedented."

"But there've been reactions before, with the AI-guided ghosts, in spite of the brevity of the shots?"

"Not this one," Halleck said, evasively.

A different one, then, Corcoran thought. *Even so, a reaction is just a reaction. It could be passive—not necessarily aware, let alone intelligent.*

Again, he reached down to 'touch' the surface of the blister. The tingling sensation was not reproduced. Instead, the surface seemed warm—although that could not possibly be a straightforward reproduction—and somehow gentle.

That kind of subjective impression was exactly what no AI could ever experience or report; it was for exactly that kind of sensation that Halleck had wanted a human register, and not just any human register but one with Corcoran's sophisticated and experienced contacts. Corcoran had no idea how to report it, though. If he told Halleck that it 'seemed gentle' Halleck would ask him what he meant—and he didn't really know. He didn't know, in fact, whether he was feeling anything at all—even the warmth—or whether it was a mere figment of his imagination.

He didn't trust himself.

He was mildly surprised by that. He'd always trusted himself before, even on Jupiter and the satellites. What had changed?

Concentrate, he instructed himself, sternly. *Mind on the job.*

In the meantime, the blur in the mirrored surface of the blister was still becoming denser, more like a cloud—as, Corcoran thought, the blister were trying to organize itself as an eye, actually trying to see something, even though there was nothing to his presence but a slightly distortion of the fabric of spacetime.

Obliged to report, Corcoran said: "It's almost as if the blister were trying to see through the lens, in the same way that I'm seeing through it. It's almost as if it were trying to form an image of me—not the lab, but me."

"Keep talking," Halleck murmured.

"It's not like it was before," Corcoran reported, letting himself ramble. "When we established communication of a sort with the rat-descendants and the insect-descendants, we knew that they'd detected the lens and knew what it was...and, for that very reason, knew that they couldn't look through it. We knew that their signals were signals, because they did their utmost to make it obvious. This is different, not just because they seemed, at first to be holding up a mirror to reflect back at me what the future intelligences could see...if, in fact, that's what's happening, rather than some purely coincidental—ordinary coincidental, not Coincidental with a capital C—phenomenon that I'm misinterpreting by virtue of my preconceptions..."

"But they have detected you," Halleck said, trying to cut to the quick. "They're not like the fifthers and sixthers, who never knew you were there. And they detected you instantly, as if they expected you…" He too was rambling. Corcoran knew that Halleck had to be excited, although his voice was flat and still conscientiously low.

"Do you think they're trying to figure out what kind of signal to display?" Corcoran asked.

That reminded Halleck of his role. "I don't know," he said, flatly.

"Has this happened before, with the test-probes? I know you don't like to tell me such things in advance, for fear of spoiling the innocence of my perceptions and reactions, but if you know anything—especially given that you think I need to be careful…"

"Just keep talking," Halleck told him, dutifully—but he relented slightly. "It's new. Could be anything. Keep looking—and touching… but be careful."

"Come on, Hal! Careful of what?"

"Try not to get stuck," said Halleck, reluctantly. Obviously, a previous ghost had 'got stuck.' Did that mean that it had been immobilized completely, Corcoran wondered, or merely that it had got bogged down?

Corcoran was about to ask that very question when his hand was *gripped*, even though he knew, and could see, perfectly well that he had no hand that was solid enough to grip, and that nothing visible was actually resting on the blister from which he was endeavoring to obtain touch sensations.

"Too late," he said to Halleck, dryly—but the grip was not in any way severe; it was gentle, as if his hand were being clasped affectionately. He didn't have the impression that he couldn't pull away. Nor, oddly enough, did he have the impression that he wanted to.

Dutifully, Corcoran issued a correction to his hasty remark. "No, it's okay; I'm not *stuck*—at least, I don't think so. But this isn't just reaction, Hal; there's definitely intelligence in it. Someone or something here is aware of the Sling, and has probably learned from other shots you've made—or will make. There's a possibility of communication here, and they're trying to act on it. Whether these are DNA-descendants or something alien, we've hit the jackpot. It really is the seventh generation, and they're not as standoffish as the fifth and sixth."

"Steady, Mr. Corcoran," said Halleck. "Let's not get carried away."

It was, in the circumstances, and unfortunate turn of phrase. At that moment, the 'blister' burst, explosively. Corcoran's ghost was suddenly flooded by a deluge of black liquid, which covered it without going through it, although that shouldn't have been possible, and somehow *gripped* it.

At the same time, the pre-existent grip on his hand tightened, affectionately—and *pulled*.

Weirdly, before he lost consciousness—which was not supposed to be possible—Corcoran had the strangest but quite distinct impression that he was not being pulled in anger or brutality, or even vulgar curiosity, and that, if possible, no harm would be done to him…

"Hal?" said Corcoran, as soon as he became conscious of himself again. "Are you there?"

Obviously, Halleck wasn't—but Corcoran heard another voice, which he remembered having heard before, but to which he couldn't put a name, shouting words he couldn't quite make out, because they were being shouted too far away from the microphone.

It seemed that several minutes passed before Halleck finally got to the apparatus. In the meantime, Corcoran dutifully took note of what he couldn't see—because, apparently, his ghost had been drawn into some tomb-like vortex of black liquid, which had robbed him of his ability to move it and manipulate it at will.

This has to be psychological, not physical, he told himself. *They can't actually make physical contact with the remote past. All they can do is play subtle games with time-independent particles and fields. They're messing with my mind, not the surrogate…which is, in its way, just as boggling.*

"Corcoran?" Halleck said, sounding like a man who has just woken up and has not yet managed to sort out the saliva in his mouth. "You're conscious?" It was not like him to ask for confirmation of the obvious; he was obviously under stress.

"Yes," Corcoran said. "I can't see anything, or hear anything except you. Presumably I'm back—but why am I still in the hood? Are the neuronal connections still in place? How long was I out? Why didn't you just disconnect me?"

Halleck cleared his throat, and then said, ominously: "It's not as simple as that."

Corcoran felt sure that his heart would have sunk, if he had been able to experience any such sensation. He couldn't feel any bodily sensation—or, come to that, any ghostly sensation. He felt as if his consciousness were in some kind of limbo, lost in space, lost in time—and, as the ancient poet had put it, in meaning.

He was, however, able to feel afraid. He was perversely glad about that. It seemed to be better than nothing.

"What happened?" Corcoran asked.

"We were rather hoping that you could tell us," Halleck retorted.

"I blacked out."

"That's what our instruments showed, but...well, we're in uncharted waters here. We're not sure how far we can trust the instrumentation. At least we have you...alive, if not...." Halleck trailed off, obviously unable to find the right word. That, too, was atypical.

"If not what?" Corcoran demanded, reflexively, although he knew that it would be futile.

"According to our monitors," Halleck said, "things inside your body—especially your head—have gone a little crazy. We're sure that it's psychosomatic, but beyond that, we don't know what's happening, how, or what to do about it. Given that you're immobilized anyway, it might seem silly to say that we think you're paralyzed from the neck down, but that's what the encephalograph readings suggest. Are you consciously aware of anything weird going on in your head?"

"I feel a little fuzzy. No hallucinations, if that's what you mean. And I can't see anything through the lens any more, although I suppose that might be down to the deluge of lack liquid. You did see the black liquid on the monitors, I suppose?"

"Yes—but it's not like paint. The seventh generation obviously has far more sophisticated control of Coincidence than the second, third or fourth. That figures, I suppose. However they moved the Earth they didn't use anything as simple as a lever or a block-and tackle. They must have a degree of control over the fundamental fields that's beyond the reach of my current theories."

Not *our* current theories, Corcoran noted, but mine. Halleck had always been reluctant to admit that even the rat-descendants or the insect-descendants understood Coincidence Theory better than he did, but now he was definitely an also-ran, and knew it.

"You're telling me that you *can't* take me out of the hood?" Corcoran said just to make sure.

"I'm telling you that we *daren't*. The future still has some kind of grip on your consciousness, and hence on your body. We're not convinced that we can pull you back without damaging you. If we're lucky, they might just be observing, after their own fashion. Like the rats and the insects, they probably think they fished you out of the remote past rather than our slinging you forwards. The resonance is effectively instantaneous, but their observation process has to go on in real time like ours. If we're really lucky, they'll respect the principle of *quid pro quo*, and when they've finished whatever they're doing, they'll give us something in exchange, even if it's only the seventh generation equivalent of a cheery hello and a picture postcard."

"Luck," Corcoran muttered, "has nothing to do with it." He knew that Halleck would fill in the second part of the judgment with the old joke about Coincidence, but he wasn't thinking along those lines at all. He wasn't thinking about fate either; he was thinking about the possible motives and ambitions of the seventh generation, whether they were Earthlife-descended or not.

They had tried to handle him gently; he was sure of that, although he wasn't quite sure how he could be sure. They didn't intend to harm him—why would they? But that didn't mean that he couldn't come to harm, and might, indeed, already have come to harm if Halleck had panicked and pulled him out of the hood while he was still connected by some mysterious non-neuronal—and presumably non-material—thread to the remote future, and the Earth that was no longer in the same orbit as of old.

Do they have any idea what they're doing? he wondered. *Or are they just groping in the dark, like us?*

He felt a touch then. He still couldn't hear anything, or see anything, but something simulated the sensation of touch within his brain. Except that it didn't really feel that it was *his* body that was being touched, or even the ghostly simulacrum of it feigned by the Slingshot. It felt like a very different kind of body: gigantic, cumbersome and approximately spherical.

That didn't feel as odd to Corcoran as it would have done to most other people. He had handled some strange surrogates in his time; he was good at adapting himself to exotic forms. That was why he had gone to Jupiter, and why Halleck had come in search of him as soon as the news got around that he was back.

"Something's happening," he told Halleck, dutifully. "I think they're fixing up some kind of relay between the lens and some other surrogate—something substantial. It's passive, but the pseudosensory information is beginning to come through."

"We can detect that," Halleck told him. "It's registering on our monitors. It's vague, though, for now."

"Give them a chance," Corcoran said. "As you said just now, this is a real-time operation. I can't hear anything, but I'm getting a glimmer of light."

It was, indeed, just a glimmer, more reminiscent of the kind of effect produced by pressure when human eyelids are closed, or of phantom phosphenes, than anything that open eyes might see—but it was changing; it was evolving. There was a distinct splotch now, and other dots.

"It looks vaguely like the sky, as seen from a spaceship," he said. "Big sun, little stars, no atmospheric scattering, no depth-perception."

He had, of course, seen the sky from a spaceship, on the way out to Jupiter, and then again—just a quick glance for form's sake—on the way back. He had done more than that, in fact; he had *felt* space, using his contacts to hook into the ship's sensors—including the deflectors that protected the swiftly-moving projectile from particles of dust. Not that there had been much dust, even while they were passing through the supposedly matter-rich regions between Jupiter and Mars—just enough to produce a slight strange tingling sensation…

"That's what I can feel!" he said "Only more so—and getting more so by the minute."

"You're not making sense, Corcoran," Halleck told him, a trifle resentfully, "and all the monitors are giving us is static."

"It's not static," Corcoran murmured. "Quite the opposite. Holy shit!" He knew that he ought to explain; indeed, he wanted to explain, but whoever or whatever was manipulating his ghost-consciousness billions of years in the future was getting the hang of it now, and the experience was unfolding rapidly, like a flower beginning to bloom in his brain. The impressions were coming too fast, and too densely-packed, to give him pause for reportage. Experienced seer as he might be, this was new. It wasn't painful; it still seemed, in some mysterious way, affectionate—but it was overwhelming. In time, he thought, he would be able to talk, but not yet.

The sensation he had in the 'skin' of his gargantuan body wasn't the same kind of tingling sensation that he's felt when the tiny particles in the not-so-hard vacuum of interplanetary space had been deflected for the spaceship's long-range armor—not similar enough, at any rate to be instantly recognizable—but it was, he was sure, a related phenomenon. The new surrogate into which his consciousness was being gradually eased was traveling through space. What looked like the sun and the stars, seen from space, really was the sun and the stars, seen from space, and what felt vaguely akin to the impact of dust particles intercepted in the surrogate's progress really was the impact of dust particles…not the cushioned impact of their deviation and deflection by a space-warping shield, but actual impacts. The surrogate wasn't armored, and it was experiencing a *lot* of impacts—which meant that it was either moving very fast indeed, or moving through space that was considerably more matter-dense than what the ancients had called the asteroid belt.

There might, of course, be a time lag between event and perception, of which I'm not aware because I'm not trying to interact. Maybe the signal's coming from way out in the system…except that…

Corcoran had told his mother the truth when he had said that he didn't understand Coincidence Theory at all, beyond the elementary ABC, but one thing he did understand was that the resonant particles, or their generative fields, had to be the same particles or generative fields, at different extratemporal standpoints. The Sling could link present Earthly matter to what was in essence, 'the same' future Earthly matter, but not to unearthly matter. If what the enigmatic members of the seventh generation were trying to link him to was some kind of deep-space probe, it had to be an Earthly space probe, and it to contain at least some matter that had once been the matter of the his own body and the machinery surrounding it. The ghost really did have to be his ghost, and the Sling's.

Maybe those rules don't apply any more, he thought. Maybe there's a way around it for more advanced theorists and practitioners. Or maybe…

The flower of consciousness reached full expansion then, and brought knowledge—or at least conviction—as well as sight. He knew what the surrogate was into which he as being linked, and knew why he felt gripped by it instead of being able to grip it as he had gripped so many other surrogates. He knew why the relationship was inverted, having no doubt at all that he was no longer bait but fish. He even knew why the seventh generation felt something for him that his own mind translated as affection. He understood, at least vaguely—or at least thought he understood—what Earthly life had become in the fullness of time—and why...

Briefly, at least, it all seemed to make sense.

For a further moment or two—or maybe longer, in real time—he looked through the eyes of the seventh generation, at the world of the edge of time, and gloried in it. Then he got back to the job, with the tongue that he was able to move again.

"Halleck!" he said aloud. "Are you still there?"

"Where the hell else would I be," the physicist retorted, intemperately. His voice no longer quiet. "Talk to me, damn it—the machines are giving me shit." Corcoran had never heard him so out of control.

"I think they're hooking me into a bigger ghost," Corcoran said, dutifully conserving a measure of objective doubt, although he had none personally. "You've only ever managed to connect me to a thin network of the particles that are presently part of me. They're trying to build me up, and they're succeeding."

"But the particles that are presently part of you must be spread all over the...oh!"

"Exactly." said Corcoran. "They're hooking me up to the entire planet. They're giving me the entire Earth—or its ghost, to least—as a surrogate body. How that involves sensations of sight and touch I'm not sure, but it makes perfect sense. They have to be able to see and hear, not just for themselves but...anyway, it does see—the Earth, I mean, not just its inhabitants. I can see the sun and the stars, and I can feel... Where is the Earth now, by the way? This might sound crazy, but it doesn't feel as if I'm in local space, unless the asteroid belt is a lot more matter-rich than it was in our day..."

Which was, Corcoran realized, not an unlikely hypothesis. The seventhers had moved the Earth. Shuffling tinier particles of matter was probably child's play. Unlike the ship he'd traveled on, back and forth from Jupiter, the future Earth wasn't being shielded from impacts with dust and more substantial meteorites—quite the opposite, in fact. Somehow, the Earth's far-future inhabitants were actually drawing matter into the planet's path, in a gradual, measured and very determinate way. But why?

His own thoughts—if they really were his own in any objective sense, became temporarily so insistent, so *loud*, that they drowned out the scrupulously mathematical reply that Halleck was giving him, relating to the dimensions of the future Earth's orbit. Whatever had a grip on him was too busy with him to pay immediate attention to Halleck.

Now that Corcoran had a reasonably clear idea of what was happening to him, he could see reasonably well, because he could interpret the information his 'eyes' were receiving. He could see the turbulent sun quite clearly, and even make out a hint of its redness. He could feel the dust that the Earth was sweeping up in its orbit…but now the experience was moving beyond that. He was becoming conscious of more things. The silence was still absolute, apart from Halleck's temporarily-meaningless jabbering. The seventhers couldn't—or perhaps didn't want to—talk to him in any language he could understand, or even offer him a bleep or two to test that part of his pseudosensory apparatus. They were trying to do something much more ambitious than merely have a chat.

They were trying to make his new ghost self-conscious: not self-conscious in the trivial, Cartesian sense of thinking and therefore being, but far more fully conscious of his vast-ghost body. They were trying to make him—or, at least, allow him—to think the thoughts of the planet, or the thoughts of a seventh-generationer hooked by means of sophisticated telepresence to the hyperconscious, active and purposive flesh of the planet.

That was not something for which Corcoran had very many experiential reference-points. To be sure, he had felt his heart hammering in his present-day body a time or two, and felt various parts of him aching, twingeing, itching, and performing a few of the other tiny shocks to which flesh was heir. All of that, however, was a mere matter of alarms and warnings, the organic equivalent of clanging bells and ailing sirens. He had never been conscious of his flesh in any broader sense, nor that of any surrogate.

No wonder they're groping, he thought.

The groping was succeeding, though. Halleck's voice began to come through clear and meaningful again, although all that the physicist was saying, at present, was: "Talk, damn it! I can't make head nor tail of the raw data. For God's sake, tell me what you're seeing, feeling!

Corcoran? Are you even bloody *listening?*" His voice was loud now, edging toward the hysterical.

"Their consciousness differs from ours," Corocran reported, able now to be tranquil and meticulous, almost as if his innate monkey madness had taken a shower in mathematical sanity. "It's totipotent. They're conscious of everything that's going on in their bodies—the functioning of every organ, maybe every single metabolic transaction—and not only their own, but the entire planet's. They're trying to give me the ghost of some such sensation...it's the *quid pro quo*, I think...the picture postcard...but it's not easy. Damn, I feel weird. I could probably cope with extended consciousness of a human body... my own body...but this...have you ever tried to imagine what it might be like to be a planet, Hal?"

"Are you sure," was Halleck's suddenly-thoughtful response, "that you really mean *they?*"

Corcoran had no difficulty seeing which way Halleck's train of thought was running. They had talked about the possibility once before, in the old days, before the disappointment with the uncommunicative plant intelligences who had finally come to the fore when the meek really had inherited the Earth. Halleck had been quite keen at one time on the hypothesis that the eventual destiny of life on Earth was what he called a *compound noösphere*: a single planetary mind, whose body was the entire planet.

Corcoran remembered, with exceptional clarity, that he had raised the objection that organic matter was only an infinitesimal fraction of the Earth's mass and that a "living planet" could never be any more than a thin carbonaceous envelope wrapped around a vast stony mantle and an even vaster iron core, but Halleck hadn't been so sure.

"The ultimate alchemical marriage," the physicist had said, "will be between the organic and the organic. We're already laying the foundation for an ultimate convergence between nanotech and silicon computer technology and organic technology. Fusion might be impossible, but we know that efficient hybridization will make enormous progress during the insect generations. In the same way that the scientific progress we made wasn't lost with our extinction, the progress the insects made will be passed on to the plants. I suspect, in fact that plant intelligence could never have developed without that legacy...that the fourthers laid the groundwork for the fifthers and sixthers precisely by means of that kind of hybridization. One day, that hybridization will reach perfection...."

That day had not come by the time the sun metamorphosed into a red giant...but that cataclysmic event had not marked the end of Earth's story, or the story of life on Earth.

Corcoran had asked Halleck more than once whether he had ever tried to imagine what it might be like to *be* a plant-descendant, perfectly hybridized with its own intrinsic and extrinsic inorganic components, awash with its own surrogates, perhaps able to make elaborate use not merely of the kind of surrogacy of which humans were capable but something far more sophisticated, perhaps based on minds that could not only comprehend Coincidence Theory but apply it, naturally and internally.

"It would be pointless," Halleck had told him. "It's beyond the scope of human imagination—even mine."

Corcoran had not doubted the judgment then, and did not doubt it now, but he also knew that the question had suddenly become urgent, and that however far his own meager imagination might fall short, he had to make every effort to extend it as far as he could. He had to make as much sense of he could of the sensations that the seventhers were attempting to give him, generously, to allow him to feel, sympathetically.

So he tried to imagine, now, on his own behalf, what it might actually feel like to be an intelligent organism that was more than an organism, but a hybrid, equipped by its own processes of growth and evolution not only with its own internal nanotech but its own external megatech, with a whole scale of permanent and natural surrogate existences stretching all the way from the molecular level of its own metabolism and neurochemistry but to an identification with all of its kind and to the entire planet that they inhabited.

He was groping, with to real chance of success, but he had to try, and he tried.

"Yes," he said, belatedly answering Halleck's question. "I mean they."

"You have to give me more than that, Corky," Halleck said, plaintively. All his efficiency had crumbled; his confusion had educed him to the inappropriate use of stupid nicknames. He even went so far as to say: "Please."

"I'll do my best," Corcoran promised. "But I think this might be one of those occasions when you have to be there. This time, I think, you're going to have to get contacts fitted and hook yourself up to your own apparatus if you really want to understand me."

"Just give me what you can," the physicist said, resignedly.

Corcoran knew that Halleck would never put himself through the intricate surgery required to fit him with contacts. It simply wasn't in him. That required a special kind of person, of which Halleck was not one, and Corcoran was. Halleck might be one of only three human beings who understood the intricacies of Coincidence Theory, but he was a physical coward as well. In any case, Corcoran thought, it was possible that the kind of understanding of Coincidence Theory that Halleck had might be more of a handicap than an advantage in this particular situation, and that he, Corcoran, was probably much better equipped than his employer, and maybe anybody, to do what he was being asked to do.

He didn't feel rejuvenated, but he did feel proud. He felt that he had a purpose. He had a sneaking suspicion that it might be a borrowed sensation, but what did that matter? If he had to borrow a sensation in order to feel, where better to borrow it from than billions of years in the future, and not merely from the supersane hybrid inhabitants of that remote era, from the entire planet.

At any rate, he was determined to try to explain it to Halleck, to the extent than it was humanly explicable, because if he could do that, he might be able to get a better imaginative handle on it himself, and secure the ghost of a remarkable, active and affectionate consciousness within his own numb feeble mind—even if it was only the picture-postcard version, and not the real thing at all.

He started out by thinking that it ought not to be too difficult to identify with the future Earth, given that he had a good idea of what a planet was like, in terms of its crust, mantle and core—but he had to abandon that kind of primitivism very quickly, because the surge of sensations that as assailing him now, confused as it as, gave the lie to that. That was the Earth of the present day; the Earth of billons of years hence was a great deal more complicated than that, in terms of its internal structure, its transactions with its environment, and its sense of purpose, its mentality, its philosophy, its emotions…

Corcoran tried so very hard to imagine, that he couldn't be entirely certain that the image he eventually formed of seventh generation was anything more than a product of his imagination, but he was sure that it wasn't a pure product, because the flow of pseudosensory information was certainly real, certainly insistent and certain making an effort of some kind to enlighten him.

He couldn't be certain of anything, but he formed some strong impressions. They were tantalizingly out of reach of his full consciousness but nevertheless sufficiently proximate to be tantalizing, seemingly *wanting* to be grasped.

Eventually, he felt able to make his attempt.

"There aren't any aliens," he reported to Halleck, his own voice now little more than a whisper. "The plants knew what the future had in store for the sun, the planet and their own descendants, and even though they were plants, or maybe because they were plant-descended, and not the offspring of flippertigibbet animals, they weren't content to sit around and enjoy the mellow sunshine while it lasted. They had a lot of work to do, but they had long time to prepare, and a much closer relationship with their technology than even the second insect generation ever contrived. They prepared for their survival of the sun's inflation, and for what would happen afterwards. They went underground…and never came out again…at least, they haven't yet, although they haven't finished engineering the surface, by any means. Anyway, they're DNA-descended, still our relatives—distant, admittedly, but not as distant as a brief glance at the family tree might suggest.

"Yes, plants and animals branched very early, and yes, it was the animal branch that had to develop intelligence first, because that's the way natural selection works. Yes, the mammals had to do the pioneering work, we monkeys as well as the rats. But then it was the insects' turn, and the insects had had an intimate symbiotic relationship with flowering plants from day one. Given time enough, and sufficient genetic flexibility, symbiosis tends toward fusion, as in the case of the fungi and algae that fused to become lichens. The fifth generation was only partly plant-descended; they were insect-descended and machine-descended too, at least in their peripherals. Motile intelligence was the seed of sedentary intelligence, and it permitted sedentary intelligences to take motile entities aboard. Maybe it was fate and maybe it was just the way it happened to work out, but there's a rationale to it."

"All that I know," Halleck put in, sounding somewhat aggrieved. "Never mind the recapitulation—move on."

"I know you know," Corcoran replied, "but I'm taking things in order, getting the story straight in my own mind, so that I can feel its narrative thrust. Bear with me. We monkeys couldn't ever have done what the sixth generation did in adapting themselves to survive the solar metamorphosis. Neither could the rats. It had to be the plants—but plants enriched by four generations of animal intelligence—an intangible seed far more valuable than their own DNA. If anything was going to survive the sun's metamorphosis, things had to go the way they did. We're not an irrelevance, a suicidal evolutionary dead-end; we're intrinsic to the process…but that's by the by. Moving on…

"There isn't any noösphere either, in the sense that you used to imagine it: no great mental fusion into a single individual. The plants *could* have done that—they're capable of vegetal reproduction, so they *could* have fused into a single great world-tree, with a single thinking consciousness—but they didn't. They chose not to. They chose to re-tain individuality, both at the physical level—including sex, the ability to shuffle the genetic deck—and at the mental level, thus preserving diversity, disagreement argument, controversy, etcetera. It was an esthetic decision, maybe a hedonistic one, but it had its rationale.

"The point is, I think, that the seventhers don't see themselves as any kind of end-point in Earthly evolution—quite the reverse. They see themselves as the true beginning, and everything that went before as mere prelude, nothing more than a matter of laying groundwork for true intelligence. Thy see themselves as something requiring fur-ther variation, further progress, and have been anxious not to narrow that potential. True intelligence, you see, in their view, is dynamic and multidimensional, involving an understanding of what's going on within and without—the without extending all the way to awareness at the planetary level—and an understanding that's always reaching, always changing. This awareness of what it is to orbit the sun, to har-vest its energy, and to harvest dust, is active, seeking, striving…

"I wish I could describe for you what that ongoing harvest feels like, Hal, but it would require a whole new phenomenology as well as a whole new vocabulary. Moving on…

"The seventhers, as I said, consider the real story of Earthlife as something not yet properly begun, which still has billions of years to run, but is nevertheless working to a deadline, with a sense of urgency, because the universe won't last forever...not, at least, in its present physical state, condemned to eternal expansion and eventual heat-death. For them, the Earth is an active agent, like the enzymes that maintain their physiology, the substratum of their intellectual being, but one that operates, obviously, on a much larger stage, on a much more extensive time-scale, on which the evolution of the expanding universe is a perceptible process, and its entropic heat-death an authentic source of *angst*.

"The plant-descended intelligences see evolutionary process and that apparently-fated dead end as a problem, which they think they need to solve, partly because they don't know whether anyone else is working on it. They don't know whether they're alone or not, and although they hope, trust and mostly believe that they can't be, given the size of the universe, in the absence of any hard evidence of extra-terrestrial life and intelligence, they figure that they have to work on the assumption that they might be. They figure that if anyone else is working on the problem, they'll be working on it in similar circumstances, with a similar sense of responsibility and urgency.

"The Earth is collecting matter as its follows its long orbit round the remade sun. It's processing that matter, and expelling it again—not as waste, except for a tiny fraction, but as spores: spores designed to withstand the rigors on interstellar travel, drifting on the initial momentum of expulsion and a boost borrowed from the solar wind. I can actually feel that process of expulsion—that process of reproduction—not simply as a physical emission but as the ghost of a kind of pleasure, a kind of ecstasy. That, more than anything else, I think, is what the members of the seventh generation are trying to communicate to me...to us...trying to help me perceive...in some small measure, to share..."

"Why?" asked Halleck, finally unable to resist the temptation to butt in, even though he must have feared that breaking Corcoran's monologue might break his train of thought.

"Because they can," Corcoran told him, sure that it was something more than a mere guess. "The fifthers and sixthers didn't have it, and couldn't have communicated it if they could, but the seventhers do and can, and they know that they won't be able to do it for long. They know that no matter how cleverly we fish, we'll never be able to contact an eighth generation."

"Why not?" Halleck demanded, defiantly, seemingly insulted by the slight to his beloved Sling."

"Because the particles will be dispersed. The Earth is a body now, accumulating, assimilating, excreting, reproducing, not in a confined way but on a universal scale. Soon—in another billion years or so—it won't be possible to find enough particles in close association to resonate, to form a ghost. You and I, Hal, and everyone else possessed of present-day intellect, will be reduced to infinitesimal fractions of seeds, on our way to the stars, one or a handful of atoms at a time."

There was silence then. Corcoran knew that Halleck was thinking about it, but the physicist didn't make any comment on the suitability or otherwise of his ultimate fate. He had regained his self-control, and that wasn't his style.

"By the way," Corcoran said. "I think I can come back to myself, now. The ghostly planet is gently fading out. I have no idea whether they think they've succeeded or not, but I guess they've done what they can, for now. They're letting me down, gently. I can feel their grip relaxing. Give me a few more minutes, though. I'll tell you when."

"The instruments agree," Halleck told him. "Your body and brain seem to be reverting to normal patterns."

Corcoran ignored that, because he already knew it. He was still grasping at the last echoes of the experience, trying to commit them to memory: not just the Earth's sight and the feel of the Earth's body and all its wondrous intricate, indescribably internal workings, but also its attitude: the way that the seventher operator, in securing him that kink with the megastructural surrogate, had sought a measure of empathy, a kind of amicable handshake, even though he was a mere flippertigibbet animal, a dirty monkey, a representative of a suicidal species.

After billions of years, they still cared. They still had a sense of kinship. They had been glad to see him, to touch him, to shake his hand. If they had been able to accept an invitation to tea with his Mum, they would have come, and would have eaten the biscuits.

"Everything seems stable this end, Mr. Corcoran," Halleck murmured.

"It's okay," Corcoran confirmed. "I'm home. You can unplug me, without any risk."

Halleck didn't take any action, of course, until he had double-checked all his monitors, but in the end he was as satisfied as he ever was, on that score at least.

"Fine," he said. "Just keep still, until we can dismantle the hood."

"Good day?" asked Corcoran's mother, when he arrived home on Friday evening. She didn't even bother to look round, at first. She was busy in the kitchen, cooking something exactly the way she had cooked it sixty years before.

When she did look round, and saw the flowers that he'd brought her, she nearly fell over with amazement.

"*You*, bringing flowers?" she said. "I never thought I'd see that."

Corcoran felt that she was overdoing the sarcasm a bit; he wasn't as bad as Halleck, after all.

"I could never quite see the point," he said. "It seemed an essentially absurd custom—like so many others."

"And now you can?" she queried. "See the point, I mean."

"A point," he said. "Dimly." *But that's how we see everything*, he didn't add. *Things only seem bright because of the woefully inadequate equipment of our senses.*

"Well, thanks," she said.

"If they could talk," he said, "they'd say the same."

"What for?" she said. "And how do you know?"

"For our appreciation," he told her. "And I know because their billion-times-great grandchildren told me so."

She didn't laugh, and she wasn't astonished. She knew that he'd spent a lot of time trying to talk to the plant-descendants of the far future, not just in the last week, but for months on end ten years before.

"You finally got them to talk to you, then?" she said, calmly, as she put the flowers in a vase and arranged them carefully.

"After a fashion," he said. "Not easy, mind. We don't exactly have a lot in common—that makes communication difficult."

You find communication difficult even with your own mother, she didn't say, even though he wouldn't have blamed her if he had. What she actually said was: "It doesn't make a lot of difference, though, does it—not to us. We still have to live our lives in the present—and according to you and Mr. Halleck, it'll all be for nothing in the end. We're going to become extinct, aren't we? Then the rats are going to take over, and after them the insects. Not a lot to look forward to, is it, even though it won't happen for billons of years?"

"You and I will be long dead," Corcoran reminded her. "As you say, it doesn't make any difference to us, and the way we live our lives."

She stood back and admired the flowers. As she did so, she seemed to absorb something from their charm, and their perfume. She smiled.

"It might," she said, "if you could be bothered to use your time machine for something sensible—like discovering next week's lottery numbers."

Corcoran sighed, at the fleeting thought that his mother really did think that discovering next week's lottery numbers was a 'sensible' way to use a time machine—but he put the critical thought out of his mind, because he didn't want it in his head just then. He could have pointed out that if the Sling were capable of obtaining information that might actually change the future, the changes thus caused could easily lead to paradoxes that might prove too much for the logical fabric of spacetime, so it obviously couldn't be capable of doing that, in order that it could exist at all. It was a circle they been round before though, and there was no point in repeating it.

"Sorry about that," he said mildly. "Halleck will keep trying, I'm sure—that and everything else. He's not the kind of man to let up once he's started, even when he knows that he can't possibly succeed—any more than the rest of us can, on that sort of level. We're all addicts of futility, after all: just dirty monkeys working for our own destruction."

"Don't be so gloomy," his mother chided him, not for the first time. She never seemed to notice the downbeat tendencies of her own world-view, but never missed any evidence of pessimism on his part, and never resisted the urge to attempt to alleviate it.

"I'm not gloomy," he assured her, and meant it—but she wouldn't have believed him even if she's taken any notice of what he'd said.

"You ought to make more effort to look on the bright side," she told him, following her familiar train of thought. She couldn't help adding, semi-automatically, not even as a joke: "Who knows what the future might bring?"

ACKNOWLEDGEMENTS

From Jeff Hecht: The inspiration for "Daybreak" came from writing about planetary science for *New Scientist*, a conversation about ice-balls with Allen Steele, and Isaac Asimov's "Nightfall".

From Guy Immega: Dr. Jaymie Matthews, Professor of Astronomy (University of British Columbia) is Mission Scientist for Canada's MOST satellite, the first to search for transits of extra-solar planets. Jaymie is a member of the Kepler Executive Council for the extended mission. He advised on "Super-Earth Mother" but is not responsible for any errors or unsupportable theories.
Dr. Diana Valencia *et alia*, authors of "Radius and Structure Models of the first Super-Earth Planet" (Harvard University), were the first to describe a new category of possible ocean planets closely orbiting dim red-dwarf stars. Dr. Valencia kindly consented to lending her name to the fictional planet in this story.

From David Conyers, David Kernot and Jeff Harris: thanks to David Brin, Julie Czernada, Sean Williams, David Langford, Ian Watson, Alastair Reynolds, Linda Nagata, Gwyneth Jones, Kevin Ikenberry and the team at *Albedo One* for their support and encouragement.

ABOUT THE AUTHORS, EDITORS AND ARTIST

Violet Addison and **David N. Smith** have written short stories for a number of successful science-fiction franchises, including *Doctor Who*, *Bernice Summerfield* and *Faction Paradox*. They've also recently written a short story for *World's Collider*, a shared world anthology from Nightscape Press. They are currently working on their first novel. *www.davenevsmith.co.uk*

Gregory Benford is the author of over twenty-five novels, including *Jupiter Project*, *Artifact*, *Against Infinity*, *Eater*, *Timescape*, and with Larry Niven, *Bowl of Heaven*. He is also a professor of physics at the University of California, Irvine, where he conducts research in plasma turbulence theory and experiment, and astrophysics. *www.gregory-benford.com*

David Brin is a physicist whose novels include Hugo Award winners *Startide Rising* and *The Uplift War*, along with *The Postman*, and recently *Existence*. His nonfiction book *The Transparent Society* won the ALA Freedom of Speech Award. His novel *Earth* is about what may be the strangest planet of them all. *www.davidbrin.com*

Jay Caselberg is an Australian author based in Europe. His work ranges from SF to Horror, Fantasy and everything in between. His short fiction and poetry has appeared in many places, including *Interzone, Aurealis, The Third Alternative* and recently at *Escape Pod, Abyss & Apex* with more due out soon. His four novel Jack Stein series was published by Roc Books. His YA Fantasy *The Jackal Dreaming* is currently available and his quiet horror novel *Empties* is due shortly. He also has a free SF Space Opera, *Binary* available online. More can be found at his website: *http://www.jaycaselberg.com.*

David Conyers is science fiction author and editor from Adelaide, South Australia. He has appeared in magazines such as *Ticon4, Andromeda Spaceways Inflight Magazine*, and *Jupiter*, as well as more than twenty anthologies. His latest book, a science fiction Cthulhu Mythos blended thriller, is *The Eye of Infinity* published by Perilous Press. He holds a degree in engineering from the University of Melbourne. Previous anthologies he has edited for Chaosium include *Cthulhu's Dark Cults* and *Undead & Unbound. www.david-conyers.com*

Paul Drummond is a stray from north of the border who was taken in by the good folk of Lancashire, England. He now lives there with his family and works as a commercial illustrator. His clients include TTA Press, publishers of *Interzone* for which he has provided many story illustrations and covers. You can see more of his work at *www.pauldrummond.co.uk.*

Meryl Ferguson is an avid naturalist (not the type who run around in the nuddy, the other kind), a feminist, a humanist and a pessimist, which is more than enough ist for one person. Her fiction has appeared in *Shimmer, A cappella Zoo*, and *Space and Time Magazine.*

Stephen Gaskell is an author, games designer, and champion of science. His work has been published in numerous venues including *Writers of the Future, Interzone,* and *Clarkesworld.* He is currently revising his first novel, *The Unborn World,* a post-apocalyptic thriller set in Lagos, Nigeria. In an effort to inspire and educate he runs the 'science-behind-the-story' website *creepytreehouse.wordpress.com.*

Jeff Harris is a science fiction writer, editor, and critic living in Adelaide, Australia. He is the assistant editor at *Aurealis* and original science columnist for *Andromeda Spaceways Inflight Magazine.* He has published two dozen short stories and articles in magazines including *Nova 70, AD, Nemesis, Science Bulletin, Aphelion, Australian Science Fiction Review* and *Antipodean SF* (e-zine) and in the anthologies *Alien Shores* and *Zombies.* His novel is *Shadowed Magic* with Chris Simmons. Honorable Mention for "Working Stiffs" appeared in Bill Congreve and Michelle Marquadt's *Year's Best Australian SF and Fantasy* and in Eileen Datlow, Terri Winding and Kelly Link's *Eighth Year's Best Fantasy and Horror.* Awards include the Fellow of the Adelaide University Science Fiction Association and Alpha Award.

Jeff Hecht writes regularly about science and technology for *New Scientist* and *Laser Focus World.* His eleven books include *Beam: The Race to Make the Laser* and *Understanding Lasers.* His short fiction has appeared in *Analog, Asimov's, Daily Science Fiction, Interzone, Nature Futures,* and *Odyssey.* His web site is *http://www.jeffhecht.com.*

Kevin Ikenberry is an American science fiction writer who still wants to be an astronaut. A former manager of the U.S. Space Camp program, Kevin works with space every day. His fiction has appeared in *Andromeda Spaceways Inflight Magazine* and several other markets. He can be found online at *www.kevinikenberry.com.*

Guy Immega is an author, engineer and entrepreneur, whose aerospace company built robots for the International Space Station and fingerprint sensors for cell phones. Guy is a graduate of Clarion West 2006, where he renewed his passion for SF. He lives in Vancouver, Canada with his beautiful wife Gayle and two rambunctious dogs. View Guy's nonfiction works at *www.kineticwords.net.*

Patty Jansen lives in Sydney, Australia, where she spends most of her time writing science fiction and fantasy. She has sold fiction to genre magazines such as *Analog Science Fiction and Fact*, *Redstone SF* and *Aurealis*. Her novels (available at ebook venues) include *Watcher's Web* (soft SF), *The Far Horizon* (middle grade SF), *Charlotte's Army* (military SF) and *Fire & Ice*, *Dust & Rain* and *Blood & Tears* (Icefire Trilogy) (dark fantasy). Her novel *Ambassador* will be published by Ticonderoga Publication in 2013. Patty is on Twitter (@pattyjansen), Facebook, LinkedIn, goodreads, LibraryThing, google+ and blogs at: *http://pattyjansen.com/*.

David Kernot is an Australian author living in the Mid North of South Australia and when he's not writing, he's riding his Harley Davidson through the wheat, wine, and wool farming lands. He writes fantasy, science fiction, and horror, and is the author of around forty short stories in a variety of anthologies in Australia and the US. *www.davidkernot.com*.

Robert J. Mendenhall is retired police officer and serves on active duty with the US Air National Guard. His fiction has appeared in three Star Trek anthologies, *The Martian Wave, Cosmic Crime Stories*, and *Night Terrors Anthology*. He lives outside Chicago, Illinois with his wife and fellow writer, Claire. Visit his website at *http://www.sff.net/people/robert-mendenhall*.

Geoff Nelder lives in England with his physicist wife within easy cycle rides of the Welsh mountains. Geoff is a former teacher, now an editor, writer and fiction competition judge. His novels including SF: *Exit, Pursued by Bee*; *ARIA trilogy*, and thrillers: *Escaping Reality*, and *Hot Air*. *http://geoffnelder.com*.

G. David Nordley is the pen name of Gerald David Nordley, an author and astronautical engineer. A retired Air Force officer, he has extensive experience in spacecraft systems operations, engineering, and testing as well as research in advanced spacecraft propulsion. As an author, he is a past Hugo and Nebula award nominee as well as a four-time winner of the *Analog Science Fiction/Science Fact* annual "AnLab" reader's poll. His latest novel is *To Climb a Flat Mountain*, from *Variationspub-*

lishing.com. He lives in Sunnyvale, CA, with his wife, a retired Apple Computer programmer. His website is *www.gdnordley.com.*

Brian Stableford has published more than seventy novels and more than twenty short-story collections, as well as translating more than a hundred volumes from French to English, about half of them antique scientific romances. A confirmed recluse, he does not do 'social networking' and has no website of his own.

Peter Watts is an ex-biologist and convicted felon who seems especially popular among people who don't know him—at least, his awards generally hail from overseas except for a Hugo (won thanks to fan outrage over an altercation with Homeland Security) and a Jackson (won thanks to fan sympathy over nearly dying from flesh-eating disease). His novel *Blindsight* is a core text for university courses ranging from Philosophy to Neuropsych, despite an unhealthy focus on space vampires. His blog is at *http://www.rifters.com/crawl/*; the surrounding website (at *www.rifters.com*) is epic but antique. Renovations are planned for the middle of 2013.

SELECTED CHAOSIUM FICTION

ARKHAM TALES

#6038	ISBN 1-56882-185-9	$15.95

STORIES OF THE LEGEND-HAUNTED CITY: Nestled along the Massachusetts coast is the small town of Arkham. For centuries it has been the source of countless rumor and legend. Those who return whisper tales of Arkham, each telling a different and remarkable account. Reports of impossible occurrences, peculiar happenings and bizarre events, tales that test sanity are found here. Magic, mysteries, monsters, mayhem, and ancient malignancies form the foundation of this unforgettable, centuries-old town. 288 pages.

CTHULHU'S DARK CULTS

#6044	ISBN 1-56882-235-9	$14.95

CHAOSIUM'S *CALL OF CTHULHU*˚ IS AN ENDLESS SOURCE of imagination of all things dark and mysterious. Here we journey across the globe to witness the numerous and diverse cults that worship Cthulhu and the Great Old Ones. Lead by powerful sorcerers and fanatical necromancers, their followers are mad and deranged slaves, and the ancient and alien gods whom they willingly devote themselves are truly terrifying. These cults control real power, for they are the real secret masters of our world.

ELDRITCH EVOLUTIONS

#6048	ISBN 1-56882-349-5	$15.95

ELDRITCH EVOLUTIONS is the first collection of short stories by Lois H. Gresh, one of the most talented writers working these days in the realms of imagination.

These tales of weird fiction blend elements wrung from science fiction, dark fantasy, and horror. Some stories are bent toward bizarre science, others are Lovecraftian Mythos tales, and yet others are just twisted. They all share an underlying darkness, pushing Lovecraftian science and themes in new directions. While H.P. Lovecraft incorporated the astronomy and physics ideas of his day (e.g., cosmos-within-cosmos and other dimensions), these stories speculate about modern science: quantum optics, particle physics, chaos theory, string theory, and so forth. Full of unique ideas, bizarre plot twists, and fascinating characters, these tales show a feel for pacing and structure, and a wild sense of humor. They always surprise and delight.

FRONTIER CTHULHU

#6041	ISBN 1-56882-219-7	$14.95

AS EXPLORERS CONQUERED THE FRONTIERS of North America, they disturbed sleeping terrors and things long forgotten by humanity. Journey into the undiscovered country where fierce Vikings struggle against monstrous abominations. Travel with European colonists as they learn of buried secrets and the creatures guarding ancient knowledge. Go west across the plains, into the territories were sorcerers dwell in demon-haunted lands, and cowboys confront cosmic horrors.

MYSTERIES OF THE WORM

#6047	ISBN 1-56882-176-X	$15.95

Robert Bloch has become one with his fictional counterpart Ludvig Prinn: future generations of readers will know him as an eldritch name hovering over a body of nightmare texts. To know them will be to know him. And thus we have decided to release a new and expanded third edition of Robert Bloch's *Mysteries of the Worm*. This collection contains four more Mythos tales—"The Opener of the Way", "The Eyes of the Mummy", "Black Bargain", and "Philtre Tip"—not included in the first two editions.

By Robert Bloch, edited and prefaced by Robert M. Price; Cover by Steven Gilberts. 300 pages, illustrated. Trade Paperback.

NECRONOMICON

#6034	ISBN 1-56882-162-X	$19.95

EXPANDED AND REVISED — Although skeptics claim that the *Necronomicon* is a fantastic tome created by H. P. Lovecraft, true seekers into the esoteric mysteries of the world know the truth: the *Necronomicon* is the blasphemous tome of forbidden knowledge written by the mad Arab, Abdul Alhazred. Even today, after attempts over the centuries to destroy any and all copies in any language, some few copies still exist, secreted away.

Within this book you will find stories about the *Necronomicon*, different versions of the Necronomicon, and two essays on this blasphemous tome. Now you too may learn the true lore of Abdul Alhazred.

THE STRANGE CASES OF RUDOLPH PEARSON

#6042   ISBN 1-56882-220-0 $14.95

PROFESSOR RUDOLPH PEARSON MOVED to New York City after the Great War, hoping to put his past behind him. While teaching Medieval Literature at Columbia University, he helped the police unravel a centuries' old mystery. At the same moment, he uncovered a threat so terrifying that he could not turn away. With the bloody scribbling of an Old English script in a dead man's apartment, Rudolph Pearson begins a journey that takes him to the very beginning of human civilization. There he learns of the terror that brings doom to his world.

TALES OUT OF INNSMOUTH

#6024   ISBN 1-56882-201-4 $16.95

A shadow hangs over Innsmouth, home of the mysterious deep ones, and the secretive Esoteric Order of Dagon. An air of mystery and fear looms... waiting. Now you can return to Innsmouth in this second collection of short stories about the children of Dagon. Visit the undersea city of Y'ha-nthlei and discover the secrets of Father Dagon in this collection of stories. This anthology includes 10 new tales and three classic reprints concerning the shunned town of Innsmouth.

THE THREE IMPOSTORS

#6030   ISBN 1-56882-132-8 $14.95

SOME OF THE FINEST HORROR STORIES ever written. Arthur Machen had a profound impact upon H. P. Lovecraft and the group of stories that would later become known as the Cthulhu Mythos.

H. P. Lovecraft declared Arthur Machen (1863–1947) to be a modern master who could create "cosmic fear raised to it's most artistic pitch." In these eerie and once-shocking stories, supernatural horror is a transmuting force powered by the core of life. To resist it requires great will from the living, for civilization is only a new way to behave, and not one instinctive to life. Decency prevents discussion about such pressures, so each person must face such things alone. The comforts and hopes of civilization are threatened and undermined by these ecstatic nightmares that haunt the living. This is nowhere more deftly suggested than through Machen's extraordinary prose, where the textures and dreams of the Old Ways are never far removed.

THE WHITE PEOPLE & OTHER STORIES

#6035	ISBN 1-56882-147-6	$14.95

THE BEST WEIRD TALES OF ARTHUR MACHEN, VOL 2. — Born in Wales in 1863, Machen was a London journalist for much of his life. Among his fiction, he may be best known for the allusive, haunting title story of this book, "The White People", which H. P. Lovecraft thought to be the second greatest horror story ever written (after Blackwood's "The Willows"). This wide ranging collection also includes the crystalline novelette "A Fragment of Life", the "Angel of Mons" (a story so coolly reported that it was imagined true by millions in the grim initial days of the Great War), and "The Great Return", telling of the stately visions which graced the Welsh village of Llan-tristant for a time. Four more tales and the poetical "Ornaments in Jade" are all finely told. This is the second of three Machen volumes to be edited by S. T. Joshi and published by Chaosium; the first volume is *The Three Impostors*. 294 pages.

EXTREME PLANETS

#6055	ISBN 1-56882-393-2	$18.95

Introduced by Hugo and Nebula Award-winning author David Brin. Featuring stories from David Brin and Gregory Benford, Brian Stableford, Peter Watts, G. David Nordley, Jay Caselberg and many more.

> *"A stellar line-up of writers presenting the most exotic worlds imaginable—prepare to have your mind blown!"* — Sean Williams, Author of *Saturn Returns* and *Twinmaker*

TWO DECADES AGO ASTRONOMERS CONFIRMED the existence of planets orbiting stars other than our Sun. Today more than 800 such worlds have been identified, and scientists now estimate that at least 160 billion star-bound planets are to be found in the Milky Way Galaxy alone. But more surprising is just how diverse and bizarre those worlds are.

Extreme Planets is a science fiction anthology of stories set on alien worlds that push the limits of what we once believed possible in a planetary environment. Visit the bizarre moons, dwarf planets and asteroids of our own Solar Systems, and in the deeper reaches of space encounter super-Earths with extreme gravity fields, carbon planets featuring mountain ranges of pure diamond, and ocean worlds shrouded by seas hundreds of kilometers thick. The challenges these environments present to the humans that explore and colonise them are many, and are the subject matter of these tales.

The anthology features 15 tales from leading science fiction authors and rising stars in the genre:

"Banner of the Angels" by David Brin and Gregory Benford

"Brood" by Stephen Gaskell

"Haumea" by G. David Nordley

"A Perfect Day off the Farm" by Patty Jansen

"Daybreak" by Jeff Hecht

"Giants" by Peter Watts

"Maelstrom" by Kevin Ikenberry

"Murder on Centauri" by Robert J. Mendenhall

"The Flight of the Salamander" by Violet Addison and David Smith

"Petrochemical Skies" by David Conyers and David Kernot

"The Hyphal Layer" by Meryl Ferguson

"Colloidal Suspension" by Geoff Nelder

"Super-Earth Mother" by Guy Immega

"Lightime" by Jay Caselberg

"The Seventh Generation" by Brian Stableford

Extreme Planets is scheduled for release in late 2013 in both trade paperback and online e-reader formats. Edited by David Conyers, David Kernot and Jeff Harris with cover illustration by Paul Drummond.

A LONG WAY HOME

#6049ISBN 978-15688236387$15.95

THIS IS THE STORY OF SEAN MCKINNEY, a young farm boy from the medieval world of Brae who longs to escape the family farm. On his way to begin study at the university, Sean stumbles into a fire-fight between troops of the local tyrant and Congressional Marines trying to overthrow Brae s corrupt and brutal government.

Saving the life of one ambushed Marine, McKinnie is taken aboard the Congressional Starship cruiser Lewis and Clark and is befriended by the starship's crew -- becoming an unofficial ship's mascot. His new friends realize that though McKinnie comes from a backwater world and is ignorant of interstellar politics, he is highly intelligent and might become a valuable asset as a covert Congressional agent. They teach him about Congressional history, including how humanity's home world was destroyed in a collision with an asteroid.

Surviving pirate attacks and deep personal losses, McKinnie grows from an innocent country bumpkin into a civilized young man, and develops a relationship with Lt. Alexandra Andropova, a young nurse in the ship's medical department.

His training complete, McKinnie embarks on several missions to primitive worlds including a return to his home world of Brae. He discovers that slavers kidnapped members of his own family, and others from Brae, to be sold to an alien machine-intelligence. Pursuing the slavers, Lewis and Clark and her crew must battle machine-controlled starships and a massive machine-controlled deep-space station in a desperate attempt to rescue the kidnapped humans.

All titles are available from bookstores and game stores. You can also order directly from www.chaosium.com, your source for fiction, roleplaying, Cthulhiana, and more.